YOU DON'T HAVE A CLUE

Latino Mystery Stories for Teens

Edited by Sarah Cortez

PIÑATA BOOKS

PIÑATA BOOKS
ARTE PÚBLICO PRESS
HOUSTON, TEXAS

You Don't Have a Clue: Latino Mystery Stories for Teens is made possible through grants from the City of Houston through the Houston Arts Alliance.

Piñata Books are full of surprises!

Arte Público Press
University of Houston
452 Cullen Performance Hall
Houston, Texas 77204-2004

Cover design by Mora Des!gn

You Don't Have a Clue: Latino Mystery Stories for Teens / edited by Sarah Cortez
    v. cm.
    ISBN 978-1-55885-692-9 (alk. paper)
    1. Short stories, American. 2. Hispanic Americans—Fiction. 3. Detective and mystery stories. [1. Hispanic Americans—Fiction. 2. Short stories. 3. Mystery and detective stories.] I. Cortez, Sarah. II. Title: You do not have a clue.
    PZ5.Y65 2011
    [Fic]—dc22

2011000117
CIP

Printed in the United States of America
April 2011–June 2011
Versa Press, Inc., East Peoria, IL
12 11 10 9 8 7 6 5 4 3 2 1

This book is dedicated to Ms. Lucha Corpi, friend, beloved mentor and pioneering genius in Latino mystery writing.

Acknowledgments

It is a great pleasure to acknowledge the gracious and bountiful help I received on various aspects of this project from the following professional librarians: Ms. Rosalind Alexander, Reference and Instruction Librarian at M.D. Anderson Library at the University of Houston-Central; Ms. Jennifer Schwartz, Manager, Adult Programming at the Houston Public Library; and Mr. Craig Bertuglia, Senior Library Specialist, Central Branch Teen Room of the Houston Public Library. I am also indebted to Ms. Adriana Gonzalez, R.N., B.S.N. for the sharing of her expertise as a nursing professional.

Table of Contents

Foreword

Award-winning poet, editor and policewoman Sarah Cortez has gathered eighteen of the most popular and talented authors of young adult fiction to provide a bundle of short stories guaranteed to frighten, intrigue and entertain readers, both young and not so young. No subtle nuancing of conflict and characters here; these stories will grab readers by the throat and send pulses skyrocketing as protagonists face villains of every sort, from other-worldly super criminals to secret neighborhood murderers, teachers who dismember their victims, Aztec goddesses that rise from the sea and professional kidnappers who may be masquerading as your very own mother or best friend. There is even a story of historical fiction speculating on an assassination attempt on Pancho Villa.

Officer Cortez is no stranger to crime and mystery, of the fictional *or* real-life variety. A veteran police officer in Houston, Texas, she is also the editor of two previous collections of mysteries, *Hit List: The Best of Latino Mystery* (Arte Público Press, 2009) and *Indian Country Noir* (Akashic Books, 2010), in addition to an anthology of teen memoirs, *Windows into My World: Latino Youth Write Their Lives* (Arte Público Press, 2007) and her own award-winning poetry collection, *How to Undress a Cop* (Arte Público Press, 2000). With *You Don't Have a Clue*, Sarah breaks new ground in a number of ways. Good story collections of any genre are hard to find, but collections of mysteries written with young readers in mind are almost nonexistent. Young adult story collections from Latina/Latino authors exclusively featuring Latina/Latino protagonists are equally rare and equally golden. Putting all of these qualities together makes this collection very special, even more so considering the accomplishments of the authors included. These are the top talents in the field. Ray Villareal's *My Father the Angel of Death*, a novel about the son of a professional wrestler, has taken the nation by storm, and so have works by René Saldaña and Gwendolyn Zepeda; in fact, the list of awards accumulated by this book's featured authors is too lengthy to recount, but a few deserve mention here: Mario Acevedo was included in Barnes and Noble's Best Paranormal Fantasy Novels of the Decade; Sarah Cortez received the 1999 PEN Texas Literary Award; Alicia Gaspar de Alba won the Lambda Literary Foundation Award and the Latino Literary Hall of Fame Best Historical Fiction Award; Sergio Troncoso won the Premio Aztlán Award as well as the Southwest Book Award. Bottom line: This is an impressive lineup of authors.

Although the eighteen stories' settings range from New York City to San Antonio, and their characters' lifestyles range from urban poverty to suburban affluence, commonalities still tie them all together. As in the lives of most teens, relationships are often at the center of life's heartache and happiness, including family relationships, relationships among and between friends, and especially relationships grounded in romance. In this collection, love for a family member or for that special someone often serves as motivation for risking total embarrassment in front of peers or even provoking the ire of a suspected killer. Also, loyalty to friends or family often results in total disregard for personal safety, and bravery often wins out over common sense in defense of others. Issues of belonging or not belonging, of feeling loved or unloved, of feeling normal or abnormal and feeling hopeful or hopeless are common across all stories as main characters attempt to solve the mysteries and personal dilemmas thrust upon them.

Perhaps the most important commonality, however, is that all the characters come home to tortillas and tamales, to *abuelo y abuelita*, to a place where they are called *mijo* or *mija* and the musical sound of the Spanish language fills the air. Like the authors, the main characters of each story are Latina/Latino, which means that in addition to all the usual characteristics of American teenagers they also have a rich overlay of language, cultural heritage and life experience that permeates their way in the world. The importance of books with characters representing the diversity of our society cannot be overstated. Its impact on young people is deep and can last a lifetime. Literature has great power to help all readers make meaning of their lives as they engage with stories in which characters struggle and succeed (or don't succeed) against the common and uncommon obstacles life places in front of them. As they process their reading, they are also processing their own life experiences, but when young readers fail to see themselves in their reading, the not so subtle message is that their lives don't count. However, when they do have the opportunity to live vicariously through young men and women with whom they can easily identify, the great power of books and reading to help them not only make meaning of their reading but also make meaning of their lives is all theirs. This is not a book for readers of Latino cultural heritage only, however, but a great book for any readers who enjoy a mystery, relish analyzing clues and solving crimes, love being scared silly or appreciate the twists and turns and delightful surprises of a wonderful story as crafted by true masters. I guarantee it.

James Blasingame, Ph.D.
Arizona State University

Introduction

Few people—of any age—can resist the implicit invitation contained in a good mystery story. And so, it is not surprising that more authors have turned to writing mystery, or crime fiction, for the young adult reader. However, a glance at both the library's shelves and the vaunted lists of writing prize-winners reveals that Latina/o authors have yet to become fully engaged in revealing their realities on the written page of the young adult mystery.

Armed with this knowledge and fueled by my own childhood and teen passion for reading crime and mystery fiction (a love which exists to this day), I conceptualized an anthology —the first of its kind—that would ask Latina/o writers to create an edgy collection of stories such as they might have enjoyed in high school or which their own sons and daughters would enjoy. Importantly, we all desired to create a collection that would speak eloquently to the complex and morally disarrayed society that teens navigate today.

As the authors created their characters and focused their plots, what emerged were protagonists that one could find in high schools around the United States: the college-bound prep school boy; the plump, not-yet-beautiful but dutiful daughter; the envious but attracted-to-ostentatious-wealth senior studying SAT vocabulary words; or the street-wise Bronx rapper with a heart of gold, to name a few. What unites all these protagonists is their desire to see justice done and a willingness to use their brains to accomplish that end.

This anthology contains stories for students at all skill levels. Whether reading a story with few twists and turns or more, the reader will be immediately pulled into the fascinating problem-solving aspect—the "gaming" or puzzle aspect—of the story. Don't be surprised at the deep discussions about the tempting array of possibilities along the right-wrong spectrum as readers consider and analyze the characters' choices, always with a dose of healthy skepticism and a growing appreciation for the vagaries of human nature.

For years, much has been made in the literature of reading about the fact that students enjoy reading for pleasure when they can pick books that interest them and when those books are engaging but accessible. With this in mind, the authors and I give you *You Don't Have a Clue*—a volume of fast plots, engrossing characters and satisfying conclusions. You'll get to follow clues, observe crime scenes, examine personalities, eliminate false leads, reflect upon the foibles and strengths of human nature, and ponder the greatest mystery of all—how to serve justice.

Sarah Cortez, Editor
Houston, Texas

No Soy Loco

Mario Acevedo

I am not crazy.

That's what I'm thinking when Dr. Kleinman asks, "When did you start hearing the voices?"

He sits on the other side of the room. With his beard, soft white hands and tweed jacket, Kleinman looks like a psychiatrist in a T.V. soap opera. Except that he wears a toupee, the first I've ever seen. It's an ugly slab of black fur that sits crooked on his head and is ringed by a crown of grayish-brown hair. I do my best to ignore the toupee but right now, the front of that hideous shag is wiggling like a couple of roaches are trying to crawl free.

Unlike the T.V. shows, I'm not lying on a couch but sitting in a chair, over by the wall and next to a big fern.

There's a weird clock on Kleinman's desk. At least, I think it's a clock because it makes a soft *click, click, click*. It's a glass pyramid that sits on a squat golden box covered in swirls. Inside the pyramid, gears twirl in rhythm to the clicking.

"Victor," Dr. Kleinman raises his voice and distracts me from the clock, "when did you start hearing these voices?"

I give him the same answer I've given to my mom and dad. To Mrs. Pérez, my homeroom teacher. To Mr. McSwane, the vice principal. The school nurse. My regular doctor. Everybody except Coach Williams. Now that the season's started, all he cares about is making the district playoffs and what happened to me is old news.

"After I got hit in the head."

Kleinman gives me owl eyes over the tops of his glasses. "Oh my. Was it a fight?"

A fight? This *güero* doc must think all we Mexican kids do is throw *chingasos*. "No, sir. We were playing catch at pre-season practice."

Dr. Kleinman cocks an eyebrow. "Practice?"

"Baseball." This time of year, what else could it be?

He goes, "Ah," and scribbles in his notebook.

"Chuy Reyes threw a ball that conked me right here." I touch behind my left ear. That *culo* did it on purpose, too. Chuy knew I was busy shagging fly balls from Tommy Wilkins. The swelling took a week to go down. "Knocked me out. I came to a few seconds later."

"Did you get a concussion?"

"I guess I did. See, I didn't go to my family doctor for a few days. Coach told me to shake it off. The doctor said I probably had a concussion, but by then I looked okay."

"And the voices?"

"I started hearing them two days later when I was in bed. It was really early in the morning." The Toshiba clock radio said it had been 2:12 A.M. "I woke up hearing a couple of people discussing something." I know what the next question is going to be so I raise my hand to keep the doc from asking. "I didn't know what they were saying because it was in a language I never heard before."

I fidget because I get antsy talking about this. Who sees a shrink except for a crazy person?

"Perhaps it was a prank?" Then the doc enunciates really slow, "A trick?"

Come on, doc. I'm in the eleventh grade; I know the definition of prank. "It wasn't a trick."

"What did the voices sound like?"

I don't know what this has to do with anything.

Kleinman goes back to giving me the owl eyes.

I look at my shoes. "Mostly I didn't understand nothing. But
one thing I remember was." Every time I have to repeat the
sounds, my mouth goes dry. "It went like: Al-kleck. Meek. Moor.
Doop." Saying this made me feel like a crazy person imitating a
parrot.

The doc scribbles in his spiral memo pad. "Go on."

I ought to type up my story and make mimeograph copies I
repeat it so much. "The voices sounded like they came from
behind a door. But they came from my left and there is no door
to my left, only a brick wall. I listened to the voices for a while."
Exactly seven minutes thanks to my Toshiba clock radio. "Then
they sounded like they were walking away."

"Was it a dream?"

"You tell me, you're the psychiatrist."

Kleinman gives a bland chuckle like it's a joke he hears a lot.
"And when did it happen again?"

"The second time was in school during home room period.
The voices sounded like they were right behind me."

"What did you do?"

"I just sat there. Pretty sure I must've been daydreaming. But
all I heard was those voices." I remember how Mrs. Pérez had
come right up to me, but I didn't see her until she was hunched
over my desk and asked me to repeat what she had just said.
Course I couldn't.

"And then?"

"I got in trouble. She marked me down for the day."

"When did you realize you weren't daydreaming?"

"After it kept happening."

"The same voices?"

"I guess. I mean the language sounded the same but sometimes it was two men talking, sometimes two women, sometimes one of each."

"Only two people?"

No one had asked that before. "No. Usually it was two but once in a while I could tell it was a discussion between several people. Three. Four. Maybe a bunch."

"And aside from the voices, you feel okay?"

The words blurt out. "I feel awful."

Kleinman's pen goes *skritch, skritch*. Will these notes go in my permanent record? Twenty years from now, are people going to say, Victor Tellez, you used to have such great hands? You were an amazing shortstop. Then you went nuts.

"Can you control these voices?"

"You mean like, turn them off and on?"

Kleinman nods.

"I wish. I mean, no, sir."

"And you have no idea what these voices are saying?"

"No, sir."

He crosses his legs and goes back to writing notes. "Please repeat what they said."

More of the crazy person parrot talk.

"Al-kleck. Meek. Moor. Doop."

Kleinman purses his lips, pushing them together like he was about to spit a watermelon seed.

A metallic buzz startles me. The noise comes from the weird clock. Kleinman uncrosses his legs. "We're out of time." He closes the memo pad and sets it on his desk.

Is this all? I don't feel any better.

The doc goes to the door and holds it open.

Mom waits for me in the outer office. Since we are visiting a psychiatrist, she got dressed up to show that crazy son or not, she is a respectable woman. "Is he okay, Dr. Kleinman?" asking like the doc had taken my brain out and poked at it with instruments.

"Victor will be fine." Kleinman's toupee makes another twitch.

My mom counts bills from her purse and gives the money to the receptionist. Sixty-five bucks for an hour's work! This doc has a racket going. That's a day's pay for my dad and he's a licensed electrician.

Now I feel like caca.

My mom's high heels tick on the asphalt of the parking lot. I slide over the clear vinyl cover on the front seat of her Mercury Comet. Mom gets behind the steering wheel. She pulls herself close to kiss my cheek.

"How is my *loquito*?"

Great. It's not enough that she slobbers on me in public, now she's calling me her little crazy one.

On the way home I stay quiet, brooding how these voices are messing up my life. I have been dropped from the J.V. roster and missed so many days of class I'm going to summer school for sure.

But it's Friday. Even though I haven't been to school since Wednesday, I'd arranged a double-date with Manny, his girl-friend and Nancy Rigby.

On the way home Mom punches the radio button. "Listen, it's Elton Juan." My mom bobs her head in tune to *Crocodile Rock* and I want to dissolve into the floor in humiliation.

The Comet halts in a plume of dust on the dirt street in front of our house. Mom lets me out so she can go shopping. I rush inside to call Manny and make sure the date is a go.

The phone is gone from its cubby in the hall and the line stretches into the bathroom. My sister Sophia's muffled voice comes from behind the door. She must be in the middle of one of her stupid marathon phone calls to her stupid friends.

I beat on the door. "Sophie, I gotta use the phone."

Her talking gets louder.

I beat harder. "Come on, Sophie. I gotta make a damn call."

She rustles and the door unlocks. It opens just a crack and she stands with the receiver pressed against her shoulder. Her eyes are narrow, snake-like. "I'm gonna tell Mom you said 'damn.'" She slams the door, locks it and goes back to her stupid talking.

I drag my feet to my room, shut the door and fall on my bed. I lay with my face turned against the pillow and wonder what I did to bring the voices. Maybe I *am* a crazy person.

Seems like a hundred years later, Sophia gets off the phone. I call Manny. He had talked with Nancy and we are still on for tonight. The gloom from the day vanishes, and I shower and afterwards, style my hair with Brylcreem.

When Manny shows up, he's driving his dad's shiny white Toronado coupe instead of the usual jalopy Rambler. Nancy is in the back seat, along with Manny's cousin Jerry and some skinny girl in hippie clothes. I sit to the left; the girls are in the middle, Jerry on the far right, the four of us crammed together while Manny and his girl Theresa have the wide front bench seat all to themselves.

We are going to a double feature at the Fiesta Drive-in. *Billy Jack* and *Boxcar Bertha*. It's still light out so we make a loop though town, cruising to University Park and back to Surplus City. Nancy has a gray sweater, tight and tempting around her big boobs. Up front, Manny cracks open a can and Theresa hands us a Budweiser.

We kill time sipping beer and smoking cigarettes like we are already *veteranos*. Manny talks about going into the Air Force. Jerry brags about the Marines and says he's sorry the war in Vietnam ended before he got to kill commie dinks.

Me, I'm hoping for a baseball scholarship but now that I am missing my junior year, it might be impossible to get on the varsity team. Without that, forget a scholarship. What keeps me from getting all moody is Nancy pressing against me, smelling nice, looking delicious.

Jerry and me put the moves on our dates. My hands wander across Nancy's back and every time they sorta wander to her front, her hands come on the defensive and push me away. Still, we keep making out.

Finally, we arrive at the drive-in. The place is crowded with Friday night couples. Manny parks right in the center though the best make-out spots are on the sides. He and Theresa have been going steady so long they actually want to see the movies.

Manny says he has to take a leak—so do I—so we *vatos* pile out and join the people heading for the snack bar and restrooms. He and Jerry burp loud and stop behind another car to pee under the bumper.

I have to get away from these *pendejos* so I hike by myself to the restroom. On my way out, I see Dr. Kleinman and a woman standing against the cinderblock wall of the snack bar. I must've given him a what-are-you-doing-here expression. For some reason, I thought super-educated people like psychiatrists didn't go to the drive-in.

He and the woman stare back, looking a little off-guard that I'd seen them.

Kleinman wears a black leather jacket and a watch cap. Good, means he has ditched that *rasquachi* toupee. The woman also has a black jacket, worn over a baggy denim jumpsuit tucked into scuffed Frye boots. Her hair touches her shoulders in a tangle of dark waves. While his face is a lump of *masa*, hers is gristle beneath tight skin.

The projection room is right above their heads. Light from the movie splashes over their faces and makes them flicker all kinds of bright colors.

His right hand is in front of his belly and holding that weird pyramid clock that was sitting on his desk. He lowers his hand and tucks the clock against his leg.

I sense an uncomfortable wall between us so I head to the car without waving hello. I feel their gazes press against my back, giving me the heebie-jeebies.

Manny and Jerry are already in the car. Nancy scoots over and gives a big welcoming smile. She wastes no time sliding her plump lips on mine, my cheek, my neck. Maybe I will get to touch those *chichis*.

Then it starts. Like the rumble of a distant train.

The voices.

No, I scream inside, not now.

Nancy shifts and leans against me.

The voices get louder, louder.

I try to ignore them. I focus on Nancy, her smell, the taste of her mouth and skin, the proximity of her boobs.

But the voices get louder, overwhelming everything until I'm blind and deaf to the world. My head is an echo chamber filled with these strange voices. Panic rakes down my spine and makes my limbs tingle.

Dr. Kleinman. He can help me.

I claw for the front seat. I snag the catch and push the seat forward. If Manny's yelling, I can't hear him. I grope for the door handle, yank hard and tumble outside.

My head seems to hover as if there's no connection to my body. I lurch toward the hazy shaft of light beaming from the projection room.

As the voices continue, an image takes over my brain. Blurry faces circle around me, mouths moving, the source of the voices. The image fades but the voices don't stop.

I stagger toward the snack bar and approach a vertical black smudge against the wall. Up close, I see it's the woman by herself.

I know I'm shouting for Dr. Kleinman but I hear only the voices. The woman makes no move. I want to shake her and have her tell me where to find Kleinman but it seems I have no arms. I'm merely a floating head, a balloon filled with a chaos of noise.

The voices shrink away. As I become aware of my body, I sink to the ground. I find myself kneeling, surrounded by the mumble of car speakers and feet crunching through the gravel. There's a stillness within me like when a fever breaks.

I look up. The woman is gone.

I go to the fountain, drink and splash water on my face and let the earth steady itself beneath my feet. Back at the car, Manny and the rest look at me like they're expecting another attack of the crazies. Except for Nancy. She's gone.

"*Vato*, she took off," Manny explains as he pops the door open.

Theresa adds, "She went to the McDonald's across the street. Gonna call her sister for a ride home."

I slide inside the backseat. Theresa mumbles into Manny's ear.

He starts the car. "I've seen this movie before." I know he's lying. "How about we call it a night, *ese*?"

"Yeah. Sure." I slump against the seat, feeling like the loser who screwed up a game.

Manny hangs the speaker back on the stand. We follow the big arrow and the word EXIT painted on the fence.

My house is easy to spot because of the yellow porch light. Manny lets me out. I don't have a watch but guess the time to be around ten. An early Friday night for a date. The Toronado drives off, laughter pluming out the windows.

My sister watches me enter. She's in her PJ's and sits at one end of the dinner table. She's quiet—a miracle for her—but her shiny eyes tell me there is trouble.

Mom is at the other end of the table, looking more stressed than usual. My dad's pacing the den, scowling and fuming in that way middle-aged men do. An open bottle of Cutty Sark stands on the counter.

I crouch beside Sophia and whisper, "What's going on?"

She whispers back. "Dad found out Mom's been taking money out of the savings account."

My throat tightens and my stomach gets queasy. Dad was saving for a new truck.

"She did it for you," Sophia says. "To pay for Dr. Kleinman."

Now I feel truly sick and go to my room.

My dad stomps out of the den, yelling, "Hey, hey."

I drop onto my bed, ignoring him.

He looms over me and glares with mean, whiskey eyes. "So where you been?"

It isn't a question; it's him lighting the fuse that will blow up into an argument.

"You were with your *marijuano* friends, weren't you? Doing drugs."

"No, Dad."

"That's why you're getting all crazy. The drugs."

My heart claws at my ribs. I tear up. I try not to but I can't help myself.

His face gets dynamite red. "Look at yourself, crybaby. Is this how you act with your *desgraciado* druggie friends?"

My eyes get blurry. "No, Dad, that's not it." It's the voices. But he won't understand. I don't understand. I start sobbing.

His neck tenses, and he clenches his fists like he wants to hit me. "Then what? It's not enough you're embarrassing the *familia* with your craziness, you're driving me to the poor house *también*."

My heart wants to rip free. "I'm sorry, Dad." I sit up and hide my face in my hands. Snot and tears slobber over my fingers.

"Sorry for what, *llorón*?"

I wait for my dad to slap me. Instead he snorts in disgust and leaves the room. Ashamed, I roll to my side, wipe my face against my pillow and let sadness drown me. The overhead light burns like a winter sun, bright but giving no heat.

This last year, I've gained thirty pounds. Gotten faster, stronger. But my muscles are useless against this misery and craziness.

A faint click disturbs me, and I open my eyes. The room is dark and the door closed. The noise came from the Toshiba clock radio changing numbers. The time is 3:43 A.M. A blanket lays over me. Had to have been Mom covering me and turning the light off.

I expect the voices but they don't come. The clock goes 3:44. Then 3:45. 3:46.

Someone shakes me awake. It's Sophia. She's wearing a dress for Mass.

My Toshiba reads 7:32. We're going early which means Mom wants me to attend confession. Breakfast is extra quiet. My dad remains in bed, sleeping off the Cutty Sark.

When we get to Our Lady of Health, Mom and Sophia stay outside while I sit on a back pew, in line for confession.

An old lady dressed in so many layers of black she must be mourning for the whole Westside shambles out of a confessional booth. I take her place and kneel. The little door behind the screen slides open. The man who gives the blessing can only be Father Theo.

I make the sign of the cross. "In the name of the Father, and of the Son, and of the Holy Spirit. My last confession was . . . " A year? Two? Three? I mumble something and finish, "ago."

No reason to waste time, so I give him the CliffsNotes reason why I'm here and explain the voices. He clears his throat, as I'm sure my story is a lot more interesting than whatever the *viejita* before me had confessed.

When I get talking about Dr. Kleinman, Father Theo interrupts, very angry. "You went to him, a Jew, before you came to me?"

"He's a psychiatrist, Father. He knows about people's minds."

"And I know about people's hearts. What's in the mind is the fruit of what grows in the heart."

I try to explain but Father Theo cuts me off. "It is guilt that bothers you. Guilt for defying your parents. Guilt for indulging in childish pursuits. Guilt for not attending Mass and confession. Pray the Rosary four times, and I'll see you here next week." He slams the little door.

I creep out of the booth and kneel in front of the altar. I've forgotten my Rosary beads, and I pretend to recite the prayers. Jesus looks down from His perch on the cross. I glance at the statues of the saints about the altar. For the first time in my life I want the comforting hug of religion and God.

Then the voices arrive, muted as whispers, as if sneaking into the church. Each voice comes from a saint surrounding me. Joseph. Mary Magdalene. Francis Xavier.

Each saint turns into what looks like a person. They seem to be wearing uniforms. Wide-shouldered jackets. Thick belts. Tall boots. Soldiers? Police?

The hair on the back of my neck stands on end. The walls close in because the voices have turned the church into a trap.

A bell clangs. The voices go silent. The saints turn back to looking normal. The trance lifts.

An acolyte is ringing the end of confession. I hustle outside into the relief of the openness. Mom looks especially pleased with herself, like confession has solved my problems. Little does she realize. Thankfully, during Mass we sit in the back, close to the door in case the voices take over the saints again.

I skip school. Not because of the voices, but because gossip topic number one will be how I freaked out at the drive-in. I wonder if I should call Nancy, but what good would it do?

By Friday, my house seems as welcoming as a prison; Mom, Dad, Sophia spying on me like wardens. I call Tommy Wilkins and get him to ask his mom if I can sleep over. Tommy says I gotta wait until Saturday night but I can come by in the afternoon.

That morning I empty the change jar on my dresser, hop on my bike and take off. I knock around town, stopping at John's Newsstand, where I browse sports and car magazines and peek at the topless *rucas* in *Bachelor's Best*.

Tommy lives near his cousins, in that yellow house where Hadley Avenue makes a big jag at Esperanza Street. He belongs to one of the few *negrito* families in town, which pretty much makes his neighborhood the black ghetto of the Mesilla Valley.

Tommy and I play catch. I enjoy the exercise, the confidence I get from using my muscles. He tells me about the team. Besides starting at second base for the J.V., he suited up for today's varsity game against Coronado. Even though we won seven to three, I get sad because I didn't play and might not ever again.

Tommy's mom is a great cook and I have a hard time saying no to anything she puts on the table.

The next morning we march down the street like over-fed ducks—Mrs. Wilkins, Tommy, his younger brothers, his two sisters and me—to the United Pentecostal Church.

The service is a lot different than Mass. Kinda informal. No acolytes. No priest in his priestly garments. No saints, no windows of colored glass, no big Jesus on the Cross in His tortured glory. Instead there's a simple cross on the pulpit. The pews and the electric organ look second-hand. The worship hall is as plain as the high school cafeteria.

People call one another *brother* this and *sister* that. There's a lot of singing and chanting.

The pastor is a skinny *vato* who reminds me of the guy who fixes flats at Big O Tires. He must've washed the grease off his hands, slicked his hair and exchanged his grimy overalls for a fraying powder-blue polyester suit.

The pastor reads from the book of Ephesians. He stops in mid-verse and starts talking about something that happened to him. He goes back-and-forth between the Bible and his story, making some point of fighting the Devil and standing for the Lord.

A woman in a beehive plays the organ. People in front wave their hands.

"Halleluiah, Brother. Amen. Shout it!"

The old ladies here aren't the meek sheep they are at Our Lady of Health. They're the first to shuffle around, hands raised, eyes closed, lips trembling in prayer.

The pastor sheds his jacket. Dark blotches stain the underarms of his shirt. He loosens his tie. Sweat shines on his forehead. He's shouting and gesturing with the Bible as if it's a knife and he's in hand-to-hand combat with Satan.

The front pews have emptied into the space in front of the altar. Mrs. Wilkins waddles down the isle and joins them. This congregation condemns the evils of King Alcohol, and their wild dancing and chanting definitely proves you don't need booze to act nuts.

They start speaking in tongues, a weird gibberish. It's supposed to be the Holy Spirit flowing through them though I wonder what Father Theo would say about this.

People beat tambourines and move herky-jerky like bumper cars. Beehive lady turns up the volume on the organ. The pastor wipes his sweat but doesn't slow his sermonizing.

I pretend I'm not staring at anything and wait for the show to end. But the speaking in tongues sounds different. It's the same gibberish only I'm starting to understand what they're saying. "Al-keck. Meek. Moor. Doop."

It's a warning.

The about-to-get-run-over-by-a-train-feeling overwhelms me.

"Al-keck. Meek. Moor. Doop."

Them. Find. Moor. Doop.

What? Them find? Find them? Are they in danger? Am I?

I feel myself turning green. Breakfast wells up. I want to run out. I turn my head to see how far I am from the door in case I have to throw up.

Then I see her. That woman who was with Dr. Kleinman at the drive-in.

She stares at me, her mouth set and serious, impassive as a stone while the music and chanting swirls around her.

I get dizzy and closer to vomiting. I shut my eyes and bring my head down.

The chanting, the speaking in tongues, the music, the image of that woman's stern eyes, circle around me like I'm on a wobbly Merry-go-round.

The pastor lowers his voice and begins the altar call. The speaking in tongues stops. People sob.

I tune it all out. Slowly my stomach settles. When the pastor gives the benediction, I glance behind me. The woman is gone.

On the way back to Tommy's house I stick close to him and his mom. I ride my bike home, paranoid, taking short cuts—along ditch banks, through holes in barbed wire fences—certain the woman is following me. Close to my house, I circle the block, wary as a hunted coyote. But I never see her.

I want everything to get back to normal, so Monday I return to school. If people talk behind my back, I don't hear them. I'm days behind in all my classes but that's okay. The work will keep me busy.

That night the voices come back. I'm alone, in bed. This time I try not to be afraid. I lay still and listen. There are a lot of strange words, but I pick out the familiar ones I've figured out already.

A hallucination takes over my mind. I am in the center of a room. Everything around me is hazy. Six figures circle around me, but they stand back so I can't make out their faces. Just as the last time they appeared, they wear identical uniforms.

The voices seem calm, like they're making a patient effort to get through to me. Again, the most I can understand is: Al-keck. Meek. Moor. Doop.

Al-keck. Meek. Them. Find.

The same warning. I feel the chill of menace. But no clue what Moor and Doop mean, or what the warning is about.

The voices say something else in the same language, and I understand every word: when you find them, let us know.

Find who?

The figures dissolve into the haze, replaced by a sphere, orbited by small moons. It's a planet I don't recognize. The planet recedes, shrinking around a star, which also recedes from me. I get the sensation that I'm traveling at great speed though I feel no movement.

I zoom past planets circling another star. One of the planets has rings like Saturn. A tiny planet grows in the distance before me.

The planet is blue and white.

It could only be Earth.

The hallucination ends with a jolt.

I'm awake in bed.

I lie motionless for many minutes, feeling off-balance. I think about the voices and the hallucination, and what they must mean. Are they giving me a warning? About what? For me? And who were those people in uniform? Why didn't they show their faces?

And where are they from? A distant planet?

It could only be more craziness.

Tuesday, when I get home from school, Mom says Dr. Klein-man has called and scheduled a visit. Said he might have figured out what's been causing the voices.

I tell my mom not to spend more money on this. She says Dr. Kleinman told her the visit is free. In fact, he's coming to pick me up in a half hour and then I'll be home for dinner. Mom smiles and I imagine a balloon over her head saying, CURED!

At four-thirty a Mercedes sedan shows up, probably the first Mercedes that's ever rolled into this barrio. Dr. Kleinman is driving and seems to be wearing the same clothes he wore when I went to his office. His toupee looks as ratty and obvious as before.

I sit up front and check out the interior. It's nice but nothing special. My uncle Memo's Chrysler Imperial is a lot, lot fancier.

We drive west on Picacho Avenue, through the west side, past the Owl Drug Store, toward the river. I've never seen a doctor's office around here as it's mostly warehouses, silos and farm equiP.M.ent stores.

The doc is quiet. By the way his brow creases, I can tell he's preoccupied with heavy thoughts. Or that toupee is really itching.

On the other side of the river, Picacho becomes US Highway 70 and goes through Fairacres. Kleinman slows and turns north. The road follows the riverbank. To the left, the ground slopes up to steep, ragged cliffs topped with mesquite and creosote. The car meanders under willows and cypress hunched over the road. We're close enough to the cliffs that the sun has dropped from view and we're blanketed in shadow. Dangling branches scrape the top of the car.

I get creeped out and wonder what the doc is up to. Am I getting kidnapped? He's taller than me but flabby, meaning I've got the edge in muscle. He tries anything perverted, I'll break his arms.

But what if he's got chloroform? Ether? A syringe of sodium pentathol? Or a blackjack he'll use to knock me out and I'll wake up shackled in a dungeon.

I'm breathing hard. My palms sweat.

Easy, Victor. Relax. Nothing bad is going to happen.

The Mercedes glides under a tunnel of willows and turns right toward an old house made of river rocks cemented together. The yard is overgrown with bramble and weeds. So forlorn and deep in the boonies, this place isn't a home but a hideout.

My suspicions sweep the area like radar. But if I'm to get rid of the voices, I have to trust him.

Kleinman parks. "Come on, Victor."

We step from the car and into a kitchen. Scabs of vinyl peel from the cabinets. The dingy linoleum floor creaks underfoot. There are pots and dishes piled in a rusted sink. The insides of the light fixtures are caked with dead flies and moths. Doesn't smell like food, rather the kitchen smells like it appears—old and musty.

It's quiet but as I follow Kleinman, I hear the familiar *click, click, click*, same as the weird clock that was in his office. He leads me to a living room cluttered with battered cheapo furniture. I figured the doc has money so why are we in this dump?

His lady friend sits behind a small card table, the cracked wooden top painted to look like an Ouija board. Stains and cigarette burns cover the scarred veneer.

Who is she? Has she been following me? I pick up a vibe from her that's as revolting as poison.

Her eyes fix on me but it's like we're separated by a one-way mirror. She knows what's going on. I don't.

An alarm rings at the back of my skull.

She wears a plaid shirt with the sleeves bunched at her elbows. Her skin is stretched across the sharp bones of her face. The weird clock is click, clicking on the table.

Kleinman offers a plastic chair. "Have a seat, Victor." He stands on the other side of the table, next to the woman.

My nerves scream danger, danger! I can't move.

"Please sit," the woman says. She's got an accent. I can't tell from where but she's not from here. "You do want us to help you?"

"The voices, Victor," Kleinman emphasizes.

The woman points to my chair. I expect to see her fingers heavy with rings like a gypsy but she wears no jewelry. She gives a weak smile and wrinkles bunch around her eyes and mouth. She appears old and frail, and I become embarrassed to think she could hurt me.

The alarm softens to a tingle. I take the seat.

The woman holds the clock and lifts the top free, separating the glass pyramid from the base and revealing a device that looks like a kitchen timer. She turns the device and lets go.

I hear gears turning, then voices.

THE voices.

The air freezes.

The timer device makes one turn and stops. The voices fade but the air remains ice cold.

"Do you understand what the voices are saying?" It's the woman talking to me.

I bring my gaze to hers. My palate is so dry my tongue remains glued to the roof of my mouth like it's stuck to an ice-tray. Working my tongue forces saliva into my mouth, and I can finally say. "Al-keck. Meek. Which means: Them. Find."

She looks at Kleinman. He looks at her. The front of his toupee makes a strange wiggle.

The woman motions for me to place my hands on the table.

I do, reluctantly. She grips my wrists with bony fingers and pushes my palms flat, her hands alongside mine.

The alarm tingle starts to buzz.

Kleinman opens his sportscoat and withdraws two daggers.

The alarm goes to red alert. I start to pull back. But the woman's grip is like steel. Her hands don't budge even as I struggle. Kleinman steps close.

My heart shrieks in panic. I pull and scream and pull. My feet scramble on the floor. I'm not going anywhere; the woman's hands might as well be iron bands.

Kleinman raises the daggers, one in each hand, like a pair of fangs.

My mind shrinks into a tiny ball of dread.

The woman's eyes glint, opaque and merciless.

Kleinman slams the daggers through the back of my hands. A thunderbolt of pain crashes through me. My eyes strain wide open, as if they can't get big enough to take in all the horror.

The woman lets go.

Blood gushes around the dagger blades. I try to withdraw my hands, but they remain staked to the table.

The woman sits back, studying me as I gasp in agony. She talks . . . in the language of the voices, and I understand every word.

"My name is Moor." Her hairline recedes. At the top of her brow, the skin twitches inside circles the size of my thumb. The skin parts and reveals pus-yellow eyeballs at the top corners of her forehead. The eyes blink and search the room before focusing puke-green irises on me.

My bones clatter in fear, and my guts feel like they're melting into my legs.

Kleinman whisks off his toupee. "And I am Doop." The skin splits above two divots on his forehead.

The woman and Kleinman stare with their horrible extra eyes, repulsive as ripe abscesses.

"That blow to your head," she says, "made you a receptor to psychic signals." She hesitates, then says, "The police on our world used you to find us."

She had said, "police" and "our world." Despite my pain, despite my terror, I now understand.

These monsters came from another planet, and their police have been trying to warn me.

Find them. Moor and Doop.

"And you have," the woman says, as if reading my thoughts. "Only we found you first." She raises a device made of glass and blue metal that she aims like a pistol. "And before you let anyone know we are here, you must die."

Panic holds me in a deadly grip, constricting like the coils of a python. Rivulets of blood seep over my hands and pool on the table. In my agony, I realize I have a decision to make.

I can let them kill me.

Or I can die fighting. Make them know my pain. Make them pay for what they've done to me.

A gush of adrenaline pries the paralysis loose and my muscles tense with fury.

The woman—or whatever alien she is—no longer has her hands on the table.

I raise my arms to lift the table off the floor, using my legs for extra leverage. Megawatts of agony sizzle from the daggers. But I ignore my anguish.

The table catches her gun and tips it backwards. The muzzle goes *zzzzittt* with a bright flash. A blast of heat slaps my face.

I ram the table against her head. The corner jabs her upper eye and it spurts like a ruptured yolk.

She howls as loud as a scalded cat, cups her eye and falls backward over her chair.

I lunge at Kleinman.

All four of his eyes get large as ping-pong balls as he retreats in a stumbling shuffle.

I smash the table on his skull, and he collapses. The tabletop breaks apart; the daggers pull free from the wood.

My mind jumps to another thought. Escape.

Embers swirl from above. The ray gun must have set the ceiling on fire. But I waste no time looking up as I turn toward a row of windows against the wall. I race toward them and leap, shielding my face with my wounded hands.

I crash through the glass. Shards snag the dagger handles, slice my hands, wrists and the back of my neck. I land on a tumble weed and the thorns sting like ants.

Jumping to my feet, I run. Blood oozes from the cuts in my neck and arms. The road before me is a black maw of shadow in the deepening gloom. I pull the daggers free and toss them aside. Arms raised, I sprint toward the road. Blood weeps from the stigmata in the palms of my hands and flows in warm sticky trails down my arms.

I hear the voices.

Al-keck. Meek. Moor. Doop.

I yell a reply in their language. "They are here. Come and get them."

I am not crazy.

No One Remembers

Patricia S. Carrillo

9:00 A.M.

Every morning she awoke to a complete absence of memory, not knowing her own name or where she was. It had been like this for a week, a somnambulant week with a family who called themselves Valdez, a week where she never fully awakened nor was sure she wanted to.

There could be no doubt that the face staring back from the bathroom mirror was hers. The dark wavy hair, pale green eyes and bright smile. Madeline ran a brush through her hair and wondered when her life would return.

Her spacious bedroom adjacent to the bath was a calming palette of blue and yellow. And since it was the only room on the second floor, there was complete privacy from everyone and the world. Her days were spent isolated in this private sanctuary, and when she would briefly awaken after long periods of slumber, she could never remember anything.

The mother had been kind and attentive to the point of distraction for the young girl. Madeline couldn't go anywhere in the house by herself without the mother watching in a constant vigil to keep her safe. A doctor had come to the house and Madeline remembered the pills he had prescribed. They were small white tablets to be taken three times a day under the watchful eye of

Mrs. Valdez. The family had been warned that if any of the pills were skipped, Madeline could have a fatal seizure.

Madeline turned on the light to the closet and chose a jean skirt and loose-fitting blouse. The clothes were slightly too large and she felt awkward. She noticed most of the clothing still had the price tags attached, but her fatigue eradicated any curiosity. Staggering down the stairs in a lethargic state, she approached the kitchen counter and sat on one of the tall stools facing a woman who was preparing a skillet of ham and eggs.

"Your morning pill is on the counter with your juice. Take it before you eat like the doctor said," the woman advised with an expressionless face and voice.

The woman worked methodically and did not engage the young girl in conversation making Madeline feel more like a stranger than a daughter. Madeline looked at the small white pill and hesitated for a moment before placing it on her tongue. She had noticed that she felt sleepy after taking the pills and she wondered if she could skip the pill this morning.

The woman noticed the hesitation and gave the young girl a piercing look. "Remember what the doctor said, you could have a seizure."

The fear that had been implanted in the young girl took hold and she obeyed and swallowed the pill with the sweet juice. A hot plate of food was placed in front of her with additional words of instruction.

"You have to keep weight on. The doctor said you are at least ten pounds underweight and that's not going to help your recovery."

Another kitchen chair slid back from the counter. A boy of about five climbed on top and looked directly at the girl's plate of food.

"Can I have cereal, Mom?"

The mother smiled at her son and prepared a sugary bowl of fruit-flavored cereal with extra milk.

"Is Maddy going with us?" the boy asked.

"You don't forget anything, Jimmy," the mother laughed. "Madeline will stay home this afternoon and rest. We'll be back before your father gets home."

Madeline chewed the eggs and took a bite of buttered toast. "If I feel better, I can go," she offered.

The mother glanced at the girl, "That is out of the question. Maybe you don't remember, but I do—the doctor said you could get lost if I take you out in public. Then, what would we do?"

At that moment a man walked into the kitchen and kissed his wife on the cheek then smiled at his son. "Ready for a big day, sport?" Then he turned to the young girl and quickly away to his wife. Madeline didn't see even a glimmer of affection in the few moments his cold blue eyes rested on her face.

He spoke to his wife, "Is she eating? She looks awfully thin."

"Everything is fine. She just needs a little TLC, and she will be good as new."

The father took his breakfast and sat at the opposite side of the kitchen. He glanced over at a large box of discarded electronic equipment beside the table.

"Am I supposed to take this somewhere?"

"I thought you could drop it off on your way to work. At the recycling center," his wife replied.

The young girl surveyed the three members of the family and saw none of the recognizable physical characteristics that should have been apparent. Madeline noted that the mother was shorter and more thickly built than herself, the father had blonde hair and the little boy sitting beside her had clear blue eyes. She felt like an outsider, not a member of the family. But it was not only the lack of physical likeness that she found odd, it was the way she felt inside. She was lost and no one cared to remember for her what her life had been like.

"What did I like to do, 'before,' I mean?" Madeline asked.

"You were just like other girls. You liked all the normal things," was the unrevealing reply from the mother.

"How did this happen to me?"

The father looked up from his morning newspaper and his face hardened. He pointed for the mother to fill his cup with more coffee. When he spoke, his voice was as harsh as his face.

"We've gone over this before. Don't you remember? You were taking anti-anxiety medication. One of the side effects is memory loss," the mother said.

"But when did it happen? How long have I been like this?"

The mother let out a long sigh and replied, "The doctor told us not to overwhelm you with details. Your recovery will take time and the best thing you can do is rest and not worry about anything."

Madeline finished eating cold ham and eggs, then felt herself becoming drowsy again. The mother noticed and suggested that she go back to bed. Madeline stood up and began to walk up the stairs. As she climbed toward her private chamber, she could hear whispers behind her. In a brief moment of curiosity, she stopped and listened to the suppressed conversation. Her head was buzzing with drowsiness, but she could make out the softly spoken words mumbled by the strangers below.

"How much longer before she goes?" the father's voice asked.

"Shh, not so loud. Just a few more days. Her passport isn't ready."

"Are you sure she's not becoming suspicious?"

"She sleeps most of the day. So far, so good," the mother answered in a faint voice.

Madeline felt a strange terror begin to swell inside her chest. The strong pull of sleep drove her to bed, and she laid her exhausted body on the sheets. While trying to stay awake to think about what she had just heard, her mind went blank and within seconds she was unconscious.

3:05 P.M.

The sound of a car door slamming shut awoke the girl with a start. Madeline opened her eyes to the brightly illuminated bedroom and noticed the clock on her bedside table indicated mid-afternoon. She sat up and felt once again the strangeness of not knowing herself or where she was.

Her mind drifted to the last words she had heard before falling asleep. The conversation seemed vague and Madeline wondered if it had even happened, but then the same sense of dread filled her heart, and she felt herself questioning her peculiar situation. Where was she going? Why were they sending her away? Why did she need a passport? She sat up and tried to focus her mind on her life past and present. If there was something tangible, maybe she could jolt her memory into working.

There were no family pictures in the room or any cards or letters that would indicate that she had communicated with friends. The room was as blank a slate as Madeline's mind. She opened up the desk drawers and saw only unused note pads and pens. Above the desk were bookshelves filled with covers that did not evoke any memories. There were no ID cards or school passes, no wallets, no backpack. The room could have belonged to anyone.

Remembering the sound that woke her up, she walked over to a window which faced the front yard. Below the rocky frame of nearby hills, she could see a neighbor's house situated across the street. It was the only other house she could see from the window. Staring out, she saw a woman being helped from a blue sedan by an attendant. The old woman struggled to gain her balance, then proceeded with cautious footsteps toward the front door. Madeline vaguely remembered the mother telling her about the neighbor.

Madeline tried to remember the old lady's name but could only think of Mrs. Somersomething. With no memories of the old woman to trigger an interest, Madeline turned her attention away from the window to the afternoon ahead of her. Walking down the stairs, she saw Jimmy playing on the floor just below the last steps and asked why he was home.

"Mom said so," was the only reply.

Madeline then had a lucid thought. She would ask the neighbor lady questions about her identity. She would have to know something about the Valdez family. "Do you want to go across the street with me?" the young girl asked.

"Okay," Jimmy answered, picking up his toy train. "Oh, we can't go outside," he added even though his eyes had widened with excitement for a brief moment. Then, he lowered his gaze when he remembered the previous instructions given to him.

"Did your mom tell you that?" Madeline asked, wondering if what she had been told at breakfast was true. For a brief moment she questioned her own ability to leave the house and felt afraid of what would happen if she did. Would she lose herself and never find her way back home again?

"She told me to say here," the boy insisted.

Feeling a sense of unexplained necessity take hold of her, Madeline assured the little boy while reassuring herself. "We're just going for a little while. Just across the street. Your mom won't mind."

Madeline went back to her room quickly to put on her shoes, then descended down the staircase remembering that it was time to take her second pill. She glanced at the kitchen counter and saw it beside a glass of water. She promised herself to take it when she returned. Next to the medication was a glass casserole dish with a sticky note attached. It indicated that the dish belonged to the neighbor. Taking the dish and Jimmy by the hand, she opened the front door and left the house for the first time that she could remember.

The sunshine felt warm and soothing. Madeline noticed as she walked that her legs were pale, even though it was warm and the climate appeared to be sunny. Jimmy, by contrast, was browned thoroughly on his arms and legs. Madeline wondered at the difference then concentrated on the house in front of her. She walked up to the front door and rang the bell.

"Hello, there," said a large dark-skinned woman from inside the house.

"Hi, we live across the street, I just came over to say hello and to bring back the dish, I think it belongs to the lady who lives here," said Madeline.

"Well, come on in and say hello to her yourself. You too, little fella," the large woman said to Jimmy. "Miss Margaret, there are neighbor kids here to see you."

An old woman turned her body away from a loud television and stared vacantly at the visitors. "Hello," she said faintly without a hint at familiarity. The old woman's face appeared featureless and tired.

"You have to be patient with Miss Margaret. She has good days and bad days, and today is not so good," the attendant said.

"What's wrong with her?" Jimmy asked.

"She suffers from memory loss, a type of dementia. Old people get it sometimes," the attendant offered, turning her attention to the small computer sitting on the kitchen counter. "I have to get her prescriptions filled by tomorrow. Excuse me, please."

Glancing over to her charge, the attendant added, "Miss Margaret, put your special necklace on. I'll be leaving for a while and you have to have it in case you need help." The old woman picked up a long cord with a plastic box connected and looked at the large red button facing her.

"That's her emergency alert, in case I'm not here. It signals the police and paramedics." The attendant broke off her conversation and turned her thoughts to the computer keyboard. "There, it's all done, and I have to get going."

Madeline felt her breath leave her body from disappointment. She needed answers to her questions and she didn't know who to turn to. She smiled and offered the casserole dish to the attendant. "We'll come back another time, when she's feeling better." Madeline said.

"I'm sure she would like that. My name is Janie by the way."

"I'm Madeline and this is my little brother Jimmy". As she said the words, it felt as if she was telling lies. Taking Jimmy by the hand, she crossed the street with a determined step. There had to be something in the house, something that would tell her who she was.

3:30 P.M.

"Do you know why I got sick?" Madeline asked the young boy.

"I don't know."

"Do you know how long I've lived here?" she asked again, hoping for a reassuring answer.

The young boy looked up with a perplexed look of his face.

Madeline kept pressing the child for answers.

"Jimmy, where does your mom keep pictures?" Madeline asked in a sweet tone.

"Pictures of what?" Jimmy said, not looking up from his toys.

"Pictures of you and me."

Jimmy looked up and stared at the girl with his large blue eyes widened. "Why would we have pictures of you?"

Madeline felt herself flinch, "I don't know. Maybe you do."

"I don't know," was the only reply. "Will you play cars with me?" he asked.

Feeling a sense of urgency overtake her, she said in a quick voice, "I'm going upstairs, let me know when your mom gets home, okay?"

Madeline raced up to her room, then remembered the pill on the counter. She ran back down the stairs, grabbed the pill and dropped it in the garbage disposal. She would take her chances of a seizure and it felt good to lift the switch to buzz the pill away. Her mind felt less cloudy than it had that morning and she needed to think. She began to ransack the bedroom for any sign of her identity. Checking under the bed, inside the closet, then through every drawer of the bathroom, she found nothing. There was no sign of her past or present.

Standing still with exasperation, she heard a faint familiar noise in the distance. It seemed to be coming from the kitchen and when Madeline went downstairs she discovered a cell phone ringing from inside of the box that the father had forgotten to take. The number on the screen was not familiar but the sound of the ring tone sparked a memory through the fog of Madeline's mind. She answered the phone with a hesitant, "Hello."

"Angie, is that you?" a frantic voice asked.

Madeline held the phone to her ear and was not sure what to say to the stranger. "This is Madeline. Who is this?"

"Angie, I know it's your voice! It's me, LeAnn. Don't you remember me?" the voice asked, as the speaker yelled into the phone.

Madeline was confused and frightened at the caller's questions. The sound of a motor could be heard from the garage signaling that the door was opening and she knew that if the mother saw her talking on the phone, something bad might happen.

"I have to call you back! Don't call me!" Madeline said without thinking. She pressed a button to end the call and slipped the slim phone into her skirt pocket. Her thoughts began to arrange themselves quickly and she felt more in control of her mind than she had for days. Thinking of the computer at the neighbor's house, she said "There has to be a computer in this house. Everyone has one, right?"

"Who are you talking to?" Jimmy asked, standing beside the young girl.

"Jimmy, where is the computer?" Madeline asked.

"Why do you want to know?"

The sound of the mother's car driving into the garage alerted the young girl further. She turned to the boy and pleaded, "Don't tell your mom I asked you anything, okay?"

"Okay," the young boy responded.

The back door to the kitchen opened and the mother looked surprised to see the girl and her son standing in the room. "I thought you would be taking a nap," she said

"I just woke up," Madeline lied.

"We went to the old lady's house," Jimmy volunteered.

The mother placed her shopping bags on the kitchen counter and stared at the girl. "You went outside by yourself?"

"Just for a minute. I saw the dish on the counter and thought I would return it. To help out," Madeline replied, trying to make her voice sound innocent.

The mother looked over to the spot where she had left the medication intended for the girl and saw that it was no longer there. "Did you take your afternoon pill?"

"I just did, so I better go upstairs and lay down."

"Jimmy, I told you to watch your sister while I went to get groceries," the mother reprimanded.

The young boy gave a blank stare at his annoyed mother and ran back to play with his toys. The mother took another inquisitive look at the girl.

"How is Mrs. Somerson? Was she feeling well?"

"Not really. She didn't know who I was, or anyone else," the girl answered

"We're having pasta tonight, your favorite," the mother said, opening the refrigerator.

"That sounds good," Madeline replied turning away from the kitchen.

The young girl quickly ascended the steps eager to discover who she was. She would call the girl named LeAnn back and maybe get the answers she was looking for.

3:40 P.M.

The cell phone was dead. The battery was down and no amount of pressing on the lifeless buttons would bring it back. Madeline stared at the useless contraption and wondered what to do next. She was desperate to call LeAnn and ask her what she knew. Pacing around the sunny bedroom, she thought of finding a charger for the phone. Trying to remember if she had seen a cell phone in the house, she recalled a cord with a large plug that had been sitting on a sofa table in the living room and that the father had been sitting on the sofa talking on his cell phone the day before.

She poked her head out of her bedroom door and took a cautious glance down the stairs. She didn't see anyone on the landing and decided to venture further down the stairs. The little boy had gone into his room to play, and the mother was in the kitchen fussing with the contents of the refrigerator. Madeline walked softly into the living room avoiding the hall leading to the kitchen and hurriedly looked for the phone charger. It was resting quietly on the table where she had remembered seeing it.

Picking it up, she stuck it into her pocket and returned to her bedroom unnoticed.

She recognized the small port on the side of the phone and tried to fit the charger into the space provided. Madeline breathed a short sigh of relief when the two pieces of equipment fit together. Plugging in the charger to a wall outlet, she attempted to turn the phone on again. The number for LeAnn was the only number that registered on the small screen as a recent incoming call and there were no outgoing numbers saved. Taking a deep breath, she pressed the send button and waited for the answer.

"Angie!" screamed the desperate voice.

"Hello, who is this?"

"It's LeAnn. Where are you?"

"I don't know a LeAnn; I don't think I do," said Madeline, becoming afraid of what she might hear next from the excited girl.

"Angie, it's me. Your best friend. Where have you been? We have been looking everywhere. You just disappeared. I've been texting and calling, but you didn't answer!"

"I'm home," Madeline offered, "I've been sick".

"You're not home. We don't know where you are. Your parents are so worried. Are you in trouble? Please tell me where you are," begged the girl.

Madeline thought about the question and realized that she did not know which town she was in or even what her home address was. "I don't know where I am," she said, feeling afraid.

"Is there something you can find with an address?"

Footsteps could be heard outside her bedroom. Madeline said a hasty goodbye to the mysterious girl and hid the phone under a stack of pillows on the floor.

"Madeline, I thought you were feeling tired," the voice accused as the door opened.

The girl sat down quickly on the bed and pulled her legs up under the folded comforter.

"I had a headache and couldn't sleep, but I took something so I should be fine." Madeline responded.

"I brought another pill for you. The doctor said if you couldn't sleep it was alright for you to take two at a time." The mother handed the white tablet to Madeline with a glass of water. "Now take it and get some rest."

Madeline could see that it was useless to argue. She took the pill and placed it inside her mouth and swallowed. The mother's expression changed from sternness to a slight smile. She left the room and closed the door behind her. Madeline felt relieved to be left alone and immediately took the pill out of her mouth. She would call LeAnn again and find out the truth. Then she heard a sound unfamiliar to her. A latch was being turned outside of the bedroom door. She was locked inside.

3:55 P.M.

The locked door would have to be figured out later, Madeline thought to herself. For now, she had to call LeAnn back. The phone rang once before the excited voice answered, this time with added urgency. "Where are you? What is happening?" the voice demanded.

"I don't know where I am, and no one will tell me," Madeline answered, feeling more lost as the minutes passed.

"You have to get outta there and call the police."

"She locked my door, and there is no where to go," Madeline replied.

The phone was quiet for a minute then LeAnn began speaking rapidly. "Your name is Angie Ramírez. You live in Chicago, and I'm your best friend. You went missing over three weeks ago when you and I went to meet Danny and his cousin at the mall. We were supposed to see a movie. You like Danny's cousin, remember? He's super cute and he goes to the high school closer to your house." LeAnn took a breath and continued. "You're sixteen and super popular. Everyone likes you, except for that girl Tiffany who thinks she's better than everyone. She tried to mess up our webpage, remember?"

LeAnn stopped then said something that seemed suddenly obvious. "You have to get on the Internet and see for yourself. You will remember everything if you see our pictures and all the stuff that our friends put there. Oh, Angie, you have to!"

"I don't think they have a computer here," Madeline said, feeling the urgency in her friend's voice.

"Then go somewhere and find one!"

Madeline stayed quiet and thought about her options. She wanted to believe that someone was trying to help but nothing the girl said was making any sense to her. She couldn't remember the boy she liked or the school she attended in Chicago. Turning her gaze out of the window, the sun was shining brightly and it did not seem possible that she could be from Chicago where she imagined snow falling only three weeks ago.

"LeAnn, what day is this?" she asked.

"It's the twenty-third of January, Wednesday."

Madeline looked down at her pale skin and thought she was very far from Chicago if that was in fact her home. "LeAnn, it's really sunny here. I have a short skirt on and today I went outside and I wasn't cold."

"You have to find out where you are so we can come and get you!"

"I'll try LeAnn. I'll try to find out something and I'll call you back."

"Take your phone with you, don't forget!"

She ended the call with her mind reeling. The Valdez family had not been unkind, just distant, and they hadn't made her feel like she was in danger. Feelings of anxiety began to overtake her and she doubted herself and her suspicions. A doctor had seen her and she had been on medication before, or had she? Why would she be with the wrong family in a town where no one knew her? She considered calling the police herself from her phone but hesitated when she considered that if she was wrong, it could cause more problems and maybe she would be put on more meds to control her behavior. And besides, she didn't know where she was. How could she tell the police to help her if they didn't know how to find her? She had a lot of thinking to do and something inside herself told her she did not have a lot of time to figure it all out.

4:20 P.M.

The lock on the door would not budge. Madeline paced about in the large space and wondered how she would be able to leave the room to find the information she desperately needed. A young boy's voice came through the wood door and surprised the girl into stillness.

"Maddy, are you in there?"

Madeline rushed to the door and whispered loudly, "Yes, yes, I'm here. If you open the door, I'll come out and play with you."

"Okay," Jimmy said as the door opened.

"Now, we have to be quiet," Madeline cautioned. "We should go to your room to play."

The girl closed the bedroom door behind her and the little boy led the way down the stairs toward his bedroom at the back of the large house. Madeline saw a back door leading to an unfenced backyard.

"These are my new ones, which one do you want?" he asked, absorbed in the array of colorful toy cars on the bedroom floor.

"I'll take the red one," Madeline said, partially sitting on the floor. Jimmy picked up two cars, one in each hand and began to make the sounds of a loud car motor as he looked around the disheveled room for the car tracks to assemble.

"Jimmy, does your mom or dad have a computer in the house?"

The young boy's focus could not be distracted from his toys. He paid no attention to the question. Madeline asked again and only received a shrug of the boy's shoulders as a response.

Turning her thoughts to the conversations with LeAnn, she questioned her predicament. Why would the girl lie to her? And why wouldn't the Valdez family give her any information?

Seeing Jimmy totally engrossed in his play, Madeline knew she had to find the answers while she had a chance. Checking first for the mother, she poked her head out into the hallway, then ran out the back door into a world that didn't know who she was.

4:35 P.M.

The sun was dimming in the west and the street was forming shadows in anticipation of the darkness that would soon follow. The Valdez house was large, creating its own imposing cover which partially concealed the girl. No one had followed her outside and the father hadn't arrived home yet. Madeline walked alongside the house wondering where she should go next. She had no access to a car and even if she did, she would not know where to drive. With great reluctance, she considered returning to the house and calling the police herself, but her fears of being misunderstood and the fact that she still didn't know her location kept her from going back.

Her heart had begun to race as she considered her only option. She had to cross the street to her neighbor's house and inquire about her location. Even if the old lady could not tell her anything, Madeleine could probably find something with a written address. Madeline crept to the corner of the building and stuck out only her foot. The front living room windows of the Valdez house were open and anyone standing inside could easily see Madeline running across the road. Madeline took a deep breath and felt her legs move quickly under her. She crossed the front yard into the street and onto the front porch to the neighbor's house imagining all the while the burning gaze of her captor's eyes. She rang the doorbell without looking back and within a few seconds, the old woman answered the door.

"My dear, what is it? I saw you running this way, is something wrong?" the old woman asked with a concerned look on her face.

Madeline looked imploringly into the woman's face and asked to be let in before she explained her situation. The old woman opened the door wider and allowed Madeline to step inside. Immediately, Madeline observed that the neighbor was alert and aware of her surroundings unlike her muddled state of mind earlier that day. For the first time, she could see the woman's personality through her concerned smile.

"Mrs. Somerson, may I use your computer?" the young girl asked, her voice cracking with desperation.

"Well, yes, that is fine, but what is wrong?" the neighbor asked again.

Madeline looked frantically around the kitchen for the computer. Spotting the screen and keyboard on the kitchen table under a stack of empty boxes and newspapers, she sat down and began to type. Nearly forgetting to answer the woman's questions, she turned her head after directing the screen for access to the Internet. "I have to find out where I am, so I can call the police," she heard herself say.

"The police? What has happened?" the woman asked, her thin voice wavering.

"I think I have been kidnapped," Madeline answered becoming more fearful as she spoke. "But I can't be sure, I just don't know anything about who I am and I have to find out before it's too late!"

"Oh, my!" the woman gasped. Without thinking she placed her hand around the plastic box that hung around her neck for security and grew silent.

The computer was slow to respond to Madeline's demands. While the screen was changing, she took the phone out of skirt pocket and dialed LeAnn's phone number.

"Hello!" the voice answered.

"LeAnn, it's me, I found a computer, and I'm going to look up the site you told me about!"

"Thank God, what's the address where you are?"

Madeline shuffled the newspapers in front of her and saw the name of the city in bold print. "The newspaper says Escondido? Where is that?"

"Let me check on my computer," LeAnn answered. "Oh, my God, you're in California near the Mexican border."

The name of the city did not provoke any memories for Madeline but the thought of being in California, thousands of miles away from Chicago shocked her.

"Can you find a street address?" asked LeAnn.

The computer screen began to form intelligible images and Madeline questioned LeAnn about the password and ID number she needed to log onto the website. Having access granted, Madeline stared at the screen in astonishment. Her face was in full color and in various photos she was surrounded by young people she could not recognize. Their youthful faces expressed innocence and joy and were in stark contrast to the girl who felt nothing but fear and doubt.

LeAnn sensed the silence and uneasiness on the other side of the phone. "Are you still there? What have you found?"

"I see myself and a lot of other people," she answered in a stunned voice.

"I'm the girl in the purple coat holding onto your arm. We were with Danny at the football game!" LeAnn shouted. "Do you see me?"

Angie looked at the computer screen and found the face of the girl in the purple coat. She had a friendly smile and was several inches shorter than herself. They had the same hairstyle and matching earrings in the picture.

"Do you see me?" asked LeAnn again. "I look kinda fat in that picture, but there are others of you and me if you scroll down!"

"LeAnn," Angie begun slowly, "what happened to me?" The pictures on the screen had brought relief that she was not imagining her predicament, but they also confirmed that she was in imminent danger.

"Angie, you left us at the mall to get something out of your car, but you never came back, we searched everywhere."

"What should I do?" the young girl asked feeling a sudden sense of helplessness.

"Where are you? Find an address!" barked LeAnn.

Angie looked around the table and saw several envelopes. Angie began to read the address to LeAnn but before she could continue, she felt a pull at her hair and the angry voice of the woman she feared. Mrs. Valdez had come to take her home.

4:45 P.M.

Her head jerked back violently and the upward force applied to her scalp caused her to rise from her chair involuntarily. Mrs. Valdez' grip was firm, her cruel fingers strong.

"Let go of me!" Angie shouted.

"You must excuse my coming into your house like this. Our daughter has a mind of her own and she's on strong medications. She knows she is not supposed to leave without our expressed permission," the woman said.

"Stop it, let go!" Angie screamed, trying to turn around to use her hands against her assailant.

"We're going home now. Sorry for the intrusion," Mrs. Valdez said.

"Mrs. Somerson, call the police. These people aren't my parents, I've been kidnapped!" Angie yelled as Mrs. Valdez dragged her to the front door.

The two fought with each other as they crossed the street. Mrs. Valdez kept her vicious grip on Angie's scalp, while holding the young girl's right arm behind her back. Angie attempted to use her left arm to free herself and to kick her captor with wild swings of her legs. Before she was dragged into the Valdez house, Angie managed to turn her body around to give one last desperate cry to the only witness. Mrs. Somerson had seen the entire spectacle from her front lawn. Standing motionless, she stared out into street with a vacant look upon her face.

4:50 P.M.

"You can't keep me here. I know what you did!" Angie screamed.

Mrs. Valdez pushed her inside the front door and slapped her face with such force that the young girl fell to the floor. "You could have had it easy, but you had to go and make trouble. Now you're going to see how hard I can be!" the woman said, towering over her victim.

Before Angie could pick herself up, Mrs. Valdez had straddled her body, holding her arms down and pressing her weight against the girl's legs. Angie convulsed her body repeatedly trying to shake off the powerful woman.

"Martin, get the injection now!" she screamed to her husband who had just arrived.

The man had a hard glare in his eyes as he returned quickly with a syringe filled with clear fluid. "Don't leave any marks on her!" he advised, handing over the needle to his wife.

"We have to call the Doc to get her outta here right now before anyone finds out!"

"I already called him a few hours ago when you told me she wasn't sleeping, I had a feeling she would try something sneaky. He should be here by five o'clock to take her."

Jimmy walked into the living room and startled the mother causing her to partially lift her weight off Angie. "Get to your room, now!" she screamed. The little boy cried in fright and ran away. Taking advantage of the loosened grip, Angie managed to move her right leg from under the woman and kicked her hard in the stomach before feeling the needle glide painfully into her arm.

"This little bitch is going to get exactly what she deserves," the woman gloated as she released her exhausted prey to the tranquilizing effects of the injected drug. "You just wait and see what's going to happen to you. All you pretty girls are good for just one thing, and you're going get plenty of it!"

Angie felt the stark terror of the helpless heading toward an unimaginable fate. Darkness filled her eyes and within seconds she was once again unconscious.

5:30 P.M.

A reassuring grip squeezed Angie's arm as she awakened slowly. Her head ached and her eyes had difficulty focusing on the face in front of hers. She felt like an eternity had passed since she had been awake and fully aware of herself.

"Is she coming to?" a man's voice said.

"It will take a while. They gave her a light dose, but she'll feel it for a few hours before her head clears up."

Angie opened her eyes slowly and saw the dim outline of a friendly face looking down at her. She was in a bed covered with blankets and was about to be lifted onto the back of a vehicle.

"Where am I?" she asked with traces of the fear she had felt before.

"You're safe now. Do you know your name?" the paramedic asked.

"Angie Ramírez," she said. "Where am I?"

"We are taking you to a hospital in downtown Escondido. You had a few hard knocks on the head and we have to make sure you're going to be okay."

A cold shot of terror filled Angie's veins as she began to recall what had transpired earlier. She tried to lift herself up from the bed to escape.

"It's okay, Angie. Lie back down. You have to rest. The people who were holding you have been taken by the police. There's no one left to hurt you."

"How did you find me?" Angie asked, feeling her eyes begin to fill with tears.

"There were a lot of people who were looking for you. When the police got the call, they came right away."

Angie let the tears flow from her tired eyes. Since that morning, her worst fears had been realized and the thought of her family and friends saving her despite the seemingly impossible odds was overwhelming. She let out a deep sigh and smiled through her tears at the paramedic.

"Will my parents be at the hospital?"

"We've already been in contact. They'll be here by morning. You just lie back and try to relax. Let us take care of you."

Angie allowed her body to relax and settle onto the gurney while it was being lifted into the ambulance. Turning her head slightly toward the neighbor's house, she saw Mrs. Somerson waving to her, and her other hand holding onto the plastic box hanging from around her neck.

For You, Mother

Sarah Cortez

That I saw my own mother burned that December day in Camargo changed my life. How could it not? If she hadn't sent me to search through the town for water, I would have been shot, then burned by the Villistas like so much firewood, as she and the other women were. But that was a cold day in December 1916 and this is a hot day in July 1923. And, I am no longer six years old.

I have grown almost to manhood, as I never doubted I would, because seeing her murderer, the famous Pancho Villa —with his jutting, yellowed teeth, his clothing covered with the blowing red dust of northern Mexico—implanted in my deepest soul the will to stay alive, so I might one day make him pay for my mother's death on that most cursed day of days.

Now I live at Canutillo. It is the hacienda where Villa lives in retirement. Even though I'm younger than most of Villa's men, I shoot well. I can kill with a knife. I keep all my equipment in careful order—cleaned and oiled. I am ready to ride hard or fight at a moment's notice. The first year here we had to be awake before four A.M. to report for his inspection, just like in the military. In this second year, *mi general* no longer gets up at three A.M. Some say that Villa chose this remote location because he feared attack by the family members of some he had killed during the Revolution. It wouldn't surprise me. But they'll have a hard time penetrating the thick walls when we can pick them off with a rifle shot as they cross the flat tortilla of the land. I protect him from being killed by others; it's my destiny to kill him. Mine, alone.

You see, Villa's most trusted men here—what's left of the Dorados—trust me. His wives, even his girlfriends in Parral, trust me. This is important because no matter how I kill him eventually, I must continue to be in their confidence after his death. As I saw my mother's hair and skirts catch fire in the stack of bound women the Villistas had shot at the request of the townspeople who didn't want the Carrancista *soldaderas* to betray those who had welcomed Villa . . . as I saw that dreadful fire sweep over her sweet face, I formed the resolve to destroy Villa completely. Absolutely completely. To wipe every trace of his accursed line off the earth. And there are many because he breeds like a dog.

This morning I awoke early. At that hour, even the insects respect the night and are quiet. I considered my plan. I had spent months figuring out every detail. I willed my body to linger unmoving on the straw pallet. There must be nothing out of the ordinary. Nothing that one of the busybody women or hordes of children might think back on later and see how I had done something to cause his fiery death.

When the first rooster finally crowed, I swung my eager legs onto the solid packed earth. It was too early for even the slightest hint of pink to curl its lips at the horizon.

After washing my face, I went to the stable. The night before we had been told how many horses to ready for Villa's ride to the christening of his friend's new baby. With a large escort of Dorados on horseback and Villa himself on a horse, I wouldn't be able to execute my plan. But I had a feeling as heavy as a molded bullet inside me, a deep certainty that today would see the fulfillment of my seven years of waiting. Why would I feel this way if it wasn't true?

Villa came to the stable, walking with his energetic step. His barrel chest radiated confidence—the same bravery that had allowed him, and us, his followers, to elude the *federales*, and even the American dog, General Pershing and his 12,000 soldiers.

He was whistling. "Good morning," he said to everyone working there. "Today, no horses. I take the car."

We put the horse blankets and harnesses back in the racks.

I went to the far end of the building where his prized Dodge sat. He walked with me.

"Well, Gonzalo, how many tanks of gasoline do we need for the trip to Río Florido?"

"Two, maybe, three."

He lingered, walking around the Dodge. His dark eyes that could shoot darts of flame when he was enraged seemed to be looking at the car in a new way. Later, I would wonder if he already felt the skeletal fingers of Death reaching for his bones. Did he know he was looking at his own black hearse?

I said a prayer. Yes, me, a murderer of many men and about to kill another. But I knew I was right. My mother had to be avenged. There was no room in my soul for anything other than this dark loyalty to her. There had never been anyone I had called *friend* and meant it.

As he walked around the car, I filled the two small, cigar-shaped tanks from the bigger supply of gasoline we always kept in another shed. Then, I strapped them to the running boards on either side of the doors. As I finished, I heard him say close behind my ear, "I hear you are doing well in classes, Gonzalo."

"*Sí, mi general.* I like the school here."

"Good. You keep studying. That is the only way to change Mexico's future," he sighed. "All that fighting we did. All those years. Corpses piled high, then higher. It didn't change a thing."

Then, he looked with great intensity into my eyes and placed his heavy hand on my shoulder. "You're the future of Mexico. Will you love her as much as we did?"

I was silent and confused. I loved no one except my mother.

Then he said, "Who knows?" He laughed, but he didn't look happy.

He paused a moment longer still trying to see my very soul. My whole body broke out in sweat as if it was raining. I was sure he would see the lie my whole life as his follower had been. That he would glimpse my deception and crack me in two with his strong arms. I had seen him do that to grown men—break them into pieces, the blood spraying everywhere. Bones, white and jagged. Their faces becoming a hole into eternity.

Instead, he walked out of the stable.

My eyes blurred and stung with the dripping beads of sweat. I remembered I must hurry.

I swung around and managed to walk nearer the hiding place I'd made when we had to rebuild sections of Canutillo. Most of the others had already left because the car was my special assignment. I alone kept it shining and clean. Many times I had changed the wheels from the wooden-spoked to the beautiful metal-spoked. Made sure the footrest for the second seat passengers would raise and lower without squeaking.

Luckily, the breakfast bell rang and everyone else jumped and ran out. I grabbed a ladder and climbed to the small hiding place in the rafters of the roof. I removed one stick of dynamite from the oily, water-proof paper. I had saved her from the many we had used when fighting and named her Aurora. I cradled her more carefully than a baby and kept her as safe as if I was her mother as I climbed down.

I removed one of the gasoline tanks and placed her resting in the crevice where she would be hidden when I replaced the tank. She was already sweating slightly. Thick drops oozed from her black shawl. How many times had I flicked drops like these to the ground with a fingernail to hear them pop as they landed? They were the drops of her promise to expedite death.

When I had helped the Villistas earlier in the Revolution, I had learned how to treat the many sisters of my Aurora. I had been smaller in size and a fast runner. I could place the sisters of death at the exact junction of railroad crossties and metal track to cause an explosion for a train that was already chugging into sight. Yes, we were famous for blowing up the trains of our enemies, the black cars coughing up broken horses and men onto the soil where we could finish them off with rifles, or simply leave them there and ride away, gaining by their two or three days' delay while they rebuilt the track and buried the dead.

In the middle of breakfast, I remembered that I hadn't done one of the most important steps of my plan. I had forgotten to let some air out of the car's tires. Aurora needed the shock of a hard jostle to wake her up.

I chewed on my tortilla and drank hot coffee to wash it down. How could I get up from the breakfast table and get to the stable without people noticing?

My mother's voice came into my ear. *Water. Go get water.* The last words she had ever spoken to me.

I was so startled I choked on the hot gulp I was swallowing and coughed it up, spraying the others across the table. Lydia, who always considered herself too much of a "lady" to talk to me, glared and brushed off her blouse. Claudia, who was barely five years old, burst into tears as she looked down at the half-chewed bits of yellow tortilla across her chest.

"Water. I'll go get water," I said as I sprang up, rushing through the kitchen and out the back door.

Breathless, I ran to the stable. Villa's insistence on strict eating times would help me. But as I ran inside, I saw one of his littlest kids—already resembling Villa with that arrogant, thrust-out jaw—at the front of the car, poking at the headlights with a babyish innocence.

"What are you doing here, *mijo*?"

I ruffled his hair and pointed him back to the kitchen. "Go. It's time to eat. Your mamá is looking for you."

His short legs took forever to get going, but he obeyed and I quickly went to work. I only had time to let air out of the rear tires. But it would have to do. No one must remember I had been gone too long from the table.

I ran back to the kitchen's rear door and soaked a thin towel in the bucket of standing water. But when I sat down, Claudia had already been cleaned up by someone else.

"Sorry," I mumbled. "Something got stuck in my throat."

She looked at me with a brave little smile while Lydia rolled her eyes.

I went back to eating, but my heart was pounding so hard that the chewing echoed in my ears loud enough to give me a headache.

After breakfast, Villa chose the men who would accompany him. Trigo, his right-hand man—the one who looked like a schoolteacher. Four others.

As they were walking to the car, one of Villa's wives ran out.

"*Mi señor*," she said to Villa, "*Mi señor*, today do not make this trip today."

He paused.

The tears welled up in her expressive eyes, "I have had a dream. A terrible dream, full of tongues of fire that grow into walls of flame. I felt my skin crackle in the heat."

He regarded her with grave eyes. Then, the slightest smile lifted the corners of his bushy moustache. He clamped a huge hand on her left shoulder and said, "Woman, do not interfere with our plans. What you felt was your own oven where you should be now preparing a good dinner for when we return."

I was standing close, so close I could have counted the threads on her dark shawl if I had wanted to. So close I could smell the starch on Villa's dress shirt underneath the black suit he was wearing for the christening. I was prepared for her to turn and extend a short finger pointing me out for what I was— a boy become a man through lies, a man ready to be torn to pieces by Villa for attempting to murder my mother's murderer. If she had seen the fire in her dream, then, perhaps, she had seen me also.

She lifted her chin at his words. One tear glistened down each cheek. She had lost; she could feel his life and vitality slipping away as a stream goes dry in summer's relentless heat. She couldn't stop Fate. She couldn't stop the deliverance of evil to evil.

He turned and slipped behind the steering wheel. Trigo sat beside him and the four others piled into the back.

I saw their several pistols, but they took no rifles. They didn't know that the beauteous Aurora would come to caress each one of them in a fiery embrace that no gun could stop. The jolting over the rocky roads would explode her in a blaze that would forever bond their hearts with her fire—as had happened to my own sweet mother.

Meantime, I would go about my regular duties at the hacienda. No one would suspect me. I would cry with the rest of them when the news was delivered. I would say *mi general* must have forgotten he couldn't smoke in the car when the spare gasoline tanks were strapped to the running boards. He must've tossed a smoking cigarette out the window, and it was blown onto the running board. Then, it exploded the gasoline. Such a huge loss. Such a senseless tragedy. Just like when I lost my mother.

I waited for news of the deaths to arrive at Canutillo. Each grain of fine sand blowing against my face whispered, "He's dead. Dead. Dead." The sun's bright rays sparkled with the promise I'd made to my mother's spirit in Camargo that winter day. Night came and grew old, and I slept badly, my insides churning with suppressed excitement when Villa didn't return on time.

Then, we found out, just as the entire world found out, that six unknown assassins had killed him as he slowed down the Dodge for that ninety-degree turn in Parral.

We boarded up the gate and stood at our posts, rifles ready, for two days. Then, Hipólito, Villa's brother, came to tell us to put down our guns.

I was one of the ones sent to get the car. Villa and Trigo's blood smelling the inside, gagging all of us. Bullet holes scarred the front and back of the Dodge. You see, they killed *mi general* by shooting him in the back like you'd shoot a rabid cur in the street from the safety of a high porch.

Before I drove the car back to Canutillo, I pretended to examine the small gasoline tanks on the running boards. Aurora was gone. Villa must have found her. It was always said he was the smartest man in México in the ways to stay alive and outwit those who wished to kill him. If Villa had returned, he would've killed me. I would have been the corpse leaking blood into the fine grit of a hot July day. No one would have prayed over me.

So, the assassins stole my chance at revenge, but they also gave me the gift of life. I will continue living here in the hacienda where everyone trusts me. I will outwit those who would kill me and destroy those whom I choose. No one with Villa's blood can be allowed to continue his accursed seed. After all, Villa's children like me. Just a series of accidents. Much easier to plan. Even *mi general* himself, wherever he is, would agree that mine is a masterful plan.

The Tattoo

Alicia Gaspar de Alba

It was one of those neon blue days in late July on Venice Beach with no clouds in the sky and sailboats bobbing on the horizon, the smell of pot and patchouli emanating from the locals who had set up shop along the boardwalk. Diana and Gina de la Torre had been looking for their little sister, Little Jay, for the last half hour. They couldn't find Little Jay anywhere and she wasn't picking up her phone.

"I told you we shouldn't ever let her go off by herself," Diana groused. "That kid always gets her ass in trouble. I'm so tired of her. She's gonna give Mami a heart attack one day."

"Hey, you guys," Gina's friend Bethany called out from one of the shops, her face dwarfed under a huge pair of sunglasses, "aren't these shades da bomb?" She had already bought *calavera* trinkets, jewelry and handmade soaps. Now she was on the hunt for the perfect pair of knockoff sunglasses.

"Tell your shopaholic friend to hurry up," Diana told Gina. "We have to find Little Jay."

One Saturday a month, Diana drove Gina to Venice Beach to sell her hand-embroidered denim handbags and cell phone holders that she made from recycled jeans and peddled under the label *L.A. Gypsy* on the boardwalk. In just half a day, Gina had made enough for a pair of nosebleed seats to the Morrissey concert at the Rose Bowl for her and her boyfriend Cricket.

"Come on, you guys, I'm starving," whined Bethany behind them. "I've got like big-time Coney Island dog cravings."

"You just wanna hang at the hot dog stand and ogle the guys in thongs pumping iron at Muscle Beach," said Gina, laughing at her boy-crazy BFF. Gina wheeled her faux-Gucci *L.A. Gypsy* suitcase behind Diana.

"There she is! Isn't that Little Jay?" Gina called out. They were standing in front of the House of Ink, almost at the Santa Monica divide where Venice Beach becomes Santa Monica Beach, and the boardwalk madness of joggers, skateboarders, roller-bladers, dog-walkers and Hare Krishnas gives way to the beer garden set.

"No way!" yelled Diana. "Tell me Little Jerk is not getting a tattoo."

Surrounded by pictures of tattoo designs, Little Jay was sitting in a high director's chair under a red umbrella with her arm extended. An Indian man with a black beard and long, wild hair blowing in the wind scrolled dark paste over the back of her hand.

Diana scuttled quickly to the tattoo booth followed by Gina and her roller bag. "Oh my god, Jay! Mami's gonna kill you!" Diana's thick black eyeliner made her black crow eyes look like they were popping out of her head.

"Get over yourself," said Little Jay. "It's just henna. It washes off." Little Jay's nose twitched with the tang of essential oils emanating from the henna paste.

"I think it's cute," said Gina, "I mean, in a Third World 'Bride and Prejudice' kind of way."

Little Jay rolled her eyes. "Whatever."

"He's doing your fingers, too? *Pinche loca*," Diana swore at her little sister. "You get more *chola*-like every day."

"Hello? What are *you* all of a sudden, Diana? A beach bunny? Just because your punker boyfriend goes to Crossroads School, don't forget where we come from, Ms. El Sereno!"

"Look who's talking, Ms. Saint Rigor Mortis School," Diana responded.

"It's Saint Wilgefortis, *chingao*. Stop calling it 'rigor mortis.' Is it my fault I got a scholarship to one of the top private schools in Los Angeles?" retorted Little Jay

"More like a combination of financial aid and Mami cooking for the school in exchange for part of your $28,000 tuition."

"Shut up, Ms. High-School-Drop-Out-I-Can't-Even-Get-Accepted-to-Cal-State."

"Bethany!" Gina called out to her friend, who was contemplating getting a tarot reading from the white lady at the next table. "Dude, get over here. Come see what Little Jay is doing. She's, like, getting a big 'ole tattoo all over her arm and hand."

Bethany approached them and pushed the fake D&G sunglasses she had just bought up on her head, scrutinizing the situation with her blue-contact-covered eyeballs. "Girl, you're gonna be in so much trouble," she said, pursing her cherry-glossed lips and shaking her head.

"Our mom's gonna flip, huh?" Gina said.

"Duh!" said Diana.

"Actually, my mom's gonna flip even more," said Bethany. "My party's in two weeks, Little Jay. And your dress has short sleeves. Will it come off by then?"

"The henna will peel off in a week or two, no worries, my friend," said the Indian man, now scrolling henna paste around Little Jay's arm, from elbow to wrist, in the shape of a peacock tail.

"It's called a mendhi," said Little Jay, admiring the intricate feathering of the design.

"Wedding mendhi," said the Indian man. "Very powerful."

"Like for getting married or something?" said Little Jay, not realizing she'd chosen a wedding design.

"Peacock mendhi is sacred to the goddess, my friend. Will bring longevity in love, fertility and good luck. You will get married young. Rich man."

Little Jay gulped at the word "fertility." What had she gone and done?

"Did he say she's gonna marry a 'young rich man' or that she'll get married young to a rich man?" Gina said to Diana.

"If it doesn't come off by the party, my mom won't let you be in the court, Jay," said Bethany, settling her big glasses over her nose again. "Oh well. Your loss."

Little Jay's head started to throb. She didn't care about not being allowed to be one of the fifteen girls in Bethany's stupid *quinceañera*. She'd never wanted to do that anyway, and the thought of having to wear that trippy lace and satin dress and dance with a guy gave her nightmares. But her mom had promised Bethany's mom that "Juanita" would be "so honored" to be in Bethany's court. It was the dumb tattoo that worried her. Why hadn't she asked what the design meant? The guy could have told her what it symbolized and she'd have gone for something else, a fire-blowing dragon image with her name in the flames or even the Dodgers logo. All she needed was some guy asking her to get married at Bethany's *quinceañera* because of this dumb wedding mendhi design. The thought of it made her want to puke. She thought they'd all like the tattoo. What a dork.

The drying paste was making the pale skin of her inner arm itch. She turned her face toward the ocean and the wind blew sand into her eyes. For a second, she felt a slight tremble under the chair. She'd been feeling it off and on all morning, a slow quivering in the ground, like an aftershock to a big earthquake, only there hadn't been a big earthquake in Los Angeles since the day she was born in 1994. She squinted against the sand, against the injustice of having to be only fourteen years old, and the youngest of three sisters, and the only one who was going to hell one day for being what she was. More than anything she wished she could tell everyone the truth. Only her best friend Roy knew the truth because he was the same way. But now he was gone for good because of what happened to him in Texas. She was completely alone with her secret.

"Earth to Little Jerk," snapped Diana, the nineteen-year-old going on forty. Little Jay wiped the tears from her eyes with her free hand.

"Did you feel it?" Little Jay said to Mendhi Man. "There was a tremor just now."

The man scowled at her and shook his head. "No, I don't think so, my friend. Please to sit still. I'm almost finished."

"We're gonna go get some hot dogs at Jodi Moroni's, alright, fool?" Diana was talking to her. "You meet us there as soon as you're done here. Don't go running off again. We gotta get home and make dinner before Mami gets back from work."

Little Jay shrugged. "Whatever."

"Don't 'whatever' me, Little Jay. I mean it. If we're not at the hot dog stand meet us back at the car. Okay?" Diana grabbed Little Jay's chin and forced her little sister to look at her.

"Okay, already. *Chingao*. Let go of me." Little Jay yanked her chin from Diana's grasp and wiggled her jaw back and forth.

"Your sister, she's bossy, eh, my friend?" said Mendhi Man when Diana and Gina had gone.

"She's a big A-hole," said Little Jay, staring at the back of Diana's long black raincoat, her glossy goth hair flapping back in the wind. From that angle, she looked like something out of a zombie movie. "Always getting in my face. Not even our mom does that. I don't know who told her she was the big shit, but that's what she thinks. Hey, how'd you know she was my sister?"

"Intuition, my friend," smiled Mendhi Man, his teeth long and yellow like piano keys.

"Anyway, it's your fault," Little Jay said, narrowing her eyes at the guy. "You could've told me this was a wedding design. I'm a dyke, okay? I'm not gonna get married unless it's to a girl, got it?"

Little Jay glanced over both shoulders, terrified one of the other customers in the booth had overheard her. You did not just come out to this Mendhi Man, Roy would have said. She half expected lightning to strike out of the clear blue sky.

"Wedding mendhi brings your heart's desire, my friend. Girl or boy, mendhi brings equal opportunity good luck." The man stood back to admire his work. "Twenty dollars, please."

Little Jay jumped down off the high director's chair with her tattooed arm in the air, and reached into her back pocket with her other hand to pull out the last two tens from the lawn-cutting money she'd saved just for a tattoo.

"Don't get it wet for at least a day," Mendhi Man said, tucking the bills into a wad of money in his fanny pack. "And use some olive oil on the skin every night for two weeks."

"Olive oil?" asked Little Jay.

"Olive or coconut. Keeps the skin supple," Mendhi Man said, smiling. "Makes the tattoo last longer. Namaste, my friend." He put his hands together in front of his chest and bowed slightly.

"Nama-what?" said Little Jay, but just then, she felt it again. The earth very definitely rolled under feet. The umbrella swayed over her head and the plastic tote box of his supplies slid back and forth across the surface of the table. Little Jay clung on to Mendhi Man for balance.

"Are you feeling dizzy?" he asked.

"That was a big one," she said. "Did you feel that?" Even the waves had gotten stirred up and for a second, she was sure there had been a shadow in front of the sun.

"Feel what, my friend?"

"Oh, come on, you didn't feel that earthquake?"

"No earthquake, my friend. You just lost your balance, I think."

"Look at the waves," she said, pointing toward the beach, but the water looked calm again, the sailboats on the horizon sat perfectly serene on the still water.

"Go home now. You have been out in the sun too long, perhaps."

"Give me a break," said Little Jay, turning to talk to an older lady in a buzz cut and a young girl in a Beatles tee who were standing there contemplating a Ganesha tattoo. "Did you all just feel the earthquake just now?" she asked them.

"There was an earthquake?" said the young girl, gazing at Little Jay over the top of her heart-shaped white sunglasses. "Cool." The girl dug her ringing cell phone out of her Mexican beach bag. "Dad, guess what," she said into the phone, "there was an earthquake just now."

"I didn't feel anything," the buzz-cut woman said to Little Jay.

"Drink some water, my friend," Mendhi Man called after her. "Perhaps you have dehydrated. It's a hot day."

Little Jay didn't mention the earthquake to her sisters and Bethany, who were all huddled at a little table next to the Jodi Moroni stand, stuffing the last of their hot dogs into their mouths and leering at the guys lifting weights in the Muscle Beach gym.

"Hey, Little Jay," said Gina, offering her a fried corndog. "I got an extra one for you, but it got cold. You took too long, dude."

Little Jay gobbled down the corndog in three bites and took the last swig from what was left of Gina's Cherry Coke. She was still thirsty, but didn't want to spend her last two dollars on a bottle of water. Bethany and Diana kept harassing her about the tattoo, but she ignored them.

"I like it," said Gina, admiring the finished tattoo. "How much was it?"

"Twenty," mumbled Little Jay.

"Maybe I'll get Cricket one for his birthday."

"Don't you have an Open House at your fancy new school this week?" Diana said. "Mami's gonna die of embarrassment if you show up with that thing."

"It's a good thing Mami's not going, then, huh?" retorted Little Jay.

As they ambled back to Diana's car parked in the Venice Pier lot off Washington, Little Jay felt troubled, like she'd forgotten something important. The dried henna was already starting to peel off her arm and she suddenly wanted nothing more than to run over to the shoreline and dip her whole arm into the ocean to wash off the stupid wedding design. Bethany was rattling on about her *quinceañera* dress and how her mom had to re-mortgage the house (whatever that meant) just to pay for the party. They were almost to the parking lot when Little Jay realized she'd forgotten her backpack.

"Oh, shit," she said aloud, "I left my backpack."

"Are you serious?" said Bethany.

"Goddammit," said Diana.

"I've gotta go back where I got the tattoo," said Little Jay.

"It's going to take you twenty minutes to go all the way back there," whined Bethany.

"No way, Little Jay, I am not letting you out of my sight again," said Diana, but Little Jay had already spun around in her Chucks and started running down the boardwalk. Behind her, she could hear Diana yelling at her to hurry up or else they were gonna leave her ass behind and she'd have to take the bus home.

"I wish," Little Jay muttered.

She ran all the way back to the House of Ink where Mendhi Man had set up his booth, but the booth was deserted. No sign of him or his tattoo pictures or his umbrella or anything. Just an empty table in the sun wedged between the tarot card reader's table and the guy making sand sculptures on the asphalt.

"Have you all seen the tattoo guy?" Little Jay asked them, panting.

"He left a little while ago," the tarot card reader told her.

"Did he have a Guatemalan backpack with him?" she asked, starting to panic.

The tarot card reader shrugged. "He had a lot of stuff," she said. "He put it all into a shopping cart, like a homeless guy."

"Maybe he did, maybe he didn't," said the sand sculpture guy, finishing the breasts on his mermaid sculpture.

"You guys!" Little Jay stomped her foot. "You're not helping. Did you see which way he went?"

"That way, I think," said Tarot Card Reader, pointing north toward Santa Monica.

"No, that way," said Sand Sculpture Guy, pointing east away from the beach.

"Great. Thanks a lot," said Little Jay. She went north, figuring that the tarot card reader probably had a better view considering the other guy had his back to the boardwalk. There were four things in her pack that she could not lose. Her phone, which had cost her several months of cutting lawns, babysitting and paper routes. Her journal, which told everything about what she was and who she had a crush on. Her insulin kit. And the gift she'd gotten from the neighbor, Ms. Fenix, for helping her clean out an abandoned old ladies' bar that she was going to transform into a literacy center for girls in gangs. She wasn't exactly sure what the thing was, other than something to hang in her room. Ms. Fenix had brought it back from Mexico and told her it was very precious. Now she'd gone and lost it because of this retarded tattoo that was going give her mom a heart attack.

"How could I be so stupid?" she muttered, dashing between tourists and baby carriages and dogs on leashes, scanning ahead

of her for a long-haired Indian man in a white beanie and white
sheet pushing a shopping cart. How hard could it be to find him,
she thought? Even in this motley crowd of weirdoes and winos,
somebody like that would stand out. For a second, she felt
another shudder in the earth and she stopped cold. Someone ran
into her from behind.

"Hey, it's you again," said the girl in heart-shaped sunglasses
she had seen earlier at Mendhi Man's booth.

"Oh, hey," said Little Jay.

"Look at my tattoo." The girl showed off the Ganesha image
hennaed to the inside of her arm. "My Nina got one just like it.
Nina, show her your Ganesha."

The older woman in the buzz cut held out her own arm.

"Can you take a picture of us?" asked the girl, pushing her
phone into Little Jay's hands.

Flustered, Little Jay took the picture. "Like mother, like
daughter tattoos," she said.

"Cute, huh?" said the girl. "But she's not my mom, she's my
godmother."

"Did you happen to see a backpack when you were there? I
think I left it by the chair."

They shook their heads in unison.

"Oh, no!" said Little Jay, her voice breaking. "I lost my bag.
I'll never find it now. Shit." She was about to let loose some tears
like a big crybaby, but the buzz-cut godmother lady touched her
shoulder and told her to stay calm.

"Look, if you concentrate real hard, you can bring it back to
you. I do that all the time and whatever I've lost always comes
back. If it's meant to, that is."

"How?" said Little Jay, desperate enough to try anything
right now.

"Close your eyes, concentrate real hard on whatever it is that
you need to come back to you. Your thoughts can work like a

magnet if you try real hard. Go sit over there on that bench, and visualize whatever it is that you want to draw back to you. You'll feel a surge when you're doing it right. That's the Universe telling you it worked."

Little Jay did as she was told. She found an empty seat on a bench next to a homeless lady in dreads smoking a joint and sat down to concentrate. She took a deep breath and closed her eyes, focusing on the black and purple stripes of the pack. She had bought it at a vintage clothes place in Pasadena, and it was small enough to use everyday but sturdy enough to use as a book bag for school. She saw the torn seam of the zipper on the front pocket and wondered why she hadn't asked Gina to fix that yet. She focused on her phone next, all the texts on it, all her friends' phone numbers stored inside it, her different games and photos. But she didn't feel any surge. Next, she visualized her journal. The entries in which she talked about liking girls, missing her friend Roy who was the only one she would ever trust with this information, the crazy dreams she'd been having about kissing the neighbor, Ms. Fenix, who had made it possible for her to get accepted at Saint Wilgefortis. Little Jay felt a definite surge over that.

"Hey, stop bogarting my smoke," the homeless lady next to her said, smacking her arm.

"Huh?" said Little Jay, opening her eyes in time to see the lady pushing off on her rollerblades, her dreadlocks flying behind her like Medusa snakes.

Little Jay felt weird, almost like she'd been transported somewhere else, to a parallel universe where things looked a little brighter and people seemed to be much closer than in the real world. She got to her feet and tried to remember what she was doing, where she was going, and it was as if she could see herself walking without actually feeling her legs moving or even her body leaving the bench.

Little Jay felt someone staring at her from behind. She turned around and saw a disabled man lying on a skateboard approaching her. He was missing the lower half of his body; he had only his head, trunk and arms and he used the skateboard to push himself around the boardwalk.

"You looking for a bag?" he said.

"What? Yes. How did you know?"

"What color is it?"

"It's Guatemalan."

"What's it got inside?"

"None of your business."

"There you are, my friend," said a familiar voice.

Mendhi Man had reappeared with his shopping cart full of stuff and her Guatemalan backpack hugging his skinny spine.

"Hey, what's going on? That's my bag."

"I was trying to go after you, my friend," he said, smiling, "but you were walking too fast for me, so I lost you in the crowd. I asked my friend Iman here to try to catch you."

Iman saluted her with one gnarly hand.

"Here you go, my friend." Mendhi Man removed the pack from his shoulders and handed it to Little Jay.

Your thoughts can work like a magnet if you try real hard, the godmother lady had told her. "That's awesome, dude," was all she managed to say.

It felt like it took her forever to make it back to the parking lot where her sister Diana was having a hissy fit waiting for her.

"You know what, Little Jay," said Diana, pasting her face so close to Little Jay's that the bits of relish and hot dog trapped in her older sister's teeth came flying out of her mouth. "This is the last time you're coming with us anywhere, you hear me? You're such a royal pain in the ass, getting lost, getting tattooed, forgetting things, taking your sweet ass time, making us wait on you like we ain't got nothing better to do. Just 'cause you're going to that college-prep school don't mean we gotta wait on you. I'm sick of it, Little Jay, okay? You hear me? I'm sick of it. Grow up once and for all, *cabrona*."

"Let's go already," called Bethany, fixing her make-up in the back seat. "You can yell at her in the car. Gina wants to stop at Wal-Mart to buy her concert tickets."

Strapped in her seatbelt in the passenger seat, Gina had her eyes closed, her white headphones on, singing out the lyrics to a My Chemical Romance tune to block out Diana's high-pitched tirade.

"Get in the car, Little Jay," Diana ordered, pulling on the strap of the backpack. Little Jay resisted, and Diana pulled harder.

"Stop yanking on me, Diana, you're gonna tear my pack."

"I said get your skinny ass in the car," Diana pulled even harder, on the front pocket this time, and tore the already frayed seam of the zipper. Little Jay watched as the precious object that Ms. Fenix had brought her back from Mexico fell out and shattered on the asphalt.

Immediately the earth shifted, a movement so definite even Diana felt it, her mouth hanging open as she looked around at the undulating cars of the parking lot.

"What the—" her words were swallowed up in the melee of people bolting out of their cars, their screams mixing with the wild barking of dogs running free of their leashes, and the roiling of sea water gathering up into a vortex between the shore and the sky. Storm clouds thickened over the beach. Rocks and planks and glass panes flew through the air as one tsunami-sized wave hovered over the pier like a gigantic dark green hand tipped with foamy white fingers. Little Jay was yanked and slapped and probed by the cold wind but she stood her ground, transfixed by the giant hand about to demolish the pier.

Instead of crashing down, the tsunami vortex opened up and something rose straight out of the sea like in one of those B movies that Little Jay loved so much. It looked like a wall of red stone rising from the sea, a huge round stone at least twenty feet in diameter, carved with shapes that made no sense but that seemed to be like joined body parts: a leg and foot, an arm and hand, a torso of breasts and loins, a head wearing a feathered helmet. The parts were scattered across the stone, like a body that had been dismembered, a woman's body cut into pieces, trussed with snakes and wedged with skulls. Little Jay realized then that it was the very thing that Ms. Fenix had brought her back from Mexico. The same object that Diana had just broken, only on a colossal scale.

"Coyolxauhqui?" she heard herself ask aloud, remembering the Aztec legend Ms. Fenix had told her about the warrior daughter of the mother of the gods who was angry that her mother was going to give birth to Huitzilopochtli, the god of war, and so attacked her at the moment of the birth in an attempt to kill the baby. But instead of a baby, she found a full-grown man in armor rising out of their mother's sacred womb, wielding a fiery serpent in his hand like a mighty sword that sliced off his sister's head and chopped up her body. From then on, to immortalize the daughter's rebellion against the mother, the sister's uprising against the brother, to remind enemies of the price of insurgence, Coyolxauhqui's severed body and head had solidified into stone. This stone was used as the base for the pyramid of the Templo Mayor where every sacrificial victim would land after he had his heart removed by the high priests of Huitzilopochtli.

This was the stone rising out of the sea on Venice Beach that July afternoon. But it did not remain inanimate for very long. In front of Little Jay's eyes, the stone came to life, the severed pieces started to move toward each other, the legs to the loins, the arms to the shoulders, the head to the neck and suddenly she was whole again. The dismembered daughter, the mutilated sister, in one piece, her feathered helmet gleaming bright gold in the sun, long peacock feathers standing out from a crown of marigolds. Her skin an ocher yellow, her armor a deep aqua blue, a tattoo of bells on each cheek, Coyolxauhqui stood twenty feet tall, the Venice pier jutting against the skull heads at her kneecaps.

"My goddess!" Little Jay said, falling to her knees.

"Can you believe this kid?" a sharp voice brought Little Jay back to earth. Someone was shaking her shoulder and poking her in the face.

"I cannot fucken believe this kid!" Diana was staring down at her, her burgundy-lipsticked mouth pursed like a prune. "Wake the fuck up, *cabrona*! You're gonna drive me out of my mind." She was shaking Little Jay's shoulder hard enough to sprain something.

"What happened?" said Little Jay, sitting up. She was still on the same bench in front of the House of Ink next to a Legalize Marijuana booth. She must have passed out.

"Seriously?" said Diana. "You're taking a nap while we're over there waiting for you for over an hour?"

"Diana, I swear, I thought I'd gone back there. After the Mendhi Man gave me back my pack—" She looked down at the bench and saw that she'd been using her pack for a pillow. "—I swear I walked back to the parking lot and you were yelling at me and then this weird thing happened, there was an earthquake and then it turned into a tsunami and then this huge round stone came out of the sea and turned into a giant goddess in blue armor."

"Tell me you didn't!" said Diana, pressing her cool palm against Little Jay's forehead. "I knew it! Your sugar's low. Look at your eyes. They're all glassy and shit. Hold out your hands."

"Diana—"

"Hold out your hands, goddammit!"

Little Jay's hands were shaking.

"Fuck, Little Jay! What were you thinking? Running back and forth on the boardwalk all day. What are we gonna do with you?"

"I don't know what happened, Diana. Honest. I passed out, I guess."

Diana opened her blue Razor phone and dialed a number.

"I found her. She says she passed out . . . Looks like it, it's right here. No, I have to get her a drink. Her sugar's low. Order something for her at Mao's. Hurry. She needs to eat."

Nothing had changed. Venice Beach was still buzzing with weirdoes and winos, the air still smelled of pot and patchouli, sailboats still dotted the horizon and her sister Diana still thought she was a hopeless loser whose only mission in life was to mortify their mother. For no good reason, except maybe she was emo, Little Jay started to cry. Crying, crying, crying like a lost kid trying to find her way home.

Diana took her by the hand and led her to the nearest store and bought her a bottle of Orangina and made her finish it before they returned outside. The sweet fizzy drink and the overhead fans of the store cleared the hot fog in her head. Her hands stopped shaking.

" . . . with your diabetes," Diana was yammering on and on as they treaded people on the boardwalk, "you could die, Little Jay. That was a really stupid thing to do. Why don't you ever think of the consequences? One of these days you're seriously gonna give Mami a heart attack. Is that what you want, huh? You wanna kill our mother?"

Little Jay was staring at her henna tattoo while Diana finished scolding her, and saw that the skin around the black crusty lines of dried henna paste was bright red, as if the sun had seared the tattoo into her arm, only instead of the peacock head and feathered tail of the mendhi that she'd paid twenty dollars for, the image had morphed into the full-bodied goddess from the Coyolxauhqui stone, wearing a feathered helmet and a loincloth of knotted snakes.

No Flowers for Marla

Nanette Guadiano

Marla went missing on a Friday last spring, when the first buds of the crepe myrtles unfurled their bright colors like alms and the showers of March washed away sins like a forgiving god. It was a busy spring as nature rushed to fill earth's canvas with color, and seniors like Marla and I hustled to fill out college applications, get our credits in order, buy our prom dresses, and plan for graduation.

She was one of the only blondes at South Ridge High, our primarily all-Latino school. In our vast sea of muddy brown eyes, Marla's teal blue ones shone as sparkling as the tropical oceans none of us had ever seen. She had shown up at our campus in the middle of junior year. No one really knew anything about her, other than her stepfather had been in the military and her mother was dead. She was an only child, an honor student, straight-laced and Vogue-Magazine-beautiful. Every guy on campus wanted to date her, but she was strictly off-limits. In fact, Marla was a total loner. People said she was a snobby white girl, even a white supremacist. I didn't believe any of it. There was something secretive and weird about her, for sure, but what it was exactly, no one really knew.

She worked part-time at a local bookstore when she wasn't busy with some extra-curricular activity like the National Honor Society, Environmental Science Club, Chemistry Club or Journalism. We were on the yearbook and newspaper committees together, and we worked in the Registrar's office during our Advisory period helping students prepare for their SATs. Marla was super-smart, and rumors of her getting into Harvard and Yale swam around campus like farm-raised catfish. Everyone both envied and resented Marla, so when she went missing, it didn't take long for people to start talking.

"They say she ran off with some college guy," Anita whispered to me during Calculus the day after the news ran a report on *Local Teen Gone Missing*. It was Tuesday morning; Marla had been missing for four days.

"What college guy?" I asked.

"I don't know. Some guy. Phillip, my boyfriend, was in the office waiting for the nurse this morning because he was trying to get out of an exam. Anyway, he says he overheard Mr. Jones call Marla's house to see why Marla was absent for three days, you know, standard office procedure, and her stepfather told the principal that Marla was missing. Her stepfather said she had never come home from work Friday night and that Saturday he'd called the cops." A little bit of spittle flew out of Anita's mouth every time she said the word 'step'. "Apparently, Marla was seeing some guy on the side. Her father, her stepfather, had seen Marla with him a few times. That's what Phillip said Mr. Bradley told the nurse."

I didn't believe a word about Marla having a boyfriend. That, I knew, was a rumor. Her stepfather was really strict. Like weird, unnatural strict. He picked her up from school everyday, and on the days she worked, he'd wait in the parking lot for her to get off, eyes hiding behind sunglasses, trail of cigarette smoke slinking out of his window like a snake. I never saw Marla talk to anybody in an intimate fashion; in fact, she was called "conceited" because she didn't associate with anyone.

"All I know is she never showed up for work on Friday," my friend Mike Cantú interjected, leaning over toward Anita and me. Mike had worked with Marla at the bookstore. He said that Friday night at nine when he left for the night, Marla's stepfather had been in the parking lot waiting for her.

Mike had told the colonel (that was what we called Marla's stepdad, though what his rank in the military actually had been, none of us knew) that he didn't know if she'd called in or not, after which Mike said the colonel's face had turned crimson and he'd sped away without so much as a thank you, leaving Mike standing in the parking lot next to a smoldering cigarette butt and the uneasy feeling that something awful was about to happen.

Wednesday morning, our journalism teacher, Mr. Farley, came back to school. No one had really noticed or cared that he'd missed class Monday and Tuesday. All anybody had been able to talk about was Marla. But when he walked into class with a scratch on his face that connected his eyebrow to his chin like a windshield crack, the buzz on campus grew to a loud swarm. Mr. Farley had been fond of Marla, creepily so. During class and yearbook meetings, I had witnessed firsthand the inappropriate looks Mr. Farley gave Marla, the unnecessary proximity, the nervous twitch of his left eye.

Thursday, posters of Marla designed and printed out by our journalism team showing her junior yearbook picture went up all over our school and neighborhoods. After questioning Marla's stepfather and several other people, including myself, the police decided that more than likely she had run away, and leads were being followed in that direction.

Then, Friday morning, a week after Marla was last seen alive, on a particularly dreary, overcast day, two bikers, cycling along the trail past the old Pearl Brewery downtown, found Marla's body under a pile of wet leaves and debris just about a half a mile from the bookstore where she had worked. News of the dismal discovery spread like a virus and that evening the news stations ran the story. Our local police chief made his official statement as we all watched riveted: "Positive identification has not yet been made, but we are fairly certain that we have, in all likelihood, found Marla Jones."

Later, it would be revealed that Marla had been so brutally beaten and her body so ravaged by the normal types of four-footed urban predators that she had to be identified by her dental records. A registered sex offender, Marcus Jacobs, who lived just blocks from where Marla's corpse had been found, was picked up and questioned in connection with her disappearance. However, he had a solid alibi, (he'd been at a sex addict's support group meeting) and was released the same day.

The police then turned their attention, as is customary, to Marla's stepfather, and the twisted rumors that had gone around campus before Marla's body was found were re-ignited. Marla had been a victim of sexual abuse, people said. It explained why she was so closed-off, why she never made any real friends. It explained her stepfather's overprotective behavior. Some of the boys on campus were also questioned. Even Mr. Farley was questioned, though nothing came of it.

The owner of the bookstore where Marla had worked held a candlelight vigil for her. Marla's stepfather, intimidating in his starched white collar and his military-style buzz cut appeared on television, asking his stepdaughter's murderer to step forward. His plea, like his haircut, was short and clipped.

Our high school was shell-shocked. Hundreds of people went to her funeral. Even though none of us really knew her, she was one of us, and we felt the impact of her death almost as much as we would have felt the death of a loved one. Maybe, because each of us knew that it could have been any one of us in that ditch. We felt the imminence of our own deaths, the fragility of our own mortality.

Parents who normally didn't care where their kids were suddenly enforced curfews. With the exception of school, my mother wouldn't let me go anywhere alone, and I didn't blame her. We felt violated as a community; we feared for ourselves and each other. In a strange way, Marla's murder had brought strangers together through the common denominators of fear and mistrust. I decided that since I had known and worked with Marla, it was my duty to write an article on her life and untimely death for the school paper. I felt sure that Mr. Farley would agree.

"I don't think that would be in the best interest of the school," Mr. Farley said, twisting his face into his signature grimace.

"What? Mr. Farley, why not? It's the most newsworthy thing that's happened in this school in decades. And besides, Marla was a member of our journalism team. We owe it to her to help bring her justice."

"What?" he asked, his face turning red like the tomatoes in my mother's garden. "What do you mean, 'bring her justice'? That's not our job, that's what the police are for."

"You know what I mean. What happened to Marla affects all of us, not just her family. I just think that we should try to do our part. Out of respect, you know?"

"No, Gloria. It is not a good idea. You need to leave this alone," he said to me. Then he walked around his desk, sat down, put his face in his hands and began to sob.

The whole thing with Mr. Farley had me totally freaked out. A grown man crying? Over a student? In front of *another* student? Bizarre. Plus, how could the journalism teacher on campus not want to do a news piece on *the murder* of one of his own students? I went home and told my mother all about it. She crossed herself and muttered a prayer in Spanish.

"*¡Ay, Dios mío!* Gloria, when are you going to learn to mind you own business?"

Papá was from Texas, but Mamá was from Mexico. Her whole belief system was steeped in superstition and fear. Someone was always watching, ready to imprison, or in the case of el mal de ojo, to kill you.

"Mamá, the whole point of journalism is to NOT mind your own business. I have to do a piece on Marla's life. I'm going to do it. With or without Mr. Farley's permission."

"Gloria, didn't you tell me *la policía* questioned the man? What if he did those horrible things to Martha?"

"Marla," I interrupted her.

"*Ay, sí*, Marla," Mamá said, rolling her eyes to heaven and crossing herself again. "And that Mr. Farley, I don't trust him." (Mamá didn't trust any white people, but I did not point that out.) "He looks funny. Like he's always watching you."

"Mamá, he has a lazy eye."

"I don't care what you call it, that man is not right in *la cabeza*," she said, tapping the side of her head for emphasis. "I don't like how he looks at you or all the other young girls at that school. And what kind of grown man cries like that in front of a child?"

Mamá was right about Mr. Farley being a little creepy when it came to us girls. Despite testosterone-driven rumors that the single Mr. Farley was gay, he did tend to stare a little too long and too hard. He liked sharing his homemade brownies with us gals after lunch, and he always took special interest in the cheerleaders. Still, I just didn't think he was capable of doing the horrible things the news reported were done to Marla. It terrified me to think about what she must have endured before succumbing to death. To think that she may have known her killer was simply unfathomable. The horror of it all infuriated me. I was doing the story, with or without Mr. Farley's permission, with or without Mamá's blessing. I owed it to Marla.

After school the next day, breaking my promise to Mamá to go straight home, I drove Papá's beat-up Dodge to The Green Leaf, the local Indie bookstore where Marla had worked and where (reportedly) she had never shown up the night she was murdered. Mrs. Fisch, the owner and manager, was at the front of the store stocking children's books when I approached.

"Can I help you?" She asked peering at me over her tiny reading glasses. She looked the part of a spinster librarian. I felt like I had tumbled back into time, into an Agatha Christie novel. I was excited and a little afraid.

"Um, yeah. Hi. My name is Gloria Cruz." I jutted my hand out a little too forcefully for her to shake. She stared at it as though it were a foreign object.

"I was a friend of Marla Jones. Well, not a friend, more of a colleague-slash-classmate. We worked on the newspaper together." With every word I spoke, I saw Mrs. Fisch harden a little more. It was like watching clay dry. Damn it! I should have rehearsed what I was going to say. I dropped my now sweaty hand to my side and pulled out a pad and pen from my backpack, which further seemed to put her off.

"Miss, I already talked to the police. I don't think I should be talking to you about any of this."

She walked toward the register. I followed her like a nuisance-child. "Please, Mrs. Fisch, I'm not asking you for anything compromising. I just want a little information. I'm doing a human-interest piece on Marla's life, you know, to honor her memory. I just want to get a feel for what kind of employee she was, how long she worked for you. That kind of thing."

Mrs. Fisch looked up from behind the register. She visibly relaxed. Pulling her glasses off of her face, she sighed deeply and then shook her head. "Well, child, why didn't you just say so?"

I shrugged and gave her my best "aw, shucks" expression. It seemed to work. Old people had a thing for sweet young people.

"That poor girl. What can I tell you?"

"How long had she worked for you?" I asked, poising my pen over my notebook like a real reporter.

"Uh, let's see. It would have been a year this April. Yes. That's about right. A year."

"And what kind of worker would you say Marla was?"

"Oh, she was a hard worker. Didn't even complain when I asked her to clean the toilets. Well, you know, it is difficult," she said defensively. "This is my own business. What with all the big chains now, a mom-and-pop establishment like mine is really a struggle. So I can't afford a bunch of extra help. Marla was only too pleased to do whatever was needed."

"I see," I nodded, not looking up from my pad. "Would you say she was trustworthy?" I asked, hoping I was easing Mrs. Fisch in the right direction.

"Marla? Oh, yes. She locked up for me plenty of times. She had the combination to the safe. She even took deposits for me sometimes. She was a good girl. Never any fuss about any boys. Never. She did her schoolwork and helped the customers. She was wonderful. I just can't understand what kind of monster could do those things to a beautiful young girl like that. She surely didn't deserve it. And when I think about how I was just going to send her home that day. If I had only called her in the morning before school, or left a message with the school. I just feel like I was to blame."

My ears perked up like a dog's. "Was she not scheduled to work the day it happened?"

"No, she was. That's just it. With the economy the way it's been, I've had to cut back. It was slow. I had a Women's Auxiliary meeting that night, and I told Mike to let Marla know when she came in that she could go right back home. She didn't have a cell phone. Didn't need one. Why, with that overprotective stepfather of hers, she never had a moment to herself." She clucked her tongue disapprovingly. "If you ask me, something just isn't right with that man. Just a few cards short of a full deck. And never a word or a smile. Just stares at you from behind those dark glasses. Anyhow, Mike had come in an hour earlier because he comes in right after school, and Marla, well, she's in all those extra-curricular activities, so it was only fair that Mike should stay and Marla should go."

My heart was racing. "Mike said that she never showed up that day."

Mrs. Fisch shrugged and sighed. "No, she didn't. She was on her way here, so I will always feel a little responsible for what happened. It's all just too awful. Listen, honey, I really do need to get back to work," she said to me.

"Of course. Thank you so much."

Mrs. Fisch nodded her head and dabbed at her eye with the corner of her blouse. I walked out of the store and into the welcome sunlight. I thought about what Mrs. Fisch had told me, and I wondered what Mike was hiding. I decided to ask him.

"You didn't tell me everything," I whispered at Mike during Calculus the next day.

"What?" he asked, leaning over and looking at me, his eyebrows raised, slight grin on his face.

"You told me that Marla had never come in the night she died. But I talked to Mrs. Fisch yesterday after school, and she said that Marla was supposed to come in and that you were supposed to send her home. Did she come in? Did you lie to the police?"

Mike's grin disappeared and his face grew redder than the cardboard Valentine's hearts still on the wall behind him.

He glanced around him like he was afraid, like someone might be listening. Satisfied that no one had overheard us, he turned back to me, meeting my glare head-on. "I can't talk about this here," he whispered.

I was growing angrier by the minute. "Stop messing around, Mike. This is serious."

"Why are you even asking questions, Gloria? That's what the police are for."

"Now you sound like Mr. Farley." At the mention of my journalism teacher's name, Mike grew even more agitated.

"You listen to me, Gloria. You are poking your nose in something you can't even begin to understand. Stop now or you'll be sorry."

Mrs. Sánchez, our Calculus teacher, cleared her throat and glanced in our direction. Several classmates turned to stare at us. Mike sat back in his chair and pulled out his textbook, pretending to pay attention to the teacher. What was in his eyes, that day, I still wonder? I thought then it had been defiance, but now, in hindsight, I think it must have been fear.

"Are you threatening me, Mike?" I asked, after a while. I had known Mike since Kindergarten, had used to chase him on the playground.

He shook his head and sighed deeply. "I'm warning you," he whispered, turning his attention back to Mrs. Sánchez.

Oh, how I wish now I had heeded it.

I had started my article on Marla's life and questionable death with the zeal of a person starting a new diet, but good intentions will only take you so far. A cookie here, a bag of chips there, and pretty soon you're back where you started, possibly a few pounds heavier. I had swerved from the path, my quest for justice if you will, first with an English paper here and there, and then math exams, application deadlines and familial commitments. Pretty soon, my notes and interviews regarding Marla were at the bottom of a pile of papers and dirty clothes in my bedroom. Searching for a phone number one night, I happened upon my journal open to my notes from my conversation with Mrs. Fisch. At the bottom of the paper, in all red caps were the words 'ASK MIKE!' It might sound silly, but at that moment I had the overwhelming sense that Marla was speaking to me, that those were her words, not mine. Suddenly, I saw that I had treated Marla with the same disrespect as her murderer, burying her under a pile of trash. Goosebumps trickled up my arms like wildfire. I knew exactly what I was supposed to do. I put the notebook in my backpack, my resolve strengthened. I would corner Mike the very next day at school.

I waited for Mike after first period, but he wasn't at his locker; nor was he in Calculus. Just my luck. He was absent.

I went to Journalism last period, busied myself with gathering together a collage for the yearbook when my friend, Lorena, ran into the room, breathing heavily.

"Oh, my god, Gloria. You're not gonna believe this."

"Lorena, what's wrong with you?" I asked, putting down my pictures.

She grabbed my hands in hers and began to cry.

"It's Mr. Farley, Gloria."

"What about him?" I asked, heart racing. I think I knew before she told me. Once something unimaginably horrible happens to you or someone you know, it's almost second nature to expect it to happen again.

"He's dead."

I felt the room spin.

It was like a runaway train, the events that followed. Apparently, Mr. Farley had taken his own life. He was found in his apartment by his landlord, after a disgruntled neighbor had complained of loud music and banging footsteps. He had overdosed on anti-anxiety medication. What had been particularly disturbing, the newspapers said, were the pictures they had found in his apartment. Lots of pictures of young girls my age, from my school, myself among them. The most damning piece of evidence was the cache of photos the police had found of Marla in different settings. School, and yes, near the Green Leaf in various natural backdrops: the burnt leaves of fall, the naked branches of winter, the unfurling blushing blossoms of spring.

It was treated as an open and shut case. Mr. Farley, in an apparent obsessive rage, had beaten and murdered Marla Jones, whom he had been stalking for an entire year. I didn't believe it for a second.

Mr. Farley, though a very strange man, did not seem to have a violent bone in his body. I could understand the pictures, though I didn't agree with them. He was a lonely, middle-aged man, with a thing for teenage girls. Okay. It was disgusting, but hardly the same thing as murder. He was a voyeur, pure and simple. He was also an amateur photographer. Why didn't the papers mention that? Why didn't they sensationalize all the pictures Mr. Farley had of animals and nature scenes, much less the pictures of his aging mother?

And what about the heavy footsteps and banging the neighbor had heard? And the loud music? Anyone who knew Mr. Farley knew he hated loud noises. He had some kind of ear problem with an aversion to high-pitched sounds. I couldn't understand how the police weren't asking the right questions. I decided to go to them. It was my duty now, to Mr. Farley and to Marla, to be sure that her real murderer was found. It seemed to me that Mr. Farley's death was incredibly suspicious, and I wondered if the police would even take me seriously. I decided it was worth a shot.

But before I'd even had a chance to drive to the police station and talk to the detective who had questioned me about Marla's reputation, something else happened that set another wheel in motion.

I was getting ready to leave school. A million thoughts were running through my head like hungry ants and I didn't notice Mike until he was at my car window.

"Gloria?"

I jumped in my seat. "Jesus, Mike. You scared the crap out of me." I looked up at him, completely taken aback. "God, Mike, you look awful. What's wrong?" He hadn't shaved in days, apparently, and his clothes were rumpled and saggy as though he'd lost several pounds.

"Can I, uh, hitch a ride to the bookstore?" He looked around nervously.

"I don't know," I said.

"Gloria," he looked directly into my eyes and moved closer to the window. I backed away involuntarily. "I'm sorry about that day in Calculus. Believe me when I tell you I had my reasons for warning you. I really need to talk to you. I promise I won't hurt you. I'm not the one you should be afraid of." He held his arms out in surrender, and for some reason, I believed him.

I rolled my eyes. "Fine, hurry up. My mother will be worried if I'm too late." His face lit up and, for a second, he looked like the Mike I had grown up with. I did not tell him that I was really on my way to the police station, nor did I confide in him my suspicions about Mr. Farley. I didn't have to.

"Mr. Farley didn't kill Marla," he said to me the second we drove out of the school parking lot. I braked and turned to him. "No, no, no. Keep driving. We might have a tail."

"Have a tail? What is that, like a spy movie or something?" My heart was hammering in my chest like a woodpecker.

Mike did not even crack a smile. "I didn't tell the police about Marla coming to the bookstore because she asked me not to."

"What? Why?"

"She was running away from home."

"What? That's ridiculous. But if that's true, then she didn't die on the way to the bookstore."

Mike looked at me. "Mrs. Fisch told the police that she told me to tell Marla to go home when she got to the bookstore. I told the police that Marla never showed up."

"But, Mike, why would you lie to the police? Marla was murdered. Do you understand that? You could be in all kinds of trouble."

Despite the lack of shocks in my father's old car, I think I could feel Mike tremble with fear.

"I promised her, Gloria. The police came asking questions before anybody knew she was dead, and I lied because she asked me to. Because I thought she'd run away. I thought I was doing the right thing. And now she's dead."

"Okay. I guess I understand. You promised her. But she's gone and you need to tell the truth. I mean, if she died on her way home, that would mean that she was abducted later than when the police figured initially that she was taken. And that would mean that Mr. Farley was still at school when she died. Which would mean that Mr. Farley couldn't have killed her. Mike, you have to do the right thing."

He rubbed his prickly face with his hands and sighed, a deep, tremulous sigh that seemed to carry the weight of the world.

"I know," he said. "I'm afraid."

"Of what? Of getting into trouble? So what? So you get a slap on the wrist. They're not gonna arrest you or anything. Mike, you have to."

"I told Mr. Farley, Gloria. The day he died. I told him. I asked him what I should do and he told me that he would figure something out. That he would help me. That he knew just the person to talk to."

The implications of what Mike was saying hit me in the gut like an actual fist. "And now *he's* dead," I said.

Mike stared at the road ahead in silence.

"And whoever did it knows you lied."

"I don't know. Maybe. I don't know what Mr. Farley said or didn't say, whether he said my name or not. But I gotta tell you, Gloria. I can't eat. I can't sleep. And when I do sleep, I dream of her." His voice fell to a whisper. "I think maybe I was in love with her."

"I think maybe we all were," I said, putting my right hand on Mike's left one.

I pulled up in the Green Leaf's parking lot, put the car in Park and turned to Mike. "Mike, why would a girl with so many opportunities right in front of her, within arms' reach, decide to run away so close to a real chance at life?"

Mike looked at me sadly, grabbed his backpack and put his hand on the door handle. "Why do you think?"

I squeezed my eyes shut against the tears that threatened me like angry children.

"Did she tell you? Do you know for sure?"

He smiled sadly. Of course, he wouldn't tell me. He wouldn't betray a dead girl's last confidence. And he didn't have to. Not really. Hadn't we all suspected? How come no one had reached out to her? How come I hadn't reached out to her? It was always there, just beneath the surface. I had always known. I guess I clung to my adolescent hope that things so vile, so evil existed only in movies and books. I hadn't wanted to know the truth. I had failed Marla. I would not fail my friend, Mike.

"Come with me," I said, reaching out for his hand again, seeing the little boy I used to chase around the playground inside the shadow of the young man in front of me.

"Mrs. Fisch is waiting. Gloria," he said, and I think I knew then that I'd never see him again. "Be careful."

I nodded, for once, at a loss for words.

I drove to the police station that afternoon and told Detective Gómez everything I knew and everything I thought had happened. He listened; I think this surprised me.

I'm not sure of all the specifics, but I know the police went to the Green Leaf to talk to Mike. Mrs. Fisch said he'd never shown up. They went to his house, where his frantic mother said that she'd gotten a call from a pay phone earlier that afternoon. Mike said he was going away for a while, for her not to worry. Maybe, he hitchhiked from where I'd left him. I still don't know. The police also went to pick up the colonel, only to find that he was gone. Apparently someone had tipped him off. Possibly, Mr. Farley? Now Mr. Farley's death was being looked at from another angle: possible homicide. Who knows? Maybe Mike was right. Maybe we did have a tail that afternoon. Thinking about that totally freaks me out. I still have nightmares. I still check my rearview mirror when I drive. I wonder if he'll ever come for me, though Detective Gómez and my gut tell me it is highly unlikely. (Mamá, on the other hand, is not so convinced.)

It's been a year since that horrible day last spring. I'm home for the weekend, getting close to finishing my first year away at college. I heard from friends that Mike is now in the military. I'm glad for him. Glad that he's okay. I also heard from my alums in Journalism that DNA evidence (which takes a while to produce results, contrary to popular television shows) taken from Marla's body had proven that the colonel was present at the time of the attack. No one else's DNA had been recovered, so put two and two together. The man is still MIA, though I'm confident that justice will one day be served.

I've decided to visit the place where Marla's body was found, which has become a virtual shrine in our community. It happens, in my culture, that a person's life is often celebrated more in death. Wreaths, flowers, signs and candles all testify to the life that was once so shrouded in secrecy and isolation. Mike had said that Marla was planning on running away. Whatever happened to Marla had been so terrible that she had risked her entire future—college, a career—to escape it. Now she was stuck here. In a town that had not been home to her. I wanted to do something for her, to honor her in some way.

Marla had been misunderstood in life; I felt that she still was in death. What she had longed for was freedom, and what she had gotten was perpetual silence.

Under the blooming crepe myrtles an altar emerges from the foliage: bluebonnets, Indian paintbrushes, sunflowers and Black-eyed Susans. There is a laminated poster with Marla's junior yearbook picture attached to a stake in the ground. I study it. Beautiful and wide-eyed, I see now the sadness beneath the veneer of rigidity, the fear in her eyes. I kneel down and close my eyes, touch the picture of her face.

I have not brought flowers for Marla. I would not presume to do so. Instead I have brought a promise. I will do in my life what Marla could not do in hers. And with every breath I take, I will swear to remember. That she *was*. Not as people choose to remember her: as an icon or a saint to be venerated. No. As a young girl with hopes and dreams and aspirations. With a desire above all else to control her own destiny. Oh, yes. She and I had more in common than either of us ever knew. I will carry her burden with mine. I have decided. I *am* my sister's keeper.

As the Flames Rose

Chema Guijarro

Sweating the little things has always been my mom's way of making me fly straight. I've just been accepted to a school for deaf kids, so naturally, she keeps insisting I grow out my hair.

I'm on the couch reading *El Llano en Llamas* when she pulls the book down, smearing red chile all over the pages. She was in the kitchen making tamales to sell at the swap meet, but now she's in front of me, hair up in a bun, her forehead sweaty and hands red like she just came out of surgery.

"Did you not hear me, Benito?" I read her lips as she says it in Spanish.

She's forgotten I'm deaf. *Again.* I've been deaf for a year now, but she still forgets. I point to my ear and the embarrassment slowly begins to hit her—she blushes and bites her lips making her cheeks puff out with little dimples. She looks as though she might say she's sorry, but I'm the one who should apologize. I should have been helping her make the tamales instead of reading. I'm not bringing it up, though, so a joke is my best option. I twirl the finger I'm pointing at my ear into small circles. It's one of those everyday gestures that coincides with sign language.

"*Loca*," I mouth.

It works. She forgets her embarrassment. "It doesn't matter that you're deaf," she says in Spanish. "I have made it clear that you are not showing up *pelón* to that school."

Mom never talks to me in English. Not in front of cops or teachers or the principle. Never. Why? I don't know. It might be something about her words being stronger in Spanish or about wanting me to practice Spanish. I asked her once, but she said I should know why. I said I didn't, but she just kept talking.

I start rubbing my scalp. I used clippers instead of a razor the last time I shaved and the stubble tickles my palm. I should argue that no one will care that I'm bald, and in my head, I'm already thinking of reasons, but I have to text them out on my phone for her and it gives her an advantage. (I stopped talking once I was too deaf to hear my own voice because I didn't want to risk sounding like a retard around people, especially not around her.) In the end, though, my handicap doesn't matter; there's nothing I can write that will make her agree with me. I go back to reading.

It takes me a while to get back into the story, but when I do, she pulls the book down again saying, "And I'm not crazy. I'm just tired."

She says "tired" with the face of someone saying goodbye at the airport, and my guilty feelings get serious. I put the book down and help her spread *masa* on the corn leaves. Around the house, it's just me and my mom. Chucho, my half brother is in jail again after being out for five years.

"Is that book from your dad's bookcase?"

I nod.

My dad left before I could crawl and has never bothered to check in on us. It's enough to say he died. But we don't. We just act like he did. The only thing he left behind is three shelves of books and old pictures of him and Mom, which Chucho burned before I got the chance to. I can tell Mom still resents him for it. There are tons of pictures of Chucho and his dad, but only a few of me as a baby. She keeps two of them framed on the shelves with my dad's books. One is of me and her, she's still young—her hair is dark and her face is a little chubby—and I'm wrapped in a blanket, a few weeks old. The other picture is of me on my first birthday, a cake shaped like the Bat-signal with one of those big number candles stuck in it in front of me. I'm blowing out the candle and Chucho and his girlfriend at the time are helping me, our cheeks puffed out and faces side by side. Other family pictures around the house are from before my dad showed up and after he left. I don't know how long he and my mom were together before they had me, but I'm glad Chucho burned them all. If we aren't worth sticking around for, he isn't worth remembering.

"I didn't ruin it with the chile, ¿verdá?" my mom says about the book.

I shake my head but there were red clumps over the pages when I closed the book. After they dry, the pages are going to be warped and stained. It's a book of short stories. The saddest stories I've ever read. In a few days, I'll scratch off the crusted-over chile and the pages will look like bandages with blood seeping through.

"Good. Your dad left those for you."

That's as much as my mom will say about my dad. I hate that she probably still thinks about him coming back. I'd never tell her, but to me, that fool's dead, wherever he is.

Even when Chucho's locked up, it's just the three of us. Alone. Both our dads are gone—his died, and mine left. This time around, Chucho will be out of the house for a while. But beyond missing him, things have already started to change: a guy who looks Mom's age showed up one day.

I was reading on the couch and saw him cross our front window with a cell phone to his ear. It was the funniest thing I'd seen all day. He was short and dressed like a *paisa*—cowboy boots and hat—and the cell phone looked out of place, like if a knight in Medieval times was wearing sunglasses. I didn't see him cross through the other window in our apartment that faces the front, so I got up to see if he was knocking. Before I could make it to the door, my mom had tapped me on the shoulder and said she knew it was for her.

He's been back four times in the past two months, but my mom has yet to give me a straight answer about him. He's never stayed long. He and my mom talk outside our apartment door for about an hour, I see him peek in and then he leaves. He's like the picture of all my friends' grandparents. Those old men you see with stern faces because they don't want you to know they miss whatever part of Mexico they left behind. Like they're missing part of themselves even though everyone in their house would be lost if they were gone. It's like he's the part of us that my dad took with him.

"He's here about your brother," is all that Mom will say, and even though I feel like he's here about all of us, like he's here to stay, I believe her.

School is distracting enough that I push everything aside. I want to pretend that I'm not sweating it, but I'm nervous. For five or six months now, I've been using the Internet and books from the library to teach myself sign language, but when me and Mom went to fill out the enrollment papers, all the kids signed so quickly that I couldn't make everything out. My name is the only thing I can sign that fast, but that's because I've been practicing it more than anything—since I'm starting over in a place where I'm sure to be the only *real* Mexican, I want 'em to get my name right. It's Benito, not Benny or Ben.

Growing up, my family always called me Nito for short, but in second grade, I was tagged with Benny by my teacher, Ms. Del Olmo. That lady was as fake as they come. She was darker than me, had more *nopales* on her forehead than me, but she still pronounced her name, "Dell-All-Moe," like she was trying to escape being Mexican.

I hated being called Benny. But in junior high, I got lucky and people started calling me Chuequito, after my brother, Chucho, who had just gotten out of prison. He was bigger than I had remembered him when he came out that time. He had always been tall, but he looked like he could run through a wall and dust himself off like it was nothing. My first really sharp memory of Chucho as an adult is imagining him lifting weights in jail. When I got his name, some of my friends had tried translating the name to Little Crooked, but it never caught on because of the respect Chucho had around the block. Getting some of that respect passed on to me changed everything. From then on, no one called me Benny. It was Benito or Chuequito. *Nothing* else.

The irony about it (yeah, I know what irony means), my brother hated being called Chueco as much as I hated being called Benny. Like a lot of nicknames, it started as a joke. He had tried out as a pitcher for his junior high baseball team, but his pitching had been so wild that the coach, whose name I forgot because he wasn't there when I started at the same junior high fifteen years later, called him Chucho "El Chueco" Barrionuevo. He ended up playing first base, and the nickname stuck.

"Sometimes you gotta live with what you get," he told me about the name. "But, at least, I'll make 'em stop thinking it's funny."

After a few days of people laughing, he tagged "El Chueco Rifa" on the side of the Thrifty that's across from the school.

When I start at the deaf school, my mom makes me promise to fly straight. She literally makes me write down, "I'll stay out of trouble." The thing about starting over, though, is that nobody knows you. Everyone looks at you and wonders where you come from and what you're likely to do. In a school where no one looks like you, where all the Mexican kids act like white kids with tans, you stand out even if you don't want to. It should be great, but I can't disappoint my mom. I keep to myself and it works.

It's not till I'm two weeks into classes that my luck runs out.

I'm sitting in first period trying to figure out if our teacher, Mr. Ackerman, is deaf. When he picks up the phone, I know he isn't. I'm sitting too far back to read his lips, but he doesn't say anything after he hangs up and keeps going on with the lesson.

"Second person," he writes on the board, "is when a character in the story is telling another character in the story's story."

He's wrong, but around me, no one is paying attention. He's copying everything from a handout to the board and only turns around after he runs out of space. Everyone signs back and forth to each other as he writes.

A few rows from me, there's a girl dressed in *chola* gear and I do a double take. She's wearing tan Dickies, Nike Cortez and a white tank top with a blue, long-sleeved button down over it. The colors don't amount to much—she's a white girl who's just biting the style—but she looks good. The shirt isn't baggy and she's got it tucked in with all the buttons done up except the top three. The Dickies aren't baggy either. You can see the outline of her legs tight against her pants as she's sitting there. Her hair and make-up are the best part, though. She's taken just enough of the style to look like a pin-up girl: brown hair flowing down the back and sides with a little poof at the top, red lipstick, black eyebrows and lashes.

I look at her and can't help rubbing my scalp. My hair's grown so much that I had to go to the barber shop for a fade. I hadn't been to a barber in two years, since the tenth grade. The top is so long that it feels weird and I'm so distracted that I don't notice when the girl turns around and catches me looking. Not being green, I smile at her. Smiling is always the best way to play it cool. It's so cool that it works. She smiles back and starts to sign something about my shoes.

She's too fast, though, and loses me. Looking down, my shoes are just my shoes. When I look up, she's signing something else. I try to keep up but get lost, again.

I sign, "Stop. You're too fast."

She chokes down a laugh—her mouth is tight, her nostrils are flaring—and she flashes me a West Coast sign—her middle and ring fingers crossed forming a W with her index and pinky.

She's playing it as cool as me, so I cock my head to the side, mouth "Oh, yeah?" and flash the sign for my brother's gang: West Street Locos.

She stops laughing and I start to think I messed up, but she points to the front and Mr. Ackerman is motioning toward me.

Slowly, like all teachers at the school, he tells me he's been calling my name for the past minute. It couldn't have been more than twenty seconds, but I don't push my luck.

He points to the white board. "Answer this."

The question is, "What is Second Person?"

I know the answer—the *right* answer—but I think of my mom: *Stay out of trouble.* Everyone in class is looking at me. Everyone, including the girl. I know exactly what Chucho would do. I picture him out of jail, walking down the block, people going up to him, showing love 'cause he made it out. I can't be weak in front of the girl, so I go for it.

I take my time, spelling out some words I haven't learned the sign for, and tell him the right answer: second person is like first person, except the author uses "you" instead of "I" to make the reader feel like they're the person the story's about.

He says I'm wrong, tells me to pay more attention, and turns to write on the board.

I'm fully committed to what Chucho would do, so I grip the desk to get up and act a fool. When I look at the girl, though, she's got a cute smile on her face and she's signing "Like" by pinching her heart.

Mr. Ackerman isn't the point, so I sign "Thank You." It looks like I'm blowing her a kiss.

At lunch, the girl is signing slower so I can keep up. She's a little giggly and says her name is Susie. When she's not signing, her hands are in her back pockets and she twists her body a little at the waist. It makes her look even cuter, so I check my posture—I lean back a little, one shoulder higher than the other, my head tilted up.

"I dressed up on a dare," she says. "People have been talking about you—how you avoid everyone—and my friend Ruby said I couldn't get you to notice me."

"Why would she do that?" I ask, but already know Ruby did it 'cause Susie likes me.

"For fun," she says. "I don't know. What do you do for fun?"

After school, my homeboy, Scribbler, picks us up in his mom's blue Berreta and we go to his house, a studio apartment in an alley behind an ampm. When Scribbler and me were in the seventh grade, we filled up the back of the ampm with our *sarreado* tags—crooked fonts and weak block lettering. I never got good, but Scribbler kept at it and earned his nickname.

Susie tells me she's never been to this side of town before. Ruby and her guy, Josh, tagged along and say they haven't either.

I take my phone from my pocket and text our conversation for Scribbler.

"You're with me and Chueco," Scribbler says. "No one's gonna do nothing."

Scribbler has been yelling since he picked us up. I can tell because his neck tightens and chest puffs up as he talks.

"You don't have to yell, fool," I text him. "They can read your lips as good as me."

He nods and keeps talking. "Besides, Ruby and her brother are Chinese and Susie's not a blonde. You don't stick out all that much."

Josh takes out his phone. "She's my girlfriend and we're Korean, but I get your point."

"My bad," Scribbler says. "But, yeah, don't sweat it. Y'all are cool hanging out."

I'd just met Josh as we were heading out of school, but until he talked back to Scribbler, I had him pegged as weak.

Scribbler's been painting the back of the ampm white, and we're checking out his progress when he taps Ruby on the shoulder. I can't see what he tells her, and for a moment, before Ruby tells us what Scribbler said, I think he might've disrespected Josh by hitting on her.

Scribbler, though, only told her about his plans for a mural.

"I'm not sure what to paint," he says. "I don't want to do the same stuff—Aztecs and pyramids and *revolucionarios*."

I translate *revolucionarios* as "Mexican Revolution fighters." After I do that, I flash to the old *paisa* that's been showing up. It's funny how we skip over people like him when we think about *raza*.

"I might do a mural about Iraq. Put in the pyramids and oil fields and stuff," Scribbler says.

Susie starts to text something, but Scribbler stops her by putting his hand over her phone.

"I know the pyramids aren't in Iraq, but how else are people gonna know it's the Middle East and not Texas?"

I laugh so hard that I don't see how Susie reacts.

Scribbler picks up a spray can. "You guys wanna try out some *placazos*."

I translate *placazo* as "tag" and point to the graffiti on the wall. They jump at the idea and take turns writing their names. Susie writes her name without the E, and we give names to Ruby and Josh. For Ruby, we just translate her name, switch the Y for an I. Josh, Scribbler calls KayJay, for Korean Josh.

The girls do their best to not smear too much paint, but Josh goes big and starts to lay his name down across the part of the wall that Scribbler's painted white. He's halfway done when Scribbler turns to look at me.

I bite my lower lip and shake my head the slightest amount.

"Cool," Scribbler says.

When we're done, we drop Ruby and Josh off first. At Susie's house, I walk her to the door and lean in for a hug. She answers back with a kiss on the cheek.

"Bye, Chuequito." She spells my nickname like I tag it, S-H-W-E-K-I-T-O.

At school, Susie tells me she wants to go tagging for real. I remember my promise to stay out of trouble, but Mom's been so secretive about that old man who keeps showing up that I agree to do it as long as it's on West Street, where it'll be easier. Mom's shutting me out, so I shut her out.

When Scribbler picks us up after school, it's just me and Susie. She tells me Ruby and Josh already had plans.

"I only asked them to be nice," she says. "I really just want-ed to hang out with you."

I blush, hoping Scribbler doesn't notice, but he does.

"What'd she say, dog? You're all blushy like *jainitas* when I tell 'em I'm gonna put them in a mural."

I wave him off and jump in the back with Susie.

Scribbler turns in his seat and says, "What? I'm your driver now?"

Susie's laughing and I beg him to drive. The sign for driving is easy to understand—you pretend you're gripping a wheel and you turn it back and forth. The sign for begging looks nothing like actual begging, so I give him the sign for praying instead—my palms together in front me like I'm five and about to go to sleep.

It works and he drives us to his house, where he hooks us up with some spray cans.

I grab a black one and tell Susie black is best 'cause it's harder to paint over, but she tucks a pink can under her arm and says, "Nothing lasts forever."

I tell Scribbler what she said, and he gives her a thumbs up.

"You need a dark hoodie," I tell her. "You gotta be cool like a ninja when you're out tagging."

She looks down at her clothes—purple sneakers, tight, black jeans and a purple peacoat.

My apartment is three blocks away, and we start walking. The sun's still out and I tell her we have enough time to grab something to eat.

Tomorrow is swap meet day, so when we walk in, my mom's in the kitchen taking tamales out of a pot and bagging them into dozens. She sees us come in and waves me over. I'm so busy texting that I don't read her lips.

When I show her the text—"This is my friend, Susie, from school"—she ignores me.

"Is this the little girl you were telling me about?"

I nod my head.

Mom talks to me in Spanish, but instead of translating, I warn Susie that my mom can be rude. I had thought of warning her on the walk over, but I decided to give my mom the benefit of the doubt. Standing in the kitchen, seeing Mom sweating over the *vaporera*, I know it's too much to ask. I apologize to Susie in advance and Mom looks at me like she knows what I'm saying.

"Can you read lips?" she asks Susie in English.

Susie nods and Mom puts her hand out. It's wet from the steam in the pot, but Susie doesn't wipe her palm after they shake.

"My name is Gabriela Barrionuevo," my mom says. "I'm Nito's mother."

Susie grabs her phone and starts to text her name, but Mom stops her. "You're Susie. Nito has told me about you."

I like that she's blunt about my having mentioned Susie, but I still blush.

"It smells delicious in here, Mrs. Barrionuevo," Susie writes. "Nito says you might need help."

Mom shakes her head. "You're lying. I'm sure he didn't say that."

Susie's eyes go wide, and I tense up.

"But it's okay. You're better than my son. He doesn't even know it's rude to not tell me what he's signing."

I look at Susie, her hands are in her back pockets, her eyes intent on my mom's lips.

We're through, I'm sure of it, but Mom puts a plastic bag out for Susie to grab. "Here, hold this while Nito tells me how you got his attention."

Susie can't talk 'cause her hands are busy holding the bags, and I mostly just nod my head. After a while of having no one to argue with, my mom starts talking about the crappy hours at the health clinic where she works.

When they finish bagging the tamales, my mom excuses herself and goes outside to smoke.

"The last girl I brought home," I tell Susie. "She kicked out in five minutes."

"So why'd you bring me?"

"Honestly?"

She nods.

"Even if I really like a girl, I can't be with her unless my mom approves."

Susie laughs, her lips puckered. "So you really, really like me?"

She's as cute as she gets, but I know my mom's right outside the door, and I don't risk trying to kiss her.

I grab some tamales and she wanders over to my dad's books.

"Do you ever read anything in English?"

"Yeah," I say, "but these were my dad's."

"Oh. Is he—you know?"

"I don't."

"You don't what?"

"I don't know. He left when I was still a baby."

"Oh," she says. "Is that you blowing out the candle?"

"Yeah."

"You're really cute."

"I was a baby."

"Yeah, but still. Is that your brother and sister with you?"

"He's my brother," I say, "But she's just the girl he was seeing at the time. I think my mom didn't want to ruin the picture by cutting her out."

"She looks more like you than your brother does."

"Me and Chucho have different dads. That's why he's so much older than me."

"Chucho's your brother?"

"Yeah."

"Where is he now?"

"Come on, I'll show you."

We turn from the pictures to go to my room, and as we walk toward the hallway, I see that the old *paisa* is at the window with my mom. They're both looking at us, their lips moving. When I spot him, the guy straightens up, stunned, but then he smiles and waves at me like he's an uncle I haven't seen in a long time. My mom looks just as surprised, but the guy is waving like an idiot and I can't help but nod at him. It's as much a "who the hell are you?" as it is a "what's up?" nod, but Susie taps me on the shoulder and by the time she's done asking who the old guy is, I turn back and he and my mom are walking across the outside hall, toward the stairs that lead down and out of the apartments.

"I don't know who he is," I tell Susie.

"It looked like he knew you."

"He doesn't. I think he might be a cop or something, asking about Chucho."

"Don't cops wear suits when they're not in uniform?"

"I don't know," I say and lead her to my room.

There, the walls are full of drawings. All the things Scribbler is tired of painting: pyramids, *revolucionarios*, Aztec warriors and hieroglyphs, low-riders, zoot suits, girls done up like pin-ups.

As Susie's looking around, I'm picking the olives out of my tamal.

She turns to me. "These are really great, Benito."

I picture Chucho sitting on his bunk, his back hunched and eyes fixed on the paper as he draws. "My brother drew them in prison."

"Oh," she says. "Why was he in prison?"

"He's there right now," I say. "He's been in and out since as far back as I can remember—for drug things, but this time he was caught after he shot a guy."

Susie's face turns sour, like I just broke up with her.

"Don't worry; the guy lived," I tell her. "My brother only shot him in the leg."

"Only?"

"Yeah. It was payback, but the guy hadn't done something bad enough to die for."

"Why the leg?" she asks like what she really wants to know is why I'm hurting her.

I'm too stupid to change the subject and I'm sure she thinks I'm bragging when I say, "It was the knee, actually."

"What?" she says, her face looking like my house stinks and she's too good for me or my family. "What's the difference?"

"Look," I say as calmly as I can manage. "You asked and I didn't want to avoid the question. It's the same reason I brought you to my house. I want you to know who I really am."

"But why would your brother do that?"

I put my tamal down. "The guy he shot had jumped me, which would have been fine, but when the guy had me down, he stomped my head into the concrete."

Susie sits on my bed.

"I ended up at the hospital for a week, and when I left, I started losing my hearing."

"Oh," she says. "How old were you?"

"It happened last year."

"Wait. You lost your hearing last year?"

"Slowly, yeah. That's why I can't sign that well."

"Are you crazy? You've only been signing and reading lips for a year?"

"Yeah. But, I mean, it's all I've been doing, so—"

"Benito, do you know how amazing that is?"

Until she said it, I hadn't thought about it. I mean, who wouldn't learn to sign this fast if they were forced to? When my guidance counselor at school said my placement tests were fantastic, it sounded to me like something you have to tell handicapped kids. Like something they tell kids on the short bus when they learn to tie their shoes.

"I don't know," I tell her. "I was just lucky that the guy didn't stomp my head any harder."

"So your brother hurt the guy for revenge?"

"Yeah, but he's always been good at figuring things out. Most *vatos* would only think of killing the guy, but he shot his knee out so the doctors would have to amputate it."

She turns toward me on my bed, sitting Indian style and putting the plate on her legs. "You make it sound like he couldn't just let it be—I mean, I'm glad he didn't kill anyone, but you were lucky, like you said. Why push things?"

"If he didn't do something back, he'd be weak."

She slaps my hands down, so I can't keep explaining, and says, "It's stupid. If he hadn't done that, he'd be here right now."

"Maybe, but at least, now, when people see that guy riding around in a wheelchair, everyone knows they shouldn't mess with me. It keeps me safe."

She starts to unwrap her tamal. "I don't know."

"It just is what it is. Sometimes you have to live with what you get, you know?"

We start to eat and I look at her as she gets up between bites to look at the drawings.

"I really like you," she says afterward, pinching her heart at me for the second time since we met. "I'm happy I came today."

"Me too," I tell her.

When we finish eating, I lend her a hoodie. As we're walking out, I see light from my mom's T.V. flicker out of her room, but I don't bother going in to see her. If Chucho were here, he'd be outside, drinking on the balcony. I miss him, but the old *paisa* pops into my head. I picture him on the couch, his hat on his knee and boots off. He'd tell me to be careful or maybe that I couldn't go out.

Outside, it's dark. Not as dark as it gets, but dark enough.

"Which places are the best to do graffiti?" Susie asks.

"Tag," I tell her.

She rolls her eyes. "Tag, then."

"You usually pick a spot and tag what fits—it's a moment-of-inspiration thing."

As mad as I am at my mom for keeping me in the dark about the old guy, I can't break my promise to stay out of trouble, so I take Susie to the safest spot I know, besides Scribblers pad, for tagging: a street that's cut off by a five-foot wall that separates houses from the freeway.

"Is it the 10 that's behind the fence?" Susie says when we get there.

I nod.

"So everyone can see it if you tag on the other side?"

I nod and start to say something, but Susie's already climbing over the wall.

By the time I jump over, she's already spraying. Cars are going by more often than I would like, but Susie keeps writing. When I think she's done, she goes back to the beginning and keeps going under her first line. A car that's passing by flashes its high beams and I'm sure we're going to get caught, but Susie goes back to start a third line. I think about dragging her over the wall, but I start reading instead. I recognize what she's tagging and decide that we have to finish it, no matter what.

She crouches down to complete the verse, and I start to cross out unnecessary words with the black can.

My chest feels like speakers thumping when we're done. We sit side by side on the pavement, our backs up against the wall, smiling and out of breath.

"You almost got us busted," I say.

"It was a moment of inspiration."

"You're crazy. But you've got good taste in music."

"You know The Smiths?"

"My brother got me into them before I lost my hearing."

"Mine too. But I've never heard anything. I just know their pictures and lyrics."

She wrote the verse in three lines and capital letters. I grab her hand and start to tap out the beat on the inside of her wrist as I mouth the words:

NOW I KNOW HOW JOAN OF ARC FELT AS
THE FLAMES ROSE TO HER ROMAN NOSE
AND HER HEARING AID STARTED TO MELT.

When I start to repeat them, she ducks under my arm and gets so close that our noses touch. I try to kiss her, but she turns her head a little. It's not till I grab her face with both hands that she kisses me back.

She never asks what I added to the *placazo*, but behind us, for commuters on the 10, the only pink letters left, the ones not crossed out, are THE FLAMES ROSE AND HER HEARING AID STARTED TO MELT.

At school, the next day, I get pulled out of class and arrested. Someone tagged the K-Mart across from the campus. The cops did a search on the names, and only SHWEKITO came back a match. Rubi, Susi and KayJay were new to the system. When Susie tells me a week later, I already know it was Josh. Since the day we tagged the ampm, Ruby hadn't shut up about Scribbler and the mural he was going to paint. It took me a while, but the only person who would want to tag the K-Mart is Josh. Not creative enough, though, he probably thought we'd like our names up there with his.

The cops act like they know I did it and want to know who was with me, but I've been here before and I tell them nothing. They talk, then yell, then bark, but I still don't tell them anything. I'm deaf and have been off the streets for a year, so in juvenile court, they only give me house arrest, ankle bracelet and all. It's nothing.

At home, though, my mom is too quiet.

When I was first arrested, she picked me up from the police department in her scrubs. On the ride home, she didn't say anything. At the apartment, she called work, said she wouldn't be going back until the next day and fell asleep on the couch. That was it. That's all the scolding I got.

By the time I have the bracelet on, I've been gone from school for a week and I don't think Mom has said three words to me. Susie has texted me every day, though, asking if she can come by. I tell her I don't want to push my luck. Ruby also texted me, saying she was with Josh when they tagged the K-Mart and wants to thank me for not telling on them. I just text back, "Don't sweat it." Josh texts me after Ruby, asking if we're cool. We're not, but I think about Susie. Josh's only fault is being unoriginal when he thought he was losing his girl.

I back off. "Yeah, we're cool. Just don't come around West Street. Ever."

I don't think Chucho would've backed off that much, but it's what *I* do.

That same day, my mom is working and I'm sitting in the living room when I see the old *paisa* walk past the front window of the apartment. I don't know if it's him or Josh or Mom being so distant that gets to me, but I beat him to the door and I scream at him. I don't know how loud or clear or shrill it comes out, but I scream at him, "Who are you? What do you want with Chucho?"

He stumbles back from the door, startled and pale, and I step out into the hallway.

I scream again, the same questions, and he reaches into the leather jacket he's wearing and hands me a letter that I ball up and throw in his face.

"Just tell me," I scream. "I'm deaf, not a moron."

"No English," he says.

I translate for him. "*Soy sordo, no imbécil.*"

"*Soy tu abuelo,*" he says.

He's too young for me to believe him, and it takes me so long to respond that he thinks I don't understand him and he repeats himself in English.

"I, your grandfather," he says.

I can't think of what to say. He looks too scared to be lying. Scared and sad. That sadness that says he's sure he's doing the right thing.

"I go," he says. "Here."

He picks up the crumpled letter, flattens it against his chest and gives it to me before walking down the hallway, the stairs and out of the apartments.

The letter is handwritten in Spanish and capital letters, an old trick that makes it so you don't have to use accent marks. I read the letter and it spells it all out—why these books are here, why there are no pictures of my dad, the identity of my brother's girlfriend in the picture. The old man who said he was my grandfather also says in the letter that his name is Benito. That my brother's girlfriend in the picture is Norma, his daughter, is also my mother, and is dead. That she had been here on a visa when I was born, and that she had lost it soon after. That when Chucho went to prison for the first time, she lost touch with my family, who had moved from the address where she wrote to us. That the books I've been reading are hers. That Chucho is not my brother and my mom is not my mom. I read the letter over and over. I can't bring myself to believe it. It's lies. I know it's lies because the only way it can be true is if everything else is a lie. If it isn't just me and Mom and Chucho.

On a Monday, Mom calls the school saying I'm ready to go back, and they schedule an expulsion hearing for the next day.

They sit us down on a long table, my mom and me on one side, five school officials on the other. The school principal, Mr. Ackerman, two teachers I don't know and the school superintendant are the school officials. The superintendant is Mexican, but I know it means nothing. He's sure to be stricter because we're both Mexican. When any of them talks, Mr. Ackerman signs what they say.

The superintendant goes first. "I understand your other son, José, is in prison, Mrs. Barrionuevo."

"Barrionuevo," Mom says. I can't hear, but I know Mom repeated our name 'cause he said it like a white guy. "My son's name is José de Jesús. He's paying for what he did and it should have nothing to do with why Benito is here."

"Okay, Mrs. Barrionuevo," the principal says. "You can appreciate that we can't have students engaging in vandalism."

Before my mom can answer, Mr. Ackerman speaks up.

"I've read the police report. Benito was charged with being tied to the graffiti, but it wasn't proven that he did it himself. He was placed on house arrest because other cases of vandalism are on his juvenile record. I don't think we should punish him for something juvenile court could not establish as fact."

One of the teachers I don't know speaks up. "But his name was up on that wall. Somehow or another, he was involved. He also didn't think helping the police was necessary, so he's the only person we can hold accountable."

"I agree," says the superintendant, "If he's not willing to help himself, then why should we?"

This is the part where they do what they want. They tell you it's your fault and they get rid of you. It's happened to Chucho and it's happened to me. It happens and you live with it, like Chucho told me way back when.

This time, though, for some reason, my mom had had enough.

"Benito doesn't know any better," She says. "His brother was too proud to be a father to him. I try as much as possible to teach him to be good, but I—I haven't done as good a job as I should."

She's talking very slowly and her lips are barely moving. Her eyes are looking straight ahead, like she's blind and talking to whoever can hear.

"I have a son in jail, a son who can't hear, and I know I'm responsible for it. Benito has been doing well in school. He has read more books in the past year than I've read my whole life. He is bilingual and is learning sign language so fast that I don't know how I never noticed he was this smart. That's why we're here, in this room—because I have never paid close attention to my son. You can't hurt him for something that's my fault."

They'll let me stay in school if I personally paint over the graffiti. We walk out to the car and before my mom can start it up, I take out my phone.

"You didn't have to do that. They wanted you to beg, but you didn't have to. I can get my GED and go do something else."

When she reads the message, she drops the phone and slaps me hard across the face.

I turn back from the slap and she's crying, her chest heaving.

"Do you really think I don't have to beg for you?"

My face is burning from her slap and I don't know what to say.

"Do you think I don't have to visit your brother every month either? Or pretend to care about those books?"

As she wipes her mascara on a tissue, I decide to talk out loud to her for the first time in the better part of a year.

"What do you mean 'pretend'?"

She's as shocked as I was when I screamed at Benito.

"I'm fifty-two years old, Benito. I know the things I have to do. You're a year away from eighteen. It's time *you* begin to think about what you have to do."

She's never put me on the spot like this, never asked me to account for myself like this, but I don't give up. "Did those books really belong to my father or to my mother?"

She grips the wheel, her hands starting to shake. I have Benito's letter folded in my back pocket, and I reach back and give it to her. While she's reading it, I start my question.

"Is that girl in my baby picture my mom?"

She reads more of the letter, and folds it back like I handed it to her. I don't know if she finished reading it, if she went past the part where Benito tells me about Norma, about my mom, my real mom, but I ask her, "Is Norma my real mom? Is she the one in that picture?"

She doesn't say anything, her hands shaking, barely holding onto the wheel.

Maybe I'm not talking clearly enough.

I go back to texting, but she looks past the phone, into my eyes and grabs me by the shoulders and presses herself to my chest, her face pressed against my left shoulder. My hands are folded under hers, but I reach up as best I can, to hug her back. She's sobbing, I can feel her body heave and her voice reverberate into my shoulder. She might be talking or just crying, but I know Benito told me the truth in that letter.

I text Susie, and she says she wants to come over.

"Not yet," I tell her.

Chucho's in jail 'cause he took care of us as best he could. I don't know why Mom, why my current mom, my long-time mom, my—I don't know why they thought I couldn't take the truth, but I know I have to do something more than be on their list of problems.

When I go paint over the graffiti, Susie comes along to help. I haven't seen her in almost two weeks and forgot how cute she is.

I open the can of paint and she says, "I'm glad they let you stay in school."

"I guess," I say. "I don't know."

"What about me?"

"I already met you. I don't need that place anymore."

"So what are you going to do?"

"We're just a semester away from graduation."

"But what about after?"

"I don't know," I tell her.

"We should figure it out," she says. And I'm sure we will.

Losing Face

Carlos Hernandez

Nice day, walking home from Bronx Science, texting Rosario, the smartest girl in school and the lady who hasn't realized yet that her destiny is to be my wife. Then, half a block away from Valentine and 203rd, I see a cop stuffing my man Remy Mo's head into the back seat. I shut my phone and run over.

The kids at school call me the cop-whisperer. Can't tell you how many times I've pulled one of my boys out of the back of a cop car. "Sorry, officers, my friend here is an idiot. Yes, of course, he'll cooperate fully with you. Yes, you will cooperate, *puto*, or it's hello, Rikers and bye-bye, Life. It was just a big misunderstanding. Have a nice day, officer." You just have to be respectful and keep cool, just talk to the po like they're people. Oh, and it helps if you don't spend your life breaking the law. That chrome you got stuffed down your pants, gangsta? All you're gonna do is shoot yourself: maybe literally, but symbolically, for sure.

I shouldered my way through the crowd—always a crowd when someone gets busted in the Bronx; people don't know how to mind their business around here—till I reached the officer, who was already halfway in the car. "Good day, officer," I said. "I am a friend of the minor you have in your vehicle. Would you mind if I inquired as to why you have taken him into custody?"

The cop looked up at me stunned. It's like he'd never heard anyone in the Bronx speak whitey before. Even though he was almost in the car, he got all the way out and came over to me. The crowd took a few steps back, left me face-to-face with John Law. "Hello there, young man. Do you know anything that might be of help to our investigation?"

I stood my ground. "What exactly is the nature of your investigation?" I asked. Smiling.

Cop looked me up and down. "Your friend, he tell you where he was last night?"

"No. I haven't spoken with him today."

"Well," said the cop, leaning in a little, "your friend's girlfriend went missing last night. Right after she posted a suicide note on Facebook. We just want to know if he knows anything about what happened to her."

"Galatea? She killed herself?" I asked. I'd never met her in person, but I'd seen pics, and Remy talked about her so much I felt like I knew her. And suicide? It hit me in the chest.

This cop was alright. I could see he saw the news affected me. He put a hand on my shoulder and said, "Don't jump the gun there. Right now she is just presumed missing. But your friend isn't exactly being cooperative." He took his hand back and became a cop again. "It's a little suspicious. It's like he's got something to hide."

Frankly, the cop was right. Remy loved Galatea with all his might. Why wouldn't he be helping them find out what happened? "Officer," I said, "would you mind if I rode along too? Maybe I can talk some sense into Remy."

The cop thought about it. The police don't usually let people ride with suspects on the way to the station. But he could see I really wanted to help. And I spoke whitey fluently. "I'll need to frisk you," he said. "Standard procedure."

"Of course," I said, assuming the position against the car. The officer did a half-assed job of frisking me—he was on my side all the way by that point—then he opened the back door.

"Move over, Mr. Colón. Your very good friend here is coming with you. You should listen to him."

Remy was wearing his default "ain't life a bitch" smirk when I got in the back with him. "Igs, man," he said. "You supposed to get me out of this. You ain't supposed to go to jail, too."

"No one's going to jail," I said. But I was suddenly pissed off. "And you know why? Because we're going to help the police. Because all the police want to do is find your shortie and make sure she's okay. Which is what you want too, right? You want to find Galatea? Make sure she's okay?"

Remy Mo's face erased itself. Then he faced forward and said, "I have the right to remain silent."

After hours of waiting around while they questioned Remy, I finally found myself sitting at a detective's desk, in a room full of detectives' desks. The name plate on my detective's desk read "Alexia Suárez-Balart." Now that's a sexy name. Spread over her desk—purposely left there for me to look at while I waited— were some blown-up, low-rez pictures of Galatea: brunette, too skinny, okay face, nice teeth, no boobs and always with a pair of Disney earrings studded in her ears. For the six pictures on the desk, left to right: Ariel, Cruella DeVille, Mulan, that pig from *The Lion King*, Tinkerbell and Cinderella's pumpkin carriage.

I heard someone coming up behind me. In heels. "Ignacio? I'm Detective Suárez-Balart." I stood and turned to face her and shake her hand.

Look, Rosario, you know you are the only woman for me. But I'm a sixteen-year-old male of the species. I would never betray you, but the body wants what it wants. And right then, my body wanted Detective Suárez-Balart.

She was older but not old, poised, professional, but open, too, and her smile was real and powerful. And she was a female Latina detective in the NYPD, which meant she was tougher than any one white-man detective—because she would have to be. Smarter, too. And I have a thing for wise Latinas.

"Detective," I said, and gave her a professional, completely un-sexual handshake. "My friends call me Igs."

"Have a seat," she said and went around to the other side of her desk. "So, Igs, what exactly are you doing here?"

"Taking care of my man Remy. And serving justice."

She sat back in her chair. "Serving justice? That's not a phrase I usually hear from young men your age."

"I'm mature for my age."

She smiled. "You certainly come across that way. But you told the officer who drove you here that you hadn't talked to Remy since last night. So I'm trying to figure out what you think you can offer my investigation."

"You need to understand your suspect, right? Know what makes him tick?"

"Remy isn't a suspect. He's a person of interest."

I put on a cockney accent and said, "Let's not quibble, love. They's a girl missing, they is, and Remy's the best lead you 'ave. But 'e won't talk to you. Don't you wanna know why?"

"That's a very good accent," she said.

I took a bow in my chair and switched back to Igs-speak. "I like to act. But you didn't answer my question."

"First, I want to know more about you, Ignacio."

"Please call me Igs, detective. My father was Ignacio."

"Hmm." She learned forward, rested her chin in her hand, thought. "Ignacio Guillermo Valencia. Why does that name sound familiar?"

"Maybe you knew him. He was NYPD. Before he skipped town with some stripper and headed for Florida."

She shook her head. "I'm sorry."

"I'm not. It taught me a valuable lesson—what kind of man not to be."

Seriously, detective. Stop smiling. I need to be thinking clearly now, for Remy's sake. "You and Remy both go to Bronx Science?"

"Yes, ma'am."

"That's a good school."

"It's alright."

"College?"

"*Por supuesto*, Mami."

"Where?"

"Maybe John Jay? Moms can afford it, and it's good for what I want to study."

"Criminal Justice?"

"Something in law enforcement. Maybe criminal psychology?"

"That's a challenging field."

"I like challenges."

She sat back in her chair again. "I bet you do."

Damn, son. Felt like I was melting. No way she was flirting with me, right? My brain said *No way, puto*. But the little *jefe* disagreed.

"I like challenges too, Igs," she continued. But now she was back to business. "And I have quite a challenge on my desk right now. I've got a missing teenage girl, and I've got to find out what happened to her."

I sat up. "You call her parents?"

"We would if we could figure out who she is. Apparently, Galatea is just a nickname."

"Weird nickname," I said. But I was also thinking *How come Remy never told me that?*

She picked up a photo on the desk, held it up. "Is this Galatea?"

"Yeah. That's the pic that comes up on Remy's phone when she calls."

She looked at me for a long two seconds, then grabbed another, held them side by side. "How about her?" she asked.

It was Galatea, too. Remy had shown me this pic of her a bunch of times, her at Yankee Stadium with a ballcap on, ponytail spilling out the back, Cruella earrings smiling wickedly. But, side by side with the other pic, I could see the girl's nose was different. And her eyes. And her smile was made from a completely different kind of mouth. "Oh, man, detective," I said. "This is gonna sound crazy. I thought that was Galatea. Remy keeps that one in his phone, too, shows it to people when he tells them about his girlfriend. I guess I never looked at it too careful."

Her voice and face went soft. "Okay. But you can now, right?"

"Sure."

She put the photos down. There was still a smile on her face, but it had gone sad. "But Remy can't, can he? He really thinks those two girls are the same person, doesn't he?"

She didn't say, "Maybe you can tell me why your friend is lying." Anyone else would've thought Remy was just trying to cover his ass by saying he couldn't identify the girl he'd been humping for months. But somehow she figured it out. People who've been around Remy his whole life haven't figured it out. Wise Latinas, man.

I leaned forward and said to her, "You ready for a sad story, detective?"

Her smile was melancholy, and so beautiful. She said, "That's the only kind we get around here, Ignacio."

You're from around here, right, detective? You know what it's like. Lot of broken homes, lot of broken people. Plenty of good people too, don't get me wrong. But poverty will eat your soul if you let it. It just chews up the best parts, the parts you need to be a good person and leaves behind the animal in you, the monster inside that will do anything to survive: steal, kill, whatever. And then it eats that too, and then you become one of walking dead. A lot of chewed-up people in our neighborhood, sitting on milk crates, drinking 40s. They literally don't know they're still alive.

Remy's moms used to be one of them, back in the day. Remy's dad was some sperm-donor she got high with one night. She worked as a cashier at a Duane Reade, which is a job you can keep even if you smoke crack. Skinny as a mis-fed chicken, losing her hair in her twenties. Killed her own womb. Remy's the only kid she'd ever have.

But she didn't even want the kid she had. He'd make any kind of noise, any at all, she'd hit him. Older he got, harder she hit. He wasn't in school yet, so nobody knew. He didn't speak a word until he was almost four.

But when he was five, he had to go to school. And then teachers started noticing the bruises. Hell, I was a kindergartener and I noticed. Especially his mouth: she loved to slap him in the mouth. I ain't no psychologist yet, but I think I know why. The mouth gives quick satisfaction to abusers. It bleeds fast, and a bloody mouth looks a damn mess. Makes you feel powerful. But mouths heal fast, too. If you don't hit too hard or too often, couple hours later no one will notice anything.

But she hit too hard. Too often. His mouth looked like an old balloon. You know, like when they've lost most of their air and they get all misshapen and sad-looking? Our assistant principal called Children's Services.

They showed up at her apartment; they told her to clean up her place and clean up her life, or she'd lose him. But then they left, detective. They left him.

The way Remy tells it, she waited a full hour. Just sat at the kitchen table, smoking and watching the clock. Then she goes to the living room where Remy's watching T.V. and yanks him off the sofa by his hair. Got in his face and hissed, "What did you tell them?"

He didn't reply. He could speak a little by then but usually didn't. And anyway, what could he say? He covered his mouth with both hands and waited.

Didn't wait long. She dragged him by the hair over to the nearest wall and smashed his head against it. Once, twice. He's five years old.

I stood up, took a breath, took a break. "Take all the time you need," the detective said. Her face was expressionless. Solemn. That helped. I sat down again.

Third time's the charm, right, detective? Remy's head went through the cheap project drywall.

On the other side of the drywall was wood and old nails. Remy's head sank like old fruit into a long rusty nail. It went so deep into his head his moms couldn't pull him off. But she tried. And tried and tried, yanking on his skull with all her crackhead might. No one knows if his brain damage happened the second the nail penetrated his skull or if his mom scrambled it trying to yank him free. But does it matter?

Ambulance came, police came, Children's Services came back; they were especially pissed. Remy went to the hospital. His moms went to Rikers.

Could've been worse for Remy. Could've come out retarded, or paralyzed, or dead. That's what he says, anyway. You ask me, Remy rolled snake-eyes.

You wouldn't know it at first. You might think he caught a break for a change. Fast-forward five years. Remy's had the same foster-home the whole time, a big family of six. Foster Dad's a contractor, Foster Mom's a Midtown office manager. They do just fine; even though they could afford to move they stay in the 'hood because that's where everyone they love lives. The four kids are all girls, all older than him, love him to death, always holding him down and smearing make-up all over his face and trying to pull dresses over his head. He's on the honor roll. Won a prize in fourth grade for a story he wrote: a boy from the projects who brings people back to life with a kiss. That right there tells you more about Remy than I ever could. The snake-eyes life he'd had up to then, and all he wants to do is help people by kissing them. Damn, son.

The foster family wants to adopt him. They start the paperwork. But then, back from the dead, his moms shows up one day at the foster family's door. Wants Remy back.

Problem is Remy doesn't recognize her.

His mom tries to laugh it off. "Do I really look so different?" she asks him. She was all the way bald now, Buddha-rolls of fat hanging from her neck. Her face was still riddled with crack-damage, but it'd been healing itself for a while now. And her teeth were weirdly perfect. Wasn't till later he figured out they were dentures.

But that's not the reason he couldn't recognize her. Five years ago she stuck a nail through that special little part of the brain that lets us recognize faces. The "fulsiform face area" it's called. I know because I've read all of Remy's medical files. All it does is recognize faces, and that's exactly the only thing the nail destroyed. Since that day, faces just blurred out for Remy, like the pixilated mugs of informants on those true-crime shows.

Remy had to start using tricks to tell people apart. Things they wore, especially stuff they'd wear every day, like hats and jewelry. The way the walked. Body language. Subtle differences in skin color, but way more subtle than black or brown or yellow or white. But the best way for him to tell people apart was voice. He developed his ears so he could hear everything about a person in their tone. He just fell in love with sound. Music. Rap and Hip-Hop especially, but Pop, too, and Rock and Blues and Motown and Gospel and even Jazz—but only Jazz with words. It was all about voice. For Remy, music without a human voice isn't music. It's just sound.

So he hadn't seen his moms in forever, and she looked so different now. Age and dentures changed her voice, too. Couldn't tell her apart from any other woman he didn't know. She had faded away, become anonymous. Should've stayed that way.

Remy's mom had become a Seventh-Day Adventist in prison, got a job when she got out as a janitor at the church on 129th. Still works there today. Seeing a shrink every week, taking the good drugs now. Told a judge she wanted to make up for being a horrible mother.

What's the judge gonna say? She'd done her time, she was clean, she was employed and she was his blood mother. She got custody. The foster family, they felt like a son had died. The dad rings Remy's mom's doorbell one day and tells her that if she ever hit Remy again he would punch her in the face until she was dead. That man is my hero.

Remy's mom, though, she wasn't going to hurt Remy anymore. Not physically, anyway. She wanted Remy to hurt her. To punish her for the evil she'd done to him. She'd cry sometimes, no reason—just washing the dishes or vacuuming, she'd start to wail, loud and showy, screaming about how evil she was and why didn't God just kill her and send her to hell where she belonged. On really bad days she'd kneel down in front of him and beg his forgiveness. Sometimes she'd beg him to beat her, with a belt or a broomstick or a frying pan or whatever, to just whack the demons out of her, so when she met Jesus in heaven she'd be pure.

House full of crazy, detective. I would've gladly grabbed a frying pan and knocked her head out the damn park, but that's not Remy. He'd just walk out the door. And stay out. Stayed every day at school as long as they'd let him. And when he had to leave school, he'd go to after-school programs for tutoring.

Remy loved to tutor, and to be tutored. Subject didn't matter. See, that's where my man met a lot of girls. Good girls, too: intelligent, sweet, maybe not so popular, maybe not the hottest *chulas* around. But Remy couldn't make out their faces anyway, so what did he care?

That's how he met Galatea. Or whatever her real name is.

When tutoring was done, he'd just hang out. All hours. Anything not to go home. And did what he had to: smoked, drank, shot up, snorted, huffed, puffed and lit up with pretty much anyone who'd let him hang. Especially liked to suck down the Remy Martin—*puto* thought it made him look money. You buy Remy some Remy, he'd do whatever you wanted. Anything. See, for Remy, the people didn't matter: he couldn't really see their faces anyway. Just one big blur of humanity for him.

The one good thing that came out of all those late nights was that Remy started freestyling, doing Spoken Word. Every other *puto* from the Bronx thinks he's a rap star, but Remy was actually good. You can hear pain, you know. You hear it and it makes you listen. Same way you have to stare at a car accident. You feel wrong for listening, but you can't help it. And pain's what makes music good.

Remy won his first Friday night at the Nuyorican Poets' Café when he was thirteen years old. You know the name of the poem that won it for him? "Face-blind."

After I finished Remy's story, Detective Suárez-Balart went to get me a Coke. I said I didn't need one, but she insisted. She insisted because she didn't want me to see her cry. Man, however long she'd been on the force, all the horrible things she must have seen and a story like Remy's could still get to her. That's a good woman right there. But what a life. Her line of work, she must get her heart broken 627 times a day.

I flipped through the pictures on her desk while she was gone. Every one of them was a different girl. Amazing. But I couldn't figure it out. Where'd he get all these pictures of all these different girls? Did he really think they were all of Galatea? And which one was the real Galatea? Which one was missing, and possibly dead?

Detective Suárez-Balart came back with my Coke. "Here you go," she said, big smile on her face. She had freshened up her make-up. Never let them see you cry, right, detective?

She peered at the pictures over my shoulder. "There was no chance Remy could tell these girls apart when we interviewed him, especially with these low-quality printouts. Their faces are too close to one another. Heck, Igs, you couldn't even tell them apart at first."

"Guess Remy's not the only one who's face-blind," I said. But something was bugging me. "You know what, detective? They don't just look alike. They all have the same haircut. Straight, just past the shoulder, a little bit of bangs, not too much, and no highlights."

"It's not an unusual style."

"Yeah, but six random high school girls, all with the same unpopular haircut, all on the same guy's phone? That's a lot of coincidence right there." I could feel my brain speeding up. "And look. In these two pictures, the girls are wearing a Yankees cap." I held up the shots: the one from the Yankees game and another outside a Papaya Dog. "The *same* Yankees cap."

She got a little closer to the pictures, which meant her mouth got a little closer to my ear. Damn, son. "They're both frayed in the same spot on the bill. They're wearing the same hat. They're *sharing* the same hat."

But I had it figured all out before she had even finished that sentence. "And you know what, detective? It's a small world."

She didn't get it right away, but she looked at the pictures, and then her eyebrows almost touched her hairline, and then she snatched all the pictures from me and rifled through them, one after the other, and then slammed them down on her desk, triumphant. She said, "It is a small world, after all."

It wasn't hard to find them, even though Remy wasn't talking. I knew where he went for tutoring. By the time I showed up in front of Detective Suárez-Balart's desk after school the next day, they had all six girls in six separate questioning rooms, complete with parents and lawyers. It wasn't no *Law & Order* drama, either: every last one of those good girls cracked in minutes.

So there are these six girls. Smart and nice, upper-middle money: but no bootie, no boobs, no boyfriends. The kind of girls who grow into women who will one day have good careers and make good money and find good men and make good babies. But right now their lives feel like they're missing out on everything. Believe me, I know the feeling. Someday, Rosario.

They find each other through their extra-curriculars, and they recognize each other instantly. They form a kind of plain-Jane Legion of Doom. They hang out all day, text and Facebook each other all night, have slumber parties on the weekends. Life is better. If only they had boyfriends.

There's this Dominican guy who comes to tutoring. Pretty tall, really handsome and dark enough to scare their parents. He's a poet, a rapper, and he's from the Bronx, a place as foreign to their lives as darkest Peru. He's smart, yet ghetto; street, yet gentle. Dangerous and safe, all in one.

Slowly, after months of tutoring, he confides in them his big secret. He's face-blind. He's so sorry for all the times he's called one of them by the wrong name. But he tells them that face-blindness is a gift. It lets him see real beauty. Even though he can't make out their faces, he knows all of them are beautiful. My man Remy knows how to sweet-talk.

They all have a crush on him, hard. How could they not? Each girl wants him for herself, of course, but no one wants to betray the Legion of Doom. These are smart girls; they can see a tragedy in the making, and six girls fighting over the same *chulo* has a *King Lear* body-count written all over it. What can they do?

At a slumber party, passing a bottle of Remy Martin—that's all they drank now—they group-thunk a plan. A brilliant, impossible plan. Remy was face-blind; he could barely tell them apart. And if they got the same haircut and dyed their hair the same and wore Disney earrings all the time, it'd be even harder for him. So what if they invented a girl who was all of them, someone they could take turns pretending to be? Thus, Galatea was born. Galatea. Yeah, now I get it.

They went to a Disney Store and bought out all the earrings it had. They made her a Facebook page and a Twitter feed so whoever's turn it was to play her could let the others know everything about their dates—with a lie this complicated, full disclosure was key. They were insanely jealous when it wasn't their turn to be Galatea and blissfully happy when it was. They made it work for six months.

Until one day Dorothy Lambert's moms went snooping through her phone and found out her perfect daughter had been sexting with a tall dark Dominican boy from the wrong borough.

The only thing Dorothy could do is lie to her moms like she'd never lied before. Her moms would believe anything as long as she didn't have to believe that her daughter was seeing some thug-life Dominican. "Remy's not my boyfriend," said Dorothy. "He's Galatea's."

Then Dorothy sends out an APB that Galatea's been compromised. These smart girls, they planned for everything. They knew their parents all talked to each other that Dorothy's moms would be following up with their moms and dads. There'd be a lot more snooping, a lot more hacked Facebook accounts. And Galatea couldn't just be erased, because that would look fishy. They had to get rid of her.

So Dorothy writes Galatea's suicide Facebook post.

The flaw in the plan: to cover themselves, the girls had Galatea friend every anonymous stranger they could. No one Remy knew, mind you; that would have made the lie harder to maintain. But when you have 3,600 Facebook friends, even friends you don't really know, someone's gonna take action when you announce that life isn't worth living anymore. Before the girls can do damage control, several anonymous tips go to the police that there's this girl on Facebook who sounds suicidal.

And Galatea's Facebook says she's "in a relationship" with this guy named Roberto Colón. Who on his own Facebook page calls himself Remy Mo. Guess where the police start their investigation?

The girls were in trouble, but they'd be okay. With the police, at least. At home, well, that's a different story. Do people with money still send their daughters to convents?

Remy and me after school at George's; he's treating for pizza. Kids at school have heard I whispered him out of jail, which is good for me. But they've also heard he was in jail, and that's great for him. Now the *puto* needs a whip and chair to keep the ladies at bay. Good for him: long as he stays the hell away from Rosario.

Around the hunk of pizza in my mouth I said, "You knew Galatea was fake, didn't you?"

He was just about to bite down on his slice. Just left his mouth open, looking at me. Then he said, "Yeah."

"Their voices. Fool your eyes, sure. But there's no way they could've fooled your ears."

"Yeah. They tried. They gave Galatea a vaguely European accent. It was hard not to laugh."

"So why didn't you tell the cops they were looking for a missing girl who didn't exist?"

Remy finally took that bite, took his time munching it. Then he said, "I didn't want them to get in trouble. I kind of loved them all, I think. It was sweet, man, all those girls thinking they could share the same guy, so they all could be in love. It touched me." He double-punched his heart. "Right here."

I sucked a little Coke, preparing the next question. "So why didn't you tell me, man? Thought I was your friend."

Remy laughed. "Your dumb ass couldn't tell them apart either. How many times I show you pictures of them? Kept waiting for the day you'd say, 'Hey now, that ain't the same girl. What's up, Remy?' Everyone thinks you so smart, but I know the truth. You better hope I don't tell them at Bronx Science how stupid you really are. Kick yo ass out on the street."

"You're the one who's face-blind," I said and sucked my drink. Lame, but it was all I had.

And anyway, it just set him up. "I got brain damage, son. You just stupid."

Puto made me spit Coke.

A Starring Role

Bertha Jacobson

If I had to describe knowing Natalia Cruz, I would say it was like riding the Poltergeist rollercoaster at Six Flags Fiesta Texas: You never knew what was coming next. But, perhaps, I should start at the beginning.

My theater class had spent the better part of my high school junior year devising a musical version for *Daughter of Fortune*, the acclaimed book from Chilean writer Isabel Allende. Even though I'm not a great singer, when it came time to produce the play during my senior year, I expected to get the main character's role of Eliza Sommers. Well, I didn't. Natalia Cruz did.

I'm not going to say I wasn't jealous at first. How could she, a new student who had just moved from Mexico two weeks before, take what was rightfully mine?

But even I could see that she had an outstanding audition. Her petite figure, long black hair, olive skin and powerful singing made her a very believable Eliza Sommers. Whereas I, with my gawky 5'8" frame, green eyes and less than melodious voice would have had to be a fabulous actress to convince the audience. I admit I was a better fit for the role of Miss Rose, the exotic British aunt who raised Eliza.

"Brianna, what are you doing after rehearsal today?" Natalia said as she approached me one afternoon.

I shrugged, still upset about what I considered her usurpation of my rights.

"Can you take me to the mall? My cousin is getting married and I need to get a gown."

Now she wanted me to be her driver? That irked me even more. Yet, I felt sorry for her. I could still remember what it was like not to know anybody in this city.

We got into my 1999 Honda Accord and Natalia immediately took possession of my dear car. She connected her own iPod to my stereo and reaching out to my back seat, grabbed the SAT guide and the Berklee College of Music catalog I kept there. She casually turned the pages.

"Do you want to go to Berklee?"

"It's always been my dream, yeah."

"You don't really sing . . . " She stopped abruptly.

The truth hurts, but I managed a smile.

"I can write songs though; some of the songs in the musical are mine."

"Really? They are good, Brianna!"

"I'm hoping for a scholarship but I need to improve my SAT score. My parents have a college fund set aside, but Berklee's not cheap." I sighed thinking about the huge government contract my uncle's company had just signed. My cousins wouldn't need scholarships or grants; they were all fixed for college.

"No, it's not. I want to go to . . . New York . . . I think." She didn't sound too assured, so she changed the subject, "Why did you pick *Daughter of Fortune*?"

Instead of answering I turned off the music and started singing one of the verses from the musical. Natalia joined in:

If not looking for riches
then why, Eliza, why?
Risk your life as a stowaway,
dress yourself as a deaf Chinese guy,

and travel the plains as a gay piano player in disguise?
What are you after, Eliza?
The love of your life.
"That Gold Rush sure was wild. Wasn't it?"

I nodded. Allende's book had all the elements for a musical comedy.

"Great idea, Brianna, you have talent." Natalia patted my shoulder.

"It wasn't all mine, there were about six of us and Ms. Lara, of course."

"Yeah, my parents and I researched the schools in San Antonio. Ms. Lara's theatre reputation is remarkable."

"Why did you guys move here?" I wanted to know.

"Crime in Mexico is out of hand."

I nodded. San Antonio had grown a lot in recent years. Many middle class families from Mexico had moved to our city trying to flee the escalating violence.

"I'm surprised you have no accent at all. Your English is great!"

"I'm just like Eliza Sommers," Natalia quipped, "I spoke English at home and Spanish elsewhere."

"Well, I guess I am the opposite." I said, explaining that both my parents were from Mexico and were adamant that we spoke Spanish at home.

A well-groomed man in his twenties approached the mall entrance at the same time we did and rushed to open the door for us. It appeared as if he had come out of a fashion magazine; his clothes didn't have a single wrinkle and were a perfect fit. He reminded me of a famous boxer whose name escaped me. Natalia Cruz went in like a queen, without thanking him or even looking at him; I mumbled a clumsy "Thanks!"

That afternoon, I learned a lot about Natalia. Her poise was impressive. She walked with the grace of a ballerina: her back straight, forehead high and feet barely touching the ground. She must have modeled at least twenty designer dresses in front of me at the most exclusive stores in the mall; and soon, I found myself fetching for her.

"Get me the lavender scarf and the pink stiletto shoes."

"Now bring me the polka dot mini dress on the display, and ask the saleslady if it comes in size zero." All without a single "please" or "thank you."

Who did she think she was, anyway? I have to admit I was ambivalent about the experience. While I didn't like the way she treated me, I was being fully entertained. Her gregarious nature kept me interested in her non-stop conversation.

When I saw the price tag on the dress she selected for her cousin's wedding, I gasped. Six hundred dollars for one dress? Frugality was not in *her* dictionary. I thought of all the cute outfits I could get at "Otra Vez," the consignment shop I often visited with Mom.

We left the last store with an array of beautiful clothes, shoes and purses for Natalia's big evening. When she bought a frosty, Natalia casually asked me to hold her shopping bags. Not in a servile mood, I was about to complain when I saw the man who had opened the door for us earlier. Natalia didn't seem to notice him, but I did. My blood froze when he tilted his head in recognition and gave me a crooked, nicotine-stained smile garnished with a gold-rimmed tooth. This time, looking past his fashionable garments, I thought he looked rather creepy, almost sinister. But when I turned my head to see if he was following us, he had vanished. Maybe I was just getting jumpy because Natalia kept talking about crime and violence in Mexico. I got more than an earful with her telling me about these pernicious thugs who stalk then abduct students right outside their school; she explained the "kidnap express" method used by low-lives wanting to get only a few thousand dollars in ransom money. She went on and on about some children in her school, the offspring of drug lords from opposing cartels, and how their parents were amiable to each other whenever they met at school-related activities, but then you'd hear on the news that the last drive-by shooting had been carried out by one of them in order to execute the other.

"What a terrible place to live!" I said feeling sorry for her. We were now sitting at the food court. Even amid the garish food advertisements and displays, I felt a darker, more ominous mood color my thoughts.

"Not very different from the Gold Rush," Natalia observed nonchalantly, imitating the British accent she used for her role as Eliza Sommers. "I even bought a hand gun and kept it in my purse for a while."

"Are you serious? Did you ever use it?" My heart skipped a beat; I had never met anyone like her.

"I almost did once. Later, when my dad's brother was brutally murdered and the anonymous phone calls started coming, I freaked out. I had a nervous breakdown and we planned my move to San Antonio virtually overnight. My parents will come and join me as soon as . . . "

I was no longer listening to Natalia's story. The creepy man, leaning against the railing not twenty yards away from us, was cleaning his fingernails with a sharp pocket knife. He looked our way and I swear he smiled at me, sending shivers down my spine. With the pocket knife still in his hand, he started toward us. I grabbed Natalia by one arm virtually lifting her from her seat and unintentionally spilling the frosty on her lap.

"What the hell . . . ?" She tried to fight me but must have noticed my fear and felt the urgency in my clenched fingers.

"Shh, don't say anything!" I dragged her as fast as I could to the ladies' restroom.

"What is wrong with you, Brianna?" She reproved me as she stood by the sink and washed the mess off her designer jeans.

Panting, I told her about the predator. Her eyes shone in alarm and all the color left her face.

"You are an idiot!" She chastised me with tears filling her eyes. She scanned the bathroom for a way out. "The last place you want to go when someone is after you is in an enclosed place like this. What do you know about survival anyway, you stupid *gringa*?"

"I have my cell phone. I can call 9-1-1 or security; it's only one man, Natalia. I don't think he's with anybody else." I pulled my cell phone out of my pocket and Natalia rubbed her forehead while thinking of a way to escape.

We heard a gentle knock on the door.

"Oh, no!" I started praying and closed my eyes while holding tight to Natalia's wet hand. Was it perspiration or water? Weird things come to my mind when I am nervous.

"Aghhhhh!" She howled.

A stronger knock, and yet another one.

"*¿Señorita Cruz?*"

It was a male voice and Natalia released my hand to open the door.

"Nooooo!" I yelled.

"*¿Está bien, señorita?*"

"Is this the man who was following us?" She asked me with her voice suddenly under control without any trace of tears or nervousness.

I nodded, not being able to utter a sound. I really had to pee now.

"Brianna, this is Martín Lugo, my bodyguard."

"*Mucho gusto, Señorita Brianna.*" His odd smile again. He was not tall at all, maybe only as tall as me.

"Your bodyguard?" I asked astonished.

"What did you expect, Denzel Washington?" She then addressed the man in Spanish.

"Estamos bien, Martín. Esta tonta pensó que me estabas siguiendo."

"Pues sí, sí la estaba siguiendo, señorita, ése es mi trabajo."

I noticed the man's candor.

"You should have told me you had a bodyguard!" I reproached Natalia. The whole debacle could have been avoided, if she had been upfront with me. My heartbeat returned to normal. Who was Natalia Cruz, and why would she need a bodyguard in San Antonio?

"I just wanted to blend in. Do you think I'll get any dates if everyone knows Martín is glued to me around the clock?"

Not expecting me to understand, she shook her head and rolled her eyes; then she checked the time on her cell phone.

"Well, I better get going. Thanks for bringing me to the mall, Brianna. It was interesting."

She took the shopping bags still wrapped around my wrist and passed them to Martín. I felt patronized when she patted my cheek, but I didn't dwell on it. I really had to pee.

Natalia was discrete enough not to tell anybody about our "adventure" at the mall and I returned the favor by not disclosing the existence of her bodyguard. Our mutual secret became a bond, and we started hanging out together more and more. I didn't bring her home because I didn't feel like explaining the bodyguard to my parents, but we became Facebook friends and would talk all the time. We were also in the same Spanish class during fourth period, so we would walk together to lunch. Martha Perales, my best friend, questioned me.

"It's just because of theater; not a big deal." That wasn't true. I have to confess I revered Natalia's glamorous lifestyle. After all, she had a bodyguard and was able to spend six hundred dollars on a single dress. She also had a brand new Lexus, good acting skills, a starring role in the play and a beautiful singing voice . . . must I say more? Yet, I sensed a dark side in her personality and I often pondered what she was concealing and who would want to hurt her.

When my parents left for a weekend church retreat and my younger sister went to spend the night at a friend's house, I invited the girls from theater to a "reading lines" party that did not turn out at all as I expected, as everybody kept texting and taking phone calls. I suggested we did the same thing we do in Ms. Lara's class. "Let's put all cell phones in a basket and give them timeout." Seeing my frustration, they agreed and by nine o'clock we were focusing on our lines.

"You know, ladies, when I was taking theater in Mexico," Natalia said, "everybody had to learn at least one additional role besides her own. That way in case of sickness or, heaven forbid, 'kidnap express' problems, the show could go on. We should do the same."

We looked at each other. Natalia's constant allusions to the Mexican violence crisis were wearing us out. Every other sentence was a reference to someone suffering from some type of atrocity, the latest news in the cartels or carnage in her hometown. In other words, the same hackneyed border news. We simply nodded and worked diligently until midnight when I suggested we watch a scary movie. All agreed, except Natalia.

"Come on, don't be a wimp," Stella teased.

Begrudgingly, Natalia twisted her mouth and sank on the couch with an indolent expression.

The movie started: A gloomy, foreboding night. A young woman in a trench coat and the sound of high heels as she walks down an empty street. Then, a sudden thump followed by another thump behind her. She turns back but can't see anyone amid the dense fog. Lightning and thunder in the background.

"Give me a break!" Natalia stopped the movie with the remote control. "This is ludicrous. Fog and rain are not necessary to commit a crime!"

"It's a movie, Natalia. Don't spoil it for us!" Luz María pled.

"Tell you what, Natalia, why don't you just lay off? We are normal teenagers; we have not been poisoned by the stupid crime in your country. If you don't like it, just leave!" Stella's animosity was pretty obvious when she stood up and jerked the control out of Natalia's hand.

"That's exactly what I am going to do, *cabrona*." Natalia's voice reached a high pitch.

"Come on, girls," I tried to mediate. I didn't want them quarreling at my place.

"See you later, Brianna." Natalia said, ignoring the other two girls and walking toward the door without waiting for me. Martín Lugo, vigilant as always, stood ready outside. I wondered if he had been standing there all evening. His face was in the shadows but I saw the tip of his cigarette light up as he inhaled. Upon seeing Natalia, he quickly dropped it to the ground and stomped it out.

The door slammed and an awkward silence filled the living room. We heard the roar of her car engine accelerating down the street and the screeching of tires as she turned the corner. We didn't speak until the sound of her engine died in the distance. Stella gave out a sigh of relief.

"She gets on my nerves!"

"You are so right!" Luz María seconded.

"And that bodyguard of hers . . . he gives me the shivers!"

Natalia had not been able to hide her bodyguard too long.

"Come on, girls, don't vilify him. He's just doing his job." I interceded.

"What is it with you and your elegant words, Brianna? Nobody uses 'vilify' anymore." Luz María lightened the mood by making fun of me.

"Well, if I don't use those dumb SAT words, I don't remember them!"

We all laughed and went back to our scary movie, but not for long. Not ten minutes later, the carbon monoxide detector in my parents' room shrieked loudly and we found ourselves in total darkness.

I walked toward the window. The street was empty and all other houses were lit.

"Maybe one of the breakers tripped," I said, keeping calm. My dad had shown me the box outside the house, next to the garage wall, but I had no idea how to fix it. I felt my way to the kitchen where my parents kept a flashlight but couldn't find it. They had probably taken it on their weekend trip.

"Luz María, are you there?" Stella's voice quivered.

"Yes, I'm here. Hold on to my hand." She, too, sounded scared.

"I don't like this. Can you do something, Brianna?"

"I'm trying!" We kept another flashlight with our camping gear, but that was up in the storage room.

"What about our cell phones?" Their tiny display lights would be enough to let us look for candles.

With my hands against the wall, I felt my way to the foyer where earlier we had placed all the cell phones inside a basket right by the front door. The basket was gone!

"I think Natalia took all of our cell phones!" I moaned.

Just then, we heard a string of explosions in my backyard.

"What the . . . !" Luz María yelled and fled to my side.

"Wait for me!" Stella wailed and tried to get to us but crashed into something and fell. "Talk to me, Brianna. Let me follow your voice." She whimpered.

The three of us cuddled together in a big hug. We were still shaking when a second succession of detonations went off. They sounded like gun shots.

"Let's get out of here!" I said and tried to open the door, but it wouldn't budge. It was locked and there was no key.

Panic-stricken, we couldn't think straight. Bawling and out of breath, we prattled nonsense. The sound of the carbon monoxide alarm took us by surprise, and we all screamed when the power returned. Sounds emerging from the T.V. that had come back to life startled us, and we looked at each other not really knowing what to expect.

The doorbell rang. We were by the door but I couldn't open it.

"Who . . . is . . . it?" I asked in a trembling voice.

"It's me, Natalia. I unintentionally took the cell phones and your keys."

Unintentionally? Bull! I thought to myself.

She opened the door from the outside and looked at us impassively. The basket of cell phones was in her hand.

"Did you ladies enjoy being scared?" She didn't sound scornful or mean, just matter of fact.

"You spoiled bitch!" Stella attempted to slap Natalia, but the zealous bodyguard materialized out of nowhere and stopped her.

"*A la señorita nadie la toca.*" He whispered, but his soft voice contained the chilling threat of what he might be capable of, and I remembered Natalia telling me that he was armed.

"I'm sorry, but you needed this lesson to understand me. It's terrifying, isn't it?" Tears burst from her eyes and soon the three of us were crying along with her.

"We're sorry, Natalia," Luz María and I said.

"I guess I'm sorry, too." Stella shrugged intimidated by Martín. I could tell her apology stemmed out of fear, not conviction.

"No hard feelings?" Natalia asked, giving us her most charming smile.

We all smiled back at her.

"Well, then, let's celebrate!" she said, producing a bottle of tequila. "There are some perks associated with an indulgent bodyguard." She turned to her fervent protector. "*Buenas noches,* Martín." Then she closed the door, leaving the man outside.

We never went back to the movie. Natalia showed us how to drink tequila shots. "*¡Para arriba, para abajo, para un lado, para el otro, para afuera, para adentroooo!*" She chanted as her hand went up, down, to the right, to the left, outwards and then she gulped it all at once. After a few rounds, we were feeling pretty giddy and a myriad of confidences started to pour out. Luz María told us about her crush on the History teacher and between hiccups, Stella started to moon us, only to reveal a green dragon tattoo on her left bun. I laughed so hard I fell off the couch.

I confessed my aversion to roller coasters and admitted I had never been able to ride the Poltergeist at Six Flags. Then, it was Natalia's turn. With a grave look, she lifted up her shirt and we all expected another tattoo. None of us were prepared for her secret. She revealed a midriff full of tiny little scars that reminded me of an abstract design. Her life had spun out of control, she explained, and she felt her problems were way over her head. Cutting herself was her way out. All of our confessions were petty compared to Natalia's. Her glamour and money couldn't make up for the pain.

When we ran out of secrets, we cried, danced, sang and continued drinking until the tequila was all gone. I must have blacked out because the next thing I remember is waking up in the morning to the alluring aroma of *chilaquiles* and *pozole*.

Martín was mopping the floor outside the bathroom, while nasty noises came from the inside. Luz María was sick.

"*Traje comida para la cruda, Señorita Brianna.*"

"*Gracias.*" I mumbled but didn't move. Somebody was drilling inside my brain.

Natalia woke up with a ravenous appetite, but I couldn't take a single bite from the culinary feast. By the time my parents arrived, all the girls had gone home and the house was impeccable, thanks to Martín's conscientious work. There was no trace of what had happened the previous night. However, Mom called me into her bedroom.

"Brianna Marie Montemayor, come over here."

She used my full name, and that was the first indication that I was in trouble. When I came in, she had her hands over her hips in her pose of a Spanish inquisitor and Dad stood by the dresser looking stern. Either she had ESP or a webcam installed at our house.

"Do you have something to tell us?"

A stagnant silence followed. I had once read that whoever breaks the silence first, loses. My parental adversaries probably knew this too because I lost.

"What do you mean?"

"Brianna, don't play games with me. I didn't raise you that way."

"The girls from drama club came to spend the night. We were practicing for the play."

"And . . . " My mother tapped her foot on the floor.

"It got out of hand?" I ventured. I wasn't about to disclose anything.

"Firecrackers? A man sleeping inside a car? The neighborhood patrol coming over?"

I didn't know anything about the patrol coming over; Martín must have handled that one himself. Mom's comments were all about outside activities, nothing from the inside. Nosy neighbors, of course! Ms. Salas came to my mind. That meddlesome lady spent all her time spying from her living room.

"It was a bad prank Natalia played on us."

"Who is Natalia?"

"Natalia Cruz is a girl that just moved from Mexico and has a bodyguard."

"Why would she need a bodyguard?"

"Her parents are important down there and they fear for her safety."

"Did you say her last name is Cruz?"

"'Cruz,' like Penelope."

She looked at Dad.

"You don't think she's related to that prominent Cruz man murdered recently, do you?"

I hated the fact that my mother kept up with Mexican news.

"She came to San Antonio when her uncle was killed." I said.

"Brianna, dear," Mom's voice changed from upset to concerned. "I know I have always told you to treat everybody fairly, but a girl with a bodyguard has no place in our lives. You may be risking your own safety. If the Mexican mob is involved, this is serious business."

"I feel sorry for her, she doesn't know anybody."

"It's not a matter of being nice, Brianna, you must protect yourself."

I bit my lip and went to my room relieved mom had not mentioned the drinking. Once there, I used my laptop to google "Cruz murder Mexico." My heart sank. Tons of hits, including gory pictures of the murdered uncle at the crime scene. I felt sick to my stomach but continued looking. I googled "Kidnap express Mexico secuestro." My mother was right. This was way over my head. I would distance myself from Natalia. Just then, I got a message from her on Facebook.

"HEY, WANT TO RIDE DOWN WITH US NEXT WEEK-END TO LAREDO FOR DRAMA CONVENTION?"

"NO THNX. THE BUS IS MORE FUN. YOU SHOULD COME ALONG TOO."

"I'M STUCK WITH MARTÍN. MY PARENTS HAVE A VILLA IN LAREDO; WANT TO STAY WITH ME?"

"THNX, NATALIA. I THINK I WILL STAY AT THE HOTEL WITH ALL THE GUYS."

I was normally more talkative, so she must have noticed my aloofness.

"R U OK?"

"MOM FOUND OUT ABOUT LAST NIGHT AND SHE'S NOT HAPPY. GTG. SEE YOU @ SCHOOL."

Unbeknownst to me, Stella and Luz María had neither forgiven nor forgotten Natalia's unpleasant hoax at my house and they were planning to retaliate. That weekend in Laredo, during dress rehearsal, all hell broke loose.

It was a scene in which Eliza Sommers is under the influence of opium to mitigate boredom as a stowaway traveling to California. A prostitute, played by Stella, comes down to the belly of the ship and helps her bathe. A bucket full of translucent shiny confetti bits was supposed to be thrown at her; instead, they threw a bucket full of dirty, sticky, smelly muck that covered Natalia from head to toe.

Martín ran to the stage and lifted her at once. He attempted to clean her up with his handkerchief but soon realized the small piece of cloth was useless. He looked around the room for the culprits and his rigid expression gave me the shivers.

Ms. Lara interrupted the rehearsal, while I offered Natalia my hotel room so she could clean up.

"This act will not go unpunished, guys, it is against school policy, you know!" I heard Ms. Lara's harsh voice as we left the hall.

Natalia showered and then borrowed some of my clothes, too big for her petite frame. Without a word, she dropped herself onto my bed and curled up into a ball. Even though her eyes were open, she was listless.

"Natalia, are you okay?" I asked, without getting a response. After a few minutes, I called Martín, who was waiting outside the hotel room.

"I may need to give her a shot." He said. "I don't have the medicine here. It's at her parents' place. Can you come with us? I need somebody to watch her."

"What is wrong with her, Martín?" I asked.

"The poor girl is a mess," he said, and I noticed for the first time that he spoke English.

Martín drove in silence while Natalia's head rested on my lap in the back seat of her brand-new Lexus. I dug into my pants to get my cell phone only to realize I had left it back in Ms. Lara's timeout basket. I wasn't familiar with the city of Laredo, didn't know where we were going and didn't pay any attention to the road. It was a beautiful day and I basked under the warm rays of the sun filtering inside the car. Natalia's lassitude worried me and I caressed her wet hair impregnated with the smell of cheap hotel shampoo. Natalia, who only used the finest products, didn't seem to care. I remembered my mom's advice and knew it was time to end our friendship or whatever it is that we had. Natalia had arrived only two months ago, yet it seemed like an eternity. She was needy and high maintenance, and her tension was rubbing off on me. This was my senior year in high school, and it should be the best time of my life.

The modern villa was sparsely furnished. Martín carried Natalia to a bedroom and gave her a shot; after that, he led me down to the kitchen to eat a quick lunch.

"Did you have anything to do with what they did to Natalia?" Martín asked me while his cool eyes scanned my face.

I didn't have time to answer because we heard someone come into the house from the garage. I expected to see Natalia's parents but instead, I faced three men in ski masks.

One of the masked men motioned for me to get into the closet under the stairs.

"You have the wrong girl!" I whimpered and looked at Martín.

"No, they don't." Natalia replied. She had walked from the bedroom without us hearing her. She was wide awake and her face was plastered with an enigmatic expression. She shoved me into the closet and just before she shut the door, Martín rested his hand on Natalia's waist. It was not a protective gesture . . . it was . . . as if they were a couple!

"Natalia!" I begged.

"Thanks, Brianna Montemayor. Naive girls like you have turned Facebook into a gold mine."

"Nataliaaaaaa!" I yelled in the dimly lit closet.

"Not my real name, of course. It's just another role I played. I really hope that your rich uncle will pay, for your sake." She answered.

A menacing silence followed.

The closet is long and empty, lit only by a single low-wattage bulb. I can stand up at the entrance but then the ceiling takes on the slope of the stairs. There is a small table and a tiny chair, like the ones little girls use to play house. On top of the table there is a writing pad, a pen and an SAT guide. Did Natalia leave the guide here as a sign of sympathy?

I have screamed and yelled to no avail. The door is firmly secured. I'm sure I won't make it back in time for rehearsal and I wonder who will play my role, or how they will justify my absence. "Kidnap express" comes to my mind, and I recall my ecstatic Facebook posting about the bundles of money my uncle would make on that new contract. Deep down, though, I expect the closet door to open at any moment and to hear Natalia's matter-of-fact voice tell me that this is just another one of her real-life lessons.

All the Facts, A to Z

Diana López

I used to go by Abigail Zúñiga, but that was before my journalism teacher kicked me off *What's News?*, the paper at my
school.

"You should try creative writing," she said.

"I don't want to make stuff up. I want to be a reporter."

"Reporters get their facts first. *All* the facts, A to Z." She
straightened a few papers, then added, "Write a retraction before
you head home. You should know how to do that by now."

She was right. I'd been writing lots of retractions. The first
was for my story about the blackout in the Freshman wing,
"Powerful vs. Powerless: Seniors Unfairly Siphon Electricity
from the Freshman Energy Grid." Was it my fault the custodian
wasn't specific when he told me the breaker kept tripping? He
never mentioned that the art teacher had turned on a hairdryer
and five fans to speed-dry the paintings in her class. And how
about my prize-worthy piece, "The School Cafeteria: Kitchen or
Coffin?" I tried to save lives with that one. I sincerely believed
Nick was case zero for a food poisoning epidemic after he vom-
ited cheese pizza all over LaTonya's backpack. I didn't know he
was about to give a speech and that standing before the public
was his number one fear. And now, I had to write a retraction for
"Coded Confession: Winning Slam Dunks Due to Doping." This
little misunderstanding happened after the starting forward told

me that "sipping the magic juice" kept the basketball team from burning out. Who knew "magic juice" meant Gatorade? I honestly thought it was a metaphor for steroids.

I turned in my paper and headed home. Luckily, it was a short walk. Cross two streets and make two lefts. I could do it with my eyes closed. I knew where the mean dogs lived and when to watch for bird poop. The scene was as familiar as my mother's *chiles rellenos*—that is, until I noticed my neighbor's car, half a block from where it should be. No doubt about it. This car belonged to Mrs. Garza. No one else had a gray sedan with a row of bobble-head bulldogs along the rear window. Then I saw Mrs. Garza herself. She was peering through some bushes. When the wind lifted her housedress, I saw knee-highs instead of full pantyhose.

"What are you doing?" I asked.

She jumped, a bit startled. "Oh, Abigail. I thought all the kids had walked home already."

"They have, but I had to write something after school." I pointed to her hands. "Why do you have binoculars?"

"These?" she said, nervously. "I was out for a walk. Trying to stay in shape. And bird watching. Yes, bird watching. It's an old people thing."

"Yeah, I guess. But if you're out for a walk, why's your car parked over there?"

She glanced at it. "So that's where it is!" she exclaimed. "Thank goodness you found it."

"You didn't know where it was?"

"Nope. Couldn't remember. First, I was bird watching and then I was looking for my car. You know how old people lose things."

I nodded. After all, poor Mrs. Garza kept losing her dogs. She'd had three this past year. They barked at all hours, and then they ran away when she forgot to close her gate. She had adopted another one last week, a big-headed white dog with watery eyes and giant paws. He drove my grandma nuts with all his barking.

"I guess I'll take my car home." She reached in her pocket and jiggled her keys.

I watched her drive away, then followed on foot, wishing I had my license already. I couldn't wait till I took driver's ed. Next summer.

My parents got divorced two years ago, so I lived at my grandma's with my mother and older sister, Belinda. Uncle Emilio practically lived there, too. He had his own place, but since he was single, he often stopped by, especially on Fridays.

"Hello!" I called as I walked in. "Grandma, are you here?" I heard the patio door. "What were you doing outside?"

"Taking care of things."

"What things?"

"Just things," she said. She took a rag from the pocket of her apron and started dusting her *santitos*. She had three long shelves in the living room, each filled with statues of Jesus, Mary and the saints. These weren't the peaceful-looking statues like at church. These were full of pain and suffering—Jesus bleeding from his hands and feet, Mary crying, John the Baptist holding his chopped-off head and blind St. Lucy, offering a platter like any regular waitress, only hers had eyeballs on it.

"All day long," Grandma complained, "that dog next door barks. At everything! Cars, squirrels, the wind. I already called la Señora Garza. She told me to get used to it. Can you believe that? Get used to it? When I've lived here for thirty-five years? I shouldn't have to get used to anything! I got a headache from all that barking."

"I don't hear him right now."

"Of course not. That crazy lady left her gate open again. He probably ran away."

I was tempted to bring up Mrs. Garza's misplaced car, but instead I said, "She sure can be forgetful."

"Today was the last straw," Grandma went on. "Let me show you what I found." I followed her to the back patio. Her foot nudged a white plastic bag. Something brown, red and oozy was in it.

"What is it?" I asked.

"A dead cat."

"That's gross, Grandma!"

"Of course, it is. That's why I put it in this bag. Who wants to see something so ugly? I found this poor thing by the fence this morning. Mrs. Garza's dog tore its belly out."

I grabbed my stomach, partly because I imagined a dog bite there and partly because I wanted to throw up.

"Don't overreact," Grandma said. "I need you to do something. Take this cat to the dumpster behind Culebra Meat Market."

"Are you kidding? Why can't we throw it in *our* trash?"

She slapped the back of my head. "Don't be a *tonta*. You want maggots all over the place next time you take out the garbage?"

"But, Grandma, that man at Culebra Meat Market is so protective about his dumpster. Remember when we tried to throw out that broken chair? He won't even let us toss in our soda cans. And don't forget you owe him five dollars."

"He overcharged me," she said.

"No, he didn't. You *under*paid. I heard you tell him you'd be back with the rest of the money."

Grandma ignored me. "Go through the alley," she said. "If you're quick, he won't see you."

She stepped inside, closed the screen door and quickly locked it.

"Are you locking me out of the house?"

"I'll let you back in after you go to the dumpster." She nodded toward the dead cat. "Hurry, before it starts to stink."

I loved my grandma, but sometimes, I hated her too. She always embarrassed me. Like the book bag she made me carry.

She had woven it from the plastic rings that hold six-packs of soda. It was so ugly! But she insisted and told me I was saving the environment. As if I cared! And then, she made me eat a jar of baby food with every meal because she believed that if the preservatives could keep the carrots orange, they could keep my hair brown. Since when did a sixteen-year-old have to worry about gray hair? How could I forget the time she sent me to Walgreen's to buy anti-aging face cream, cans of Ensure, Rolaids, *Reader's Digest* and these little strips she wore on her nose to keep from snoring? And with my bad luck, I ran into Analisa from my fourth period class. She was buying something cool. Diet pills, I think. When she saw my basket, she asked, "What's all that old people stuff for?" How humiliating!

That's how I felt with this dead cat I was lugging to the dumpster. One hundred percent humiliated.

Luckily, when I reached the alley, the market's back door was closed. I tiptoed to the dumpster and slowly lifted the lid, but before I could throw in the cat, I heard, "What are you doing?!" When I turned, I saw the Culebra Meat Market man waving a corncob at me, his mouth all greasy from the butter. "You think this is public property?" he yelled. "What you got in there? Hey, come back! I know who you are. You're that Zúñiga girl. Tell your grandma she owes me five bucks!"

I ran as hard as I could, nearly reaching my street before noticing I still had the cat. I tossed it over a fence. Let someone else bury it.

This time when I got home, everyone was there—Mom, Belinda and Uncle Emilio.

"What do you think?" Mom asked as she twirled in a new black dress. Before I could answer, she said, "Wait, let me put on my accessories."

"You bought accessories, too?" Belinda said. Then she turned to me, "I can't believe she spent money on new clothes *and* accessories."

My uncle sat on the sofa, watching the afternoon news.

"Emilio," Grandma said, "go outside and turn on the front sprinkler. Make sure no water gets on the sidewalk."

"Okay. I'll go during a commercial."

Grandma switched off the T.V. "Commercial time," she said.

My poor uncle went outside, grumbling to himself.

Then Mom returned. She wore a pendant made of big red stones and a black *rebozo* with roses printed on it. She had new heels too.

"You look like a babe!" I exclaimed.

"She looks like a woman of the streets," Grandma said.

"How much did all that cost?" Belinda asked.

Just then, Uncle Emilio stepped inside. He was soaked.

"Oh, I forgot to mention," Grandma said. "I need a new washer for that spigot. It squirts all over the place. Maybe next week you can fix it." My uncle sighed as he removed his shirt. Then he picked up the remote, but before he could push any buttons, Grandma said, "In the backyard tree, there's a plastic bag stuck on the branches. Been there for days. It's driving me crazy. I don't want the neighbors to think I'm so messy that I got trash in my yard. Get the ladder and take it down, will you?"

"Ma," he said, "I want to watch the news."

"What news? There's a traffic jam on the Loop, but you're not in your car, so why do you care? Everything else is about gang shootings. Are you in a gang? No! So what does it matter?"

"*Ya, ya . . .*" he said as he headed outside.

"So how much did all that cost?" Belinda asked again.

"It doesn't matter," Mom said. "I have a date tonight. It's been a long time since I've gone on a real date, so I want to look nice. I can spend my money however I want."

"*After* you meet your children's needs," Belinda argued. "Isn't that right, Abigail?"

"I meet your needs," Mom said. "You have a roof over your head, don't you? You have food in your belly. Clothes on your back."

"But what about my senior trip? I *need* to go. It's an educational opportunity."

"To Cancún?"

"Yes, to Cancún. There's lots of history there. We'll be taking a day trip to the pyramids."

"And you'll be taking night trips to the clubs," Mom said. "I know what people do there. I already told you. I'm not paying for an extracurricular trip. If you want to have fun, then get a job and earn your own money."

"Even if I got a job today, I wouldn't earn enough. I need the down payment by Monday."

Most of the time, I hated being the younger sister. Belinda had beaten me to all the cool stuff like wearing make-up and dating boys. But luckily, she made all her mistakes first, too—taking government with Mr. Domínguez, the meanest teacher on campus, and failing to save money for her senior trip. No way was I taking Mr. Domínguez, and no way would I be broke when senior trip time came around. Being two years younger than Belinda meant I had two years to save my money.

Uncle Emilio stepped in again. He had a big welt on his forehead. "There was a bee's nest in that tree."

"I know," Grandma said.

"You knew? Why didn't you tell me?"

"If I told you, you wouldn't have climbed up there. You're always a wimp about bees." She examined his forehead and pinched out the stinger. Then she went to the utility closet and pulled out two mousetraps. "I heard some noises in the attic. I think we got rats. Set these up, and when you're finished, I got one for the garage, too."

"Wait a minute," Emilio said. "Can't I relax for a while?"

"If you want to relax, then go home."

Poor Uncle Emilio. It was Friday. He hated to be alone on Friday, so he grabbed the mousetraps and made his way to the attic.

"How about you?" Belinda said to Grandma. "You have money, right? Can you lend me some for the trip? I'll get a job when I return. I'll pay you back."

"What makes you think I have money?"

"You get social security checks, don't you? I know you cash them."

"Of course, I cash them. I need money for my medicines. And to pay for my stone and my plot!" Sickness and death always silenced us. "I'm sorry, *mija*, but I don't even have a roll of pennies to spare."

Belinda stomped out and slammed one of the doors in the hallway. She must have startled Uncle Emilio because we heard him shout, "San Antonio Alamo!" It was his way of cussing.

"What happened?" we said as he loped back.

"What do you think happened? That stupid mousetrap caught my finger." He held it up. His finger was bleeding a bit, but mostly it was black and blue.

"You want an icepack?" I asked.

He nodded, so I went to the fridge and put some ice in a Ziploc bag. Hopefully, it would help the swelling.

Soon after I returned to the living room, the doorbell rang. Mom opened it and introduced us to a very handsome man—her date. I wished my boyfriend looked like that. Okay, I didn't have a boyfriend. A couple of times, I'd gone out with a guy named Justin. He didn't have a car, so we had to take the bus everywhere. Justin had held my hand and kissed me, but a bus stop littered with cigarette butts and wadded burger wrappers didn't exactly inspire romance. At least we were still friends—on Facebook.

Mom's date politely greeted us but Grandma just grunted and eyed him suspiciously. Finally, she said, "My daughter's not really a woman of the streets. She just likes to dress like one."

"Don't start," Mom warned.

"Well, look at you, showing half your *chichis*. I don't want this man to think you're easy."

"Oh, my God!" Mom cried.

"It's okay," the man said, a bit amused. Then he turned to my grandma, "I promise to treat your daughter with the utmost respect."

"Well, you better. You'd be wasting your time anyhow, if you tried some hanky-panky. She's going through the change of life, you know."

"That's nobody's business, Ma."

"And even if she weren't," Grandma continued, "she can't have babies. So if you want a family, forget it. The doctors took out her womb last year. She had a horrible case of end-of-mitosis."

"You mean endometriosis," I corrected.

Grandma slapped the back of my head. "Don't talk back to me!"

"Will you excuse us?" Mom said to her date. "Wait in the car? I'll be there in a minute." After the drop-dead gorgeous man stepped out, Mom went straight to Grandma, got in her face like a tomboy about to fight. "How can you ruin this for me? You know how hard it's been since the divorce. How vulnerable I feel. For once, Ma. Stay out of it. I just want a fresh start here."

"Looks like you're starting fresh to me," Grandma said as she deliberately looked at Mom's cleavage.

Mom clenched her fists and growled. I could tell she wanted to punch Grandma, but that was a line she'd never cross.

"Come on," Uncle Emilio said. He put his arm around Mom and walked her to the door. "Go have fun. Don't let this get to you." She nodded and headed out. As soon as her date's car cleared the street, Uncle Emilio turned to Grandma. "You're mean," he said. "It's one thing to make me do all your ridiculous chores, but embarrassing my sister that way? That's criminal. I can't believe you act like this in front of your *santitos*." He waved at them, and I imagined them bowing in agreement. "Someday," Emilio said, pointing his swollen, purple finger, "someone's going to teach you a lesson, Ma." With that, he left, letting the door slam behind him. He was too mad to remember the shirt he'd left on the sofa.

Grandma didn't have time to react because Belinda marched into the room carrying a glass jug. It was huge, the kind used for *aguas frescas*, and it was full of dollar bills. "You liar!" she yelled. "Look at all this money here."

"Where did you get that?" Grandma scolded.

"From your room! Your closet! You know where it was."

"Why are you going through my things?"

"Because I knew you had money. And here it is."

"Grandma," I said, "if you have all that money, why don't you pay back the meat market man?"

"Because he overcharged me!"

"You must have a thousand dollars," Belinda said. "But you're so selfish. You won't even give me cash for Cancún."

"That's right. I won't," Grandma said. "That money's for my retirement."

"*Please!*" Belinda begged. "*Please* give me some money. All I need is the down payment. You've got plenty right here."

"No!" Grandma slapped Belinda's hands from the jug. She dropped it, but luckily it didn't break. It just thudded and rolled.

"I can't believe how mean you are!" Belinda said as she ran out the door. Every time she got mad, she ran out. She'd go to her friend Sandra's house. When she was super mad, she'd call

Dad to pick her up. I had a feeling he'd be picking her up tonight.

"*¡Desgraciados!*" Grandma hissed. "Those people don't appreciate a thing."

I kept my mouth shut. I wasn't about to make things worse.

Grandma picked up the jug and carried it to her closet, while I settled on the couch to watch T.V. I enjoyed watching news shows. Someday I wanted to wear spiffy designer suits and report earth-shattering events on *Dateline* or *60 Minutes*. Before I could find a program, though, Grandma returned with a wad of bills in her hands. "Come on," she said. "Let's go to La Estrella. You can order some nachos and I can order some beer."

Some people might say that hanging out with Grandma on a Friday night was a lame way for a sixteen-year-old to spend her time, but I would have to disagree. After a few sips of beer, Grandma relaxed. She loved to gossip about Mom, Belinda, Uncle Emilio and all the neighbors. I'm sure she gossiped about me too, but why worry about it? Grandma never read books or watched movies. She didn't have a job. Most of her friends were mad about some trouble she stirred up. If it weren't for *chisme*, she'd have nothing to say. So I listened and laughed, and because I let her go on and on, she let me order nachos and a greasy burger. Yup, sometimes I hated my grandma, but sometimes I loved her, too.

After a couple of hours, we returned to the house and heard barking. "*Qué curioso*," Grandma said.

"What's strange?" I asked.

"All the barking next door. I thought that dog ran away. Didn't la Señora Garza leave her gate open?"

"Maybe she came back and closed it before he ran out."

Grandma didn't say anything, but she shook her head as if disagreeing. When we arrived at the front door, she mumbled, "Hmmm . . ."

"What is it?"

"The door's not locked." She reached in her purse and pulled out the black case that held her glasses. She slowly opened the door and stepped inside, pointing the case the way cops point revolvers. "First impressions count," she whispered. Then she scanned the room just like every detective on *CSI*. "Clear!" she said for the living room. "Clear!" for the kitchen. "All clear!" for the bedrooms. After her search, she flipped on the living room light and with horror, cried, "*¡Mis santitos! ¡Se fueron!*"

Sure enough, the shelves were empty. Dust outlined circles where the statues once stood. Every saint had disappeared.

Headlines popped in my head: "Holy Relics in Unholy Hands" and "The Case of the Vanishing *Santitos*: Miracle or Crime?" Honestly, I didn't know what could have happened to them. Were they stolen or, like Uncle Emilio had warned, was God teaching Grandma a lesson?

"Call 9-1-1," Grandma ordered. "We've been burglarized!"

I almost did, too, but then I remembered what my journalism teacher said—reporters get the facts, *all* the facts, A to Z. Why would a burglar steal the *santitos* but leave the T.V., laptop and—I ran to Grandma's closet—a giant jug of money? Furthermore, I saw no broken windows or pried-open doors. And, upon closer examination, I discovered Mom's *rebozo* draped over the sofa where Uncle Emilio's shirt used to be, and a note on the coffee table from Belinda that said, "I'm with Dad."

"This was no regular break-in," I said. "Someone in the family stole the saints."

Grandma's dismay turned to anger. "Why would they do that?"

"Because you pissed them off," I said. "And the first element of a crime is motivation. The second element is opportunity, and Uncle Emilio, Belinda and Mom have all been here." I pointed out the evidence. "Which brings us to the third element—means. Don't they all have house keys?"

"Since when did you turn into Warlock Holmes?"

"*Sherlock* Holmes," I corrected.

She slapped the back of my head. "Don't talk back to me!"

Just then, headlights turned into our driveway. We heard a car door and a few minutes later, Mom stepped in.

Instead of asking about the date, Grandma dove into accusations. "Did you come back to the house after we left?"

"Yes," Mom admitted. "I forgot my purse."

Grandma crossed her arms. "So where are they?" she demanded.

"Where are what?"

Grandma nodded toward the shelves.

"Your *santitos*!" Mom exclaimed. "What happened to them?"

"That's what *I* want to know."

"You think I took them?" Mom laughed. Grandma stared at her like a skeptical cop. "Look," Mom said, "they were fine when I left."

"So they weren't missing yet?" I asked.

"No."

"Are you sure?"

"Yes, I'm sure. I grabbed my purse, saw *La Virgen* and felt guilty. Can you believe that? I was just going to dinner, but that statue made me feel like such a sinner. I'm actually glad those things are gone."

Grandma tensed up, so I patted her arm to reassure her. Then I took a notepad from my purse. "And what time were you here?" I asked Mom.

"Around seven-thirty." I scribbled it down. "What's up with you?" she asked. "You're a detective now?"

"A reporter," I said, "and I'm getting all my facts, A to Z." I thought for a moment. "When you came by, did you notice Uncle Emilio's shirt or Belinda's note?"

"His shirt was right there," Mom said, pointing to the couch. "But I didn't see any note."

"So it had to be Uncle Emilio or Belinda," I concluded. "They must have stolen the statues sometime between seven-thirty and nine o'clock."

I might have written "Saints Pawned to Fund Senior Trip" or "Swiping Saints: One Son's Quest to 'Teach a Lesson'," but I knew better now. No way was I ever writing another retraction. I called Belinda to get more facts.

"What?" she snapped.

"It's me, Abigail."

"Oh," she apologized. "I thought you were Mom or Grandma. What's up? You want Dad to come get you?"

"No," I said. "I just have a few questions to ask."

"About what?"

"About Grandma's saints."

"What about them?" Belinda said, clearly annoyed.

I decided to try the direct approach. "Did you take them? They're gone."

"Gone? Like stolen?"

"Yeah," I said. "So did you take them?"

"No, I didn't take them. Why would I want those ugly things? They creep me out. If I wanted to steal something, I'd steal Grandma's money. I might steal it anyway. I can't believe how selfish she's being."

"Okay, okay," I said, trying to calm her down. "So they were here when you dropped off the note?"

"Yes."

"Are you sure?"

"How could I miss them? Haven't you noticed? Those things *stare* at you."

"Then it must have been Uncle Emilio. He's the only other person who has access to the house."

"Don't go blaming him," Belinda warned. "He was there too. He stopped by to pick up his shirt while I was packing a bag. Then he and Dad stood outside and talked for twenty minutes. They still act like *compadres*, you know? We all left at the same time, and I'm telling you, the saints were there. Dad honked the horn to rush me, and as I dropped my note on the coffee table, I saw them. They were scolding me or something. As if they knew I was going to bug Dad for cash. *Adiós*, I say. Those things got an opinion about everything."

"They're just statues," I said.

"They're 'touched,' Abigail. Grandma takes them to church and gets them blessed."

"Maybe," I said, shaking my head at her silliness. "I just have one more question. Did you lock the door when you left?"

"Not sure."

"Well, think about it. What were you carrying?"

"Lots of stuff. I'm spending a *whole* night. A girl needs things. I remember switching off the lights, but I don't remember if I locked the door."

"And what time did you leave?"

"A quarter till nine. Now *that* I remember because Dad wanted to catch some cop show, so he ran a couple of stop signs."

I hung up with Belinda and wrote down the new clues.

"Well?" Grandma and Mom wanted to know. "Who was it? Belinda or Emilio?"

"Neither," I said. "They both have alibis."

Whatever happened, I realized, happened between eight forty-five and nine. Not much of a window. Maybe the burglars were just getting started when we showed up. Maybe they ran off when they saw Grandma's "gun." But how could I verify that? I looked at the notes scribbled on my pad. Finally, I had all the facts, A to Z, but I still didn't have any answers.

The next morning, I found Grandma at the empty shelves. "Do you think they left me?" she asked. "Do you think they walked out to punish me?"

"They can't walk," I said.

"Of course, they can. They're *santitos*."

She slumped onto the couch and sat like a zombie for two hours. I hated how miserable she felt, so I decided to treat this like a kidnapping. I skipped the step about filing a missing person's report and went straight to combing the streets with a photo. We didn't have any milk-carton worthy portraits of the saints, but I did find a couple of pics—one with Uncle Emilio as a pimply-faced teenager and another with Belinda, Mom and me dressed as the girls in Fanta soda ads. The saints were in the background, but even with our heads in the way, you could still see them.

I canvassed the streets, sifting through merchandise at every garage sale and pawn shop, questioning every *viejita* working in her garden and every *viejito* working on his car. No one had seen Grandma's saints. Finally, I decided to make posters. "Have you seen us?" it said with a close-up from the pictures. I included our phone number and then nailed the posters to the poles right next to the "missing dog," "most wanted" and "yard sale" signs. A whole week passed by, but no one called.

Meanwhile, Grandma started watching T.V. She *hated* T.V. She said that it was like putting your head in the microwave, that it made your brain cells melt. Yet there she was, watching show after show, but not laughing at the jokes or crying at the sad parts. She lost her spirit. She was as hollow as a *flauta* without the meat. Mrs. Garza's dog barked, but Grandma ignored it. Belinda want-

ed a prom dress, senior ring, new purse, bikini, pedicure and sub-
scription for *Glamour* magazine, and each time she asked for
money, Grandma just pointed to the *aguas frescas* jug, no comment. And she also had no comment when Mom went on a second and then a third date with the handsome guy. Grandma even
left Uncle Emilio alone. He didn't know what to do with himself.
He changed the washer in the spigot, fixed a torn screen and balanced a wobbly ceiling fan all without being told. It was creepy
peaceful in our house, and I hated every minute.

"Grandma," I said one day, "you want me to go to Walgreen's
and get you something?" I tried to think of some embarrassing
old-person stuff. "Do you need any Depends?"

She looked at me. "Why? You think I have incompetence?"

"Incontinence," I corrected. And that's when I realized how
bad things were—Grandma didn't slap the back of my head and
she didn't scold me. She was forgiving, she was nice, she was a
total stranger now.

Another week went by, and I feared the worst. Those saints were
gone. Gone forever. Nevertheless, I went through the neighborhood to replace any missing or ruined signs.

When I got to one of the bus stops, this kid said, "You the
one looking for those statues?"

"Yeah."

"I know where they are," he admitted.

"You do?"

He nodded. "I saw them a while back."

"Why didn't you call?"

"No reward," he said. "You're supposed to offer a reward. You
know, a finder's fee."

I glanced at the posters put up by other people. All of them
mentioned rewards. How could I be so dumb?

"So where did you see them?"

He didn't answer, just held out his hand.

"Okay, okay," I said, reaching in my pockets. "All I have is three bucks."

"That's cheap," he complained, but he took the money anyway. "So I wanted to rip off a Snickers bar," he said, "but then I saw *him*." He pointed to St. Francis in the picture. "That guy scared the hell out of me."

"Are you kidding?" I laughed. "He's nearly bald. He's got little birdies all around him. He's like the god of gardening or something. You sure those other statues didn't creep you out?"

"Those guys? They're cool. They're like the dudes in my video games."

"So where did you see them?" I asked again.

"Culebra Meat Market. You know where that is?"

Of course, I thought. It all made sense. We'd been avoiding that place and getting our groceries from the HEB instead because Grandma owed the meat market man five bucks. When he saw me trying to dump the dead cat, he probably decided to get back at her. But how did he know where we lived? How did he know we'd be gone? Was he stalking us?

I marched straight to his store. Sure enough, all the *santitos* were displayed in a glass cabinet by the register. A sign said, "Saints for Sale." The original fifteen dollars had been scratched out and replaced with ten dollars, which was now reduced for the "super low cost of $5 each."

"You're that Zúñiga girl," the man said, this time pointing a melting Eskimo pie at me. "Your grandmother owes me five bucks."

"Is that what this is?" I said. "Ransom?"

He looked totally confused.

"You stole her saints," I explained.

"What are you talking about? I didn't steal anything."

"Yet here they are."

"These?" he tapped the glass cabinet. "You know what they say—one man's trash is another man's treasure. I found these in my dumpster one morning. I've been trying to sell them ever since. But they're possessed, I tell you. And not by the Holy Spirit." He shivered a bit.

"So who threw them in your dumpster?"

"You really want to know?"

I nodded.

"Okay," he said, "follow me." We went to his office. He had a desk, a file cabinet and five security cameras, three focused on the dumpster. No wonder he knew when I was there. He had more surveillance for the dumpster than for the store. "I back up all my video files," he said, flipping through a box of DVDs. He found the right one and put it in the player. Sure enough, I saw myself tiptoeing with the dead cat. He fast-forwarded. On the video, the sun went down; the street lights switched on. And then . . .

"Mrs. Garza!" I exclaimed. "Mrs. Garza stole the saints!"

I rushed home, grabbed Grandma and pounded on Mrs. Garza's door.

"It was you," I said when she answered. "I saw the surveillance tape from Culebra Meat Market. You stole my grandma's saints and tried to throw them away."

"Is this true?" Grandma said. "Why would you do such a terrible thing?"

Mrs. Garza put her hands on her hips and glared at us. "Payback," she said. "I lost three dogs, thanks to you. At first, I wasn't sure. I'm a *viejita*. I forget things. So I blamed myself when I lost the first two dogs. But with the third one, I was careful. I know I kept the gate closed. *And* locked. But he disappeared too. Well, I wasn't going to take any more chances. Someone was responsible and that someone was you."

"That's why you had your binoculars," I realized. "You were spying on the house."

"I had to pretend to leave," Mrs. Garza confessed. "So I drove off and hid my car down the street. That's when I saw your grandma opening the gate and letting out the dog. It took two hours to get him back."

Everything made sense now. Grandma's complaints and then her surprise when we heard barking the evening the saints disappeared.

"I didn't plan to steal them," Mrs. Garza said. "I went over to have some words, but when I got there, the door was open and the house was empty. That's when I got my idea. Let you worry about the saints the way I worried about my dogs."

"You think a dog is equal to a saint?!" Grandma yelled. "Do dogs pray for you? Do they keep you honest? Do they . . ." She didn't get to finish because Mrs. Garza slammed the door in her face.

I couldn't help smiling. Grandma was her old self again.

So I learned some stuff about Grandma, but I also learned about investigating, too. Cover all leads, be patient and, above all else, offer a reward on your posters.

After Mrs. Garza slammed her door, Grandma and I went to Culebra Meat Market. The shop owner offered to return the statues for five bucks. Grandma grudgingly gave him the cash. He seemed pleased to finally get his money, but he seemed more pleased to be rid of the *santitos*. We took them home, put them back on the shelves, and in no time, Grandma was embarrassing and scolding us again. The saints, for some reason, brought out the worst in her, which was fine by me. Anything else was straight out boring.

After things got back to normal, I wrote about my adventure and gave the story to my journalism teacher. "I know you can't put this in the school paper," I said, "but any fact checker will tell you that it's one hundred percent true."

She nodded, pleased. She said I didn't have to take creative writing after all. Clearly, I knew how to solve a mystery and get at the truth.

So I'm writing for *What's News?* again, only this time I don't put my name on the stories. I put A-Z. Those are the initials for Abigail Zúñiga and those are the facts—that's right—*all* the facts, A to Z.

Hating Holly Hernandez

R. Narvaez

Hating Holly Hernandez was easy.

She was the most insufferable, insidious, inane girl in all of Flatbush High School of Science.

I would do anything to never again sit behind her in Pre-Calculus, Advanced Biology, Creative Writing or Advanced Spanish, being forced to inhale the pungent strawberry scent of her shampoo and conditioner; forced to watch the perfectly coifed back of her auburn hair bounce when she giggled or raised her hand, which is far, far, far too often; or forced to reply to one of her cruel "Hello, Xanders," accompanied by teeth that while imperfect had a dangerously pleasing quality to them.

Damn that Holly Hernandez.

At the climax of our incarceration in junior high school two years ago, she was dubbed Most Humanitarian, Most Fashionable and Most Likely to Succeed. The former two I could not quibble with, for I care neither for humanity nor have I ever spent a moment worrying over my sartorial deficiencies. But the latter, Most Likely to Succeed, a title that recognizes one's obvious destiny to change the world, and the fact that it was not bestowed upon one who justly deserves it, truly enflamed my testicles.

We were the only two from our beleaguered, under-funded junior high school to pass the entrance exam for this vaunted school. Now, every day at Flatbush her popularity grows, as does

173

my ire. And so I have resolved, *by the great beard of Zeus* that I will crush Holly Hernandez, if it is the last thing I ever do.

Option 1: Drugs. I could manufacture methamphetamines and plant them in her little red backpack then anonymously alert security. But my secret lab was demolished when my landlord converted the basement into three studio apartments.

Option 2: Gossip. I considered spreading news among her friends that she had AIDS, was carrying her father's baby, or was a homophobic racist. This proved impossible since none of her friends were my friends, since indeed I had no friends.

Option 3: Academics. *Eureka!* Using funds I won playing online poker, I procured the answers for the upcoming New York State Regents Biology Exam. It would be simple enough to place them in her little red backpack and alert the proctor.

And thus Holly Hernandez would be destroyed.

On the morning of the exams, I awoke before anyone else in my family, even my vigilant Abuela. I walked into the bathroom and gazed at my own fiendishness.

"Good morning, Jawbreaker," I said to my reflection, and then broke mighty wind.

Short, dry, curly hair. A face pockmarked with pizza-red pustules. A fat, flat nose whose only use is to prop up spectacles thick as glass brick. And then my most distinctive feature: shining out from between my thick, gibbous lips: the tinsel-shiny railroad across my teeth, perpetually on display, since I have been cursed to be an open-mouth-breather because of my asthma. In sixth grade, bullies dubbed me "Jawbreaker," and so I proudly took the name for myself, eliminating the power of my foes to demean me, even using it as my online handle.

"You fine-looking villain," I said. "Today shall be the day of your greatest victory."

In my excitement, I took forty-five minutes to shower and had to run to the bus stop.

I rushed to the fourth floor computer room to meet Mr. Backhaus. We quickly exchanged envelopes. I shuffled downstairs and stopped off at my locker to pick up my lucky Incredible Hulk action figure. I had to find space for the figure in my duffle bag —its presence during any exam I took was essential.

I arrived in the designated exam room just in time, voluntarily taking the seat behind Holly Hernandez. She wore her favorite red pullover and starched white shirt. I knew it was her favorite because she had written as much on her various online profiles. In front of her, she had a dozen number two pencils on display, each sharp enough to perform delicate micro-vascular surgery.

I put my duffle bag on the floor and got out my one nubby pencil. I enjoyed marking my answers with deep, dark, round dents until they were shiny with graphite.

Then I dropped the pencil on the floor, creating the pretense I needed to transfer the answers from my duffle to the obnoxious little red backpack. But just as I began to slowly bend, Holly Hernandez whipped her scented hair around, smiled and said to me, "Hiya, Xander!"

I grunted a reply. I preferred not be called by my silly birth name. But once again I refused to correct her. She could never know me for who I really am.

"Are you ready for this?" she said, perkily. "I've been studying every night for weeks!"

I grunted a reply.

"You're so good in this class," she said, even more perkily. "I'm sure this test will be no problem for you!"

I grunted again. Time was running short. But then the proctor Mr. Straczynski, my old World History teacher, came in and began writing on the board, causing Holly Hernandez to stiffen to attention, much like a trained Labrador.

The moment had arrived.

I bent to pick up my pencil and reach for the inner area of my duffle where the answers were hidden.

But they weren't there.

Perhaps the envelope had shifted while I shuffled to class. *No!* It wasn't on the other side, or under my comic books and video games. *Where in Hades?*

I stretched my cumbersome body and reached both hands into my bag. The answers were gone.

My locker. The answers could be nowhere else.

I extricated myself from my chair. Then Mr. Straczynski said, "The exam starts in three minutes, young man. Hurry back."

Insolent fool.

My locker was on the same floor, but all the way on the other corner of the building. I shuffled as best I could in my loafers, which tended to slide on the linoleum floor, and almost collided with Ms. Curtis, my Pre-Calculus teacher, just coming out of the stairwell. She mumbled an apology. *Dazed harpie.* In any case, I quickly dialed the combination.

But . . . the lock was already open.

Not again. What new humiliation had the school bullies concocted for me now? Skid-marked underwear? Week-old ethnic food?

I jiggled the handle, already contemplating seven types of revenge.

I don't think I ever could have been prepared for what I found.

There, hanging from the silver hook that branched out from the top of the locker, was a severed human arm, still dripping with blood.

My stomach began to gurgle, and I felt a quake throughout my body.

"Holy crap!" someone yelled, and I recognized the voice of Mr. Licata, head of security at Flatbush. "Don't move a muscle, geek. I got you!"

At that moment I wet myself, just a little.

The rest of my life flashed before me. Prison. Tattoos. Marriage to an inmate. No Ivy League, of course. No senior-year escapades with zaftig French women—*au revoir!* No more of Abuela's inimitable *rellenos de plátanos*. And worst of all—no recognition of my genius. At most, an interview for some documentary about fallen teens that once had great potential.

I slumped to my knees and felt actual tears build up behind my eyes.

"Xander had nothing to do with this, and I'll prove it!"

I turned. It was Holly Hernandez. My nemesis. My plague. My tsunami.

Her red sweater fit perfectly.

She asked Mr. Licata to seal the school immediately, to prevent anyone from leaving. She was sure the culprit was someone near, since the arm was still *fresh*. And they needed to find the owner of the arm, to see if the person could still be saved.

Why was she was defending me?

Mr. Licata obeyed like a good Rottweiler. No doubt because she had helped him before on so many occasions.

The Mystery of the Somnolent Substitute.

The Secret of the Shrinking Varsity Sweaters.

The Curse of the Janitor's Closet.

She had solved them all.

"Xander," she said, touching me on the arm. Touching. Me. "Are you alright?" she said.

I could only mumble in the affirmative.

"Don't worry," she said. "We'll get to the bottom of this!"

Her searing touch on my person was distracting. But still something more was troubling me. Save for the severed arm, there was nothing else in my locker. My textbooks, my tennis shoes, my acne cream—all gone.

Whoever placed that body part in my locker also had the answers to the Biology Regents exam, and thus could brand me a cheater and get me expelled.

In his slick windbreaker, his police whistle swinging, Mr. Licata told Holly Hernandez that he trusted her, but, he said, "I'd like to talk to your friend anyway."

He grabbed my arm. He was cruel, cold, concrete.

I turned and saw Holly Hernandez, and she was looking at me with—*was it annoyance? pity? disgust?*

I was being forced to confront the beast in his own domain.

I sat in Mr. Licata's personal Abu Ghraib. His office was dedicated to the art of corporal punishment. Every inch of wall featured a different kind of paddle or bat, some new, some ancient, some obviously well worn.

But I had been pummeled by the best. Mr. Licata could not intimidate me.

He took off his jacket and bared his simian arms. He rifled through his file cabinet and retrieved a fat file—no doubt my voluminous school record.

"Xander Herrera," he said, scratching his cormorantal belly. "A junior. Good grades, very good grades. Transferred several times in grade school. They called you 'precocious' and 'imaginative.' We know what that means. Oh, look at this, one teacher thought you might be mildly autistic."

He laughed and looked up at me, seemed to wince, then changed his gaze to somewhere behind me. Perhaps deciding which paddle he would delight himself using on me.

He questioned me—*When had I arrived at school that morning? Had I been in any fights recently? Did I use drugs?* He told me the police would arrive soon and that I should tell him everything before they arrived.

I mumbled my answers—not to his satisfaction.

He picked a small billy club from a shelf and began to tap it slowly on the edge of his desk.

"I'm your pal," he said, tap-tap-tapping. "I know all about you, Xander. I can help you out. Let you go your own way in this school, if you know what I mean. I just need to know whose arm you cut off there and why."

How strange. Mr. Licata thought I did it, and yet he wanted to make a deal.

I was about to mumble another reply, when someone rapped quickly on the door and then opened it.

My albatross, my ache.

"Mr. Licata," said Holly Hernandez. "I have a plan!"

Before he could speak, she quickly outlined a strategy. More than 800 students were in school that day taking exams in forty classrooms, run by forty proctors. The school had notoriously tight security, so she discounted outsiders. Including staff and security that meant about 900 people were in the building. All of them suspects. But only one of them had just committed a violent crime.

"They can't have gone very far!" she said. "We need to lock down the school!"

Mr. Licata had put down his billy club. Now he was nodding like a bobble-head doll.

Just then one of Licata's minions bumbled in. "Sir, you better come see this. Hi, Holly."

I followed Holly Hernandez and the Neanderthals into the hallway and there, stumbling in from one of the stairwells, was Vice Principal Katz, his cheap, three-piece suit covered in blood.

"Help," he kept saying. "Help."

Holly Hernandez and I were sitting in the principal's office. The walls were decorated with cheap jazz posters in elaborate wooden frames. Principal Williams walked in wearing a black turtleneck, black pants and black thick-framed glasses.

"Holly, always good to see you. Even in these circumstances," she said.

"It's always good to see you, ma'am. And how is Mr. Williams?" Holly Hernandez said.

"He loved that scarf you knitted him. Wears it just about all the time."

"I'm glad!"

I believe it was only my spectacles that prevented my eyes from rolling out of my head and onto the floor.

"Holly, I can't thank you enough for your quick thinking," she said. "Your father's men are searching the building as we speak."

Her father was a detective on the metropolitan police force. Of course, she actually knew who her father was. Of course, he actually recognized her existence. And, of course, they solved crimes together, no doubt in between potato sack races and roaring bouts of checkers.

"I've been able to examine the arm," Holly Hernandez said, holding up a crime scene investigation kit she apparently kept in her little red backpack. "The arm was definitely severed within the last hour! The victim was white, male, I'd say an adult, athletic—"

"And left-handed," I mumbled.

"Yes, Xander!" she said.

"It was a right arm with a watch on the wrist," we both said, though I mumbled and she exclaimed.

"Excellent, Xander!" she said, then she turned to Principal Williams and asked about the vice principal.

"Well, he was going to the bathroom when he was knocked out from behind then blindfolded. He says he was being held in the wood shop, he thinks, because of—"

"—the smell of sawdust and glue," said my affliction.

"Yes, exactly, but it was darkened, and he heard something being dragged, and then the sound of one of the power saws being operated right near him, and then he was . . ."

"Splattered," I said. Audibly.

The principal looked straight at me. "Xander, Miss Hernandez says you had nothing to do with this incident, and her word is gold with me. Despite what I know about you, and despite your poor attitude. But I expect you to stay . . . out of the way while this investigation is going on."

I nodded and leaned forward to take candy from her desk. It was a sour gummy worm and would wreak havoc with my braces. But I didn't want to reach for another candy and ruin the drama of the moment.

"Keep up the good work," the principal said to Holly Hernandez.

I was torqued into a tiny seat in a detention room. It smelled of yesterday's pork chops. I had been told to wait there indefinitely. My mind raced to put the pieces of this puzzle together.

Was the vice principal intended to be a second victim?

Why had the arm been placed in my locker, of all lockers and hiding places?

Who held those exam answers and my fate in their blood-soaked hands?

I felt powerless. A billion tons of unrecyclable anguish polluted my heart. Dark considerations filled my brain.

1. I could jump out the window—if only I had the means to saw off the gates.

2. I could sever my own arm to engender sympathy.

3. I could contact my family.

None of these would serve.

I considered jumping out the window again, when, in my lowest hour, my mortal enemy walked in, smiling a smile completely devoid of guile, that somehow made me feel . . . *comforted*?

"Xander!" she said.

"Holly Hernandez," I said.

"They found a severed foot in the art studio on the sixth floor. Could be from the same victim."

"How grisly," I said. "And all the way on the other side of the building."

"Exactly. That's why I need your help."

I froze in my seat. My bowels went cold. Here was the vaunted, the lauded, the perfect Holly Hernandez asking *me* for help.

"We have to get into the guy's locker room!" she said.

By the Furies.

It smelled of fecal matter, cloying cologne and millennia of cheese-filled socks. I dreaded the boy's locker room not just for that, but for the years of humiliation I had faced there.

Holly Hernandez asked me to lead her to the shower. This took a moment, as I had elected never to shower in school no matter how much sweat I had excreted that day. I decided to divert myself with a question I had been wanting to ask: "So how do you know I didn't put the arm in my locker?"

I anticipated her saying that while anyone as intellectually superior as I might be tempted to sever an arm, he would never let himself so easily be caught.

But she said, "Well, I saw you in the computer room with Mr. Backhaus this morning! You would never have had time to get to the wood shop and then to the test room in time!"

"Oh," I said.

We found the shower room, and Holly Hernandez extracted a spritzer from her crime scene investigation kit.

"Popi gave this to me for Christmas! Isn't it neat?"

"Neat?"

The spritzer was decorated with daisies. She found a puddle where someone had recently showered. She began to spray the tiles with her mawkish device.

"Xander, please shut off the lights!"

I did as commanded, and into the darkness, I said, "When I found the arm, how did you happen to be there so fast?"

"I can sense trouble. It's just something I've always been able to do. Plus, you screamed."

"I did not."

"Yes, you did. Heard it on the other side of the building!"

"Did n—"

"Blood!"

"Blood?"

"See the bluish-green light! My theory is that our perp is most likely male, due to the preliminary psychological profile I am compiling, and after committing his sick deeds, he must have been completely . . . *splattered* and needed to get cleaned up!"

"Ergo, the locker room," I said.

If this perpetrator took the time to clean himself, did he also take the time to examine the materials he stole from my locker? I prayed not. I saw then the irony of ironies that my greatest rival was perhaps the only person who could get me close to this "perp," so I could find those exam answers before anyone else. She had no idea how she was secretly helping *me,* her arch-nemesis. Also, she probably had no idea that I had crowned myself as her arch-nemesis.

I mused on this, but then suddenly Holly Hernandez announced that she had a plan. She immediately got on her little red cell phone.

"Popi," she said into the phone. "We need everyone in the auditorium now!"

She told him that in order to ensure no one escaped and that we all kept an eye on each other, the class on the top floor north would collect the classes to the east and then the classes to the south and west and then they would all proceed to the classrooms downstairs in the same spiral, and down and down, like a growing train of juvenile academia, until all 900 people in the building sat together in the auditorium.

Very clever. She was flawless. Per usual.

We went to exit the gymnasium through the pool—the fastest way to get to the auditorium—but that door was locked. However, the door to a small anteroom nearby appeared open.

I offered, "That room should lead us to the back stairwell."

"Yes, I know!" said Holly Hernandez.

"I've studied the school's floor plans extensively."

"As have I!" she said.

She led the way, and I followed her bouncing tresses into the dimly lit anteroom. It was filled with safety vests and lifeguard accoutrements, an orgy of oranges.

"Wait," she said. "The pool's been closed for renovation!"

"¿Qué?"

"So no one should have had to move those vests!" she said, and tip-toed to a disarrayed pile of orange. Behind it, we made a horrific discovery.

There, partially wrapped in a tarpaulin, was a body. In parts. With parts missing.

"It's Mr. DiBona!" Holly Hernandez said.

"The architectural art teacher."

"He's dead!"

"I concur."

"Wow, you didn't scream this time, Xander!"

"I'll have you know I never—"

But before I finished the dim light went out and the door to the room slammed.

I confess—this time I did scream.

As insidious as I am, I have no desire to be in a pitch-dark room with a dead body. Let alone a locked dark room. Holly Hernandez used her cell phone light to find the door. It was locked from the other side.

We attempted to put our shoulders to it, and then something clattered on the floor, and we were plunged back into darkness.

"My phone!" she said. I heard her fumbling on the floor. "It's broken! Xander, let's use yours to find the door at the other end!"

In the blackness, I felt myself grow hot. "I don't have one."

"What?"

I said, louder, "I don't have a cell phone. We can't afford one. And I wouldn't want anyone to call me anyway."

I heard her sigh, then sit on the floor.

I asked her if she was alright. She was rifling through her backpack. She withdrew something, unscrewed it, then drank.

"Have some, Xander."

I reached in the darkness for her approximate location.

"That's not it."

"Oh, sorry."

"That's okay. Here."

"Thank you," I said, moving the water bottle to my mouth. But what was inside it was not water.

I coughed. "What is this?"

"Vodka. Strawberry-infused."

"Oh, my."

"It's never too early!"

"But you're—"

Holly Hernandez, Most Humanitarian.

Holly Hernandez, Most Fashionable.

Holly Hernandez, Most Likely to Succeed.

"I'm not perfect, Xander," she said. "I know everyone thinks that. But I'm not."

"Oh."

I had no idea what to say in such a situation. My archenemy had a weakness, a vice, an easily exploitable vice.

And yet somehow I knew I would do nothing to exploit it.

I gave back the bottle, and she took it quickly, closing it, then opening it again and taking another gulp. Then she closed it and put it back in her bag. For a second it seemed as if I heard her sniffle. Which frankly would have annoyed me beyond sanity. But then, suddenly, she took a deep breath, and said, "This way!"

She took my hand, which was somehow wet, perhaps from condensation from the bottle, and led us to the door on the other side of the room. It opened easily.

"Let's go," she said.

Every seat in the auditorium was filled. Hundreds of high school students, with their tumescent urges and issues, herded through the building, not told why, and, worse, not fed lunch. The savages were restless.

Holly Hernandez led me to the stage. She went to the man I knew to be her father. Detective Hernandez. The man I would have been happy to accuse of impregnating her. He appeared to be intelligent. Wore loafers, blazer, tie with cartoon characters on it. No doubt a gift from his gifted offspring.

He reported that another body part, a foot and calf, had been found in the basement. She nodded, then she turned to the audience. "These are our suspects! All 900 people here! But we can quickly narrow down the list!"

She showed no sign of having done shots of vodka—

"The perp had to have keys to access several locked rooms, such as the wood shop and the pool supply room, and that means someone on the staff or faculty! Therefore, every student is excused! But please remain seated until I finish!"

—she was clear, cogent, commanding the audience without the crutch of a microphone or podium—

"Therefore, that leaves more than 40 suspects!"

—I never hated her more.

Her father approached her. "Nena, I may be able to help there. We've kept the majority of the faculty and staff confined to classrooms since this morning."

"Aha! Who was not confined?!"

He handed her a list. She scanned it, then announced: "Will the following please come up to the stage: Ms. Curtis, Mr. Licata, Mrs. Lavish, Vice Principal Katz, Mr. Straczynski and . . . Xander Herrera!"

My stomach turned cold. *BETRAYER!*

"Popi, why is Xander on this list?!" Holly Hernandez stood right in front of her much taller father. His eyebrows twitched. His nostrils flared. His mouth crumpled.

"I know he's your friend, *mi vida*," the father said. "But we still have to consider him a suspect."

"If he stays on the list, I'm going home!"

Was she actually pouting?

"Okay, okay, *negrita*," her detective father relented. "Mr. Herrera does not have to be a suspect at this time. But keep where I can see you, young man."

My intestines unclenched. She had defended me for the second time that day. I owed Holly Hernandez now. *I owed her.*

As the real suspects marched on stage, I felt reprieved and had a wicked vision of the band playing "Pomp and Circumstance." Oh, Jawbreaker, what a wicked funnyman you are.

She paused in front of our math teacher, Ms. Curtis. Impossible. Too unimaginative.

"It's not Ms. Curtis!" announced my former nemesis.

"*¿Por qué, mi vida?*" said her father.

"Although we found evidence of blood in the boy's shower room, a female could have gone there to defer suspicion. But Ms. Curtis has not changed her clothes. She only has three outfits and she wears each one three to four days in a row. Today, she has on her plaid skirt and red polyester blouse—but she just started this outfit's cycle yesterday."

Oh, very good, very good.

Then she paused in front of Mr. Licata, the brute. I could see him enjoying a rousing bout of dismemberment.

"It's not Mr. Licata."

"*¿Por qué, nena?*" said her father.

"He still has the same blood-stained shirt he had on a few hours ago! Our perp definitely took a shower! Mr. Licata . . . has not!"

Enamored with the teen detective's charm, the barbarian actually smiled at that.

Fine, fine. Then she paused in front of Mrs. Lavish, one of the lunchroom ladies. She always gave me extra tater tots after school, in exchange for unfiltered cigarettes, so I liked her. But I could see her with a power saw.

"It can't be Mrs. Lavish," said my former bedevilment, "because operating the power saw requires some hand strength, and as we can see by her wrist braces, Mrs. Lavish is afflicted with carpal tunnel syndrome!"

Ah, of course. Why had I never noticed those?

"That leaves Vice Principal Katz and Mr. Straczynski! As I said, the perp had to clean the blood off himself. And both of you smell of soap, and have wet hair!"

Katz was quick to counter, "I can't believe this. I showered because there was blood all over me."

"That could have all just been a diversion. How about you, Mr. Straczynski?"

"I swim in the pool every day before lunch. Everyone knows that."

And then she paused. And I saw it on her face. She really didn't know which one had done it, and she was stuck.

In that moment I had an epiphany. The modus operandi appeared like Athena from the sea. I had it—I had what I needed to help Holly Hernandez.

I stepped forward. "Ms. Hernandez, the answer is obvious to you, but before you finish, may I take a crack at being a junior detective? If you don't mind?"

She mumbled, still perkily, "Yes, of course, Xander!"

Her father looked at me as if I were something he found on the bottom of his shoe, but he allowed this because he was his daughter's father.

I began. "Miss Hernandez knows that the body parts of Mr. DiBona were scattered throughout the building, in extremely separate areas. Vice Principal Katz, does that remind you of anything?"

"No, not at all," he said. He clearly wanted to kick me.

"Hmm. Well, that's because you were a marketing major, if memory serves, your knowledge of history is miniscule. What we need is a scholar of medievalism. Of Dark Age methods of revenge and torture."

I turned to our last suspect.

"Mr. Straczynski, I must say, both Ms. Hernandez and I remember quite well the extensive lecture you gave last year on William Wallace, who was drawn and quartered, and his body parts sent to different parts of the country." I put my face in his face. "Why, Mr. Straczynski, did you kill and dismember Mr. DiBona?"

"You little geek bastard!"

He lunged at me, but one of Detective Hernandez's fine officers held him back.

It was over. Holly Hernandez looked at me with . . . *jealousy? pride? lust?*

In a few moments, a security guard came up to Detective Hernandez and said, "We've found these hidden in a file cabinet, sir."

He handed over blood-covered overalls.

"That seals it!" said Holly Hernandez.

And he handed over the stuff from my locker. I took a step forward, but Detective Hernandez immediately told an officer to hold it all as evidence.

On the stage, Mr. Straczynski poured forth with a confession. He and Mr. DiBona had been working together on a reproduction of a medieval peasant's home for months, planning and building every day before the start of classes. That morning they had argued over the placement of a *louvre*. One pushed the other, there was a shove, some grappling, then more shoving. Among all those tools and sharp edges. Somehow, suddenly, sadly, the architectural teacher was dead. Mr. Straczynski at first sought help, but when he spotted Vice Principal Katz, he decided instead that he'd rather not get caught. He approached the V.P. from behind and knocked him out, then took both victims into the nearby wood shop, where he proceeded to saw his buddy, the architectural art teacher, into pieces. The scattering of the body parts was a flourish he couldn't help adding.

I was waiting for the bus when Detective Hernandez pulled up in a car in front of me. *What fresh hell is this?*

And then Holly Hernandez got out of the front seat and handed me a stained bag with my possessions in it. My textbooks, my tennis shoes, my acne cream. The Regents answers.

She said, "Thank you so much for you help on this case . . . Jawbreaker!"

"Zounds!" I yelped.

"That's your online name, isn't it?!"

"But, but . . ."

"You still owe me $150 from Texas Hold 'Em online two nights ago. From the chats we had during our games, I was able to deduce you wear braces, attend Flatbush High and often sit behind a girl who—what were your words?—is 'distractingly redolent of strawberries'!"

"*Incroyable!*" I muttered. I felt a warmth toward her then, something amicable, amusing and a little amorous.

"I'm PoohBear1000!"

Of course!

"I hope we can be friends!" she said.

I smiled, showing all of my brilliant aluminum.

Then she said, "But if you ever try to put test answers in my backpack again, Jawbreaker, I won't be so nice! Later, gator!"

I grunted a reply and stood there, breathing through my mouth. And then she got in her father's car and they drove away.

I arrived home that night and took a shower. My grandmother served me spaghetti *con pollo,* my second favorite meal of hers. My mother ignored me and watched her *novelas.*

As I walked to my room, Abuela yelled for me to put on pants. I grunted and I went to go online.

To my surprise, I found that I had received an email. It was an invitation from Holly Hernandez. A party at her house.

A party.

With all those cretinous friends of hers?

Certainly not. I moved my mouse to delete it. But then I thought, *What better place than her inner circle to get close enough to Holly Hernandez to destroy her?* I would win the day yet.

I replied in the affirmative.

Carbon Beach

Daniel A. Olivas

Hernán Tafolla stared into Detective Ana Urrea's eyes. At sixteen, Hernán stood as tall as the detective, whose light brown eyes reminded him of the hot chocolate milk he drank each morning before walking to school. Deep. Rich. Delectable. As he and the detective stood off to the side, five police officers milled about the beach, not too far from the man's head that poked out from a mound of sand a few yards from the constant tide. If Hernán squinted, the head looked as though it had been severed from its body. But no. Nothing so exotic here. Just a dead body, covered up to its chin in sand. As the detective asked questions, Hernán could hear the waves hitting the wet sand, sea gulls calling out to each other and the Sunday traffic emanating from the Pacific Coast Highway up past the beautiful homes. He heard an officer say that David Geffen lived in the house directly in front of the head. Hernán had discovered it shortly after walking through the public access way from the sidewalk to the sand. He finally had a driver's permit and had driven all the way to Malibu from the Valley to enjoy some solitude with an early morning stroll on the beach. The head had been covered by an inverted, blue ice chest, like the one Hernán's uncle Rudy always brought to Shadow Ranch Park in Canoga Park for family fiestas. At least, that's what Hernán told the police and then Detective Urrea who now questioned Hernán with greater depth as they waited for his mother to get there. Detective Urrea blinked, once and then again, shielded her eyes—those beautiful eyes—from the bright August sun. Her lips moved slowly and Hernán noticed that she had nearly perfect teeth, white and straight, except for a bit of red lipstick that had smudged onto one of her upper front teeth. She wanted Hernán to try very hard to remember if he'd seen any suspicious persons nearby. Hernán furrowed his brow, went deep into his memory, trying to come up with something. He knew then that he loved the detective. No doubt. A perfect love for a perfect woman. Hernán had to win her over. He was already part way there with this remarkable discovery of the man's body. Who else would have bothered to look under the ice chest? Only a dynamic, mature-for-his-age, quick-thinking, young man. Yes, Hernán would help in the investigation and Detective Urrea would have no choice but to return his love. And because Hernán knew a lot about the man's death—too much, if truth be told—he would have every opportunity to make Detective Ana Urrea his. All he needed to do was remain calm. What was that word his English teacher taught the last week of school? Insouciance. Yes, that's it. In-sou-ci-ance. He must demonstrate insouciance, a lack of concern, indifference. That way, no one would be suspicious. Hernán never failed to do something once he set his mind to it. And he wouldn't fail now.

The Librarian

Juan Carlos Pérez-Duthie

Those few who first spotted her, swore she had driven into town like a derelict tumbleweed right ahead of one of that spring's last major sandstorms. It was Deming's biggest news in a while, the "Sandstorm of the Century," or at least that's what our local T.V. station called it.

When I finally saw that car, it was unlike any I had ever seen in my life (well, I'm only eighteen, but still, most people, even those my age, were thrilled by it). Old Mr. Dimas, the school janitor, described it as a black 1950 Packard four-door sedan. And it was a sight to behold as it came into Deming, followed by a veil of mocha-colored dust that had been conceived in the Chihuahua Desert and that now threatened to devour not only us, but our county, Luna, as well as the neighboring Hidalgo and Doña Ana counties. All of New Mexico, some feared.

In the end, though, it wasn't the monstrosity the media had predicted. The storm and its offshoots lasted a day, as the winds and its ribbons of particles choked everything in sight, bringing darkness to the sun as if someone had dimmed the lights till they went black. Yet, that day in Deming was remembered more for another reason: because it was the day Mrs. Vasconsuelos, our school librarian, was found dead.

Poor Mr. Vasconsuelos told everyone who would listen, that she had died in the bathtub at their home that afternoon, and that because of the howling of the wind, he had not been able to hear anything abnormal, if indeed there had been something to listen to coming from that room.

"She had been in the library, working till the last minute, storing away computers and covering books, sealing windows with the help of some students, hoping to minimize the damages of the sand," the school principal, Mrs. Goddard, said to the local newspaper, *The Deming Headlight*.

Between sobs, the widower explained to a reporter on T.V., "When she got home, she was exhausted, so she went to soak in a nice bath. She mentioned that, as the storm approached, she had met a woman parked on the side of the road, and asked her if she needed help. The woman said no, but was so appreciative, she gave my wife a gift. I don't know what the gift was. Anyway, once she got in the bath, I noticed a long time had gone by, and she didn't come out, so I opened the door and saw her there. Still. Her skin looking bluish, her hair dripping wet and covering half her face. It was crazy, but it seemed she had drowned, which didn't make sense, because the water had drained out."

Due to the storm, Mr. Vasconsuelos had been unable to call for assistance. He tried 9-1-1, he explained to the police, but was told no one could make it to his property until after the winds subsided. With his windows shut, there was no way to see who was outside that would be able to help, if anyone, and to open the door would've meant having the furious desert fly in. A clinic and a hospital both said no one could drive there either. Not even the paramedics or the firefighters were allowed to respond to calls. His wife's beloved school also failed him; no one answered when he dialed. In the end, there was nothing else to do. He sat on the floor of their bathroom, resting his body against the bathtub, holding Mrs. Vasconsuelos' lifeless hand while he cried.

The news of Mrs. Vasconsuelos' death shocked everyone at the school, as was to be expected. Especially since the day of the storm, the gym had been used as a shelter, and our librarian and some teachers, as well as students, had spent the early part of the day getting everything ready for the mess expected from the sands. The next morning, Mr. Vasconsuelos called to inform Mrs. Goddard of his terrible loss. A loving obituary ran in the paper two days later, remembering the forty-six-year-old Colombian librarian as someone totally in love with books and with helping students love them, too.

Mrs. Vasconsuelos was a humble woman, a devout Catholic (like us) who had studied at an all girls-school in New York City, and had moved to New Mexico to work on an Apache reservation when she thought God had called her to serve others. Instead, life had a different surprise in store for her, since the man who had found her a place to live in Deming, Victor Vasconsuelos, born and raised in New Mexico, asked her out shortly after he got her the exact townhouse she was looking for. And from that day on, they were inseparable.

Some people whispered that, since there was no one else in the house, and she was a relatively young woman, he was the only real suspect. But most folks did not share that sentiment. They sensed his all too palpable grief. Gossip of another kind also spread: that she had been poisoned, or committed suicide; that stuck in the drain a little glass ampoule, split open, had been found. A death pill, it was said.

Four days after the storm, on the morning Mrs. Vasconsuelos was to be buried, Hermine Rinkel came to our campus looking for work. The black Packard parked outside the administration building immediately drew the attention of those few people who remained on the premises. You see, from middle school to high school, everyone had been given the day off so they could attend the funeral. The teaching staff and administrators, too, but a skeleton crew remained, and it was Marlene, the substitute receptionist, a.k.a yours truly, who Hermine first met.

"I come to see about a job," she said with what I detected right away was a foreign accent. I thought the woman sounded like a villain in a cartoon or in an old movie. Still, I liked the air she exuded: one of total calmness, serenity, sporting a dress that probably cost less than what one would think, but the regal way in which she carried herself made an impression. Reading glasses cascaded down the tip of her nose and threatened to fall, but they never seemed to leave the edge. Her eyes were blue, not a typical sky-blue, mind you, more like a deep sea blue, and her hair was reddish, more copper now, with age having removed some of its luster. She had a bit of sun damage on her fair skin.

I welcomed her warmly and extended my hand. (It just felt like she would be someone who expected to shake hands.) After Hermine reciprocated, I then retrieved some papers out of a drawer in the receptionist's desk and gave them to this cool-looking woman who spoke funny. "Here is a list of the job openings available, and these are the forms you have to sign if you're interested in any of them," I said.

Hermine smiled while nodding and retreated to a seat to study the pages. But her disappointment took no time in showing on her face when she stood up and she stated that there really wasn't anything there that could make use of her qualifications.

Knowing that such a fine lady from abroad was not a common occurrence in Deming, and that the school would most likely benefit from someone of her background, I tried to find out what she would like to do.

"My profession, my life, has been books. I was a librarian in Zurich for over twenty years," she said proudly. Hermine did not go into details as to what she was doing here now, or how she had even heard of Deming. And I didn't dare ask.

"Oh, Ms. . . . " I proceeded to look at the pages where Hermine had signed her name. "Ms. Rinkel, there is an opening that I imagine we will have to fill, although it has not been posted yet and I don't know if I'm supposed to say this. It is that of school librarian. We just lost the one we had. It was during the sandstorm. Such a freaky thing."

Hermine listened intently as I told her this.

"Now . . . that is terrible, young lady," responded Hermine, who then pulled out from her large purse a black folder with some papers inside. "And these are my credentials."

"Please, call me Marlene," I said to her, trying to make her feel more comfortable. "And I will give these right away to the principal. I think she'll be thrilled to have you!"

With a slight bow and a smile that illuminated her face, Hermine turned around and headed toward the door. Then she stopped and looked back at me.

"Nice name . . . Marlene," she said, still smiling. "Like Dietrich."

After I clocked out that afternoon, I went out to find Mr. Dimas, our janitor, a walking encyclopedia of names. I told him what Hermine had called me. And right away he had an answer. "She has compared you to a German actress, that incredibly beautiful and well-dressed woman, Marlene Dietrich."

I felt kind of proud with what I had accomplished, holding the fort while everyone else was at the funeral; I just hoped that the principal would not get pissed off at me for having taken the liberty to tell Hermine about Mrs. Vasconsuelos' unfortunate death. But, the truth was, that we were going to need a librarian, and here was this woman, who had just, oh my God, dropped from the sky!

The next day I went back to class. And there was still sand everywhere. The library remained closed, and we would all be sad whenever we walked by it, whispering as if we had been inside, talking books with Mrs. Vasconsuelos, asking her for help with our term papers, seeking her out for anything from a broken heart to a chat about college admissions.

Sometimes she reminisced about the land of her parents, the city of Cali, in Colombia. They had left there when they were very young and sought a better life in New York City. The Bronx, to be precise. Or she spoke about the skyscrapers in Manhattan, and how on clear nights, they seemed to be bridges to the stars. She had grown to love the desert, with all its strange creatures, both ugly and beautiful, but especially the plants and its flowers. She liked when cacti blossomed amid rock formations, making everything look like a pop-up picture book.

It was said that she and Mr. Vasconsuelos had once thought of retiring in Brazil, where they had allegedly adopted two small children, twins. Mami told me this, from hearsay. But apparently, it was true, for after one vacation in 1974 in South America, Mrs. Vasconsuelos came back very sad and withdrawn. The story goes that, after traveling several times to this small cattle town, she had adopted the twins. The town's name, Candido Godoi, I sort of remembered from seeing a T.V. special on it, and screaming at Mom one night "That's it! That's the place the Vasconsuelos went to for their kids!"

The children never made it out of Brazil though. On their way to the airport, the car the Vasconsuelos were driving was hit from the back by a small bus that had lost control. Half of their car was crushed, and in it, the twins. Mr. and Mrs. Vasconsuelos returned to Deming and never talked about it, not to anyone, as far as I know. They wouldn't even acknowledge that they had been in Brazil. But our journalism teacher, Mr. Sawyer, had found a little news item detailing this horrific car crash in that Brazilian town involving two Americans from New Mexico.

Some people really have bad luck, I guess. Mr. Vasconsuelos being one of them. First, he lost his children, and now his wife.

It was enough to make anyone go crazy. After her death, we seldom saw him anymore, except occasionally at the market. He had even stopped going to church. So sad, since he and his wife never missed mass.

After a few weeks, our collective grief began to subside, in great part thanks to the charm and wit of Hermine.

Little sandstorms continued sporadically, hinting that summer was just right around the corner. Our principal, Mrs. Goddard, had taken an immediate liking to Hermine, and even congratulated me for having tended to her so well that day when most everyone was at the funeral, and for having mentioned our need for a librarian to her. In a short time, Hermine was not only working as our invaluable researcher, just like Mrs. Vasconsuelos, but she was also sponsoring a German Club, something we had never had before.

In spite of her pale skin, she was fearless with the sun. She organized camping trips and always wore big straw hats to protect herself from the rays. We went hiking in the desert, examining stones and flowers, looking for fossils, spotting birds and lizards, spiders and scorpions. She made us, those of us in her German Club, and those who frequently visited the library seeking her expertise in so many areas, learn in a new way, coming to view knowledge as valuable for its own sake. She was relentless in her research.

One Sunday after mass, we were invited by Hermine to her house. She was proud that her charming adobe bungalow had been restored by the previous owners to its 1943 glory, with polished hardwood floors and a working chimney. She showed me her fine hand-painted German porcelain and everywhere was a profusion of orchids.

I was expecting to find cuckoo clocks and to be offered Swiss cheese, but no, there was nothing clichéd about her. What struck me as sort of unusual was that there were no photos of her as a young woman, no pictures of Zurich, of relatives or friends. It was as if she didn't have a past, but lived in a perpetually frozen present. She also had many books, mostly in German. Some in Latin, Spanish and a good selection in English. Too much stuff to fit in that Packard, I thought.

"Since you are still not of age, I am sorry to inform you that we will not be having good German beer today," she teased us. "Instead, we will enjoy freshly made lemonade and pastries. Today we have Apfelkuchen, or apple cake, and Zimtkuchen, or cinnamon cake."

Those sweets . . . were . . . to . . . die . . . for.

She was in such good spirits, joking, laughing and sharing stories about her childhood in Switzerland. Until Marco, my friend, asked her about World War II. He said he had to write a paper for his world history class, and wanted to know if she had any experiences that she could relay to him. For the first time in several months, Hermine became tense. She didn't say anything for a moment, and finally, after she had seemingly gathered her thoughts, she explained that she had been in Zurich all the time and had tried not to read the news so as not to get depressed about what was happening.

"Whose car is that?" were the first words Tommy Arrow, one of our food suppliers and an Apache, asked me at the reception desk one morning.

"The Packard parked outside? Oh, that belongs to our librarian, the one who has taken Mrs. Vasconsuelos' place," I explained.

"You don't say . . . And how long has she been here, Marlene?"

"In town? Since the day of the last storm, the big one."

"Now that's interesting," he said, stroking his chin and looking down at the lapis ring on his hand. "For I could swear I saw that same car, during one of last year's big storms, in Doña Ana County. It's quite a unique car, you know, so I remember it well."

I didn't know what he was getting to, but I had a feeling it was not good.

"In fact, I remember commenting about that car to some of my *compadres* there, you know? 'Cause I travel quite a bit, because of my work, you know, and, some of them also praised the car, but said they had seen it in other towns, always when there were storms. Some lady drove it."

With those words, he looked at me, as if signaling me to provide more information, but I did no such thing.

"You take care, Marlene, I gotta run. And keep an eye on that Packard, you know what I mean?"

No, I don't know what you mean, I thought to myself.

Still, he had piqued my curiosity.

That afternoon, when I finished work, I stopped by the library to see Hermine.

"Well, hello there, beautiful Marlene," said Hermine, beaming. "How may I assist you?"

I thought of something quick.

"You know, that paper Marco was working on, I kinda liked his idea, and I'm thinking of asking him to let me work with him on it, and I figured that maybe you could provide us with some reference books here about the war."

A smile colder than the Alps slowly etched itself on her face and stayed there, no words coming out.

"Why, of course, let me see what I can dig up for you and Marco. Why don't you come back the next day you work, and I will have them ready?"

"Thanks! That will be the day after tomorrow."

"Fine then, I will have the materials for you."

The phone at her desk rang. She picked it up and covering it with her hand, excused herself in a low voice.

I waved goodbye.

"Marco, I asked her to get us some books. I told her I wanted to do the history paper with you."

"And why did you do that?"

"I guess I had some questions about her. You know, Tommy Arrow, the Indian man who sells us supplies and stuff, he told me he'd seen her car before, in other towns, and that people would talk about it, because they all remembered her coming in with the storms."

"Huh, kinda like here . . . "

I shrugged and replied, "Not sure."

"Why does she have all that German stuff at her house if she is Swiss? I don't get it. Switzerland was neutral during the war."

"Was it?"

"Duh, yeah!"

"Oh, hush, you know history has never been my strong subject. Seriously though, there's something not right here."

"Hey, I have an idea. Let's go into the downtown library, and dig up some stuff on her!"

I paused before I answered, feeling I was betraying her.

"I guess there's no harm in looking around."

"If we're gonna go, we gotta do it soon. They say another storm is coming."

"Okay, I have to see her in two days, to take out a few books she's going to get for me, but after that, we can go downtown."

On the day we had agreed, I stopped by the library to see Hermine. And strangely, she was not there. It was the first time I had seen her miss a day.

"She went to the library downtown, to look for some books we didn't have," Mr. Sawyer, the journalism teacher, told me. "I needed to do some research of my own, so I offered to take over for her for a few hours."

"Mr. Sawyer?"

"Yes?"

"How would you go about finding information on someone?"

"Someone well-known?"

"No, not really."

"You could start with the microfiche system in the library, searching for a specific time period or geographical area, if you have enough data. And the librarian, of course, can help you with that."

A day later Marco and I spent hours going through these boring black and white microfiches, moving the reels back and forth, checking *The Deming Headlight* daily and other publications that were available only in print. We searched for sandstorms, their occurrence in Deming, then in other towns of our county, then in other counties, and finally, in other states. Nothing unusual. Except . . .

"Hey, Marlene, check this out . . . "

"What?"

"This story, from 1976, refers to a major sandstorm in Las Cruces. It was a mile high, like a tidal wave of dirt."

"And?"

"An odd incident occurred. Some townspeople there remembered seeing a fancy car preceding the storm."

"Let me guess."

"Yeah. Our Packard."

"And, another thing Marlene . . . "

"What . . . "

"There was only one death registered. At a school."

We both stared in silence at each other. Marco and I kept reviewing the film strips, and a pattern emerged. Although the car was not mentioned again, every time a sandstorm had been reported, an unexplainable death had occurred as well. In New Mexico, Arizona, Colorado. Even northern Mexico. And in all these cases, the victims had been women who had adopted children.

"Do any of these stories say where these children came from, if they were from the States or from abroad?" I asked.

"No, except for one woman in Mexico, who is described as a Brazilian-German national."

Two words came into my head: Candido Godoi.

"Marco?"

"Yes?"

"Let's go ask the librarian here to help us find info on a town in Brazil."

"In Brazil? Why? What does that have to do with anything?"

"Come on."

"Candido Godoi is a small municipality in the state of Rio Grande do Sul."

We listened attentively to what the librarian downtown had found for us.

"It has an ethnically homogenous population of German descent, and one other characteristic which has made it quite unique in the world: it has the highest incidence of twins anywhere."

"I am not following this," Marco said.

"Hush," I replied. "Ma'am, please keep going."

"In the mid-1970s, the town became known to the outside world when twelve pairs of twins were apparently kidnapped and taken out of the country. They were brought to the United States and to Mexico. They were supposed to be—oh, this is good, kids, this is good!—the pride and joy of Dr. Josef Mengele and his assistant, a nurse."

Those names didn't mean anything to me, but Marco, as usual, knew something about them. I could see it in his expression.

The librarian continued. "That man was known as the Angel of Death, and he used to do horrible experiments on people in the concentration camps during World War II. He specialized in experiments on twins."

Marco and I didn't say anything. I was not sure what to make out of all this, but I could see on my friend's face the same expression Tommy Arrow made in the school administrator's office when he asked about the Packard outside.

"What are you thinking?" I said to him.

"Ma'am, are there any photos in that book? Any of Mengele and of this woman?"

"Let's see."

She flipped the pages and, indeed, there were some black and white photos. Then she stopped at one.

"This says it is allegedly Doctor Mengele, at a beach in Brazil, with his assistant . . . "

"Can we see?" Marco asked, turning his head around to catch a glimpse. She passed the book to him and we stared at the picture.

"That . . . that woman," I managed to say while trying to get a hold of my nerves.

"Looks like our librarian, doesn't it?" Marco said.

"Can you please make us a copy?" I said. "And let's hurry back Marco, there's another storm on its way."

Before she left to photocopy the page, the librarian addressed us. "May I ask, what is your interest in this photo?"

Marco answered right away.

"We're working on a history paper."

"Oh, I see," she said, before entering another room.

We wondered if she had put two and two together. Hadn't Hermine been at this library the day before? Surely this woman must've helped her. With one look at the picture, she should've recognized her instantly. The photo depicted a prettier version of Hermine, a younger one, but it was she.

"We have to go, we have to go!" I said.

As we stepped outside, however, the sun had begun to disappear under a cloud of sand. Once again, the desert was encroaching on us.

"Where's Ms. Rinkel?" I asked Mr. Sawyer in a hurry when I saw he was at the library again.

"She left a note here, with a copy for us. Mrs. Goddard has hers."

"What does it say?" I was about to start heaving. That's how anxious I was.

"Well, I guess there's no harm done in telling you a bit of faculty news, since you brought us Ms. Rinkel. She's gone to another town, but she doesn't say where. An emergency, it seems. A friend of hers who had adopted children lost them in an accident, and she is going there to console her."

Mr. Sawyer look at me as if he wanted to ask me something, but he didn't. Instead, he took out an envelope from a drawer.

"Here. She left this for you, Marlene."

I thanked him and walked out into the hall. Just then I saw Marco approaching. He saw my face and knew immediately something had happened.

"What is it? What's going on?" he asked.

"She's gone."

"Gone? Where? When?"

"To another town. To . . . visit a friend."

Marco noticed the envelope in my hands.

"Is that from her?"

"Yeah. But I haven't opened it yet."

I tore open the small ivory envelope and pulled out a note. I read it in silence.

"Well?" Marco was eager to know.

"She says thank you for the job. She says I have a bright future ahead of me, maybe one like her, in research."

The Red Lipstick

L. M. Quinn

The sound of car horns and screeching tires told me there was another traffic jam outside on Whittier Boulevard. I waited for the crunch of metal, but it didn't happen. Instead, *norteño* music started up from the liquor store next to us, drowning out the traffic noise.

My papi yelled at me from inside the garage to print out the López invoice for the work done on Mr. López' blue Chevy. I found the invoice in three seconds and printed it out, something my papi and his workers couldn't do. Computers were a mystery to them, just as fixing a car was to me.

I was also good at finding things—like lost keys and Mami's watch—when my nose wasn't buried in a book or staring at *CSI* or Hercule Poirot on the T.V. I adored the fussy *gordito* Belgian detective Poirot with the awesome grey brain cells he used to track down and catch all of the bad guys who came his way. There was no "grey" in his brand of justice, though. If you did the crime, you paid. *¿Lógico, no?*

Speaking of mystery, there was a real-live one happening at my papi's garage right here in Montebello, California. Auto parts had gone missing over the last three months, and it was costing my papi money he couldn't afford to lose.

Since my first day of work last Monday, no parts had been taken. My papi said that I was good luck and he was glad to have me here.

"Working at the garage this summer will help your papi save money until he hires a new bookkeeper in the fall," my mami had said the evening before I'd started working at the garage.

I protested at first because my summer school drama class started mid-June, but Papi would let me take time off work to attend. She'd thanked me for agreeing to help out with one of her special *lleno de amor* hugs that made me forget I was a fifteen-year-old *gordita morenita* who wore glasses and braces, when I longed to be like the brilliant (but chubby) Belgian detective. Nobody noticed how much you weighed when you were famous.

"You got the invoice, Yoli?" Sergio, my papi's favorite worker walked up to my counter with Mr. López shuffling after him in his baggy beige windbreaker and dirty white sneakers.

Sergio had worked for my papi for eight years, never missing one day for sick leave or for sleeping off a *cruda* every Monday like the other workers. Many of Papi's customers asked for Sergio to work on their cars. Everything he fixed, stayed fixed.

I nodded and handed Sergio the invoice so he could explain the charges in detail.

While they were talking, I ticked off on the inventory screen the auto parts that had been used for Mr. López' car, noting that the inventory total didn't balance because of the stolen parts.

I waited for Mr. López to leave and followed Sergio into the garage. A sharp, smell of oil and sweat filled my nose forcing me to breathe through my mouth as I headed to the vending machines at the back wall. I wanted a soda and chips to keep me going until my two o'clock lunch hour today.

"*La chismosa gordita* stuffing her face again." The comment from one of the workers was low, but loud enough for me to hear and bring a warm flush to my face.

"¡*Ya! Déjala en paz*," said Sergio, loud enough to be heard over the off-on-again of the hydraulic jack.

Sergio, father of five girls and with a wife suffering from MS in a wheelchair, came to my defense as he often had since I started working here, always telling me to ignore the guys' comments, and how I was going to be *una señorita bien bonita* one day.

The other workers didn't like having the boss' daughter in the garage. To them, I was a spy and would rat on them to my papi or to their families. Sure, I could tell everybody about how Lalo cheated on his girlfriend or Pepe spent part of his weekly paycheck gambling at the Bicycle Casino and then told his wife the check was short that week because my papi had cut all of the worker's hours to save money. But I didn't gossip. I watched and listened, just like Miss Marple and Sherlock Holmes did in some of my favorite mysteries.

"I want to be a detective," I'd told my best friend Laura last year in the high school cafeteria.

She rolled her eyes and shook her head, causing her frizzy black shoulder-length hair to bob up and down, and her glasses to slip down her pug nose.

"No way your *papis* are going to let you do that. Besides you know nothing about being a detective."

"Wrong. You know I've read every detective and mystery book in the library, and I'm going to study police science at Cal State L.A. after I graduate. I already sent away for a catalogue to see what courses they offer."

Laura just kept rolling her eyes and shaking her head as I'd watched the fork clutched in her chubby fingers shove a second piece of chocolate cake into her mouth.

Yesterday in drama class, I had almost told Laura about the unsolved mystery at my papi's garage, but something held me back. I'd wanted to solve it first before boasting about my super-detection skills. But once I had shown Laura the proof, she would be my biggest fan. She was like that.

"Yoli? We're going to lunch now."

Sergio smiled at me through his tiredness and patted my arm as he headed out the front office door with my papi to eat lunch at the Playa Baja on Beverly Boulevard like all the workers did every day at noon. Lalo and Pepe followed them a few seconds later, looking at me like I was a *cucaracha* on the wall. The potato chips I was snacking on didn't look so good anymore. Those two guys could make anyone lose their appetite, which was probably a good thing in my case.

I went into the closet where the parts were stored noting the hundreds of black, oily fingerprints on the boxes, shelves and walls from the guys grabbing parts to be used on their jobs.

Brilliant British detectives like the *güerito,* monocled Lord Peter Wimsey used fingerprints to catch criminals, but all the guys in the garage left prints here, including my papi, so there was no way to trap the thief using prints.

"Yoli! Where are you?" Mami's voice echoed inside of the empty garage an hour later.

"Coming."

I turned off the light inside the parts closet and locked the door. A lot of good that did. All of the workers had keys, too.

"They have to be able to get to the parts at all times in order to do their job," Papi had said when the parts started to go missing, even though Mami tried to reason with him.

"You know that it might be one of the workers, don't you? They're the only ones who have keys. *Es lógico.*"

"The guys are like family. I want them to feel trusted. My father always did the same at the garage with his workers before me, and it worked for him. It has to be someone from outside, not one of my guys."

Mami just shook her head and stayed silent. I could see pinkness creep into her cheeks—never a good sign—but she didn't want an argument.

"Okay, it's possible it is one of them. If the stealing doesn't stop, I'll call in the police."

Mami and I took the bus on the corner to Tía Lucy's house in Pico Rivera where we were going to be treated not only to a lunch of my *tía's* killer green chile and cheese tamales, but also to a make-up party. My *tía* sold Avon stuff like make-up, lipstick, perfume, all of which my mami bought from her saying she'd rather support her own family than give her money to Penny's.

I liked the make-up party with my mom and aunt's friends painting their lips and eyes all colors and sending sexy *piropos* to one another.

"Close your ears," they said with hoots of laughter to me and two other young girls there. We put our hands over our ears, but we could still hear everything. And soon we were all laughing together.

"Here's some red lipstick. It didn't sell too well, but it would be perfect for you to use in drama class, *¿verdad?*" My *tía* handed me a box filled with a dozen golden tubes, only one of which had been used as a sample. There was a blood-red fingerprint on the side of that tube.

Two days later, I was working at the garage, and waiting for a parts delivery.

Laura dropped by to tell me that our drama class dress rehearsal had been rescheduled for that afternoon at one o'clock. She'd stopped by my house and gotten my make-up bag and costume for me.

"You need to show up in costume and full make-up. I can't wait for you because I got to go to the dentist, so I'll meet you in class."

I had just enough time to let Papi know I'd have to leave early, put the new parts in the parts closet and then take the bus to the auditorium.

Riding the bus in costume and make-up was always a thrill. I wasn't Yoli, *la gordita*, but a comical housekeeper, a Hawaiian dancer or a pretty teacher, depending on what role I was playing in the school drama that year.

"Hello? Parts delivery."

I came out of the restroom behind the counter with my hands still covered in white grease paint and red lipstick, and helped the guy load the parts into the closet, checking off the numbers on the invoice to match the parts.

I didn't have time to enter the new parts into the computer, but I could do it when I got back from the rehearsal. I tucked the grease-paint and lipstick-smudged invoice under the keyboard so I wouldn't forget where I'd put it.

Before locking the closet door, I managed to wipe away the grease paint and lipstick from the outside fronts of the boxes. I'd do another wipe when I got back to catch any remaining stains on the bottom and sides of the boxes.

A half-hour later, knees and hands shaking, I stood behind the dusty curtain on the stage waiting for my cue to enter the scene. Once on stage, I forgot about being nervous and became my character, Mrs. Hudson, Sherlock Holmes' trusty housekeeper.

We were doing an adaptation of the *Hound of the Baskervilles*. The hound was only sound effects, but it still was pretty creepy when his howling blasted out between our spoken lines.

Dress rehearsal went really well. Mr. Molina, our teacher, told us that he hadn't ever seen such good work so early in a rehearsal. I couldn't wait to tell my *papis* all about it over dinner tonight. They knew I loved my drama classes. I felt glamorous and powerful when I performed in front of an audience, my lines perfectly spoken. Acting out different roles would also help me big-time when I had to do undercover detective work—something my parents didn't know yet.

I got back to the garage about five, booted up the PC and took the invoice from under the keyboard.

When I unfolded the sheet, something was different. The grease paint and red lipstick blotches had been smudged even further with black grease and what looked like a pencil eraser trying to remove some of the checkmarks I'd made. The number of new parts checked off on the list was not as many as I remembered.

My pencil sat in a small blue and white pottery vase among other pens. The normally clean pencil eraser was now blood-red.

Just then, Pepe came out of the parts closet holding two boxes and headed into the garage.

I went into the closet and looked at the boxes on the shelves noting a few empty spaces toward the back where more than two boxes had been removed. The other guys had probably used parts today too, so there was no way of telling what was missing until I entered what they'd used.

At six o'clock, the guys were gathering up their things to leave when I finished entering all the parts used that day. Three of the new and most expensive parts missing.

"Come on, Yoli. Time to go."

My papi turned off the lights in the garage and put on his jacket. He had dark circles under his eyes and a few wrinkles on his face I hadn't noticed before. I wanted to hug him and tell him I loved him and that everything was going to be okay.

Instead, I logged off the PC, grabbed my backpack and followed him out feeling bad that everything wasn't okay and that I'd have to tell him that more parts had been stolen today.

My hands looked like prunes. I'd been scrubbing them for ten minutes to get the red lipstick off. That lipstick just didn't want to go away. It would take days of scrubbing before it would fade from my hands. If only I hadn't used my fingers to apply the color on my lips. Maybe that was why Tía Lucy couldn't sell this color.

I went into the living room to say goodnight to my *papis*. Mami was already asleep in front of the T.V., one of her *novelas* playing softly in the background. I kissed her on the cheek and she opened one eye and smiled at me before closing it again.

Papi was finishing the bookkeeping on last month's accounts, mumbling under his breath. He leaned over and gave me a kiss, then hugged me.

"You're doing a great job with the accounts, *hijita*. I'm proud of you. I only wish I had a detective in the family to put a stop to the stealing."

I kept silent, hugged him back and then headed for my bedroom to finish my drama homework before going to sleep.

Somehow, I was going to find the thief and prove what a great detective I was to both Laura and my papi. No more auto parts were going to be stolen on my watch.

The following day at breakfast, I told my papi that it was probably a good idea for one of us to be at the front desk at all times so we could keep an eye on the parts closet. He agreed with me, so I packed my lunch everyday to eat it at my desk, and Papi took over the desk when I had to go to drama class once a week.

The workers grumbled about having to find one of us to get the parts they needed, but they stopped a few days later, once they got used to the routine.

For the rest of the month, no parts went missing.

The following Monday, I was running late to my last drama rehearsal before our two public performances, so Sergio offered to give me a lift to Montebello High School on the way to pick up his wife, Lupe, for one of her weekly doctor's appointments.

I got into the passenger seat of his old, white Ford pickup that needed painting and a new set of tires. My teeth rattled every time we hit a bump, and I had to wriggle around to avoid the spring poking through my seat cushion.

Lupe's MS was getting worse and she would need total day-care in addition to some different and very expensive medication soon, according to Sergio. And with five daughters to support, the oldest one just starting high school, Sergio was going to have to look for a night job to pay for all of the extra expenses.

It didn't look like he'd be getting a new truck any time soon. I wished I could give him one for always being so nice to me, a shiny, new red one with a big dashboard. He could put tiny framed pictures of Lupe and his kids on it, instead of taping them to the worn, cracked leather dashboard of this truck.

I felt really bad for him and his family, and told him I would pray for them. He thanked me with a smile, but his shoulders didn't straighten up and the smile soon disappeared. The way he sat reminded me of the way dogs sat at the pound, knowing you wouldn't take them.

Turning onto Cleveland Avenue, he pulled up to the front of the high school and double parked next to an SUV to let me out.

It was when I took my backpack from the storage space behind the seat that I saw the red lipstick stains on the floor. There was no mistaking that color, but I had to be certain.

"Wait, Sergio! I dropped my pen."

I bent down closer to the floor, my stomach tying into knots, and ran my finger across the stain that left blood-red lipstick marks on my fingers. The stains must have come from the bottom of the new boxes from which I hadn't yet wiped off the lipstick, boxes that should be taken into the garage for a job and nowhere else.

"Thanks, Sergio. See you tomorrow."

I watched his truck rattle off, unable to move. How could he steal from Papi? But he had. I'd seen *la tristeza y desesperación* in his eyes when he talked about his wife and having to get another job, just like those actors in Mami's *novelas* whose mother or childhood sweetheart was dying and who would do anything to save them.

Would I steal if I needed money and had my family depending on me? I didn't have an easy answer. It was a grey area in the right or wrong of a case that my favorite detectives hadn't encountered and, certainly, never explained.

But it wasn't right what Sergio had done, no matter how much I wanted to see it otherwise. And if Papi called the police and Sergio got caught, he and his family wouldn't survive for sure. Sergio would go to jail.

I struggled with my lines during rehearsal, my mind being more on my own mystery than on Sherlock Holmes' case.

By the time Papi picked me up after rehearsal that afternoon, I knew what I had to do before any more parts went missing.

I put the letter telling Sergio I knew what he'd done on the front seat of his truck just before he left for the day. In it, I told him that if he stopped taking the parts, I wouldn't say anything to my papi.

The following day, Sergio called in very early and left a voice-mail message that he was sick. Then he and his family disappeared.

One night after dinner the following week, I overheard my papi telling Mami that Sergio had probably gone back to Mexico where he could get less expensive treatment and a full-time healthcare worker for his wife. He hated to lose his favorite mechanic, but that family always came first.

I kept my promise to Sergio not to tell, but one day soon everyone would figure out he had been the one taking the auto parts. What he did was wrong. It still made me feel bad he had to steal and then run away to protect his family.

Being a detective wasn't easy. For sure, even the great Hercule Poirot must have had some sad days with cases like this one.

Back Up

Manuel Ramos

It's not that I thought Dad was a creep just because he was a cop. It was weird, that's all. He'd be out busting the bad guys, getting worked up behind the stuff he had to see every day like women all bruised and black-eyed, and burned kids and old men pistol-whipped. And the dead people. He saw plenty of those. He did that for years, and he started drinking heavy, a regular booze hound. And I remember him coming home in his uniform and before he hit the bottle he'd take off his gun, unload and wipe it clean, and tell me and my brother Martín that if he ever caught us fooling around with his piece that he would "kick the living hell out of us." We were like seven and ten so that scared us, of course, and made us want to get our hands on that gun all that much more. We never did, though. He kept it locked up and the key stayed with him. When he eventually took us target shooting and tried to teach us how to deal with a gun, he jammed us with rules. "Never load a gun unless you intend to use it. Never point a gun at anyone unless you intend to hurt them. Never shoot at someone unless you intend to kill that person." His favorite rule? "Stop. Look. Be Careful. Be aware of where you are and who's around." By the time he preached his rules, we had moved on and it was no big deal. And by the time I made it to Cunningham High, no one hardly ever brought up Dad's cop job.

That was before Dad made detective and before Martín was arrested and sent to the Youth Correctional Facility, or the YCF, as the old man called it. I missed that guy, but truth is, he was a mess-up, big time. Martín never grew up, never figured out what to do with himself, and when he got into drugs, that was it for my big brother. Now, he's sitting out his sentence. The judge showed no mercy (even though Dad was on the force) and sentenced him to farm work and boredom at the YCF until he turned eighteen. That was the first time I knew that my mother's heart was broken. *Pinche* judge, like my Dad said, just loud enough for the asshole to hear him. But Martín will get out later this year. Whether he wants to come home is another question. What's there to come home to, right?

The second time my mom broke down, was when they forced Dad off the force. Even I did not see that coming. And then they started fighting all the time until he moved out and they filed for divorce, and there I was, trying to finish high school when I didn't really care about nothing, Dad turned into a stranger, my mom wouldn't quit crying and life was like one big drag.

But I didn't mean for this to be a downer. I like to write in my journal and so I just let it rip; whatever pops in my head ends up in my book. Sometimes it comes out all cheery and sappy and sometimes I can't believe the stuff I put down. I been doing it for years, but not even Jamey knows about it. He'd just say that it's so gay, but I know it's what I need to chill sometimes, and gay ain't got nothing to do with it.

Jamey's real name is Jaime Rodriguez, but no one calls him that. And I'm Miguel Resendez, but you can call me Mike. Mike and Jamey—we been buds since he moved to El-town (our neighborhood is Elvin Heights, but it's been known as El-town from the years when the OGs cruised Braxton Avenue in their low-rider Chevys and Mercurys). He sauntered into Mrs. Hyde's second-grade class looking like a tall, skinny version of George

López, all dark and big-headed. Jamey and Mike—Cheech and Chong. That's what some of the jocks call us, behind our backs, but we don't care.

Jamey and I are a good team. He's tough, not afraid to mix it up if he has to. We've had to back each other up a few times, usually against the El-town Cutters. They finally left us alone, but there were plenty of times when Jamey and I had to throw down. We been knocked out, cut up, even shot at, but we never gave in. So now there's a truce between us and the Cutters, and most of the guys who used to hassle us are getting beat up by my brother in the YCF, or cruisin' in their wheelchairs, or dead. It's all good now. Except that my life still sucks.

Jamey and I talked one day a few weeks after Dad split.

"You don't know where he is?" Jamey said, although I think he knew the answer.

"Him and Mom had a big fight. He ran out of the house saying that everyone could shove it. He must have gotten drunk. He came home the next morning, early. I could hear him stumbling around. But he didn't stay long. He got his stuff and moved out. It's like he blames us because he screwed up. What I really don't like is that he won't talk to us, he won't explain what's going on with him."

Jamey shrugged. We had skipped last period and were sitting around our table in Corey Park, the place where we wasted a lot of time, sometimes with others from school but most often just the two of us.

"What do you think happened? Didn't your pops say nothing?" Jamey spoke like he was picking his words all careful. I didn't answer right away. I looked at the carved heart with the initials AB/MR that I had carved into the table months ago, when me and Andrea were still an item. "You got to admit, that was extreme, even for your old man." I jerked my head and glared at Jamey.

Where was he going with this? "I mean, shooting Cold Play when he didn't have any gun. He's a clown and all that, but still."

I pushed Jamey off the table bench.

"Shut up!" I never had been mad at Jamey, but I was pissed right then, real pissed. Me and Dad weren't exactly Father and Son of the Year, but he was my old man, and no one had a right to talk about him, except me.

"Hey, dude. Damn. Cool it." Jamey picked himself up. He clenched his fists, then let it go. "Catch you later, jerk face." He walked away. I almost shouted at him to come back. Almost.

The night it all came down, I was alone in the house. Mom's text said that she was visiting Grandma Herrera over in Clifton; she might stay the night; something about Grandma not feeling well. Dad apparently had stopped by, there was a dirty plate and half-filled coffee pot on the counter, but he hadn't left a message.

I felt sick, like the flu or something. I listened to a mix of Dad's oldies. *Too many teardrops for one heart to be crying. You're gonna cry ninety-six tears. Cry, cry, cry.* I had always liked that song even though it made no sense. What was so bad about ninety-six tears? I turned off the CD player and sat in the dark and the silence. I thought about throwing up, or maybe smoking a cigarette, but I didn't do anything. I just sat there, for a long time.

Finally, I switched on a lamp and picked up a newspaper from the end table where it had gathered dust for weeks. *MAN SHOT BY POLICE EXPECTED TO RECOVER.* A smaller headline announced: *Resendez on Administrative Leave.* I didn't have to read the story to know what else it said.

Officer Resendez and his partner, Officer Sandra Moreno, were driving through the alleys in the Horseback Hill area when they saw a man crawl out of a basement window and sneak through a backyard. The police officers waited in the darkness and made their arrest.

Slam-dunk. Dad and his partner Sandra must have been all smiles. They had busted Hank Garcia, the so-called Zebra Burglar because he wore a black-and-white bandanna around his head. The cops wanted that guy, for months. The story was that he and his gang had broken into hundreds of homes and businesses over the past two years, and some people had been hurt, seriously.

But the arrest went bad. They were calling in the details when Fred Jackson showed up. He was a low-life most of us knew as a cheap hood who gave himself the nickname "Cold Play." According to Garcia, Dad immediately left the car and started waving his gun at Cold Play. *I was sitting in the back seat, handcuffed. The cop and this other guy were saying something behind the car, I don't know what. It sounded like an argument. Then I heard the blast of a gun, and it seemed like the whole inside of the car lit up. I twisted around to my left and I could see the cop holding his gun, standing over the guy who was bleeding in the street. The second cop, who had been in the front seat, rushed out. I heard her say, "What did you do, Carlos?" Then they messed around in the dark for a long time. Finally, more cops showed up and they took me away. It didn't look right, that's all I know.*

There had been an internal investigation by the police department and the district attorney's office. The newspapers had a great time quoting the criminals, who had no problem slamming Dad and the police in general. Jackson's story, told from his hospital bed, was that he had been walking home after a night of partying when he stumbled on Dad's police cruiser. He admitted that he had been drinking but denied that he had done anything to provoke the cops. *That one pig, the Mexican, he shot me like I was a sick dog. Any soulful man he saw that night was gonna get shot, and that turned out to be me. I want him to pay. Someone has to pay for what happened to me.* The Elvin Heights Echo had a photograph of Jackson in his hospital bed, a bandage wrapped around his head. The caption read: *Fred Jackson, aka Cold Play: Innocent victim of police shooting?*

I had to laugh. Cold Play had never been innocent of anything. He was one of those white guys who tried to act ghetto, gangsta bullshit. We thought he was stupid. And his nickname was another joke. The guy probably didn't know that he had named himself after a white music group—music that he would never listen to. But then I guess a guy who needs to give himself a handle didn't give a damn about what I thought.

They put Dad on administrative leave while the investigation dragged on. Dad kept telling us that it would be straightened out, that the investigation would go nowhere, but even he admitted that the Department wanted no more of him. My dad had a reputation for being an aggressive cop; quick to retaliate and much too likely to draw his weapon. He had been involved in two other shootings, and he was the subject of a half-dozen citizen complaints for excessive force. Each time he had been cleared by the Police Review Board, but the complaints stayed in his personnel file. Dad didn't know what to do when he wasn't being a cop, and it showed. One day he told us he was quitting the force. That was when the real trouble started between Dad and Mom.

My cell rang and vibrated.

"What?"

"You cool down?" Jamey asked. We hadn't talked since I had shoved him off the bench.

"I'm okay. You?"

"I'm not the one been screwed up. Your old man home yet?"

"He's been around but I haven't seen him. Now Mom's gone, too."

"You're on your own?"

"Nothing new. Look, I'm beat. I need some sleep."

"Let's get together tomorrow, okay?"

"If you want."

"Yeah. Terry told me to act right. Like, you're under pressure or something. 'Poor baby,' I said."

"Screw you."

"Yeah, right. We'll hook up tomorrow."

"Later, dude. Easy."

Terry was his on-again, off-again girlfriend. She had more common sense in her pudgy little finger than Jamey had in his whole family.

I sat in the dark for a few more minutes. Eventually I shuffled to my room and flopped on the bed.

About an hour later I threw a few clothes and candy bars into a backpack. I picked up my cell, slipped a cap on my head. I locked all the windows and doors. I snared cash from the envelope I had taped under my bed (about $500 saved from my part-time gig as a busboy) and I wrote a note that said, *I'll be back in a few days. I need to get my head together. Don't worry. I'll be okay.* I signed it "Miguel." I stepped out the door and walked up the street and it was as though I saw the houses and lawns and driveways for the first time. I looked back at the house and realized that it looked like every other house on the block. I kept on walking even though I didn't know where I was going.

I had to wait forever but eventually I caught the bus at the corner of Wilder and 40th. It took me downtown, which seemed as good a place as any to spend the night. I seriously thought about staying on the bus until it got to the edge of El-town, out near the old airport. But then what?

As I debated my short-term future, my cell rang. It was the old man.

"Yeah?" I said.

"Mike. Where are you?"

"I'm on my way to Jamey's. We got some math homework. He always needs my help with that stuff. Where are you?"

"I'm at work. Overtime, under the lights. I had to take a construction job. An old friend put in a good word for me with the foreman and the union. They need a lot of men to get the new courthouse back on schedule. It's crazy out here. Ironic, me working on a courthouse, huh?"

"I guess."

"I can't talk too much, Mike. So you gotta listen good. You and your mother have to be careful. Sandra let me know that Cold Play put a target on my back. I can handle that, but I'm worried about your mother and you."

I wanted to say that if he had never left, maybe he wouldn't have to worry so much.

"Mom's at Grandma's for a few days. I'll call her and let her know. She won't take your calls."

"I know. I know. What about you?"

"I'm good, Dad. Jamey and me been in tight spots before. This is just Cold Play doin' it macho for his suck-ups. No sweat, Dad. Seriously."

"Yeah, I know, you're a tough guy. But this Cold Play is just enough of an idiot to try to do something. You should be okay at school tomorrow. I'll pick you up after, and give you a ride home. About 3:30?"

"No way. I'm not in middle school. I can deal with it. I'll be with Jamey. I'll walk home the long way, by his house. We'll be careful. I thought you had to work, anyway?"

"Yeah, I do. I probably can't get to the school until 4:30. Wait for me, inside. I mean it, Mike."

"I said I'd be okay. I can take care of myself."

"This is serious, Mike. This guy is crazy. He tried to kill me once, that's why I had to shoot him. And he won't let it go. Now that I think about it, I'm going to pick you up in the morning and take you to school. I'll be there by seven-thirty."

I shut the cell. I didn't answer it when he called back.

I called Grandma's number but no one picked up. I texted Mom—*Dad sd b careful. Cold Play threats. Stay @ Grandma a few days.* I didn't mention that I had run away.

I patted my backpack and felt the gun. Jamey and I bought it a long time before, when we thought that we needed extra protection from the Cutters. I never had to use it, but I figured that it would be a good thing to have as I walked the streets when I . . . well, I wasn't sure what I was trying to do, I only knew that I had to get out of the house and away from everyone and everything. I needed a change, and I was doing the only thing that might cause that change.

That night was rough. I roamed the streets, confused, sneaking around like a thief, heading for cover whenever I saw headlights. I avoided everyone—the homeless guys, the hookers, the other runaways. Dad's message had put a little panic in my head. Maybe Cold Play was looking for me. What if he found me? What would I do? I decided to leave town, hit the road.

I crashed not too far from the Main Street Mall, down a flight of stairs that led to the small shop where Downtown Barbers had been for years, below street level. I leaned against the door and tried to get comfortable. I had to move broken glass and old newspapers. I made sure no one could see me from the street. I cleaned the area as best I could.

That's when it hit me. What the hell was I doing? I had a warm bed at my house. Food. Cable. I should be going to school in the morning, spending time with Jamey and maybe talking to Andrea, if she would only give me a chance. What did I expect to accomplish scrunched up in a ball hidden away like a bum, a gun pressing against my ribs? Or on the run like an orphan? Did I think I could fix everything on my own? Take care of Cold Play? Get Dad's job back? Get Mom and Dad back together?

The wind picked up. It whistled across the deserted streets, pushing trash and dirt into my concrete cave. I shivered, occasionally drifted off. The night dragged on.

I nearly jumped out of my shoes when my cell buzzed. Jamey. The screen flashed 5:38 A.M.

"Mike? I'm in a jam. You got to come."

"What is it? What the hell . . . "

"Cold Play grabbed me when I left Terry's last night. He said he couldn't find you so he settled for me." It almost sounded like Jamey laughed at his own words. "He finally got me to call you. He says you have to do something."

"What does he want? Are you okay?"

He waited a few seconds. He shouted, "Call the cops, your dad! Don't come . . . "

I heard what must have been Jamey getting punched and a loud "Oh!" Then it sounded like the phone had been dropped. A gruff, almost hoarse voice said, "Kid—If you want to see your buddy again, you better listen good. It's your old man. You get him to come and talk to me, and your pal walks out of here okay. If Resendez ain't here in another hour, Jamey's dead. And you're next."

"What? What do you mean?"

"Don't be stupid, kid. Get your old man here to the football field, at the high school. One hour, six-thirty. You get him here. And tell him he better be alone or this punk is dead, and then you. I know where you and your old lady live." He hung up.

I immediately punched in number 1—Dad's speed dial. He answered on the first ring. I guess he wasn't sleeping either. I tried to explain what was going on but all I could get out was a jumbled mix of crying and half-sentences. He finally had to shout at me, "Michael! Get it together! Goddammit! What is going on?"

It took longer than I wanted but I managed to convince Dad that Jamey was in trouble and needed his help.

"You stay where you are. I'll send Sandra for you and I'll go meet Jackson. I'm gonna bust his ass for good."

"How?" I was so mixed up. It sounded like Dad was talking as though he was still a cop. He just couldn't give it up.

"I can't explain now. I've got to get to the football field. Jamey's in real danger. I hope I'm not too late. Wait for Sandra."

My stomach tightened and dry heaves jerked my upper body. I couldn't think straight for a long time. I sweated and shivered, imagined terrible things about Jamey, my Dad and Cold Play. Confusion mixed with the wind whipping around me. *I should do what Dad said*, I thought. *But, I can't let down Jamey. It's all my fault.*

That stuff went on in my head until I finally settled down and figured out what I needed to do. I grabbed the gun, stuck it in my pants, made sure I had my money and then I ran up the stairs from my hiding place. I left everything else for the barbers. I tore down windy Main Street heading for the high school and the football field. The gun hindered my running so I pulled it from my pants and held it while I ran. If anyone saw me they'd have to call the police—crazy teenager running through the dark with a gun. There was no traffic but some lights had been turned on in a few of the stores and buildings. I heard Jamey's voice as I ran—worried but still telling me to stay away, to let my Dad handle it. Jamey had been willing to get hurt, maybe killed just to keep me out of danger. I saw a bike leaning against a tree in a yard. I didn't slow down as I approached the short picket fence. I jumped over the fence, grabbed the bike, ran it to the gate and took off. A dog jumped at me from behind, but I left him barking and howling.

The football field appeared in the night like a giant sleeping black bear. A wire and plywood fence surrounded the field, and the gate was chained and locked up. But I didn't have a problem getting in. The fence had more holes than Grandma Herrera's old aprons, and it was no big deal to get inside to the asphalt strip that circled the field. I left the bike at the fence, found a break in the old wire and crawled in and stayed low, looking for any sign of Dad, Jamey or Cold Play.

When I saw them, I stopped breathing for a few seconds. They were in the end zone under the scoreboard, the darkest place on the field, maybe thirty yards from me. Cold Play must have thought he would be safe there, and the truth was that no one could see him from the street, outside the fence. Dad knelt on the ground, his hands behind his head. Jamey was also on the ground but he was lying down and I didn't see him move. Cold Play strutted around them, holding a gun pointed at Dad's head.

I moved to them, on hands and knees. I thought I inched along slow, so as not to make noise, but in just a few seconds I was close enough that I could hear Cold Play cussing and threatening my father.

"You thought you could burn Cold Play and that'd be it? You dumb pig. Get ready to kiss your ass goodbye, Resendez. Tonight you pay for messing with me."

"I already said I'm sorry that happened. We can do business together, man. I know stuff that you can use, and I want in on the action. Don't you understand?"

Cold Play swung the gun at Dad and hit him on the jaw. Dad dropped to the grass, next to Jamey. Cold Play held his gun with both hands and aimed at Dad.

I stood up and waved at Cold Play. "Hey, asshole. Over here, you dumb son-of-a-bitch." I jumped up and down. He stumbled backwards, surprised I guess. Dad screamed something I couldn't understand. Cold Play aimed the gun and before I could do anything, he shot at me. The bullet landed a few feet to my right. I hollered although I didn't even think about it. It just came out. I rolled to my left and dug into the ground. I aimed my gun in the general direction of Cold Play.

Dad's rules rolled through my head. *Stop. Look. Be Careful. Be Aware.* It was too dark and I couldn't take the chance that I might shoot Dad or Jamey. I couldn't see Cold Play anyway. I rolled some more and picked up my head to take another look. I saw no one. I waited a few minutes. Nothing moved except the tips of the grass in the remaining breeze from the windy night. A piece of paper floated across the field and jammed itself against the fence, where it quivered like something dying.

I started to crawl to the end zone, slowly and quietly, and had gone only a few yards when I heard the footsteps behind me. Then I felt the gun at the back of my head.

"What a night for old Cold Play. A trifecta. The pig, his kid and another kid just for grins. Yeah, a great night." I smelled booze and a sickly, sweet odor of something else coming from Cold Play. It's strange, but I didn't feel afraid. That might sound like bragging, but I'm just saying that right then, when Cold Play had his gun pressed against my skull and I waited for the final flash or whatever it was that would happen when he pulled the trigger, right then, I could see clearly, make out details in the dark; I could hear each sound in the night, any little bit of noise, even the beating of Cold Play's crazy heart. And I knew I could handle it. My only thought was that I still needed to do something to help Dad and Jamey. I hadn't finished and I hadn't helped, and that bothered me.

The shot sounded like every movie gun blast I had ever heard, like every explosion in Grand Theft Auto, like every argument Mom and Dad made me sit through. I collapsed on the ground, heaving and breathing deeply but feeling like my lungs were blocked off. Cold Play fell next to me, blood flowing from his mouth, a gurgling noise coming out of his nose, tiny red bubbles covering his lips.

Dad reached down and picked me up. He hugged me and I think we were both crying.

"How . . . ?" I stammered.

"The dummy didn't think that I might have a back up. Hidden in my boot. I was waiting for my chance. You gave it to me, Mike."

"Jamey?" I said.

"He's hurt, beat up pretty bad. But he'll be alright."

I looked over Dad's shoulder. The sun was coming up over the downtown buildings. A half-dozen cops were running into the field. Four of them surrounded us, two checked out Dead Play. Sandra stepped forward.

"Carlos, you alright? I told you to wait for back up. ¡Cabezón!" She slugged him on the shoulder, then she smiled. "Your boy, he okay?"

An ambulance raced onto the field and Jamey was loaded aboard and then hauled away. Sandra called his parents.

There were more questions but I didn't say too much. Dad had to tell the story of what happened at least three times to different cops and detectives. It looked like the cops didn't know how to deal with Dad. At least, there wasn't a question about it being self-defense. Finally, they let him take me home. Sandra said she would make sure the bike I had "borrowed" would be returned. She grabbed my gun, too.

Dad took me to the motel where he was sleeping. He could tell that I was tired, completely beat, so he didn't ask me any more questions or dig into what I was doing on the street, with a gun, or what the hell did I think I was doing at the football field. He saved all that for the next day, and when he was finished with me he called Mom and told her what had happened. Dad and I talked a lot waiting for Mom. I think he needed that. Then she picked me up and took me home where I had to deal with another lecture, then more crying from her, and finally hugs and kisses.

A few days later, Jamey and I were able to talk without anyone else around.

"So, your dad is still a cop, undercover, eh? That's wild—crazy but cool, know what I mean?"

"Yeah, I know exactly what you mean. He said not to tell anyone, not even you."

"You serious? You know you can trust me. Who else you got?"

"Yeah. It's all good. I think he expects me to tell you."

"There you go."

"Anyway, Dad and Sandra had been trying to stop the burglary ring for months. Cold Play and that Zebra guy are just part of the gang. The burglaries are a small piece of what they're into. When Dad had to shoot Cold Play the first time, it gave him an idea, an excuse to put himself on the street in civilian clothes. A way to get inside the gang."

"But they didn't find a gun. The story was that Cold Play didn't have a weapon."

"Dad explained that. When Cold Play got shot he managed to kick his gun down the sewer drain and Dad and Sandra acted like they couldn't find it. Dad has been trying to make contact with one of the leaders of the gang, someone who doesn't think much of Cold Play. Dad said his own rep is shot now, and everyone thinks he's dirty. That's how he wanted it."

"He should have told you, or your Mom at least."

"He thought it was too dangerous for us to know. But it didn't matter anyway. Cold Play made his move."

"Your dad stopped him. Ain't his cover blown?"

"Maybe. Maybe not. Since Cold Play is dead, there's only a few who know the real story. You for one."

Jamey tried to smile but he looked nervous.

"Dad shooting Cold Play gives him some cred with the gang. Cold Play wasn't too popular. That's why you can't say anything, Jamey. *Nada.*"

He extended his hand and we knuckle-bumped. Jamey would never tell anyone.

"But your mom and dad are over? This didn't fix it?"

"No way. If anything, she hates him worse now. He almost got me killed, according to her. I've tried to tell her it wasn't his fault. He saved me. But that's not the way she looks at it."

Jamey nodded.

"When you get those stitches out?" I asked. "They are ugly, bro. How can Terry stand to kiss that face?"

"Hey, man. She's all over me now, like syrup on a pancake. Nothing better than a good beating so women will act nice and accommodating. Too bad nothing happened to you that you can use on Andrea. You missed your chance. You should have got wounded, or something. At least."

"Yeah, too bad. Maybe next time."

The Right Size

René Saldaña, Jr.

The one called Jimmy stays behind with me, my baby brother, Chino and our dad in my parents' bedroom. His back's to the bedroom door, the gun waving this way and that, but mostly pointing in the general direction of Dad, the obvious one to aim at, I guess. This guy Jimmy probably thinks Dad is the greater threat among the three of us, but he's dead wrong. Dad couldn't hurt a bug, much less a guy with a gun who's aiming it right at his face. I'm not knocking Dad. He's a real good father, would give his life for any one of us kids (is probably thinking he just might have to today), but his whole existence he's always told us it's always better to turn the other cheek, to walk away from a fight. He's built solid, is a construction guy, but wouldn't swat at a fly for nothing. I'm not saying he's a pansy, but I'm thinking we're in a heap of trouble here. I overhead Mom once say I was kind of small for fourteen. Right now would be a good time to grow half a foot and pick up some muscle. No such luck, though.

This guy Jimmy says to us, "Flat on the floor. And don't none of you look at me, or so help me, I'll . . . " He most likely finishes that sentence the way I think he's going to: with a "or so help me, I'll cap you." Or something else just as criminally hardened like that. Whatever he says I can't hear because as soon as he said hit the ground, I'm blocking out everything that comes after. Scared stiff, when I see Chino and Dad drop onto the floor, I follow suit. I dive fast, no worries. The carpet feels soft on my face, and I see a dead, dry spider where the carpet meets the baseboard. The sun coming in through the window is warming my back.

I turn my head to see Dad kissing the floor, too, but he's trying to talk some sense into Jimmy. Like I said, Dad wouldn't lift a finger, not even against a punk like this Jimmy guy waving a gun. His words, a whisper, are clear enough for me to hear. Dad says: "Listen, whatever you two want with my boy out there, well it can't be this bad. Is it money? We can take care of it, if it is." By his *boy out there* Dad means my older brother Tommy. I don't know how he fits into all this, but it doesn't surprise me one bit that Tommy's somehow involved, and he's managed to tangle us in it, too. That's Tommy for you. Always has been trouble. The proverbial "black sheep." For instance, he dumped school when he was just starting out his tenth grade year. Just up and quit. Came home one day with a backpack full of books, a ton of homework and a scowl on his face. He sat at dinner that night and announced that this kind of silliness was for the birds, and that he wasn't gonna take it. He said he'd go in the next day and hand in the books to his teachers and turn in his notice at the office. He was sixteen, old enough to quit if he wanted to, and he did. Nothing Mom or Dad could say to change his mind. It's not that he was dumb; it's that he's driven in a completely different way. Always something doing with him. Always set his sights on something ahead, just around the next corner. Right then, though, he couldn't quite figure out how any of this school work was going to help him in his future as a body shop guy, and school didn't offer that line of study.

He did just like he said. And by the next evening he'd not only jumped the school ship, he'd also secured (his word) a job at a local body shop, starting out at the bottom, he said, a broad smile across his face, sweeping up the joint, wiping down the toilet and all the while in between, he'd be putting the tools back where they belong. "That way," he said, "I'm learning what each one is, and what it does." Within two months, his boss man Joe had him helping with little jobs (pounding out dents with a mallet, spreading and smoothing the Bondo) and a few months after that, he was showing what he knew and what he didn't on an old junker of a truck a friend of Joe's brought in. A freebie for the guy, but he'd have to take or leave what Tommy gave him. It turned out not so bad, according to Tommy. That night he put together a little computer show for us with pictures he'd taken all along the way, and he even made popcorn for us. Like he'd said, not a bad job.

But the whole time he's working, he's hanging out later and later nights after work, and with older guys. Talking big to Dad, like he's gonna get his own wheels, something cheap and needing work, but something he can drive whenever and wherever. Dad tried setting him straight, but then Tommy pulled the old "I'm a man making my own cash" card and threatened to move out. Mom was the hard-nose of the two of them, and she said to Tommy, "Much as it hurts to say so, Tommy, I think you're right. You either start paying rent here, *mijo*, or you move out and be your own man like you say you are." I hated to think it, but man, it was Mom, not Dad, who wore the pants in the house. I know, it's not how you want to see your dad, but man, all my life it was just like this: push come to shove, he'd shy away. But Mom was strong.

Well, her challenge that night seemed to shut Tommy up in a snap. Or so we thought. For the next week he kept quiet about the car or being a big-time money-making man. On Friday night, though, we heard an awful rumbling out front, and when we went to look, who else but Tommy was polishing up this rust bucket of a car with a broad smile that belongs only to him in the whole family. He was beaming.

And over dinner, he said he'd found a place to live, too. Nothing fancy, he said, but good enough for me, close to work and cheap. That weekend, he packed his stuff, loaded it into the car and drove off. Sure enough, Mom cried. And Dad shut himself in his workshop. Chino and I couldn't quite decide how to make the best use of all this new, extra space. A room for three that in a day turns into a room for two can confound a guy. But we managed, eventually. Like good baby brothers do, we adapted.

I'd also heard, on the grapevine and so I didn't put too much stock in it, that Tommy was messing with dope. Not doing it, but selling it. I had no clue Mom and Dad knew, but over dinner one evening, Dad asked him point-blank what was up with that. Tommy denied it left and right, that all that was bogus. He wasn't into any of that. But he cut the night short, not staying for dessert or coffee. Dad took him at his word then, and that was that.

Until, of course, today. Chino and I had just come home from school and Dad was getting ready to mow the lawn when Tommy's car screeched to a stop in front of our house, he jumped out, leaving the driver's side door open wide, and booked it inside. He didn't get a chance to explain anything to us before a second car slammed on its brakes and skidded to an abrupt stop right behind Tommy's, just missing slamming into it by inches. Two guys got out, looked over their shoulders, approached Tommy's car slowly, and I noticed one of them had his hand in his coat pocket. I'd seen enough movies to know the outline of what he was gripping in the pocket was a gun.

Tommy closed the front door and peeked out the hole. "Hide," he said.

"What's going on?" Dad wanted to know.

"Where's Mom?" Tommy asked.

"At work, why, Tommy? What trouble are you in?"

"Dad, I'm so sorry. But I didn't know where else to go."

Tommy was jittery, his hands aflutter. He peeped out the hole again, turned to us and said, "Hide. Now!" That's about the time he shoved me and Chino into our mom and dad's bedroom, then came back for Dad, pulling him in by the arm, begging him to please hide with us. "I'm so sorry, Dad," he said, then the front door flew open, there was some screaming between these guys and Tommy, and then the one named Jimmy found us in the room, and now we're all lying flat on our stomachs, scared stiff, but at least I hadn't peed all over myself, like I thought somebody fearing for his life might do. Splayed out on the floor, though, my heart is beating harder than ever, like I'd just run five miles at full speed, non-stop.

There's a lot of yelling coming from the living room, where the other bad guy, the one with his hand in his coat pocket earlier is with Tommy. Tommy is screaming back that he has no idea "where the stuff is, man, I swear it, on my mother."

At those words, Dad winces. I see his jaw muscles screw up tight. And I think Tommy's got no right bringing our mom into this mess, not even as an idea in the abstract, whatever his mess. Isn't it enough that he's jammed us right into the middle of it, hasn't thought about our safety in coming here with those thugs trailing him, and now to mention Mom's name—what a jerk.

Dad swallows hard and tries to reason with this Jimmy idiot again, who's shifting from foot to foot, like he needs to go to the toilet bad. He keeps cracking the door open a bit and trying to get his bearings straight about what's happening out in the living room with his buddy and Tommy.

"Listen, son," Dad tells him.

Jimmy stomps over to Dad, kicks him in the face, leaving a gash on his forehead that oddly doesn't bleed. Chino starts crying, and Dad whispers to him, "*Mijito, no llores.* It'll be over soon." Stupid Jimmy goes back to the door. I'm wishing that Dad had been a Navy Seal in a former life, but all he does is dab at his forehead, then looks at his fingers. Does it a second time to make sure, I guess, that he's really not bleeding, and he shrugs his shoulders. Weird.

But how does he know that Jimmy and the other one aren't going to deal with us in a bad way? I mean, look at where his attempt at peaceful negotiations has gotten us so far. And man, that cut still isn't bleeding. Freaky.

"It'll be okay, Chinito, stop crying now," Dad whispers again.

That's when Jimmy bounds over a second time, Dad seems to cringe, ready for another blow, but it doesn't come. Instead, Jimmy bends and grabs Dad by the collar of his shirt and drags him to the opposite side of the bed. Dad manages to land on his side, and he's looking right at me under the bed, nodding a reassuring nod at me and Chino. I'm thrown off my game right then because instead of looking like he's about to mess his pants, he's got the calmest look on his face. Weirder still, he gives me another nod, a more noticeable one this time, and he blinks an eye. Like he's got a plan and he's letting me in on it. Trouble is, I got no idea what he's thinking. But, at least, now I'm paying better attention.

He turns his face away from us and begins crying to himself. I'm telling you, it's like he's the biggest sissy boo-hooing, and then it gets worse: he starts sniveling. I can hear him slurping up the boogers in his nose. I've got no clue what's going on. And then I see Jimmy's boots marching back toward Dad. This time though, he goes down to one knee beside Dad. I see something glinting in Dad's left hand, then it's gone.

Dad's saying something to him, something I can't make out. Apparently neither can Jimmy because he bends in closer to hear what Dad's saying, and then there's a quick jerk to Dad's shoulders, and then he's on his knees. Next, I hear gurgling, and I'm about to cry out for Dad, but that's when I see Jimmy's body slump onto the floor. His throat is slit and blood is gushing out of the cut, spurting onto our tan carpet.

That's when I feel the warmth of my urine under me, and I'm embarrassed that I've wet myself like this. I feel a shaking at my shoulders, and I turn away from Jimmy's lifeless face and all that blood gathering in a pool around his face and chest. When I look up, I find Dad staring down at me with something in his eyes I've never seen before, something hard and cold mixed together. "Sorry you had to see that, boys, but he gave me no choice. This is our only chance." I see he has Jimmy's gun in his hand now, his grip on it not so tight, not so loose either, but just right, at home in the palm of his hand. Then he tells us what's what: he wants us to climb out the window, run to the neighbor's, and call the cops. "Soon as you get in, lock the door behind you, too. You got me?" he asks, looking at me.

When I don't answer, he says, "You okay, *mijo*?"

I look down at my pants and feel like crying. "Never mind that. Now get Chino out of here safe. I'm gonna go see what I can do for Tommy. When this is over, I'll come get you. Make sure it's me or the police before you open the door. I love you, boys." He slides open the window, pops the screen real quiet, then he kisses me on the forehead, and Chino too. "Now go," he says. I want to tell him I love him, too, but he's already turned toward the door, not looking back.

We're just out of the window when we hear the gunshots. I wet myself again. I didn't know you could do that, one right after another. This time the stream of warmth ends up in a puddle at my feet. But I know enough to grab Chino and throw us to the ground. I try shoving him first, then me as far under the hedge as I can. I can't scream out for Dad like I want, like I know I should. Can he be dead? And what's up with Tommy?

I hear the doorknob turn, then the screen door squeak open. It's Tommy stumbling out, his face all torn up, blood splattered on the front of his shirt, a trickle of it oozing out of his right ear. Startled, to say the least. Lost, even. He looks down at us, I mean right at me, in my eyes, and must not see me, or if he does he just can't make sense of his baby brothers cowering under the bushes, because he staggers all the way back to his car and falls into the driver's seat. He throws up onto the dash, then he starts wiping it up with his hands.

A second or two later Dad comes out, and I can hear the sirens now. Dad looks toward the neighbor's house, and when I make a move to get up, he sees us. He lays the gun down on the sidewalk and walks over to us. He says, "*Mijo*, you and your brother alright?"

"I peed on myself again, Dad," I say.

"What?"

"I . . ."

"It doesn't matter. What matters is that you're okay. You're okay, right?" He pulls us out from under the hedge, where I've somehow managed to cram us in pretty tight. Once out, he holds us both real hard, and Chino and me are crying into his chest. That's how short I am. I feel his hand rubbing at my hair over and over, and listening to his heartbeat calms me down some. I guess I'm just the right size, after all. "Shh, shh, shh," he keeps saying, almost like a song.

Then the police get there and they've yanked Tommy from his car. They are jamming him up against the trunk of his car. He had fixed the junker up nice and fine, the color of it a sort of metallic purple that changes colors to dark purple, even black depending on where you're standing looking at it, and how the light of the sun hits it. Right then, I notice it's closer to black than to anything else. Tommy's sniffling, trying to explain something to the officer. Another two cops come over to us and ask whether we're okay, then one of them jumps back at the sight of the gun on the sidewalk. Dad's man-handled some when he tells them he'd discharged the firearm and that they'd find two bodies inside.

Dad's just about the coolest customer explaining to them what all had transpired in the span of the last twenty minutes. Down to how he'd killed the first guy and then the second. He doesn't leave anything out that I can tell. But it's hard to hear what the officer handcuffing him is saying because now a couple EMTs are checking me and Chino over pretty good, making sure we're okay. I tell them I need to change my pants, but one of them says the house is a crime scene now and it isn't possible to get in there, so my EMT gets into the back of the wagon and comes back out with a towel. I wrap it around my waist and don't think how odd that looks, how obvious it is that I'm trying to cover up my messed pants.

A cop checks in on us, tries to explain to us what's happening with Dad and Tommy, and that they've gotten hold of Mom. That she's on her way. She'll meet us at the station. That we shouldn't worry. But whatever. Cleared by the EMT, Chino and me are taken to a squad car, put into the back seat of it and are pulling out when I turn to find Dad, see him in the back of another car, and he's still super cool. He nods in my direction, and for a brief moment, I think, *I must've dreamed it all, Dad slicing the throat of the one called Jimmy, shooting the other one dead, all that blood. Because how could Dad have made all of that blood happen and right now be so calm?* But Chino next to me is whimpering, and the smell of urine coming off me is so noticeable that I know it's all for real.

I'm still looking at Dad, who turns in my direction and nods for me to take care of my brother. He mouths, *You're okay.*

And you know what, things will be okay. Oh, not so hunky-dory for Tommy, I'm sure, but for all that had just happened, all that I had just seen and heard, I would be alright. My dad just told me as much in that look of his. So calm am I then that not even the sight of either Jimmy's or the other guy's corpse being brought out of the house on a gurney bothers me. These punks were the problem; Dad the solution.

I lean back in the seat, wrap an arm around Chino's shoulders, pull him tight to me like Dad had done earlier and whisper to him, "It's all okay now, bro. You cry. You let it all out. Everything's going to turn out good. Dad said so."

My dad *had* said so, and in my eyes he was no wimp no more. He took good care of us today. And would from here on out. We'd be good, alright. No worries.

Nuts

Sergio Troncoso

"Sit over here, Ethan. I don't wanna sit next to those jerks," Zendon Wong hissed to Ethan García. The cafeteria at Pierpont Prep was a hothouse of smells. The scent of Mexican food sliced through the air. Orange-colored rice steamed a scent of wet sand. Tacos as stiff as cardboard were stuffed with a glittery beef. Peals of laughter, squeaky pleas and chairs and tables scraping into place resounded through the air. The first lunch period of middle school kids was exiting, and the second lunch period of high school kids was announcing its arrival with a roar.

"I wanna hear every detail. Everything, before she gets here."

Zendon glanced around nervously, reassuring himself he wasn't within earshot of anybody, or that Phoebe Radley was not yet hunting for him. It was never hard to miss Phoebe in a crowd: her curly red hair bounced like Medusa's snakes on top of her head, and she was tall and athletic. "Ethan, she took my pants off."

"What?"

"Keep your goddamn voice down."

"She came over to my house. My parents were still at work. I didn't want her to come over. She said we could study together," Zendon said, staring at his best friend with his serious eyes.

"And?"

"Well, I don't know. Told her I had a Geometry test."

247

"Get outta here."

"She kept kinda rubbing against me. For once I wish my spoiled sister hadn't decided to hang out with her friends at Famiglia." Zendon was already six feet tall, one of the tallest sophomores at Pierpont Prep, but spindly, like a giant toothpick, with straight black hair and aviator-type glasses which gave him the air of an athlete, although he was far from athletic. Whenever he and Ethan were alone in the hallway, Zendon unleashed a litany of astonished whispers. "Phoeb, you know, started doing stuff."

"Holy Crap!"

"Shut up."

Ethan scanned the room. No one was paying attention to them. He shoved half a taco in his mouth, gulped milk and wiped his face with a napkin. Dr. Gavin, his Pre-Calculus teacher, waved from the other side of the cafeteria, and Ethan remembered Science Olympiad this weekend. "You can't stop now, man. Give it up."

"Okay, but . . . I didn't know what she was doing. I told her to stop, but before I knew it she was on top of me," Zendon whispered in what for him was the softest of whispers, still staring at Ethan. They had always told each other everything. They had been best friends since third grade at The River School, when the two had discovered their mutual obsession with Harry Potter. Two years ago, when Ethan announced he was applying to Pierpont Prep, and Zendon realized it was Ethan's first choice, Zendon made it a point to focus his parents on this school. Pierpont Prep's academic renown made it easy. But while Ethan was sailing through the alma mater of two Nobel Laureates, four mayors of New York City and three Pulitzer-prize winners, Zendon did his best.

"She raped you, Zen. Phoeb freaking raped you."

"Shut up. It was nice," Zendon said, glancing over his shoulder while stealing another look at Ethan's deep brown eyes and his infectious grin. For some reason, this saddened him. Did Ethan really like him? Zendon remembered a certain moment in the movie he had seen last night, when Juno prompted Bleeker to take Katrina De Voort to the prom. Juno didn't mean it either; she *couldn't* have meant it. But Bleek was clueless.

"Hey, retardos," Joshua Epstein said, hovering over Ethan and Zendon, orange tray in his hand. Joshua towered over them even though he was also a sophomore, a boy-man with jerky movements and a singsong voice. His eerie, self-possessed grin alerted everyone to brace themselves for an unpleasant surprise.

"Get the hell out of here, Epstein," Ethan said, staring at Zendon who was trying to lose himself in his tacos. Joshua was also in Science Olympiad, but at the last contest he had spent half the time making plans with friends (Ethan not included) for a weekend at his parents' country house in Litchfield.

"You wish. Hey, Ethan, what would happen if I shoved this pecan pie in your fat mouth?" Joshua sneered, a small dessert plate balanced in his palm an inch from Ethan's face. Ethan turned white.

"What is wrong with you?" Zendon blurted out. Already on the edge of his seat, he was ready to knock the pecan pie from Epstein's hand.

Joshua knew the danger. What an inspired way to undermine Ethan García's supreme confidence! Joshua glanced at the row of tables in the cafeteria; no teacher was nearby, but Zendon's high-pitched retort had turned a few heads. He dropped the pecan pie on his tray. "See you on Saturday, García."

"He is such an asshole, I hate him," Zendon said, his eyes boring a hole into Epstein's back as he lurched away. If he had had a knife on his tray, he might have hurled it between Epstein's shoulder blades. "You okay?"

"Yeah, I'm fine," Ethan said, his forehead damp and suddenly cool. A shiver scampered up his spine.

"Let's get outta here and hang out at the lounge."

Zendon and Ethan shot up in unison, and dumped their trays into metal slots. On the other side of the wall, cafeteria workers grabbed them, flung the leftovers into gray garbage barrels and dropped the plates on wet conveyor belts. With clinks and clangs, students threw their utensils into separate bins. Ethan had often heard Spanish among the workers, and he wondered how many of them were Guatemalan, Honduran, Colombian or Mexican, like his father. He could understand snippets of what they said, yet whenever he read a passage in Mr. Vega's Spanish honors class, his accent horrified him. It was as bad as Epstein's.

"I'll be there in a sec, let me get something from my backpack," Ethan said, slapping Zendon between his shoulder blades and shoving him playfully forward. The Student Lounge, the social center at Pierpont Prep, was reserved for the high school. It was half the size of the cafeteria, but with nooks for hanging out, sofas of all sizes, bean bags and dozens of oak chairs meant to fit under heavy study tables. Students shoved and clustered the furniture every which way. Cushy benches adjacent to its walls displayed the forest green and gold of the school. Hundreds of numbered student lockers, assigned yet unlocked, lined three of its four walls. Pierpont Prep glorified its honor code. Indeed, it was rare when something went missing from the Student Lounge. It was the Grand Central Station of their high school. Yet, the unspoken rule was to keep anything you truly valued with you at all times, or simply to leave it at home.

"Want a cookie?"

"Sure, why not? Your mom's, right?"

"Yeah. She'd also still take me on the subway to school if I let her. So, Phoeb, man."

"Please don't tell her anything," Zendon said, watching the glass doors to the Student Lounge swing open and close with a whoosh like heart valves. He munched on the soft, chunky chocolate chip cookie, and finished it in three bites. "Not a freaking hint. She's on my back as it is."

"Maybe you can get her on her back and–"

"Hey, stop fooling around."

"Something . . ."

"You okay? You're really red, like, strawberry red."

"Zen, I can't breathe," Ethan gasped, grabbing his throat and patting his chest. In a matter of seconds, his face had turned a bright crimson, his chest heaved and his eyes, bulging out of their sockets, begged for help.

"You choking? Hey, stop fooling . . . Ethan, Ethan!"

Ethan collapsed onto the floor, smacking his head on the side of the table. Before he passed out, Zendon heard only a hoarse, but clear "EpiPen" from his friend's mouth.

"Help! Get the nurse! He's allergic to nuts! Run!" Zendon screamed at a startled girl in front of him as he jumped to Ethan's locker and yanked open his backpack. In his mind raced one thought, 'Get the EpiPen. Get the damn EpiPen.' But it wasn't there! Ethan's EpiPen was gone.

A crowd gathered around Ethan, and another girl, Lilah Havermeyer, was holding his head. Ethan, semi-conscious, wheezed, his breath but a whisper. No air seemed to reach his inflamed lungs. Zendon shoved everyone aside and yelled, "Anyone have a goddamn EpiPen! He's going into shock! An EpiPen!" The baggie with the chocolate chip cookies lay at Ethan's feet, half of them crushed by onlookers. Ethan's face was turning blue. Beads of sweat dripped from Zendon's temples.

"Here," someone said from behind, shoving a yellow EpiPen box in front of Zendon's eyes. He ripped open the box, and out slid the practice gray EpiPen, exactly like the one he and Ethan had used as kids at River to give each other "shots" during recess. His hands trembled. Zendon grabbed the actual EpiPen, flicked off the cap from the clear yellow plastic casing—in the back he heard someone mutter, "Holy shit!"—and stabbed Ethan's thigh through the jeans with a shot of adrenalin. In the next moment, the nurse appeared with another EpiPen in her hand, and teachers moved the crowd away from Ethan and out of the Student Lounge. As Zendon almost hyperventilated on the floor next to the sofa, he glimpsed a red-faced Dr. Gavin on his cell phone shouting instructions to a 9-1-1 operator on how to get to the Student Lounge. Someone patted him on the back, but Zendon only craned his neck in search of Ethan's face through the forest of legs and arms.

"Can you breathe okay?" asked Carlos García, a husky fifty-year-old with gray temples, a crew cut and an Apple MacBook case still dangling from his wide shoulders. His navy blue parka gave him the appearance of a New York cop at the Thanksgiving Day parade.

"He's fine. Don't worry," Sarah Mondschein said soothingly, rubbing her son's temple as he lay smiling on his bed, above which still hung the yellow cloth T-rex that had also stood guard over his crib. The walls of Ethan's and Jonathan's room were covered with posters of a Gemini rocket launch from NASA, Alpha Centauri and nearby stars, details about the planets' compositions and a dinosaur family-tree from the American Natural History Museum. Above Jonathan's bed was a whimsical red cloth pterodactyl also on the wall since he had been a baby. Last year Ethan's impetuous younger brother had repeatedly stabbed it with a pencil.

"You don't think they let him out of the hospital too quick? Cancelled my lecture as soon as I found out," Carlos said to his wife. He sat at the end of the bed and squeezed Ethan's foot. "But mom told me by the time I got to the hospital you would already be back at the apartment."

"Dad, I'm okay. Really. See, I can breathe."

"Thank God. What the hell happened? That school has got to get its act together about nuts. You could've died! I'm calling the headmaster tomorrow, I'm gonna meet with him–"

"Dad, really, no. Don't . . ."

"Carlos, please, I think it was my cookies. But that's just not possible," Sarah said, staring at her son on the bed. She turned to face her husband. Her blue eyes glistened with tears, yet she remained composed, her body straight and sleek in her off-white silk blouse and black wool skirt.

"What? *Your* cookies? You mean the ones you baked him this morning?"

"It's not possible. I know what I put in them. I've been sending him with those cookies for years," she said, her voice cracking.

"I want to know what happened," Carlos said, glowering at his wife. The hairs on the back of Ethan's neck stood up whenever he saw that death-look on his father's face. It reminded him of the cover of his father's favorite book, *Zapata and the Mexican Revolution*, with the smoldering glare of the peasant leader in blood-red and black. It was the best I-don't-take-shit-from-anybody look Ethan had ever seen.

"Please. Dad. It's okay. Just—"

"Tell me what happened."

"Zendon and I were finishing lunch. We were at the Student Lounge. I grabbed the cookies from my backpack and as soon as I ate one I couldn't breathe."

"Nothing else? What did you have for lunch?"

"Mexican food. That's it."

"I bet it was 'Mexican food.' And?"

"Well, Zendon gave me the EpiPen shot. They took me to the hospital and I'm fine. Mom was there pretty much as soon as I arrived. She had to leave work, a big meeting," Ethan said, searching his mother's still-ashen face.

"At least Zendon has his shit together," Carlos growled, staring at the pile of clothes on the small gray armchair tucked in the corner next to the window. "Why don't you take it easy? You're not going to school tomorrow, are you?"

"I'm fine, Dad. I don't want to miss anything. Really, I'm okay. The headmaster already emailed me and said they're talking to the cafeteria people; he wants to see me when I get back. He wants to find out what happened, too."

"I bet he does. Goddamn idiot."

Carlos and Sarah walked out and left the door inches from being closed.

"It's not the cookies. It can't be the cookies. Carlos, I know what I put in them. I know," Sarah said, marching to the kitchen, her back to her husband.

"I had to cancel the 'Battle of Celaya' lecture. The 'Battle of Celaya,' mind you. Jeannie emailed the students on record, but it was only an hour before and God knows how many still showed up." He was angry at his wife, whom he had loved since the day he saw her at 'Latin America and Underdevelopment' by the famed Fernando Enrique Cardoso in Morningside Heights, a class that had determined so much of who he was today.

"Here. Here's everything I put. The cinnamon. The empty bag of Hershey's chocolate chips. The flour. The sugar. Nothing in this house has nuts!" She was glaring at the items on the white Formica counter as if daring anything to move so she could crush it with her fists.

"I know that. I know that."

"I've made those cookies for him hundreds of times. I feel like throwing up."

"Look, let's go over everything. What you did. Everything."

"I mixed the dough the night before. Just like I always do. Added the chocolate chips. Got up early, because I had a seven-thirty meeting, and I thought it would be nice for the kids to get up to warm cookies in the oven." Sarah yanked out the garbage can and rifled through its contents. The foil top of a Yoplait yogurt smeared her blouse, but she ignored it. "I wrote what we were missing on the grocery-store list: one percent milk, eggs, Diet Coke, chicken fingers, broccoli, cauliflower. Carlos, here's the list! Before I left, I took the cookies out, wrapped three cookies in foil twice and left them on the counter. I did not poison my son!" Sarah collapsed onto the kitchen floor, one black pump off her foot and jamming underneath the stove. Tears dribbled over her porcelain cheeks. The garbage can had toppled over next to her knees.

The doorbell buzzed. A second later the latch turned sharply. Jonathan, in black jeans, black jacket, his hair spiky and streaked with yellow, strode in and dumped his backpack on the rug. ("You look like Pepe Le Peu!" his father had opined three weeks ago.) "Hey, what are you guys doing here?"

"It's for me! I got it!" Ethan shouted into the hallway and shut his bedroom door. He had recognized Zendon's phone number on caller ID, and suddenly remembered his cell phone was out of power after the flurry of calls and texts from his friends earlier at the hospital. It was almost 10:00 P.M. Moments before his father had lit into Jonathan about "his attitude." The shouts still reverberated against the walls.

"You okay? Coming to school tomorrow?"

"Yeah, I'm fine. Fully recovered. Thanks, man. I owe you one. I thought you'd call earlier."

"I know, I know. Freaking Phoeb, man. She came over after the commotion in school. I told her I was too upset. She said she was lonely, and needed to talk to me. She followed me home. I really didn't want to talk to her. I mean, by the time the ambulance came you seemed okay, but I was still worried."

"Thanks, man. I'm fine. I hope you get a medal. You deserve it. I left my backpack and all my stuff in the locker, my homework. I don't even know what we have due tomorrow."

"I got it. Picked up everything from your locker, your homework from your teachers. Mr. Vega told me to tell you not to worry about the homework. I told him you wanted it anyway. All your other teachers were the same. 'Tell Ethan not to worry about tomorrow.' I'm sure all week you're golden. I was gonna bring your backpack after school—can I just bring it to school tomorrow?—but Phoeb, man."

"Hey, thanks. You're like my guardian angel. What happened?"

"She told me she loved me. Can you believe that?"

"Oh, man."

"She was crying. She was screaming. My parents weren't home, thank God. She said she was really lonely and nobody liked her. She said 'Sookie' betrayed her too. I don't know what the hell she was talking about. But Phoeb's not bad, when you get to know her. Just a little clingy and spacey. You know, sometimes she goes off the 'deep end' and you feel like you're talking to a wall. She wasn't making a lot of sense. Told her I really was not in the mood. But she kept at it. Said I didn't love her. Burst into tears. So we did it."

"You *what*?"

"Yeah, I mean, she was so upset. She kept telling me how she needed someone to love her. How she had to have someone love her. I didn't feel sorry for her—well, not that much. You know, Phoeb's got a nice body."

"You're right about that. So you did it?"

"Yeah, and it made her happy," Zendon said, pausing. "I liked it too. And she gave me those big green eyes, I think she was happy about it. I mean, it felt like if I didn't do her, she might do something terrible to herself, or to me. I wasn't scared, really. And I wasn't doing her, like, a favor. I just wanted her to calm down, to leave. She was vigorous, let me tell you."

"Vigorous, huh? Lucky bastard. So you and Phoeb, huh?"

"It's not like we're going out. We're definitely not going out. I'm just trying to make her happy. She told me before my parents showed up that she has felt abandoned all her life. She's just lonely."

"Who isn't? Mr. Happy-Maker."

"Shut up."

"You got to fill in the blanks tomorrow. My brother just walked in. See you."

Ethan pushed his way through the front doors of Pierpont Prep, half an hour before the first bell rang, and waved to the security guard Emiliano, a Dominicano who loved to talk about baseball. Ethan followed the serpentine route to the nurse's office, down the main stairs, through a few hallway and past the black-box theatre. Mrs. MacIntyre sat behind a desk, and as soon as she saw Ethan she pushed herself up and shuffled to the side of her desk and hugged him. A big, sloppy, suffocating hug. The school's nurse was two hundred pounds of affection.

"Ethan, Ethan. How do you feel? Thank you for coming in early."

"I'm fine. Really, Mrs. MacIntyre. I'm okay. Just wanted to check in. My parents said they sent you an email, too."

"Yes, yes. What a scare! Thank goodness you're alright. Zendon's a good friend. What a job he did! If I see him in the hallways, I'm going to give him a big hug, too!"

"I know," Ethan said, smiling and imagining how mortified Zendon would be. He had to tell Zen that Nurse MacIntyre was looking for him.

"So, we've talked to the cafeteria staff. And I know about the cookies. But the headmaster is having meetings with the staff about redoubling our efforts to know the ingredients in everything we give to the students. Frankly, I think we should be a 'nut-free' school. Period. I don't understand 'nut-aware,' or why the reluctance. It could be we have to change food vendors to guarantee our food is nut-free. Maybe the school's worried about liability issues. But the cookies. Isn't that what you were eating when you had the allergic reaction?"

"Yes, but my mom says she didn't put anything in the cookies she hasn't put in before. She's made those cookies for me hundreds of times. She won't allow any nuts in our house." How could they think it was his mother's cookies?

"Well, I'm sure we'll get to the bottom of it." Mrs. MacIntyre did not tell him, but the incident had brought back unpleasant memories of something that happened two years ago. An eighth grader, Melissa Cohen, had collapsed in Biology class, and died. Nobody had ever found out how she had ingested potassium cyanide. Had it been on purpose, a prank or just a terrible mistake? That had been a horrible day at Pierpont Prep. Yesterday when the news came that a student had collapsed in the Student Lounge, hearts were racing, and many immediately relived their most awful memories at the school. "You have your EpiPen? Remember, you should always carry one with you."

"Yes, I had two in my backpack. I'm fine, really."

"I don't want you doing anything strenuous today, and I've already emailed Coach Johnson and you're excused from gym class today. Free period."

"Oh, that's great. Thank you, Mrs. MacIntyre. That'll help me catch up on homework."

"You let me know if you don't feel well."

"Okay, thanks."

Zendon handed him the backpack a few minutes after Ethan had stepped into the Student Lounge after meeting with Mrs. MacIntyre. During his morning classes, friends and semi-friends made it a point to see how Ethan was, what had happened and how he was feeling today. Chloe Schwartz had shouted at his back, "Hey, you owe me an EpiPen!" and he had turned quickly enough to see her wave at him around a corner. He had already heard two different accounts of the day Melissa Cohen died. By his English Literature class just before lunch, he was tired of the notoriety.

Alito, of all people, smiled eerily at him. Ethan wondered if he was imagining things, or if he was already too jaded by high school to give the benefit of the doubt to a kid like Alito. Alito wasn't too bright, and certainly it irked him that Ethan, Jewish and Mexican, was at the top of the class.

As Ethan waited in the lunch line—Italian meatballs, linguini, steamed broccoli, Caesar salad—different thoughts flashed in his mind. *It was the cookies, but it couldn't have been the cookies. Was it the bad Mexican food? What had almost killed him yesterday? What exactly?* His father had texted him that they were meeting with the headmaster to discuss what happened, to try to figure it out. Ethan was supposed to stop by the headmaster's office today before he returned home. He hoped his sometimes hot-headed father would not make a big deal out of it. He was fine. Yes, he was fine. But the linguini and meatballs in front of him seemed oddly forbidding. What hidden dangers lurked in the cafeteria and at Pierpont Prep? He had always assumed he was safe in school. But a kid had died two years ago in Biology class. She had turned a reddish purple, according to a student who had been there. Not twenty-four hours before, Ethan had been sprawled on the floor of the Student Lounge, gasping for breath. Was this school cursed?

For his free period, instead of the Student Lounge, Ethan went to the school's library. The lounge reminded him of yesterday's close call, yet he did quickly check his locker to look for his EpiPens. Zendon had mentioned something about not finding them in Ethan's backpack yesterday, in the panic. The EpiPens weren't in his locker, nor anywhere nearby. After lunch, the lounge's floor had been swept clean. He dumped the contents of his backpack on an empty table at the library, and the box of two EpiPens was missing. He could've sworn he carried it in the front pocket of his backpack. Ethan knew he had placed the box of EpiPens in his backpack at the beginning of the school year, and he had assumed they were still there. Had he taken them out? When he had been at The River School, the EpiPens (which his mother religiously renewed every year at the pharmacy when the expiration date loomed) had provided him with an elusive comfort as a kid: he had his magic medicine, if something happened, if he ate a walnut, pistachio or pecan by mistake, his EpiPens would save him. But in ten years, Ethan had never used one EpiPen. Every year box after box of expired EpiPens had been dumped in the garbage.

Now as a teenager, Ethan thought of these shots of adrenalin as a nuisance he flung into his backpack to appease his mother, or shoved in his jeans pocket when he met his old River buddies for dinner and a movie. *What a waste of time!* he had thought. Until now. What had happened to his EpiPens? The library was empty except for Mrs. Litvak, the cheery librarian who seemed to like the lower–school kids much more than the high schoolers. She glanced at him warily, as if to say *Why are you here?* At the table with his homework binders and textbooks, Ethan felt strangely naked under the florescent lights.

Ethan finished his math problem set, and had about ten minutes before the bell rang for his next class. On the stacks about a foot from his head were Pierpont Prep's yearbooks, dozens of them going back to the 1940s and 50s. He picked up a couple of recent yearbooks and flipped through the pages absentmindedly, glancing at the pictures of the soccer team, lacrosse, Science Olympiad, Model UN, theatrical productions and the individual head shots of freshman who were now juniors, eighth-graders who were now sophomores. These were the kids in his current class. Their faces had lost, in some, the baby fat or wide-eyed look of—what would you call it?—innocence or naiveté. Ethan had remembered his River graduation, and how promising the future seemed to be, and how proud his parents were that he would be attending historic Pierpont Prep. Ethan's accomplishments especially meant a lot to his dad, who had grown up poor on the Mexican-American border. "You won't be carrying the baggage I had when I went to the Ivy League," his father had told him. Ethan still believed a bright future was before him, even though the competition was fierce at Pierpont Prep. K-through-8 River had been the cocoon of his childhood. High school was the beginning of the real world.

Ethan flipped a page, and a name caught his eye: Melissa Cohen. He stared at the dead girl's eighth-grade head shot. Her hair was richly black and curly, and layered beautifully around her face. Her skin was pale, her teeth seemed perfect and together with her high cheekbones and easy smile they made her a true beauty. She would have been extremely popular in high school, and he guessed she must have been one of the most popular girls in her grade. How could this poor girl end up dead? Why wasn't she walking the halls of Pierpont Prep today? In Ethan's mind, he imagined asking Melissa Cohen to a movie or to Five Napkin Burger for a Saturday lunch.

Ethan studied the yearbook's index and discovered other pictures of Melissa Cohen. In one she was hitting a volleyball, and he recognized many of the girls of the eighth-grade volleyball team, including Sarah, Joaniko, Phoebe, Alyssa, Grace, Olivia and Hayley. Oh, man! If the head shot created a mysteriously beautiful aura around Melissa, the action shot, her lunging for the volleyball, made her look sexy. Her breasts were already developing. Her legs were long and muscular. This girl would have been hot by sophomore year! If Melissa had had half a brain, with that body and face, no doubt Ethan would have asked her out. Another picture had 'Melissa Soupy Cohen' in an apron and hairnet at a soup kitchen for the school's community service project. Ethan slammed the yearbook shut. What was he doing daydreaming about a dead girl? Wasn't that a bit sicko? He shoved the yearbook back onto the bookshelves, and the bell rang.

Ethan returned home, to their co-op apartment on the Upper Westside of Manhattan. It was quiet in the afternoon, and usually this was his favorite time. His weird little brother rarely came home straight from school. His parents were at work. He was alone to look at their view of the Hudson River from the twenty-first floor, to relax in his solitude. But all day at school, he had felt eyes were on him. Eyes behind his back. Eyes following him, even when nobody he knew had been in the hallways. This strange sensation was more than just friends and acquaintances asking him how he was feeling and what had happened yesterday in the cafeteria. That had been a mild nuisance. He had ignored it after a while, or simply answered crisply by giving the blow-by-blow of what he thought they wanted to hear. No, this extra feeling, these eyes at the back of his neck, felt more sinister. As if somebody wanted to warn him of impending danger, but couldn't, or wouldn't. As if somebody wanted to harm him.

In the stillness of the apartment, Ethan shrugged his shoulders and kicked off his sneakers. He was getting paranoid, he thought. What happened yesterday had been an accident. Hadn't it? True, he didn't quite know what had happened, what exactly he had ingested that had caused his near-death experience. Today he had stopped by his locker in the Student Lounge, and uncharacteristically cleaned it out, left not a book or a notebook, not one pencil behind. Why hadn't Pierpont Prep ever put locks on these lockers? Ethan had stared at the other students joking around, slamming their lockers shut, half-full with their junk. Did they realize some maniac could just open a locker and leave an unpleasant surprise behind? Why did these kids trust everybody around them, their teachers, administrators, janitors, even other kids? But again it was those eyes that preoccupied him, following him, warning him, wanting to warn him, threatening him.

Ethan turned on his MacBook his father and mother had bought for his birthday last year. He opened his news page on Yahoo! and checked his Facebook profile; a few friends had left well-wishes on his wall, and Lilah had sent this long, somewhat sappy note to his Facebook private mailbox. Wow. Did Lilah like him? She was a babe, and certainly a girl his parents would approve of, one of the smartest and most level-headed sophomores at Pierpont Prep. Hey, maybe he should go into anaphylactic shock more often. Finally, Ethan checked his Gmail account. Among the emails notifying him he had won the Nigerian lottery (again!) and advertising pharmacies with cheap prescriptions for 'V-i-a-g-r-a and C-i-a-l-i-s,' was a strange email that did not seem to be spam. It read:

From: Doable HePrey doableheprey@gmail.com
To: Ethan Garcia ethangarcia@gmail.com
Sent: Thu, Mar 18, 2010 3:36 P.M.
Subject: I like you, let me know
Dear E:
    I like you a lot. Can't say who I am yet. But I just wanted to ask you. Do you like boys? Everything depends on it. Please let me know.
Me

What the hell was this about? Was this someone's idea of a stupid joke? Ethan imagined one of many idiots who could have sent this email, some friends trying to get under his skin, or a jerk simply wanting to psyche him out. He wouldn't put it past Epstein to pull a stunt like this. Some of the kids at Pierpont Prep were not exactly moral human beings.

Ethan typed up an email to play along. 'I love juicy boys,' he wrote and asked coyly whether they should meet at Riverside Park. Of course, he didn't like boys, but if this idiot wanted to play a cat-and-mouse game, Ethan could turn the tables on him somehow. His finger hovered over the Send button, then, he stopped. Those eyes again. They seemed to be burning a hole into the back of his neck.

At once he remembered an old *Seinfeld* episode, in which a Columbia student reporter thinks Jerry and George are gay, and they keep uncomfortably explaining, to the camera and to each other, that there is nothing wrong with it. There *was* nothing wrong with being gay. Ethan didn't really care if someone was gay, straight or bi. Maybe this poor sucker, who didn't have the guts to ask him directly, was just another scared kid at Pierpont Prep. Perhaps, he was reaching out and Ethan's little ruse would be the last straw in this guy's miserable existence in the shadows. What would be the point of hurting someone like that? Would he want someone to play with his emotions? So Ethan erased his sentences and instead sent this email:

```
From: Ethan Garcia ethangarcia@gmail.com
To: Doable HePrey doableheprey@gmail.com
Sent: Thu, Mar 18, 2010 5:42 P.M.
Subject: RE: I like you, let me know
Dear Doable:
     I'm sorry to disappoint you, but I like girls.
I hope this doesn't hurt you, because I don't
mean to. I'm sure you will find someone you like
who also likes you for who you are. I know it's
tough, and I assume you're at PP just like me.
But don't worry. High school gets easier as
you get older (I hope!), and all of us are just
trying to make it out alive.
     Take care.
     Ethan
```

Belle

Ray Villareal

When Todd Cepeda walked inside Gino's Pizzeria, his eyes were immediately drawn to the girl sitting by the window. She wore a turquoise sweater, navy-blue skinny jeans and black, high-heeled boots. Her auburn hair was cut in a bob, and it rounded her smooth-skinned face. Todd tried to recall if he had seen her at school. He didn't think so. He would remember a babe like her.

He had gone to Gino's to pick up something for dinner. His mother had called to let him know that she'd be working late and wouldn't come home until after eight o'clock. Todd would have to be on his own for supper. That was fine with him. This way, he could eat whatever he wanted. Tonight it would be pepperoni pizza.

Todd turned in his order. While he waited, he looked back at the girl. She was sipping a Coke and reading a book. He wanted to introduce himself to her, but he wasn't sure how to go about it. He thought of the dopey pick-up lines his friend, Carlos Escobar, used whenever he hit on girls. *I need to call heaven 'cause they've just lost one of their angels.* That was pretty lame, but not as ridiculous as *I'm a thief, and I'm here to steal your heart.*

Todd made his way toward the window and pretended to look at the passing traffic. Then he turned and gazed down at the girl. "What are you reading?" he asked.

The girl looked up and smiled. She turned her book over and showed Todd the cover. "*The Metamorphosis* by Franz Kafka."

Well, at least she didn't tell him to get lost.

"For class?"

"Uh-hm."

"Do you go to North Oak Cliff?"

The girl hesitated. "Yes."

"Me, too." *Come on, Toddy boy, keep it going.* "Junior or senior?"

Again the girl hesitated before answering, "Senior."

"Really?" Todd regarded her curiously. "I'm a senior, but I don't think I've ever seen you at school."

The girl winked. "Maybe you just haven't looked hard enough."

Was she flirting with him? Todd's heart fluttered. Good-looking girls didn't usually come on to him. Todd didn't think he was ugly; just not the type girls took a second look at. He nudged his head in the direction of her book. "Who do you have for English?"

The girl's expression grew blank for a moment. Then she said, "Um, you know, the one they call . . . 'Bulldog'."

Bulldog? Todd couldn't think of any English teachers at his school the kids called Bulldog. Ms. Chavoya was too young and attractive. Mr. Berry? Too effeminate. Mrs. Forehand? She had white, curly hair and wore wire-frame glasses that hung at the tip of her round nose. She looked more like Mrs. Santa Claus than a bulldog. The only other person Todd could think of was Mrs. Lindsey. Mrs. Lindsey had a doughy face with sagging jowls and deep circles under her eyes. "You mean Mrs. Lindsey?"

The girl's face brightened. "Yes, that's her. Mrs. Lindsey."

"No kidding," Todd said. "I have her third period. When do you go to her?"

The girl's smile disappeared. She dog-eared the page she was reading, closed the book and slipped it in her purse. "I have to go." She rose from her chair.

Toddy boy, you blew it. Everything was going fine, but somehow you said the wrong thing. "Listen, I, uh, have a car. If you want, I can give you a ride home."

"That's alright," the girl said. "My house is on Edgefield, not too far away. But thanks anyway." She started toward the door.

"Wait. What's your name?"

The girl wavered. "Belle."

"Belle what?"

"Just . . . Belle," she said and left.

Todd tried placing her face again. His locker was on the second floor, same as Mrs. Lindsey's classroom. Surely he should have seen Belle at school by now.

His food order number was called. Todd grabbed his pizza, got in his car and headed home.

When he turned left on West Tenth, he spotted Belle crossing the street, walking toward the Vista Ridge Apartments. Todd pulled his car to the curb and watched as she stopped in front of an apartment door. She took keys out of her purse, unlocked the door and went inside.

Wait a minute. Didn't Belle say she lived on Edgefield? In a house? What was she doing going into an apartment on West Tenth Street?

He sighed. *Toddy boy, that's what they call the 'ole brush-off.*

It wasn't the first time he had been rejected by a girl. At least Belle had been more subtle about it. That flake Naomi Garza told him, point-blank, that she wouldn't go out with him because she thought he was boring.

When Todd got home, out of curiosity, he dug up last year's yearbook. He thumbed through the underclassmen pages and studied the photos and names. Strange, there was no one named Belle. Maybe she had flunked her senior year. Todd searched the senior class pages. No Belle there, either. Nothing particularly unusual about that. It was possible Belle was new to North Oak

Cliff High School, so she wouldn't have been pictured in last year's yearbook.

After he ate his pizza, Todd started on his government homework, but he couldn't concentrate on it. His thoughts were on Belle. Senior Fall Ball was coming up, and he still didn't have a date. At the beginning of the year, he thought he might ask Debbie Tyler to go with him. But lately, her face had broken out with so many pimples that the guys had started referring to her as Freddy Kruger. Todd knew he could score big-time points with the guys if he showed up at the dance with Belle on his arm. He hoped she didn't have a boyfriend.

Before giving himself too much time to think about it, he rushed out of the house and drove to the Vista Ridge Apartments.

He pulled his car in front of the apartment complex. It was dark, but Todd was certain he had the right place. He drummed his fingers on the steering wheel, not sure what he would say when he saw Belle. He thought of a worst-case scenario. She might become furious that he followed her and accuse him of being a stalker. Todd would explain that he had seen her going into the apartment by accident. He would apologize for the intrusion and promise never to bother her again. On the other hand, she might welcome his persistence.

"Chicks like for you to chase them," his friend Carlos had said. "It's part of a game they play."

Todd stepped out of the car and walked up to the door. No guts, no glory, he thought and rang the bell.

The outside light came on, and a shadowy figure peeked out of the curtain. The door cracked open with the security door chain in place.

"Whachoo want?" a woman asked in a thick, Spanish accent. Her face was hidden behind the door. A brown Chihuahua stuck its snout through the door and barked a high, "Yap! Yap! Yap!"

"Hello, my name's Todd Cepeda. I go to North Oak Cliff with Belle. May I please speak with her?"

"Belle ees no here," the woman said.

Bummer.

"Can you tell me when she'll be back?" Todd asked.

The little dog bared its teeth and growled. "You no unnerstan'," the woman said. "No Belle leef here." She slammed the door and turned off the exterior light.

Todd stared at the door, dumbfounded. *No Belle lives here?* He stepped back and gazed at his surroundings. He had seen Belle enter this door, 117, the second one from the left; he was almost positive of it. He looked at the street sign. 900 W. Tenth. This was the place alright. What was going on?

Then it hit him. Belle had an overly-protective mother. She probably screened all of her daughter's male visitors. Since Belle hadn't brought him home, her mother didn't recognize him, and she wasn't about to let a stranger inside. He would try to meet up with Belle at school tomorrow.

The next day, Todd kept his eyes out for her. He looked up and down the hallways and in the classrooms, but didn't find her.

When he arrived at his English class, Todd saw Mrs. Lindsey standing outside the door, greeting her students. *Bulldog*, he thought and snickered.

He approached her and asked, "Mrs. Lindsey, which of your classes is reading *The Metamorphosis*?"

The teacher gave him a puzzled look. "Kafka's *The Metamorphosis*? None this year, Todd. Why do you ask?"

Duped again. "Oh, nothing," Todd said, blushing. "I met a girl named Belle who said she was in your class and that you were having them read *The Metamorphosis*."

Mrs. Lindsey wrinkled her brows. "I don't have any students named Belle."

Of course she didn't. That girl had strung him along, and Todd fell for it like a hormone-raging fool. First, she'd flirted with him. Then she lied about who her teacher was and where she lived. Belle probably wasn't even her real name.

"I did have a Belle in my class once," Mrs. Lindsey said, "but that was a few years ago. Poor girl. Suffered such a tragedy."

"What do you mean?" Todd asked.

Mrs. Lindsey sighed. "Her house burned down, and her family was killed."

A chill ran though Todd's body. For a split second, he wondered if he had met a ghost the day before. "Did Belle die in the fire, too?" he ventured to ask.

Mrs. Lindsey gestured for Todd to move out of the way to let Allison Barnes and Peter Logan through. "No, she managed to get out in time. Unfortunately, she was so traumatized by what happened that she dropped out of school. Too bad. With less than a semester to graduate, too. She went to live with some relatives in Houston."

That ruled out the ghost theory. It was obvious they were talking about two different people. Todd's Belle, if that was her name, was still in school, and she had a mother who was very much alive.

He was about to go inside the classroom when Mrs. Lindsey said, "By the way, if you happen to drive down Edgefield, just before you get to West Davis, you can see the vacant lot where Belle's house used to be."

At lunchtime, Todd shared his story with the guys.

"There's nothing weird about it," Carlos said. "The chick didn't like you prying into her business, so she fed you a line to throw you off."

Todd poked the brown glob on his lunch tray with his fork. The glob jiggled, and a thin cloud of steam escaped from it. Todd accepted that the food in the North Oak Cliff cafeteria wasn't exactly gourmet, but this was the first time he couldn't identify the main entrée. "But why would she say that she lived on Edge-field, the same street where another girl named Belle's house burned down?"

Nelson took a sip of his milk and let out a burp. "Maybe she's a ghost. You know, like the Lady of White Rock Lake."

"She's not a ghost," Todd scoffed, not wanting to admit that he had entertained the same thought.

"How do you know?" Nelson asked. "Did you touch her? If she was a ghost, your hand might've gone through her."

Todd couldn't tell if Nelson was being serious. Nelson loved to talk about auras and spirits and paranormal activities.

"No, man. I spoke with her. I didn't fondle her," Todd said sharply. He dipped his bread in the cream gravy on his mashed potatoes and took a bite. Not tasty, but certainly better than the brown junk.

Nelson turned to the guys. "They say that people driving around White Rock Lake late at night have seen a woman hitch-hiking in wet clothes. When they stop to offer her help, she tells them that she was in a boating accident and needs a ride home. When they arrive at the address the woman has given them, they turn and look in the back seat, but she's no longer there. They go up to the house and ring the doorbell. A man answers, and after they explain what happened, he says, 'My daughter drowned at White Rock Lake'."

Rolando cracked a smile. "I think Nelson might have some-thing there, Todd. Maybe Belle's ghost led you to that apartment. I bet that if you were to go back and ask the woman what hap-pened to Belle, she'd tell you that Belle died in the fire."

Todd pushed his food tray aside, leaned back in his chair and crossed his arms. "Aren't you guys listening to me? Belle's not dead."

Nelson sniffed. "I still say she's a ghost."

After school, Todd made his way to the parking lot. When he rounded the corner of the building, he was surprised to find Belle sitting under a live oak tree, reading her book. He wondered if he should confront her, ask her why she lied to him. He decided against it. Belle didn't owe him an explanation. After all, he was the one who had approached her at Gino's Pizzeria and asked a bunch of questions she probably felt uncomfortable answering.

Belle looked up from her book and wiggled her fingers. "Hi, Todd."

He flinched. "How do you know my name?"

"I don't know," she said with a shrug. "You must have told me yesterday."

Todd couldn't remember telling her his name. Maybe she had done some snooping, too. She might have asked some of her friends if they knew him. Todd's insides warmed at the thought that a gorgeous babe like Belle would want to know more about him. He looked at her student ID badge. It was decorated with flower stickers, but he could still see her name. Belle Segovia. So Belle really was her name.

"Still reading that book for Mrs. Lindsey's class?" he asked.

Belle rose and brushed the grass off the back of her pants. "I prefer to think that I'm reading a book for myself rather than for a teacher. If I feel that I'm reading it for myself, I tend to enjoy a book better."

In other words, Liar, you're not reading The Metamorphosis *for Mrs. Lindsey, are you?* But out loud, Todd said, "That's a good way of looking at it. Is it a good book?"

Belle picked her backpack off the ground and slipped it around her shoulders. "It depends on your definition of good. It's about a man who turns into a bug."

Todd laughed. "Are you serious?"

She handed him the book. "Here, keep it. It's yours. Read it when you get a chance. I think you'll like it."

"But don't you need it for class?" Todd asked.

"Not really," she said. "I've read it so many times, I know it by heart."

Of course she didn't need the book for class—at least, not Mrs. Lindsey's. Todd couldn't understand why Belle was acting so mysterious, but he decided it didn't matter. She obviously liked him. She had even given him a present. He figured that later she would confess that she really lived at the Vista Ridge Apartments and that Mrs. Lindsey wasn't her teacher. She would explain that she was always careful about giving out too much information to guys she'd just met.

Steeling his nerves, Todd asked, "Listen, are you, uh, planning to go to Fall Ball?"

Belle giggled. "Fall Ball? What's that?"

Was she still messing with him? Everyone knew about the Senior Fall Ball. It was promoted during the morning announcements daily. Posters of the event hung in the hallways and in the cafeteria. "You know, the dance," he said.

"A dance?" Belle's eyes grew distant, dreamy. "I haven't been to a dance . . . " She caught herself. "Wait a minute. Are you inviting me to a dance?"

Todd felt his chest tighten. This was the part he hated most about asking girls out. The very real possibility of being rejected. "Yeah, well, I mean . . . if you'd like to go."

"When is it?"

She sounded interested. Good. "A week from Saturday," Todd said, trying to keep his voice steady. "Seven o'clock at City Place."

Belle smiled. "Sure, I'd love to go."

A surge of elation rushed through Todd. He had hit the jackpot. Won the lottery. He had just scored a date with the most beautiful girl at North Oak Cliff High School.

"But I'll have to ask my parents first."

Todd's ego took an instant nosedive. He had heard this line before. When he'd asked Angela Mason to go to the movies with him to see *Scarlet Dreams*, she initially said yes. Then on the day of their date, she fed him the my-parents-won't-let-me-go excuse. Later, Todd learned that Angela had gone to a party with Bobby McIntire that night instead.

But Belle did seem genuinely interested.

Todd fished his cell phone out of his pocket. "Let me have your number, and I'll call you."

Belle reeled back. "I don't . . . I mean, we don't have a phone," she said.

Another lie. Who didn't have a phone these days? But Todd decided not to press her. After all, she had accepted his invitation to go to the dance. Maybe. "How will I reach you, then?" he asked.

"Don't worry. I'll find you," she said. "See you."

"Wait. Let me give you a ride home," Todd offered. Then, unable to resist, he added, "You live on Edgefield, right?"

Belle gave a start of surprise. Then she composed herself and said, "I . . . I'm not going home right now. I've got to run a few errands. But I'll let you know about the dance."

Todd watched her saunter down the sidewalk. He considered following her but changed his mind. Whatever she was keeping from him wasn't any of his business. He stared at the book she had given him. A story about a man who turns into a bug. That was probably a lie, too.

That night, Todd began reading *The Metamorphosis*. He wasn't much of a reader. Except for the sports section in *The Dallas Morning News*, he didn't do much reading outside of school. As it turned out, Belle was telling the truth about the book; he found the story so bizarre, he couldn't put it down.

While he read about Gregor Samsa, a man who wakes up one morning to find himself inexplicably changed into a monstrous insect, Todd thought about how cool it was to know a girl who read these kinds of stories. *Toddy boy, I hope she's not leading you on.*

The next day, he took the book to school. If he saw Belle, he would tell her how much he was enjoying it. To his disappointment, he didn't see her.

When he got to his English class, Mrs. Lindsey noticed the book in his hand. "It's good to see a student reading *The Metamorphosis* without having it assigned," she said.

Todd held the book in front of her. "It's about this guy who turns into a giant bug."

"Yes, I know," Mrs. Lindsey said. "It used to be on my required reading list."

Thinking that he might yet be able to track down the elusive Belle Segovia, Todd asked, "Do you know which teacher's teaching *The Metamorphosis* right now?"

"No one," Mrs. Lindsey answered without hesitation. "The English Department changed its curriculum a while back, and we haven't used it since."

Todd wondered why Belle claimed she was reading *The Metamorphosis* for school when no English teacher at North Oak Cliff was teaching it. And where was Belle? He hadn't seen her anywhere. He even asked some of the girls—Claudia, Brenda, Leticia and a few others if they knew her, but it seemed no one had ever heard of Belle Segovia.

On his way home from school, Todd decided to drive down Edgefield Avenue. As he neared the intersection of Edgefield and West Davis, on the right-hand side of the street, he saw an empty lot between two houses. He pulled his car over and got out. The lot was covered with weeds. Concrete steps and a walkway led to what must have been the porch. Across the street, an old man was working in his garden.

Todd walked over to him. "Excuse me, sir. I don't mean to bother you, but can you tell me anything about the house that used to be over there?" He aimed a thumb at the vacant lot.

The man straightened and removed his gloves. He pulled a handkerchief from his back pocket and wiped his forehead. "You talking about the Segovia place?"

Segovia. Belle's last name. Todd gulped. "Yes," he said, almost whispering.

"Burned down 'bout six years ago," the man said. "Why do you ask?"

Todd cleared his throat. "I, uh, I'm a student at North Oak Cliff High School, and . . . I'm a reporter for our school newspaper, the *Over the Cliff*." He couldn't believe how easy the lie flowed out of his mouth. But then, he had been learning from an expert. "We're, um, writing articles about the neighborhood, and my journalism teacher asked me to find out about the Segovia house."

The man took another swipe at his forehead with his handkerchief. Then he blew his nose and stuck the handkerchief back in his pocket. "Nothing much to tell," he said. "An old extension cord under a rug is what caused the fire. Least that's what I heard."

Todd nodded. "Did you know the family?"

The man put his gloves back on. "Not too well, but they seemed like nice people. 'Course, I didn't talk to them a whole lot. They spoke very little English. But they were always friendly. Most of my neighbors are."

"What about their daughter, Belle?" Todd asked. He turned his head, afraid that the man might see something suspicious in his eyes.

The man scrunched up his mouth and made a serious face, as if he was trying to come up with an appropriate answer. "From what I heard she went to live with an aunt and uncle in San Antonio."

"Houston," Todd corrected him.

"Oh, you know the family?"

"I've . . . met Belle," Todd muttered, still refusing to lock eyes with the man.

The man grinned. "Pretty girl. Used to see her every afternoon, walking that little white poodle up and down the sidewalk. Poor Chico. He died in the fire, too."

They chatted a few minutes more before the man excused himself to return to his gardening. Todd thanked him for his time.

"Sure thing. Good luck with your article." As Todd headed toward his car, the man said, "If you happen to see Belle, you tell her Mr. Huckaby said hello."

Belle sat on the couch with her arms crossed, her eyes seething contempt.

"You are not going to that dance!" her mother told her in Spanish. "You hear me? I knew there was going to be trouble the moment that boy showed up at our door."

Belle turned her head but didn't say anything.

Chico paced back and forth in front of her, his eyes wide with alarm. "Yap! Yap! Yap!"

"Shut up, Chico!" Belle's mother grabbed a magazine and tried to swat the dog.

Chico jumped out of the way. "Yap! Yap! Yap!"

"*Mija*, we're just trying to protect you," her father said in a calm voice.

Good cop, bad cop, Belle thought. They had their roles down pat. Belle's mother, the temperamental interrogator; her father, the gentle mediator.

"Papi, we're just friends," Belle said. "That's all. I can have friends, can't I?"

"No! No friends!" her mother interjected.

"Yap! Yap! Yap!"

"*Mija*, why don't you take Chico for a walk?" her father suggested.

Good idea. Belle couldn't stand being cooped up any longer. She grabbed the leash from the coffee table and hooked it on the dog's collar. "Come on, Chico."

"And don't talk to anybody!" her mother warned.

Todd watched Belle come out of the apartment with the Chihuahua. It was the same dog that had met him at the door a couple of nights ago. Todd had been parked outside the Vista Ridge Apartments for about twenty minutes, trying to piece together the Belle Segovia puzzle. He felt as if he was back in Mr. Mondragón's ninth grade algebra class, working on a word problem.

Write an algebraic equation and solve. A girl named Belle Segovia says she's a student at North Oak Cliff High School, but no one's ever heard of her. She says she lives in a house on Edgefield, but she actually lives in an apartment on W. Tenth St. Another girl named Belle Segovia used to live on Edgefield, but her house burned down six years ago and her family and her dog died in the fire. Who is Belle?

Perhaps it was time to confront her, to find out the truth. Todd noticed that the lights in the apartment were turned off. No one seemed to be home. Belle's parents were probably shopping or something. He weighed his options. He could wait until Belle returned from walking the dog and surprise her at the door. Bad idea. What if she exploded with anger at being called a liar and then her parents showed up? It could turn into an ugly scene. Todd also thought about driving up to Belle while she was walking her dog. He would pretend that he just happened to be passing by. Then what? Would he tell her that nothing she said was adding up?

He would have to think this through some more. Todd turned on the ignition and drove home.

He didn't see Belle at school the following day. Nor did he run into her the day after.

Senior Fall Ball was a week away, and Todd still didn't know if he had a date. He had begun to wish he had never invited Belle to the dance. Tickets were twenty-five dollars—thirty, if you bought them at the door. That was a small fortune, especially for someone who didn't work. Todd's mother didn't allow him to have a job.

"You have the rest of your life to work," she told him. "Right now, school comes first."

Todd's allowance varied from week to week, depending on the chores he was given. Tomorrow was Saturday, which meant that he would spend the day working on the yard, mowing and trimming the hedges. That would bring in a few extra bucks. But he didn't know if he wanted to spend his hard-earned money on someone he couldn't rely on—or trust.

On Monday morning, Todd found Belle sitting on the retaining wall in front of the school. She smiled as she watched the students walk past her on their way inside the building.

"There you are."

"Hi, Todd." Belle raised her cheerful face toward the sky and took in a deep breath. "Isn't this a glorious day?"

It was seventy-two degrees and the sun was shining, not bad weather for the last week in October, but Todd didn't think there was anything particularly glorious about it.

"I've been looking all over the place for you," he said. "Senior Fall Ball's this Saturday, and I need to know if you're planning to go with me."

Belle's cheerfulness faded. "I'm sorry, Todd. I wish I could give an answer, but I'm still not sure if I can go."

Todd glared at her. "You told me you wanted to go to the dance." Then, more bluntly, he added, "Or was that just another lie?"

Belle blinked with surprise. "What do you mean 'was that just another lie'?"

"You know exactly what I'm talking about." Todd was fed up with her cat-and-mouse game. "I know Mrs. Lindsey isn't your teacher, and I know you live at the Vista Ridge Apartments on Tenth Street."

Belle hopped off the retaining wall. Her face grew hot with resentment. "Have you been spying on me?" she snapped.

"Only enough to know that you're not who you say you are." Todd looked at her ID badge. Her name was visible, but the flower stickers covered the year. An answer to a question that had been gnawing at him suddenly hit him. He eyed her skeptically and asked, "Are you really a student here?"

Belle snatched her backpack from the wall. "I don't have to listen to this," she said and stormed off.

"Hey! School's the other way," Todd called, but he had a feeling Belle wouldn't be returning. If his hunch was right, she hadn't been a student at North Oak Cliff High School in years. He fired a parting shot. "By the way, Mr. Huckaby told me to say hello to you."

Belle whipped her head around and gaped at him, pop-eyed. Then she hurried away.

During second period study hall, Todd asked for a pass to go to the library.

The reference section had copies of past yearbooks. Todd pulled down the one from six years ago, turned to the index and read the names. There she was. Segovia, Belle—67, 180, 187, 224.

On page sixty-seven, next to someone named Mark Scott was a photograph of Belle Segovia. Her hair was longer, but it was definitely her. That would make Belle twenty-three or twenty-four years old. After his visit with Mr. Huckaby, Todd had suspected something like this, but still his heart skipped a beat when he realized how old she really was.

Belle's extracurricular activities were listed beside her name: Spanish Club, National Honor Society and Theatre. Todd turned to page 180. LITTLE THEATRE, it read at the top. There were photos of scenes from the school play, *The Importance of Being Earnest*, including one of Belle portraying Lady Bracknell. The other two pages showed her in group pictures with her organizations.

Why was Belle pretending to be a student at North Oak Cliff High School? Todd recalled Mrs. Lindsey saying that Belle had dropped out of school shortly before graduation. Was Belle somehow trying to relive her senior year? Something else caught Todd's attention. On the faculty page under the name Ruth Lindsey, someone had scribbled BULLDOG.

In a panic, Belle threw her clothes into her suitcase. She had to leave. Immediately.

"Didn't I tell you to stay away from that boy?" her mother scolded. "I told you he was going to bring trouble. But you didn't listen to me. You never do."

"Don't be so rough on her," Belle's father said. "She tried. Didn't you, *mija*? It was the boy's fault. He wouldn't leave you alone."

Belle scrambled to stuff the wadded-up clothes from the dresser's bottom drawers into her bulky suitcase. She compressed her lips into a straight line, refusing to answer. She had to get out. She couldn't take a chance on being forced to return to *that place*. The place she had been sent because of Tío Roy's and Tía Lydia's lies to the judge. The place of endless corridors and heavy metal doors.

When she clicked the suitcase shut and stood up, she stared at the narrow panel of mirror on the back of the bedroom door. She could see Chico wrestling with a T-shirt she had dropped on the floor, his short tan legs almost engulfed by the expanse of soft cotton, his bright black eyes relishing the sport. He was her third dog named Chico and she hoped he'd live longer than the others.

But other than Chico, no one else's reflection could be seen in the mirror.

"As soon as you finish packing, I'll call a taxi to come pick us up," Belle's father said in his gentlest voice, almost whispering in her ear.

After school, Todd drove to the Vista Ridge Apartments. He wanted to talk to Belle. He didn't know what he would say, but he wanted answers.

When he arrived, he stopped at the apartment mailboxes located on the front side of the building and looked at the one for 117. SEGOVIA it said in a red label above the apartment number.

Todd walked to the apartment and noticed that the door was ajar. He pushed it open. "Hello?"

No answer.

He entered the apartment. The cream-colored walls were bare. A brown couch with a broken armrest and frayed upholstery was pushed against a wall. A coffee table and a T.V. stand made up the rest of the living room furniture. The gold carpet was covered with dark stains, and Todd detected a faint odor of urine. The bedroom door was open, so Todd went inside.

"Can I help you?" a voice asked.

Todd jumped and a girlish squeal escaped from his throat. He spun around and saw burly man with a five o'clock shadow standing by the window.

"I, uh, was looking for the people who live here," Todd managed to say.

"You mean the girl?" the man asked. "She's gone. Skipped without paying the rent."

Todd's eyebrows shot up. "Really? The family moved out?"

"Aren't you listening to me?" the man said gruffly. "There ain't no family. Just the girl." He stared at a carpet stain and swiped it with his foot.

Todd thought about the woman who had answered the door the first time he came by. "Are you sure about that?"

"I should be," the man said. "I'm the apartment manager." He walked out of the bedroom and made his way to the living room. He noticed the broken armrest on the couch and made a face. "Good riddance to her, I say. That girl's a real loony tune." He made circles around the side of his head with an index finger. "Always talking to herself, you know? I'd pass by her apartment and I'd hear her. She'd speak in her normal voice. Then she'd change it and start talking in Spanish. Then she'd make her voice go deeper and keep talking." He shook his head. "Good looking gal, but what a wacko."

"So there was never a family living here?" Todd asked, feeling goosebumps blossom on his arms.

The man let out a sigh of frustration. "Like I said, it was just the girl. Her and the dog."

Valentine Surprise

Gwendolyn Zepeda

Even though Valentine's Day was coming up, it was another slow Saturday at work. I was setting up a big pink and red display on the counter, making a bunch of teddy bears and baby chickens look like they were having a tea party with teacups full of jelly beans, trying to keep busy despite the lack of customers. I was wishing for the thousandth time that I'd applied for a job at the new outlet mall on the edge of town. But for some reason I never did, and now all the after-school and weekend shifts there were taken and here I was, stuck at Debbi's Glamour Gifts on stale old Main Street.

My boss, Debbi, used to be okay—she'd let me read books at the counter when it was slow—but she's in a permanent bad mood since they opened the outlet mall. I guess it's because hardly anyone spends money here anymore. And really, I can't blame them. This town was pretty lame until the outlet mall opened up and now everybody's glad that they don't have to drive all the way to Austin to get normal jeans. Debbi mostly sells flowery dresses, mom purses and jewelry with big pearls and fake diamonds. They have all that at the mall, and better stuff, plus cinnamon pretzels and gelato, and everything there is in one big building with a brand-new parking lot all the way around it. Meanwhile, Debbi's store is in a dusty old house, so there's no central heat or air, and there's never enough parking in front, so customers always have to park at Burber Brothers' Grocery and walk across the street to get here. So, really, when you add it all up, there's pretty much no reason on earth for *anyone* to be at Debbi's.

In fact, at that moment, on the Saturday I'm telling you about, the only people there were me, Debbi and this kid from school named Joseph Melado. And I knew why *he* was here: Because he hates crowds. He told me that last year, when we had to do a history project together for Fourth Period.

Most of the kids at school don't talk to Joseph because he has to go to ACE sometimes—that's for kids who have dyslexia or depression or whatever—and because he dresses weird. He always wears boots and this big brown coat that looks like it came from somebody's grandfather's closet—even when it's not too cold. But he told me it's because he likes being warm and doesn't care what anybody thinks about how he looks. And I can respect that. He's actually pretty smart—we got an A on the project we did together—and he's not crazy or anything, so I say hi to him in the halls, even though people make fun of him. But they're the same people who make fun of me because I'm not pretty enough and I don't wear the newest jeans from the outlet mall, so I don't worry about it.

And I didn't mind that Joseph was in the store that day, taking his time looking at every single thing Debbi had for sale. He'd told me when he came in that he was looking for a gift for his mom and couldn't figure out what to get her, but he didn't need any help.

So I told Debbi we should just leave him alone and let him take his time. So she left me alone at the counter and went to the back, to the stockroom. I could hear her back there, gossiping with her sister on the phone. It sounded like she'd be a while.

Meanwhile, I was really getting into my display, filling up tea cups with all the different colors of candy and trying to make the teddy bears and baby chicks look like they were deep in conversation. I guess you could say I was bored. Debbi was picky about her displays, and it was kind of surprising that she was letting me do this one, considering that it would be the first thing customers saw when they walked through the door. So I wanted to do a good job.

I was trying to get the biggest teddy bear to sit up straight in his little iron chair when the bell on the front door rang and Tyler Farmhausen walked in, wearing his letter jacket and a really cute hat.

Tyler is the hottest guy at school, but that's not why I care about him. And it's not because his family has tons of money from their ranch, either. See, the thing is, he's not your typical football player or rancher's son. He's also interested in writing, like I am. He sits next to me in English, and he was my partner for our sonnet assignment last semester. He let me do most of our poem, because I write "just like people in books."

He says I'm the smartest girl in the school and always asks for my opinion on his class work. See, he doesn't judge people by their looks and their clothes, like some of the other guys on the team who call me "The Flats" and stick plastic surgery ads into my locker. And Tyler has really green eyes and a really nice smile. Not that that's the most important thing. But it is something you can't help but notice about him.

"Hi, Lindsey," he said as he came through the door. The sun shone through the glass next to our Open sign and hit his hair, making it look almost gold.

I said, "Hi, Tyler. Can I help you find anything?" like Debbi makes me to say to all the customers, but in a way that would show him I really meant it.

He came right up to the counter, close enough for me to smell his cologne, and said, "Actually, yeah, you can." He leaned over the counter, close enough so I could see the freckles on his nose. "I'm looking for a Valentine's present for this girl. But she doesn't know that I like her. So it's got to be a secret admirer kind of thing. And I don't know her that well—I only know that she's real nice and real smart."

He smiled at me then, with that smile I was telling you about. It made my stomach feel kind of strange, like when you drink a lot of soda too fast and you can feel the bubbles all the way through. He said, "So I need your help, Lindsey. I want you . . . I mean, I want this girl to really like the gift I pick out. So I need you to tell me what you think she'd like."

"Okay. Yeah. I mean, yeah. Okay." That sounded stupid, I know, but I totally could not think of anything else to say. Was it just my imagination, or did it sound like he was talking about *me?*

There was no way, though. Yes, he thought I was smart and nice, but that didn't mean he *liked* me. I didn't know what kind of girls Tyler liked, but it was probably cheerleader types. At least, it probably wasn't girls who had to wear glasses instead of contacts and who had to walk to work every day after school.

Then again, why else would he be here? And why would he be telling me all this stuff about the girl he liked? If he meant some other girl, he'd be buying her something at the outlet mall, right? It was almost like he came here to tell me this story, on purpose, so that I'd know that he liked me.

There was only one way to find out, and that was to keep talking to him.

I set down the teddy bear that wouldn't sit up straight and saw that my fingers were trembling. Get hold of yourself, Lindsey, I told myself. Out loud, as casually as I could, I said, "Sure, yeah. Let me show you some of the new bracelets we just got. And, um . . . Can you tell me a little more about the girl?"

The bell on the front door had to ring again, right at that moment, of course. I looked over to greet whoever it was, figuring it was most likely Mrs. Schmitt, who came in almost every day and never bought a thing. But I was wrong. It was a girl from school—a girl who I hate.

Crysta Morgan thinks she's better than everyone else because she has blue eyes and naturally blonde hair and because her family owns some dumb restaurant where she's the hostess and wears a stupid barmaid uniform that all the men in town love. And because her parents always fly to Chicago on business and sometimes they take her with them. And, of course, she's a cheerleader and part of the Homecoming Royal Court. Girls like that always are.

But none of that is why I hate her. The reason is: once I was walking down the hall after Second Period, and Crysta and her friends were standing by their lockers. As I passed them, I heard one of them say, "Low-income Lindsey."

It wasn't Crysta who said it, but when I turned back to see, she was laughing really loud, along with all the others.

She walked through Debbi's front door and I knew right off the bat why *she* was there and not at the mall. She'd only been in the store twice before, and both times, earrings and bracelets had come up missing. But I didn't actually see her steal anything, and other people had been in the store at the time, so Debbi never did anything about it.

Crysta was wearing a really short skirt with tights and high-heeled mini boots, even though it was pretty cold outside and jeans would've been smarter. She was carrying a big pink purse and a large whipped-cream-topped drink from the only trendy coffee shop in town. I looked at her but she didn't look at me, so I didn't feel the need to say "Can I help you find anything?" She went right to our purse display, over by the front window.

I didn't like taking my eyes off her, but I wanted to get back to Tyler. He'd drifted down the counter to my other side and was examining our revolving rack of fake flower pins. I walked over that way, but when I reached him, I didn't know what to say. The moment between us had been broken. Plus, the conversation we'd started wasn't exactly one I wanted to continue when someone like Crysta could overhear.

But I wanted to say *something*.

"Those are nice," I told him, even though the fake flowers totally weren't. "But what about something more like this?" I came out from behind the counter and went over to a table that was covered with soaps and candles and our cheaper rings and bracelets. I did that for a couple of reasons: There were actually a few cute things on that table, one, and because picking something like that would show that I wasn't obsessed with money. And, three, that was the table Crysta had taken the earrings from last time she was here, so standing right next to it would keep her away, kill two birds with one stone.

Tyler followed me over and shuffled through the merchandise, but then something behind me caught his attention. I turned and saw Crysta smiling at him and holding up the teddy bear I'd just set down. She was flirting with him! I turned back to Tyler to see how he'd react.

He didn't do anything. He looked away from her and didn't even give her a polite smile.

Good, I thought.

"So," he said to me, "which of these bracelets looks best? Which one would look good on a girl with dark brown hair and big brown eyes?" He smiled at me again, then picked up a band of red and gold beads and held it near my wrist. His finger brushed my thumb.

I have dark brown hair.

I heard myself giggle and the sound echoed against the store's wooden walls. "That one's pretty, yeah," I said. My hand felt warm where he'd touched it.

"Yeah, I think that looks nice." He didn't move his hand away from mine. My chest felt all fluttery and it seemed like everything around our hands was shimmering.

Behind us, there was a crash.

I turned and saw one of our stand-up racks lying on the floor with purses all jumbled on top of it. Next to that, there was a puddle of brown liquid, topped with a little dab of whipped cream. Next to all that was Crysta. "Dammit!" she said.

My thoughts exactly. Next to me, obviously startled, Tyler jerked his hand away from mine.

"What in the world is going on out here?" That was Debbi, coming out of the stockroom with her phone in one hand and a snack cake in the other. "What are you kids doing?"

I hated that she said that, lumping me in with everyone else, as if I'd been doing something wrong.

"This rack fell over and almost landed on top of me!" Crysta said.

"Oh, my word," said Debbi. She set her snack cake on the counter and pushed her phone into the neckline of her blouse. "Let me help you." She hurried over to where Crysta was standing, looking like she'd just been the victim of some crime. "Lindsey, go get the mop."

I went into the stockroom, to the closet in its corner where we kept the cleaning supplies. As I pulled the mop out of it, I heard the bells on the door ring, twice in a row. I rolled the mop bucket to the front room just in time to see the tail end of an old brown coat exiting the store. Joseph. I'd totally forgotten he was in the store.

I looked around. Tyler was gone, too.

Debbi had her arm around Crysta, who was giving an Academy Award winning performance, trembling and hiccupping like she'd just escaped death.

"Poor thing! Are you okay?" Debbi said.

Crysta nodded. "I'm fine. I think I'll go now."

"Well, let me give you the money to buy another coffee," Debbi said. "Or maybe a coupon . . . " She let go of Crysta and walked toward the register, where we kept the coupons and store credit slips.

"No, that's fine. I'll just be going now," Crysta said, hoisting her purse on her shoulder and turning to the door. She was in a hurry to leave now, it seemed.

There was a small clatter near the register. I turned and saw that Debbi had knocked over one of the teacups in my display. And then I noticed something else.

My teddy bear—the big one that I'd been trying to put into the chair . . . the one that Crysta had been holding a few minutes ago . . . was gone.

I turned back to Crysta, who now had her hand on the front door.

"Stop," I told her.

She and Debbi looked at me. I let go of the mop handle and walked to the front door, blocking Crysta's way. "You took something," I told her.

She stared at me, no longer scared and innocent, but with the same snooty face she always wore at school. "What?"

"What are you saying, Lindsey?" said Debbi.

"There was a teddy bear on the counter. Now it's gone. She stole it," I said.

"What?" said Debbi. Her blonde eyebrows lifted in surprise.

Crysta snorted. "I didn't take anything. I don't have your stupid bear." She lifted her hands to show that they were empty. "Who do you think you are? First, your stupid rack almost falls on me, and now you're trying to . . . "

I scanned her with my eyes, then realized what she must have done. "Your purse," I said. "You put it in your purse." It was big enough to hold four or five teddy bears, and who-knew-what all else.

"What? I did not!" Crysta practically yelled. But she sounded really suspicious.

Debbi must have thought so, too, because she walked over to us and said, really serious and quiet, "Honey, I'm gonna need you to open up your purse and show us."

With a roll of her eyes, Crysta opened her purse and held it out for Debbi to see. I was close enough to see inside, too. The purse was jammed full . . . with make-up, gum wrappers, a phone . . . but no teddy bear.

Debbi sighed. "Oh, my word. Honey, I apologize."

Crysta turned and smiled at me. It was an evil smile. "*She's* the one who owes me an apology," she said.

"You're right," Debbi said. "Lindsey, please apologize to our customer."

"But," I said. "But she's . . . " She was lying. I knew it. Somehow, she had stolen that bear. I'd seen it in her hands.

"Lindsey. Now."

Feeling like I was being forced at gunpoint, I muttered an apology.

Debbi offered her more coupons, but Crysta just smiled another evil smile and went out the door. I watched her go, but couldn't see the teddy bear anywhere on her.

When she was out of sight, Debbi turned to me. "Lindsey, you're lucky I don't fire you right now."

"What? Why? What'd I do?" Apparently, Debbi was mad about the missing merchandise, and she was going to take it out on me.

"You accused a customer of stealing. Not even to mention that a customer almost got hurt on your watch, and you didn't do anything about it!"

"What?" I couldn't believe what I was hearing. "Debbi, she totally knocked that rack down on purpose!"

"Why would she do that?"

"To create a distraction! So she could get away with stealing the teddy bear!" Even as I said it aloud, I knew that it didn't make sense.

Debbi launched into a lecture about customer service, and I replayed the incident in my mind. If she'd been planning to steal something, why would she make a big mess and draw all that attention to herself?

Because, I realized, she wanted attention. From Tyler. She wanted him to stop talking to me and rush over to help her.

And I'd been so distracted by Tyler that the teddy bear had been misplaced in some other way, maybe.

" . . . and so you're going to clean up this mess, and then that teddy bear's coming out of your paycheck," Debbi said.

"But, if she didn't steal it, then it's not gone," I said. "It has to be around here somewhere. I'll find it." That teddy bear could cost two hours of my salary.

Debbi considered, then said, "Yes, you need to find it. And then it's *still* coming out of your pay, to teach you a lesson. You can't be rude to customers or accuse them of stealing, even if they're girls from school that you don't like. And if you *don't* find that bear, I'll have to assume *you* were the one who took it, and I'll have to double dock you for it."

"But that's not fair," I said. It wasn't fair for me to be humiliated in front of Crysta and then lose two hours of work, on top of that. Four hours, if Crysta took the bear. And I still believed that she did, somehow.

It wasn't fair at all. And it didn't make sense. But Debbi had said her final word on the subject, and I didn't want to lose my job. So I shut my mouth, and my boss went behind the counter and opened the register, apparently to make sure I hadn't lost any money.

It didn't make sense, I thought as I mopped the sticky mess off the floor. It wasn't fair.

And then the bells rang. The front door opened and Joseph came in.

"Hello. May I help you find something?" Debbi asked automatically, even though he'd just been in the store.

"No. I just wanted to give you this." Joseph reached into his coat and pulled out . . . the missing teddy bear! He placed it on the counter in front of Debbi, who was too surprised to say anything.

I practically ran over to the counter. "Where'd you get that?"

He coughed and looked down at the floor, obviously nervous about having to speak to an audience of two people. "I was outside just now, and Tyler was there, too, but he didn't see me. Crysta came out and I heard her tell him, 'Low-income Lindsey said I stole the teddy bear, but then I showed them inside my purse and she had to apologize to me'."

"Low income . . . what?" said Debbi.

"And then what happened?" I asked Joseph. My heart was beating hard. His story had started bad and would undoubtedly end even worse.

"Then Tyler said, 'You shouldn't have told me to steal the bear, Crysta. You should have just pointed out a pair of earrings. What if I'd gotten caught?'"

That was it, then. Tyler had stolen the bear. For Crysta. "Then what happened?"

Joseph shrugged. "Then they left."

Debbi's mouth was hanging open. "Tyler Farmhausen? I can't believe it. He's always been such a nice young man."

I didn't want to believe it, either. But, apparently, it was true. I asked Joseph, "So how'd you get the bear back?"

He coughed. "Oh, I heard Tyler say that he didn't make it all the way to his truck . . . that he'd left the bear in the Burber Brothers parking lot and come back to check on Crysta, since it was taking her so long to come out of the store. So, um . . . When I heard that, I went to the parking lot and found it, then hid it in my coat and brought it back here."

"Wow," I said. "You did all that?"

"Yeah. Well, I didn't want you to get in trouble for something that wasn't your fault."

"Wow," I said. I was in shock. Tyler had pretended to like me in order to steal for his girlfriend. His girlfriend Crysta, the girl I hated. He'd tricked me, for her. I felt really, really stupid.

It wasn't fair.

It didn't make sense.

"Yes, thank you," said Debbi. "We really appreciate your help. Here . . . " She opened the register and fished around in the drawer. "Have a coupon. Ten percent off your next purchase."

"Thanks," Joseph said. And then he turned and walked out the door.

The teddy bear lay on the counter where he'd left it, looking up at me with its glassy eyes.

"You know, you could have at least thanked that boy," Debbi told me. "He didn't have to do that for you."

She was right. I hadn't even thanked him. And he was probably all the way across the street by now. "Can I . . . Do you mind if I . . . "

She nodded. "Go ahead. Hurry."

Outside, I saw Joseph's brown coat across the street, already disappearing between the pick-up trucks at the edge of the grocery store parking lot. I hurried to the crosswalk and had to let a couple of cars pass before jogging after him.

I'd lost sight of him by the time I got across the street, but went in the same direction I'd seen him go. And then I ended up next to a big, blue minivan, and I heard a familiar voice coming from the other side of it.

"I can't believe you did that! Why'd you have to go back?" It was Crysta. I peered through the minivan's windows, but they were tinted too dark so I had to creep around the back of it to see her and Tyler.

But it wasn't Tyler with her. It was Joseph. He was standing next to Crysta, next to an old, brown Chevy Malibu.

"I told you, Crysta, it wasn't fair for you to get Lindsey in trouble like that. She didn't deserve it. And you didn't need that bear, anyway. I got you enough stuff." He reached into his big brown coat then and pulled out earrings, bracelets and necklaces . . . all stuff from the back of our store, where he'd been shopping the whole time I'd been talking to Tyler in the front. He put them in a pile on the hood of the car and said, "Why'd you even go into the store? I told you to stay here and wait."

"And *I* told *you*, I wanted to make sure you got me something good!"

"Well, that should be enough for you," he said, pointing to the pile of stolen jewelry.

"We'll see," she said. Then she leaned over and *kissed* him. Crysta Morgan kissed Joseph Melado.

What was the world coming to? Where was the shy boy from the dyslexic class who hated crowds, who wore an old coat to keep warm? I used to feel sorry for Joseph, and now here he was, using his old coat to steal and rubbing his hands all over the popular girl's butt. And Crysta was obviously loving it. With her eyes closed and her face pressed to his, she used one hand to undo the top button of his shirt, as if she'd done it a hundred times before. Joseph turned her and pushed her body against the hood of his Malibu. She ran her hands through his hair and made little noises in her throat.

It looked like they'd be there for a while. I started to feel uncomfortable watching them, so I stepped back behind the minivan, leaving them alone with their fake diamonds and their secret love. I would go back to the store and tell Debbi what they'd done. I'd let her walk over here and confront them so she could see the evidence for herself this time.

I took a long look around the parking lot and the surrounding area. Tyler Farmhausen was nowhere to be seen, and neither was his big white pick-up with the duallys. I would have recognized it a mile away. So, obviously, he was long gone and had nothing whatsoever to do with Joseph and Crysta's crimes.

After looking both ways at the corner, I walked slowly back to Debbi's Glamour Gifts.

There were two hours left on my shift. I knew I'd spend them thinking about hands touching under red and gold beads, and listening for the bells over the door.

Glossary of Spanish Words

Abuela—grandmother

Aguas frescas—fresh fruit drinks

Adiós—goodbye

Ay Dios—oh God

¡Ay, Dios mío!—oh, my God

Ay, sí la cabeza—oh, yes, the head

¡Bien padre!—phrase used to express complete approval, as in "excellent" or "very fine"

Bite—hip-hop slang for plagiarizing or copying a style

Buelita—abbreviated term of endearment for Abuela, meaning grandmother

Buenas noches—good evening, good night

Cabezón—a hardheaded person; stubborn

Cabrona—jerk, bitch

Chichis—slang for breasts, or boobs

Chilaquiles—tortilla, cheese and hot pepper based dish

Chile—a pepper or a pepper paste, salsa or powder

Chingao—slang version of "chingado," or fuck

Chingazos—vulgar slang for blows in a fist fight

Chisme—gossip

Chismosa/o—someone who gossips

Chola/o—a gang member

Chola/o-like—gang-like

Chucho—a hypocorism for Jesús; Chuy is also a hypocorism of Jesús

Chueco—crooked; *chuequito* is the diminutive form and expresses affection

Chula/o—a flirt, a sexpot, a player

Colibrí—hummingbird

Comida para la cruda—food to help with a hangover

Compadres—literally "co-parents," used to refer to close friends

Coyolxauhqui—Aztec warrior goddess

Cruda—hangover

Cucaracha—roach

Culo—asshole

Déjala en paz—leave her be

Desesperación—desperation

Desgraciado/os—wretched; disgraceful people

Dorados—the personal bodyguards of Pancho Villa. All were chosen by Villa himself for bravery, resourcefulness and loyalty. Literally, the "Golden Men"

El llano en llamas—a book of stories by Mexican author Juan Rulfo that is set in Jalisco immediately after the Mexican Revolution. It has been translated as, *The Burning Plain*

Ese—hey, you

Es lógico—makes sense

Familia—family

Federales—the troops employed by the Mexican government

Gear—hip-hop slang for clothing and accessories

Gordita/o—chubby

Gracias—thanks

Gringa/o—foreigner from a non-Spanish speaking country

Güera/o; Güerita/o—blond; light skinned, fair-haired; term of endearment

Hijita/o—daughter, son; term of endearment

Jaina—Chicano slang for woman or girlfriend. Sometimes spelled haina. Jainita is the diminutive form

Jefe/a—the boss, the leader, the commander-in-chief; mother

Lleno de amor—full of love

Llorón—crybaby

Loquita/o—crazy girl or boy

Macho—manly with possible connotations of silent strength and bravery

Mal de ojo—the evil eye

Mami—Mother

Marijuana—pot head

Masa—dough, in this case, corn dough or *nixtamal*, for the tamales

Mensa/o—colloquial term for "dummy"

Mi general—my General

Mi vida—"My life;" term of endearment

Mija/o—abbreviation of mi hija or mi hijo, meaning my daughter or my son; term of endearment

¡Mira!—look!

Mojadita/o—"wetback;" in the diminutive, term of endearment

Morenita—brunette

Mucho gusto—nice to meet you

Nada—nothing

Nadie la toca—nobody touches her

Negrita/o—black person, African-American; "Little black one;" term of endearment

Norteño—from the North of Mexico

Novelas—Spanish-language soap operas

Órale—expressive term indicating agreement, okay or "right on"

Otra vez—again

Paisa—short for *paisano* (countryman); term used to describe Mexican immigrants that have a provincial or indigenous look to them. In recent years, it has also been used as a pejorative meaning dim-witted

Papi—father

Papis—parents

Para arriba, para abajo, para un lado, para el otro, para afuera para adentro—chant used when drinking tequila shots

Pendeja/o—"fool," dumb ass

Pensó—he/she/it thought

Pesadilla—nightmare

Pinche—an all-purpose insult; insignificant, lousy, miserable, worthless

Pinche loca/o—goddamn fool

Piropos—compliments

Placazo—Chicano slang for graffiti, tattoos, or more specifically, a graffiti artist or gang member's alias/nickname

Policía—police

¿Por qué, mi vida?—why, my dear?

¿Por qué, nena?—why, girl?

Pozole—hominy and meat based stew

Puta/o—gigolo/prostitute. Like most profanities, may be used either as a term of derision or affection

Qué curioso—how curious!

Quinceañera—Mexican version of "sweet 16" party, celebrated at age 15, and often involving a special Mass, a dinner and dance, a "court" of fourteen ladies in waiting—each with her own escort—and a groom-like escort for the birthday girl. The birthday girl's dress, dinner and dance can be almost as expensive as a wedding

Rasquachi—low-brow, crude, gauche

Refín—food, chow

Raza—literally, race; also used in northern Mexico as a synonym for people, regardless of race

Rebozo—shawl

Rellenos de plátanos—stuffed plantains

Revolucionario—revolutionary

Rifa—Pachuco slang to describe something exceptional; similar to the use of "rule" in U.S. slang

Rucas—chicks, girls, women

¿Sabes qué?—you know what?

Santitos—little saints

Sarreado—a derivative of *sarra*, which is slang in northern Mexico for ugly, mean or unfortunate

Se fueron—they're gone

Secuestro—kidnapping

Señorita—miss

Señorita bien bonita—good-looking young lady

Siguiendo—following

Soy sordo, no imbécil—I am deaf, not an imbecil

Soy tu abuelo—I am your grandfather

Spaghetti con pollo—spaghetti with chicken

También—also

Tía/o—aunt; uncle

Tonta/o—silly, dummy

Trabajo—job

Tristeza—sadness

Vaporera—a large pot that cooks with steam

Vato(s)—Pachuco slang for man; a derivative of *chivato*, which is slang for an informant and in formal Spanish is a goat that is between six months and a year old; dudes

Verdá—an informal version of the word *verdad* (truth) that is common in Mexico

¿Verdad?—right?

Viejita—old woman

Veteranos—veterans

Ya—enough

Zoot suits—the typical dress of Pachucos, Mexicans born in the United States during the 40s and 50s who, as a means of resisting assimilation, embellished the fashion of the time and created their own slang, sometimes mixing English and Spanish. The word zoot suit itself is a reduplication of suit. A zoot suit has a jacket with wide padded shoulders and coat tails; pants with wide legs and narrow cuffs; and is accessorized with a suit and/or wallet chain and a fedora with a brim that is wider than usual and has a long feather tucked into its band.

Contributor's Biographies

Mario Acevedo writes the Felix Gomez detective-vampire series for Eos HarperCollins. Mario's debut novel, *The Nymphos of Rocky Flats*, was a national bestseller and was chosen by Barnes & Noble as one of the best Paranormal Fantasy Novels of the Decade. His vampire character is featured in the comic book series *Killing the Cobra* from IDW Publishing. His short fiction includes a contribution to the anthology, *Hit List: The Best of Latino Mystery* (Arte Público Press, 2009). Mario lives and writes in Denver, Colorado.

Patricia S. Carrillo is a native of the Central Valley of California. Her undergraduate degree is from California State University of Fresno. After completing law school, Patricia opened her own practice in Fresno. Her first novel for young adults, *Desert Passage*, was published by Arte Público Press in 2008. Patricia lives in Sanger, California.

The poetry of **Sarah Cortez** in *How to Undress a Cop* (Arte Público Press, 2000) brings the world of street policing to the reader in a way that poet-reviewer Ed Hirsch describes as "nervy, quick-hitting, street-smart, sexual." She won the 1999 PEN Texas Literary award in poetry. She edited *Windows into My World: Latino Youth Write Their Lives* (Arte Público Press, 2007), an anthology of short memoir reflecting the diversity of growing up Latino in the United States, which received the 2008 Skipping Stones Honor Award for being "an exceptional book promoting understanding of diverse cultures." Ms. Cortez edited the fiction anthology, *Hit List: The Best of Latino Mystery* (Arte Público

Press, 2009) and *Indian Country Noir* (Akashic Books, 2010). She brings her heritage and blood as a Tejana with Mexican, French, Comanche and Spanish roots to the written page. She was born, lives and is a police officer in Houston, Texas.

Alicia Gaspar de Alba serves as the chair of the César E. Chávez Department of Chicana and Chicano Studies at UCLA and is also a professor in that department. She has published eight books, including the novels *Sor Juana's Second Dream* (University of New Mexico Press, 1999), which was awarded Best Historical Fiction by the Latino Literary Hall of Fame; *Desert Blood: The Juárez Murders* (Arte Público Press, 2005), which was the recipient of both the Lambda Literary Foundation Award for Best Lesbian Mystery Novel and the Latino Book Award for Best English-Language Mystery; and *Calligraphy of the Witch* (St. Martin's Press 2007).

On the academic side, Alicia has published *Chicano Art Inside/Outside the Master's House: Cultural Politics and the CARA Exhibition* (University of Texas Press, 1998) and the edited volume *Velvet Barrios: Popular Culture and Chicana/o Sexualities* (Palgrave, 2003). Her writing has been translated into Spanish, German and Italian.

She was born in El Paso, Texas, and has lived in Iowa City, Boston, Albuquerque and Santa Barbara. She currently lives in West Los Angeles.

Nanette Guadiano is a writer and teacher. Her poetry has appeared in several publications, including: *Borderlands: Texas Poetry Review, Border Senses, The Texas Poetry Calendar, Literary Mama, Big Land, Big Sky, Big Hair: The Best of the Texas Poetry Calendar (Anthology) and Voices Along the River (Anthology)*. Her creative nonfiction has appeared in *Fifteen Candles: A Tale of Taffeta, Hairspray, Drunk Uncles and Other Quinceañera Stories* (Harper Collins 2007) and *A Cup of Comfort for Single Mothers* (2007). Nanette is a native Texan and lives in San Antonio.

Chema Guijarro is a graduate of University of California, Riverside Palm Desert's MFA in Creative Writing and Writing for the Performing Arts program. Prior to writing fiction, he was a print reporter covering courts and law enforcement in Imperial County, California. He currently resides in Riverside, California.

Carlos Hernandez is a writer and educator living in New York. He cowrote the novel *Abecedarium* (with Davis Schneiderman), wrote the novella *The Last Generation to Die* and has penned short stories published in *Happy, Interzone, Fiction International* and *Cosmopsis*.

Bertha Jacobson grew up in Chihuahua, Mexico, and moved to the United States after graduating from high school. She left a career in Software Engineering to raise a family and now freelances as a Federally Certified Court Interpreter in San Antonio, Texas. Ms. Jacobson is an active member of the Society of Latino and Hispanic Writers of San Antonio, The Society of Children's Writers and Illustrators and *Las Mujeres*, a writing group sponsored by Our Lady of the Lake University. She publishes both in the English and Spanish. Her short story "A Broken String of Lace" was included in *Hit List: The Best of Latino Mystery* (Arte Público Press, 2009). Her short stories in Spanish have appeared in *Poetas y Narradores Anthology Collections* published by the *Instituto de Cultura Peruana*.

Diana López, a native of Corpus Christi, Texas, is the author of *Sofia's Saints* (Bilingual Review Press, 2002) and the middle grade novel, *Confetti Girl* (Little Brown, 2009). Her interest in writing for teens comes from nine years of teaching sixth and eighth graders in the San Antonio Independent School District. Her fiction has been featured in several journals and in the anthology *Hecho en Tejas* (University of New Mexico Press, 2007). She also wrote a chapter for "Twin Wells: A Texquisite Corpse," a serialized murder-mystery published in *Texas Monthly* in 2008. Currently, she teaches at St. Philip's College in San Antonio.

R. Narvaez was born and raised in Brooklyn, New York. His work has been published in *Mississippi Review, Murdaland, Plots with Guns, Spinetingler, Hit List: The Best of Latino Mystery* (Arte Público Press, 2009) and *Indian Country Noir* (Akashic Books, 2010).

Daniel A. Olivas is the author of six books including *The Book of Want: A Novel* (University of Arizona Press, 2011), *Anywhere But L.A.: Stories* (Bilingual Press, 2009) and the bilingual children's picture book, *Benjamin and the Word / Benjamín y la palabra* (Arte Público Press, 2005). His writing has appeared in many publications including the *Los Angeles Times*, *El Paso Times*, *Exquisite Corpse*, *MacGuffin*, *THEMA* and *La Bloga*. Olivas is the editor of *Latinos in Lotusland: An Anthology of Contemporary Southern California Literature* (Bilingual Press, 2008). He has been widely anthologized, including in *Sudden Fiction Latino* (W. W. Norton, 2010) and *Love to Mamá* (Lee & Low Books, 2001). Since 1990, Olivas has practiced law in the Public Rights Division of the California Department of Justice. He makes his home in Los Angeles.

Juan Carlos Pérez-Duthie is a Miami-based writer and journalist, currently pursuing an MFA in Creative Writing at the University of California, Palm Desert Campus. Born in San Juan, Puerto Rico, he writes in both English and Spanish for various publications. He holds a Master's Degree in Journalism from Universidad Torcuato Di Tella, Buenos Aires, Argentina, and a B.A. in Communications from Fordham University, New York City.

L. M. Quinn works and lives in Los Angeles. Fiction is her passion, but she has also published book reviews, essays and travel writing in *Travel 50 & Beyond* and *ELLE* magazines. Her short story "A Not So Clear Case of Murder" was included in *Hit List: The Best of Latino Mystery* (Arte Público Press, 2009).

Manuel Ramos is a lawyer and former professor of Chicano Literature and a recipient of the Colorado Book Award and the Chicano/Latino Literary Award. He is the Director of Advocacy for Colorado Legal Services, the statewide legal aid program and the author of seven novels, five of which feature Denver lawyer Luis Móntez. The Móntez series debuted with *The Ballad of Rocky Ruiz* (1993), a finalist for the Edgar® award from the Mystery Writers of America. His published works include the noir private eye novel, *Moony's Road to Hell* (2002), several short stories, poems, non-fiction articles and a handbook on Colorado landlord-tenant law, now in a fifth edition. Recent publications include a story entitled "The Skull of Pancho Villa" in the anthology *Hit List: The Best of Latino Mystery* (Arte Público Press, 2009); and the story "Fence Busters" in the award-winning anthology *A Dozen on Denver* (Fulcrum Publishing, 2009). His novel entitled *King of the Chicanos* was published in May 2010, by Wings Press.

Rene Saldaña, Jr., teaches in the College of Education at Texas Tech University, in Lubbock, Texas. He is the author of *A Good Long Way*, *The Whole Sky Full of Stars* and *Finding Our Way: Stories*, among others.

Sergio Troncoso was born in El Paso, Texas, and now lives in New York City. After graduating from Harvard College, he was a Fulbright Scholar to Mexico and studied international relations and philosophy at Yale University.

Troncoso's stories have been featured in many anthologies, including *Camino Del Sol: Fifteen Years of Latina and Latino Writing* (University of Arizona Press, 2010), *Latino Boom: An Anthology of U.S. Latino Literature* (Pearson/Longman Publishing, 2005), Once Upon a Cuento (Curbstone Press, 2003), *Literary El Paso* (Texas Christian University Press, 2009), *Hecho en Tejas: An Anthology of Texas-Mexican Literature* (University of New Mexico Press, 2007), *City Wilds: Essay and Stories about Urban Nature* (University of Georgia Press, 2002) and *New World: Young Latino Writers* (Dell Publishing, 1997). His work has also appeared in *Literal: Latin American Voices, Encyclopedia Latina, Newsday, The El Paso Times, Other Times* and many other newspapers and literary reviews.

His book of short stories *The Last Tortilla and Other Stories* (University of Arizona Press, 1999) won the Premio Aztlán for the best book by a new Chicano writer, and the Southwest Book Award from the Border Regional Library Association. His novel, *The Nature of Truth* (Northwestern University Press, 2003) is a story about a Yale research student who discovers that his boss, a renowned professor, hides a Nazi past.

Ray Villareal is the award-winning author of *My Father, the Angel of Death* (Piñata Books, 2006), *Alamo Wars* (Piñata Books, 2008) and *Who's Buried in the Garden?* (Piñata Books, 2009). He graduated from Southern Methodist University with a B.A. in Elementary Education with an emphasis on Bilingual Education and a Master of Liberal Arts. He lives in Dallas, Texas, with his wife, Sylvia, and their children, Ana and Mateo. He works for the Dallas Independent School District as an instructional reading coach.

Gwendolyn Zepeda was born in Houston, Texas, in 1971 and attended the University of Texas at Austin. She was the first Latina blogger and began her writing career on the Web in 1997 as one of the founding writers of the entertainment site Television Without Pity. Her first book was a short story collection called *To the Last Man I Slept with and All the Jerks Just Like Him* (Arte Público Press, 2004). Her first novel was *Houston, We Have a Problema* (Grand Central Publishing, 2009) and her second novel is *Lone Star Legend* (Grand Central Publishing, 2010). Zepeda has also written two award-winning bilingual picture books, *Growing Up with Tamales* and *Sunflowers*.